A Shadow Life

Leta McCurry

ISBN: 10:0692772391
ISBN-13: 978-0692772393

Embers Press
Grants Pass, Oregon

Other books by Leta McCurry

HIGH COTTON COUNTRY

DEDICATION

For Louise and Millie.
A woman without sisters is like a bird without wings.
Author Unknown.

CONTENTS

ACKNOWLEDGMENTS

Thanks to Susan Abel, my incomparable Advance Readers Club, and the Women's Fiction Writers Association for beta reading, encouragement, and inspiration.

And to Catherine Rourke, "The Editorial Intuitive" – Professional Manuscript Evaluator, Book Editor, and Word Surgeon, whose perception, diligence, and guidance empowered me to tell a better story.

And always, appreciation to Dale for patience and calm amidst all the craziness.

"There's something about a closet
that makes a skeleton terribly restless."
John Barrymore

Part One
Mattie Hawkins

June 1, 1938 – May 24, 1943

1 – CALVIN
Menard, Texas — Wednesday, June 1, 1938

The kerosene lamp burned low in the silence. Mattie Hawkins was the only one fully awake in the deep hours of the night. She stared at the plain pine coffin holding the remains of her husband as flickering shadows, like ghosts on the prowl, moved softly among the small group keeping wake. In that raw box lay her life and Laney's, snatched away as suddenly and surely as if they had been picked up by a tornado and blown to kingdom come.

How could God let this happen—in an instant—with no time to prepare? Could she have done anything to change it?

Only two days ago—the morning had started like any other except it was Calvin's birthday. About mid-morning, Mattie stopped working the iron pump handle and leaned against the kitchen counter to catch her breath. She took a tin dipper from its nail on the wall, filled it with the cool water she had drawn from the pump, and drank deeply. Patting the sweat from her face with the bottom of her apron, she smiled at her five-year-old daughter, Laney Belle, playing with homemade A-B-C blocks under the kitchen table.

"Whatcha doin', dumplin'?"

"I spelled cat, Mama. See?" Laney patted the blocks lined up on the raw pine floor.

"You sure did," Mattie said. "You're so smart."

"And pretty," Laney giggled. "Daddy says I'm pretty just like my mama."

I might be pretty to look at on the outside, but I'm ugly on the inside, Mattie

3

thought. How come her neighbor women had a dozen babies one right after another and she could barely produce one?

Laney was the only living child from Mattie's five pregnancies over the last five years. The others were either lost early or stillborn. There wouldn't be any more babies either. Doc Crouch had taken Mattie's husband, Calvin, aside and made sure he understood that getting his wife with child again would likely mean her death.

Tears sprang to Mattie's eyes as she watched her daughter. Her arms ached for babies. Sometimes her breasts felt full and heavy like they did when she was in a family way, but she knew it had to be her imagination.

And it wasn't just babies she missed. She missed the warm coupling with her husband. Mattie understood why Calvin didn't hug, kiss, and cuddle her like he used to. It was just too hard for him to start something she couldn't finish. Calvin loved her, but she sometimes wondered where her husband found relief for his needs. Best not think about that.

"Hey, dumplin', you know what today is?" Mattie hung the cup back on the nail.

Laney's big blue eyes got even bigger. "Is it my birthday?"

"No. You just had your birthday in April, on the second—remember? But it's Daddy's birthday and we're going to make his favorite molasses layer cake."

"Is it a surprise?" Laney scrambled out from under the table, scattering blocks every which way. "Can I help?"

"It is a surprise, and you know I can't make that cake without your help.'" Mattie opened the doors to the bottom shelf of the Hoosier cabinet shoved against the wall and pulled out big containers of flour and sugar. "Laney, run out to the henhouse and get me two eggs. Can you do that?"

"Okay, Mama." The little girl dashed out the door, gawky arms and legs flying.

Mattie put butter and baking soda on the table and began rummaging in the top shelf of the cabinet. Frowning, she laid her index finger across her lips and tried to think. Now where did she put the molasses? *Oh, fiddlesticks! Calvin used the last of it on his flapjacks a few days ago.*

"Did I do good, Mama?" Laney carefully laid the eggs on the table.

"You done wonderful, honey, but you know what? We have to walk to town for molasses."

Just what she needed—a mile walk to town and back. It was so hot just about every living thing was hunkered down somewhere in whatever shade that could be found. Well, nothing for it but just to get it done.

"Put on your shoes and socks, Laney."

"Do I have to? Can't I go barefoot?"

"Its hotter'n blue blazes out there. You need your shoes. And hurry or we won't get back in time to make Daddy's cake."

While Laney went for her shoes, Mattie took off her apron, pulled on a slat bonnet and tied a bow under her chin. The underarms of her dress were dark with sweat, but no use putting on a fresh one. She'd be wet and sticky again before she got to town anyway.

The buildings on the edge of town, shimmering and dancing in the heat, looked much more than a mile away, but Mattie mopped her forehead with her hanky every few minutes and trudged on.

The heat didn't seem to bother Laney. Where did the child get all that energy? Mattie was encouraged by the sight of her daughter hopping and skipping ahead, her fine blonde hair as soft and white as a summer cloud, her rugged little body toasted nut brown from playing in the sun. But, still, a constant prayer always hovered in Mattie's mind. *Lord, don't let my girl grow up weak and sickly like me and my mama before me.*

Just as Laney was the only child of Mattie's many pregnancies, Mattie was the only surviving child of her mother's many miscarriages and stillbirths. Mattie had been a sickly child and caught everything that came along. She missed so much school she was unable to keep up and stopped going in the third grade. Mattie watched Laney closely for any sign of illness or weakness and fret herself into a panic if Laney even had the sniffles. So far, thank the Lord, Laney was as wiry as a wild pony and as hardy as a desert cactus.

It was already plain Laney was going to be a beauty with her big eyes... a blue so pale they sometimes looked gray like ice frozen on the lake, her impish dimples, and blonde hair that was still cotton white but starting to show streaks of a light shimmering gold. She wouldn't have any trouble getting a husband when the time came. Not like her mother. Most girls married at fourteen or fifteen, but Mattie was an old maid of twenty-four when she met Calvin.

It wasn't because she was ugly that men hadn't come courting. Her mirror showed she was pretty in a pale, sparrow-like way. It was because she rarely left the house after dropping out of school and really didn't know any of the local boys.

Then one day Calvin drove into the yard, asking directions to Opal Satler's boarding house. He was a young widower whose wife and baby had died in childbirth and he had come to take a job at the Menard Farmers & Merchants Bank, owned by a cousin. Six months later Calvin and Mattie married.

"Can I have a penny candy, Mama?" Laney turned and waited for Mattie to catch up.

Mattie's stomach muscles clenched so hard it felt like she had swallowed a rock. How to explain to a five-year old that times were so hard every penny was precious? President Roosevelt could talk all he wanted about times getting better, but he hadn't paid a visit to the Texas Hill Country lately. Calvin was one of the lucky ones to have his bank teller job but, still, it was barely enough to scrape by. And it didn't bear thinking about how much they owed Doc Crouch for Mattie's constant sickness.

Mattie sighed. "I don't see how we can buy candy today, dumplin'."

"Then can we go see Daddy?"

"Well, maybe, if he's not busy. We'll see."

Mattie pulled Laney to the side of the dirt road as she heard a car approaching from behind. An older black Ford sped past, sending a blanket of fine dust swirling in its wake. Mattie choked and coughed deeply. She leaned forward, placed her hands on her knees, and focused on breathing.

"Lord-a-mercy!" she gasped. "Old Man Fallows is sure in an all-fired hurry today!"

"Did we get Daddy a present?"

"I made him a new shirt out of them flour sacks I've been savin'." Mattie coughed and spit, then took Laney's hand as the child skipped along beside her. "It can be from the both of us since you ..."

The frantic honking of a car horn and the screams of people and horses shattered the quiet afternoon like an exploding cannon ball. An eerie moment of complete silence followed, then shouting, and Mattie could see people running. A cold, dark, dread squeezed Mattie's chest. Calvin. *Calvin!* Wheezing and gasping, she clutched Laney's hand and broke into a run. *Don't think about breathing. Get to Calvin.*

The black Ford was perched at a crazy angle, its front end poking skyward from the top of the shattered frame of a farm wagon. A man in overalls lay sprawled in the street, moaning, his leg at a funny angle. Mattie recognized a local farmer, Roscoe Spranger.

Off to the side, Old Man Fallows sat in the dirt, his face buried in his hands, his shoulders jerking like he was being slammed in the back with a sledge hammer.

One horse, making a noise that made Mattie sick to her stomach, lay bleeding and covered by the splintered boards. Behind the horse a big pile of what looked like bloody rags leaked a dark liquid onto the sand. A woman's bonnet lay in the dust and a man's arm stuck out from the rag pile. The arm was covered by a yellow-and-blue plaid shirt sleeve, just like the fabric Mattie had used to make a new shirt for Calvin only a month ago.

Mattie stared at the arm in a stupor, barely aware of someone grabbing Laney and carrying her away. There was a gunshot and the struggling horse's head flopped to the ground. Mattie fought for air, her lungs sounding like honking geese, as white-hot terror seared her chest. She tried to scream Calvin's name as she threw herself at the bloody rags in the wreckage. Grabbing the hand as she fell into blackness, she realized with horror it wasn't attached to anything. The hand was falling with her into the void.

Then she felt someone holding her and something cold and wet on her face. Sheriff Doggett was propping her up, his arms tight around her.

"Here, Mattie, drink some water." Mattie recognized the voice of Elsa Kroger from the general store. Mattie swallowed obediently and cautiously tested her breathing, relieved when at least some flow of air found her lungs.

"Laney," Mattie croaked.

"Laney's okay. Near scared to death, but Otto sweet-talked her and took her to the store for a soda pop and some candy."

Mattie didn't want to speak his name. If she didn't say it, everything would be all right. He would be behind his teller's cage, working like he always was.

"Calvin?"

Mattie saw Sheriff Doggett's chin quiver for a second. "Calvin and Old Granny Halvern. Both of them."

Carter Bagley, the banker, knelt in front of Mattie. "It's my fault, Mattie." He was shaking like a dog climbing out of a cold creek and his voice was hoarse. "Granny Halvern was in the bank and she had a weak spell. I asked Calvin to walk her over to the general store so one of the

Kroger boys could take her home…" Carter choked and bowed his head.

"That old fool, Fallows, come roaring into town too fast. He spooked Spranger's horse," Sheriff Doggett said. "Calvin and Granny were just crossing the street. The horse and wagon ran over them, then the car ran right up on it all. I'm so sorry, Mattie."

Sorry.

Sorry wasn't what she needed. She needed her husband to rise up whole again out of that ugly pine box. She needed her life back. She needed the words for her little girl when she came home in the morning. Words to tell Laney there wouldn't be any more Daddy for piggyback rides, wading in the creek, reading fairy tales and singing Laney's favorite song, "Ragtime Cowboy Joe," at the top of their lungs.

Who was going to give her words for that?

2 – THE TROTTERS

Mattie Hawkins sat in a rocking chair in the shade of the front porch, hollowed out, mind and body numb, still wearing the clothes she had worn yesterday and through the night, sitting with neighbors watching over her dead husband.

Horrible, horrible to sit for hours with the dead. What good did it do the dead? Or the living? But it was what was done, had always been done, holding a wake for the dead. All the neighbors, except Clara, had gone home to get ready for the funeral.

Mattie paid no mind to the sweltering heat baking the bare dirt of the yard, or the mingled sweat and tears dribbling down her face. *Don't come home, Laney.* But she would, anytime now, from spending the last two days and nights with little Lizzie Kroger in the living quarters above the general store.

"Mattie, won't you come in and rest awhile? Maybe sleep a little?" Clara, opened the screen door. She looked as weary and rumpled as Mattie. "It's gonna be long day. The undertaker'll be here soon to pick up... Calvin. And Laney should be coming."

Mattie shook her head. "I don't know if I'll ever rest again."

How could she rest when the hard fist of grief had squeezed her heart down to the size of a hard little marble? When every time she closed her eyes, she saw that hand and arm? When Calvin was about to leave home for the last time for the short trip to the church house and the funeral?

"At least eat a little something."

Mattie had eaten nothing since breakfast with Calvin—was it three

9

mornings ago now? She couldn't eat. Her belly was too full of raw terror.

"No, I…" Mattie stood suddenly and reached out to grasp Clara's arm for support. She inhaled sharply as the black hearse stopped in the front yard in a cloud of swirling dust and the undertaker and three helpers climbed out. Horace Lund, the undertaker, walked up the porch steps, hat in hand.

"I purely am sorry about all this, Miz Hawkins."

Mattie nodded and squeezed Clara's hand. Clara put her arm around Mattie's shoulder.

"We'll just take him on over to the church." Horace motioned his helpers into the house and entered behind them.

They came out bearing the pine box between them. Mattie lay her fingers across her lips and sobs shook her thin frame as the men slid the box into the hearse. Before they were out of sight, the Kroger car arrived and stopped by the front gate. The door burst open and Laney came flying up the steps.

"Mama! Mama! Guess what?" She threw herself into Mattie's arms, almost knocking her down. Mattie swallowed her sobs and stiffened her back.

"What, dumplin'?"

"Mr. Otto give me candy and Big Red strawberry soda pop and ice cream." Laney's eyes were wide as she jumped into her mother's arms. "And I got to play with Lizzie's new doll. Can I spend the night again, Mama? Miz Elsa says I can. Anytime I want."

"Of course you can." Mattie hugged Laney as Elsa trudged up the steps. To Elsa she said, "I can't thank you and Otto enough."

"We all do what we can in time of trouble," Elsa replied.

"Go on in. Clara's inside."

As Elsa disappeared through the door, Mattie led Laney to a bench under an old oak tree across the yard and lifted her onto her lap.

"Did you miss me, Laney?"

Laney's white-blonde curls bounced as she nodded. Deep dimples popped into her chubby cheeks. "I missed Daddy, too."

"Oh, Laney!" Mattie hugged her daughter so hard Laney started squirming. *Don't cry now.* "Laney, be still and look at me, honey." Mattie couldn't help it. Tears rolled down cheeks.

"Don't cry, Mama." Big tears pooled in Laney's eyes as she reached up and patted Mattie's cheek.

"Laney, you have to listen to me now. You understand?" Laney nodded so Mattie continued. "Sometimes people get hurt real bad. Remember last week when you fell off the swing and hurt your knee?"

Laney nodded again. Mattie's tongue felt so big and thick in her mouth she thought she would choke. *Lord, help me find the words.*

"Remember yesterday when we went to town and everybody was running and yelling?"

"And the horsie was hurt and they had to shoot him? And I got to go to Lizzie's and have candy and ice cream?"

"Well, yesterday, in town, Daddy got hurt real bad."

"Did they have to shoot him?" Laney's chin quivered.

"No, honey. Nobody shot Daddy, but you remember Flower, your little doggie that was hit by a car?"

"And she had to go live in doggie heaven so she could get well?"

"Yes. Daddy got hurt like that." Mattie tried to control her voice, but it was shaking like a tree branch in a hard wind.

"Did Daddy go to doggie heaven, too?" Tears trickled down Laney's cheeks.

"Oh, Laney!" Mattie cupped the little girl's chin in her hand and looked directly into her eyes, so large, so blue, so trusting. "Daddy went to people heaven. He went to be with Jesus."

"When's he coming back?"

Mattie felt herself shattering like a glass dropped on stone and knew she could never be put back together. *But, Laney... hold together for Laney.* Mattie struggled to force herself to speak. Her words were thin like vapor.

"He's not coming back, Laney."

"Not ever?"

Mattie couldn't hold on. She shrieked her pain and despair like an animal caught in the jaws of a trap. Laney burst into tears and wailed as loud as her mother. Clara and Elsa rushed out and threw their arms around them.

* * * *

In mid-afternoon, Mattie stood on her back porch staring blankly toward the north. She couldn't see Rest Haven Cemetery from there but she knew what it looked like. Hot, dusty, a few scrubby trees, and two new graves. Old Granny Halvern and Calvin.

That morning Mattie had stumbled through washing herself and putting on her Sunday go-to-meeting dress and hat and washing and dressing Laney. Mattie hadn't fully grasped the funeral service or the kind words whispered to her. It felt like she was standing off, watching it all happen to somebody else.

The screen door creaked and Carter Bagley stepped out.

"Mattie, I know how hard all this is," he said. "Calvin was a good man and it's a crying shame this happened."

Mattie couldn't reply. There was nothing to say. Carter took Mattie's hands in both of his. "I know you have to figure some things out, so I just wanted you to know that your bank balance is twelve dollars and forty-two cents. Calvin being family and all, I'll go ahead and pay his salary for the whole month. That'll be a hundred and thirty-five dollars. That's the best I can do, Mattie."

"Thank you."

"I know that won't last long. Do you have any family you can go to?"

"No. No family," Mattie said. "I have no one. Just Laney."

"I wish I could do more, Mattie." He patted her on the shoulder and turned back into the house.

Mattie stood watching Laney sitting with Lizzie Kroger under a pecan tree across the yard. She was faintly aware of the sound of her neighbors gathered in the house and front yard. It was the third day that Mattie hadn't eaten, but the smell of the abundance of food brought in by the community didn't tempt her. Laney hadn't eaten anything today either. *I have to eat something so she'll eat. And to keep my strength up for her.*

Mattie turned as the screen door creaked again.

"Mattie." The preacher stepped up beside her and laid an arm across her thin shoulders.

"Thank you for everything, Brother Ripley."

"I wish I could do more. I feel so helpless when something like this happens." He patted her shoulder then moved to lean against the railing. "Do you have any thought as to what you'll do now?"

"I don't know what to do, Brother Ripley." Mattie's raw voice sounded like a frog croaking. "They's a little money, but what with the undertaker, and the rent being thirty dollars a month, and we're paying ten dollars a month on the furniture and another twenty on Calvin's car, plus doctor bills and everything else, it won't last long."

"I know Calvin's folks are gone. What about any of his brothers or sisters?"

"He had an older brother killed in the war in France. His younger sister married and moved someplace up north. I don't know where."

"Is there anyone at all in your family, Mattie? Anyone to help you?"

"No. Nobody."

"I thought that was the case. I took the liberty to talk to Sam at the furniture store and Mose down at the car dealership. They'll take the furniture and car back so you won't have no more payments on them."

"Don't matter none." Mattie sighed. "I can't drive and it don't look like I'll have a house, so I have no use for the furniture."

"Several people have handed me money to help pay Harold, so I think the undertaking might be taken care of. I've talked to some of the church members and here's what we've come up with," Brother Ripley said. "Ma and Pa Trotter's kids have scattered every which way and they're getting up in years. Ma could use some help around the house and they have plenty of room. They're willing to have you and Laney, at least as long as they can. How does that sound to you, Mattie?"

Mattie wasn't sure how old the Trotters were and, as far as she could remember, she had never heard their first names. Everybody called them Ma and Pa. Mattie hung her head. *Lord, a charity case.* But, she had to think of Laney.

"I'll do what I can to earn my keep, but when the money I have is gone, I won't have no way to help out."

"I talked to the deacons and we're going to bring it before the church for a vote to take up an offering for you and Laney on the first of every month. It probably won't be a lot but it will be something." Brother Ripley stood and put his hand on Mattie's shoulder. "Doc Crouch has volunteered to tend to you and Laney without charge, and Brother and Sister Kroger said they'll donate five dollars' worth of food and goods every month."

Mattie covered her face with her hands and sobbed so hard her body shook. The generosity of these poor people was almost more than she could bear. She had no doubt the church would vote in favor of the offering, but Celery Creek Baptist was a poor church. They could hardly pay the preacher except with canned goods, produce, and whatever help he needed around the parsonage. And the Krogers were struggling small-town merchants.

"I feel so shamed that I need help." Mattie wiped her wet hands on her dress. Would there be a time when she was so dried out no tears would come? "I thank you, Brother Ripley. We truly appreciate it."

"Thank the Lord for it, Mattie. Thank the Lord."

3 – MOVING ON

Mattie gathered an egg from the last nest and put it into a bucket with the rest. Breathing heavily, she collapsed onto a stump in the hen yard and lifted her face to the sun. One year. One year without Calvin.

Mattie watched Laney throwing a stick for the Trotters' ancient hound dog, Twister. Mattie wouldn't have believed it could happen, but it did. The two of them had finally run dry and hadn't cried for the last few months, at least on the outside.

Laney was no longer the bouncy, happy child she had been, but she had just finished first grade. The teacher said she was a good student and a fast learner—one blessing to be counted. Maybe she wouldn't grow up to be as ignorant as her mother.

Mattie pressed her hand against her back and stretched. Ma and Pa Trotter, who Mattie had learned were seventy-five and seventy-eight years old, had welcomed Mattie and Laney and treated them like family. The past year with them had been as good as could be expected.

Ma was getting more and more feeble, so almost all the cooking and inside cleaning fell to Mattie. Pa, too, was slowing down. Mattie noticed it was later and later in the morning when he got out to feed and milk the cow and slop the hog. And, the garden he planted in the spring wasn't even a quarter of the normal planting.

As good as they had been to Mattie and Laney, lately something wasn't right. Mattie had walked in on the Trotters in deep conversation several times and as soon as they saw her, they stopped talking. Mattie was edgy with fear. She knew whatever was coming couldn't be a good thing. She had tried to ease into a few questions, but the old couple always seemed flustered and talked about something else.

Mattie stood, wiped the sweat from her face with the bottom of her apron, and picked up the bucket of eggs. "Laney," she called. "Would you like to come in the house for a glass of cool buttermilk?"

"Okay, Mama." Laney threw the stick one more time for the panting dog.

When Mattie and Laney walked into the kitchen, Ma and Pa were sitting at the kitchen table and Mattie suspected they weren't just passing the time of day. She had an uneasy feeling they had been waiting for her. There was an envelope on the table between them.

"Mattie," Pa said without looking at her. "Come set a spell."

Ma was busily wiping her hands on a dishtowel and didn't look at Mattie either.

"Laney, it's so hot in here, why don't you go play jacks on the front porch? Here, take a glass of buttermilk with you."

Mattie quickly poured a small glass of buttermilk from the pitcher in the ice box. Then she sat down, folded her hands on the table and waited, her heart jumping like a big toad frog into her throat.

"Mattie," Pa said. She glanced at Ma and held her breath as she saw tears pooling in the old woman's rheumy eyes. "Mattie," Pa started again, swallowing hard, his big Adam's apple barely visible in the folds of his turkey-gobbler neck. "You know you and the girl are welcome here."

Mattie nodded, held mute by fear. She moved her hands to her lap under the table and clenched her fists so hard her ragged nails bit into her palms.

"But me and Ma, we're gettin' to where we can't do for ourselves anymore. Not that you haven't been a big help. You have. It's just that…"

"It's the kids," Ma said in her watery little voice. "Malva Jean and Joe Ray." Mattie knew this was their daughter and son-in-law who lived a few miles outside Hot Springs, Arkansas. "They worry about us and they know you won't be here forever."

"We're gettin' way too old to keep up this place," Pa said gruffly.

"And Malva Jean and Joe Ray, they been building a room onto their house for us for the last three months." Ma picked up the envelope from the table. "And now it's finished."

Mattie's legs were shaking so hard under the table she could hear the heels of her shoes clacking against the pine floor. Her tongue was sticking to the roof of her mouth, so she just nodded.

"And we got an offer to buy this place from our neighbor to the west. It's a good offer. Too good to pass up." Pa spoke fast, words piling on each other, like he couldn't get his say done fast enough.

"I…" Mattie started, but it sounded like "Aakk," so she licked her lips and started again. "I understand. You have been so good to us. You have to do what's best for you."

Ma's lower lip trembled. "You're like a daughter to us, Mattie, and we love that baby, but life is just running out for us. All our kids say we ought to go to Malva Jean. We gotta go."

"Yes, of course. How long?"

"Joe Ray can come for us in mid-July. So about six weeks," Ma said.

Six weeks! How could she figure out what to do in six weeks? Where to go? All the other church members had families and too little room and too little money to care of their own. There were no jobs for women and even if there were, nobody would hire Mattie. They all knew how poorly she was, what with her weak chest.

Why did you have to go and get yourself killed, Calvin? Mattie was startled by anger she hadn't felt before. *What am I supposed to do? Can you tell me that, Calvin?*

4 – REVIVAL MEETING

The following Sunday a week-long revival began at the Celery Creek Baptist Church with a visiting preacher, G.T. Ford, out of Ardmore, Oklahoma. Pa had trouble starting his old Model A, so they were late and could hear the congregation singing "There's Power in the Blood" before they even got out of the car.

As they filed into a pew near the back, Mattie was the last one in, taking the seat nearest the aisle. Special church doings were as much a social event as a spiritual one, so it gave people in the community a chance to visit and catch up on gossip. Local non-members swelled the numbers attending the nightly service, but real strangers were rare. That's why the man in the too-small, rumpled suit stood out like a fox in the henhouse.

Mattie spotted him across the aisle as she opened her song book. She couldn't read the words of the songs but she knew them all by memory; she just held the song book so people would think she could read. Mattie looked around for friends she hadn't seen for a while. The man was gazing at her so intently she almost dropped her song book. A shiver raced over every inch of her skin. Mattie looked straight ahead for the rest of the service, but she was aware of the man watching her.

When the service was over, the man hung around on the fringes of groups of people visiting with each other. Several of the men shook his hand. Mattie gritted her teeth. *Come on, Pa, let's go*. She didn't know why the stranger gave her such an uneasy feeling, but he did, and she sighed with relief when the old couple walked to the car.

The following night at the revival, every muscle in Mattie's body was as tense as a starched Sunday shirt. When she didn't see the strange man, she inhaled and exhaled deeply, her shoulders and back relaxing a little. There came a rustle of movement and, without turning around, she knew it was him settling into the pew behind her. She could feel him there as surely as if he reached out and touched her.

At home after the service, while Pa went to check on the livestock, Ma, Mattie, and Laney settled around the table for some leftover cornbread and cold buttermilk before bed.

"You was jumpy as a toad on a hot rock at church tonight," Ma said. "The Holy Spirit working on you about something?"

"No. I don't think so. Just nerves, I guess, with all that's going on."

"I wish things was different, Mattie, but I don't know what else to do."

Ma took out her false teeth and put them in her pocket as she attacked her bowl of crumbled cornbread and buttermilk.

"I know, Ma, but you have to do what you have to do."

"We'd take you and Laney with us to Malva Jean's, but there just ain't room, honey. Malva Jean has six kids of her own and now us."

"You've already done more than I could have expected, and Laney and me, we truly thank you and Pa. I don't want you to feel bad."

"I can't help how I feel."

"Did you notice that strange man who's been at service the last two nights?" Mattie said. Why did even talking about him make her feel nervous?

"I did see' im. Wonder who he is?"

"Did you think there was anything funny about him?"

"No, can't say I did, 'ceptin' he was looking you up and down."

"I saw him." Laney held her spoon halfway to her mouth. "I don't like him. He's a bad man."

"Well, Laney, we really can't say," Mattie said. "We don't know him. He could turn out to be a really nice man." But Mattie didn't believe it.

"I don't like him," Laney repeated and went back to eating.

The stranger sat behind Mattie again the following night. He made her so jittery she had no idea what Preacher Ford's sermon was about. Her hands shook and her heart tapped in choppy jerks and starts. What was wrong with her?

Just before the last prayer of the night was amen'd, Mattie grabbed Laney's hand. Careful not to look at anyone, she led Laney out to the car and settled in the back seat. The stranger walked out of church behind Ma and Pa and stopped them about halfway to the car. Watching them, Mattie held her breath. Who was he? What did he want? Why was he talking to Ma and Pa?

As the three of them approached the car, Mattie tried to sink low in the seat, a cold dread coiling around her heart like a snake. She pulled Laney close to her side.

"Mattie," Pa said. "This feller here is Harley Faddis."

"Evenin', ma'am."

Harley grinned and in the twilight Mattie saw dark tobacco stains along his gum line. She looked back and forth from Pa to Harley Faddis.

Harley was not a tall man, the top of his head barely reaching Pa's ear, but he appeared to be solid and strong. His thick black hair was slicked straight back from a hard-angled face that made Mattie think he must be part Indian. Not a bad-looking man, all in all, but it was his eyes that made Mattie grip the Bible in her lap. They weren't crossed, but they weren't exactly right either... like maybe he saw everything twice. Mattie shuddered.

"Mr. Faddis here would like to come callin' on you, Mattie," Pa said. "He's gonna take supper with us tomorrow night before service."

Mattie couldn't speak or even shake her head. She sat frozen like an insect trapped in a web with a big spider crawling toward her, fast.

5 – HARLEY

"Purty nice car," Ma said, looking out the window as Harley drove into the yard the following afternoon. "It looks just like Opal's car."

Mattie looked over Ma's shoulder as Harley climbed out and crossed the yard, taking his hat off as he approached the porch. Opal Satler operated the local boarding house, and it did look like the car she drove around town... even had the same dent in the right rear fender. But why would this man be driving Opal's car?

"Laney's right." Mattie shuddered. "I don't like him either. I don't want him calling on me."

"Why?" Ma sounded surprised. "He's a nice-enough-looking man."

"I don't know why." Mattie lay her fingers across her lips as she watched Harley. There was nothing really bad about him that she could see.

"Maybe you should give the man a chance." Ma patted Mattie's arm. "Things being the way they are, could be he's an answer to prayer."

Nobody could live up to Calvin, but Ma was right. *Things being the way they are.* Maybe she was being silly. Maybe she just wasn't used to a man's attention. How would she know how men acted or how she was supposed to feel since she had never known anyone but Calvin? Maybe she was too quick to judge. She should give the man a chance. Maybe her shivers about him were uncalled for. Still, she jumped when he knocked on the door.

"Come on in," Ma said, pushing open the screen door.

"Evenin', Missus." Harley stepped inside, then turned to Mattie and nodded. "Ma'am."

"Mr. Faddis." Mattie was unable to keep the tremor from her voice.

21

Those odd eyes. He was looking at her like he wanted to swallow her whole.

"Supper's ready." Ma took Harley's hat, put it on a table by the door and turned toward Mattie. "Better call Pa and Laney to the table"

Mattie rushed to the back door and stepped onto the porch. Couldn't she just keep going and not look back? Grab Laney and run? No. No place to run. *Things being the way they are.* Mattie gripped the porch post to steady herself.

"Pa!" she called. "Laney!" They came out of the barn, Laney holding Pa's hand. "Supper's on," Mattie said.

As the platters and bowls of fried chicken, last summer's canned corn, fresh sliced tomatoes, green beans with pork fat, and cornbread were passed around the table, Mattie noticed that Harley filled his plate to overflowing three times. He ate two-handed, a fork in one hand and a slab of corn bread or piece of chicken in the other, shoveling food in almost faster than he could chew, mostly with his mouth open.

Watching him, Mattie lost her appetite and laid her fork on the edge of her plate. She glanced at Laney who was sitting, unmoving, fork suspended in one hand, mouth open, eyes glued to Harley.

Calvin had taught Laney—and Mattie, too, for that matter—what manners were. Calvin told them that his mama, Miz Lucy, always preached to him, "We may be poor, but we don't have to act like it. Good manners don't cost anything." So she had taught Calvin to be a gentleman, poor but polite.

Finally, after two slices of fresh peach pie, Harley pushed his plate back. He hadn't said a word while he was eating. Now he patted his stomach and said, "Mighty fine grub, Miz Trotter. Thank you."

"You're welcome, Mr. Faddis," Ma said. "But I don't have as much skedaddle in me as I use-ter. Mattie cooked supper." Mattie tried to sink down in her chair. She did not want this man thinking she had gone to special trouble for him. She had just fixed what Ma told her.

"Well, well," Harley said and dug at his big teeth with a fingernail. "Purty and a good cook to boot."

Mattie kept her head down and stared at her hands in her lap.

"And, respectful, too," Harley added. "I can't abide a forward woman."

Pa cleared his throat and asked, "What is it you do, Mr. Faddis?"

"It's Harley. Y'all call me Harley. I have my own business. I'm in metals."

"Metals?" Ma questioned.

"Yes, ma'am. Iron, steel, all kinds of metal."

"Oh," Granny said. Nobody at the table had any idea what Harley was talking about, but it sounded important. But why was he dressed so shabby? His car was decent, though.

"Where you from?" Pa asked.

"Over to Junction. Born and bred."

"It's cooling down outside, Mattie," Granny said, pushing up from the table. "You and Harley go set in the porch swing a spell. Me and Laney can ready up in here."

"No." Mattie jumped up. "I'll clear up. You rest."

"No. No. You go on now. Laney's gonna help. Ain'tcha, honey?" Laney nodded as Ma fluttered her hands to shoo Mattie and Harley out.

Mattie couldn't see any way out of sitting in the swing with Harley, so she led the way to the porch. She sat so far against the arm of the swing it punched painfully against her side, but it wasn't far enough to keep Harley's bulky thigh from resting against hers. Pulling out a plug of chewing tobacco, he cut off a piece with his pocket knife and pushed it into his jaw. Mattie looked away and shivered.

"Mattie your name?"

"Yes," she whispered.

"You're a right purty gal." Harley grinned. Mattie didn't reply, so he added, "I hear tell you're a widder woman?"

Mattie nodded.

"Never been married myself." Harley spit a stream of tobacco juice over the railing. "Been thinking a lot about it lately, though. I think it's time I got hitched."

Still Mattie said nothing.

"Don't talk much, do ye?" Harley scraped his boot against the floor and set the swing to moving. "Well, that's good. I can't abide a chatterin' woman, flappin' her lips all the time."

Harley explained how his business took him about the countryside and into the big cities, like Dallas and Houston.

"I got customers," he said. "Just about more'n I can handle, so I stay busy. I figure it's about time I got myself a wife, but it's hard to find a good woman, what with me workin' just about night and day. You know what I mean?"

Mattie wanted to shake her head, no, she didn't know what he meant, but she nodded. Just then Pa and Ma walked out and sat in rocking chairs on the other end of the porch. Laney followed them out and climbed into Mattie's lap.

Mattie buried her face in Laney's soft hair and closed her eyes. *Lord, let me open my eyes and none of this be true. Let it be Calvin setting here next to me, like it used to be.* She held her breath, trying to close her ears as Pa said, "Look's like this summer's gonna be a scorcher."

"That's what everbody's sayin' up and down the state," Harley replied.

"You travel a lot, do ye?" Pa asked.

"Yeah. Business takes me all over."

Ma creaked her rocking chair. "Brother Ford's preaching a good revival, don'tcha think, Harley?"

"Yes, ma'am."

"You a churchgoing man?" Ma peered at Harley.

"I purely wisht I could be but with all the travelin', it just seems I'm not around a church when the doors are open."

Pa pulled a big pocket watch out of his bib overalls, looked at it, stood and stretched. "Speakin' of church, we better be gettin' on. Meetin's gonna be startin' purty soon."

"How 'bout you ride with me?" Harley stood and held his hand out to Mattie.

"I..." Mattie began. She wanted to say no, tell this man to leave, but the words wouldn't come... *things being the way they are.*

"Laney can come with us," Granny said.

Laney threw her arms around Mattie's neck. "I want to ride with Mama."

"I better ride with Laney," Mattie said to Harley.

"Then both of you come." Harley reached over and took Laney off Mattie's lap. Laney immediately burst into tears and reached for her mother, kicking her legs. Harley slid one arm down to control her kicking and stepped off the porch. "You comin'?"

"Yes," Mattie said, her voice raspy as she felt the familiar squeeze on her lungs. She leaned over, putting her hands on her knees. *Slow. Calm. Breathe. Easy now.*

"What's the matter with you?" Harley said.

"Nothing." Mattie stood upright, inhaling deeply. She took Laney out of his arms. "Just lost my breath for a minute. I'll get my purse and Bible."

"Here's the way I see it," Harley said as he drove down the lane toward the main road. "They ain't no use beatin' around the bush and wastin' time. I need to be gettin' back to work, so here it is. I need a woman and you need a man. Ain't that about right?"

"I…" Mattie swallowed hard. No more babies, Doc Crouch had said. It's too risky. "I don't think I can…" Mattie's face flushed hot and she bit her lip. "What I mean is…"

"Well, I hear you ain't gonna have anyplace to live here directly. Did I hear wrong?"

"No." Mattie answered barely above a whisper.

"I don't necessarily hanker to be saddled with a young'un, but you're a better lookin' woman than I expected to find. I'm offerin' to marry you."

"But I can't…"

"What's all this stammerin'? Tell me whatcha gonna do? You ain't got no place to go. You better make up your mind. I'm not hangin' around more'n another day or two. No call to waste my time. So tomorrow. I'll come by tomorrow afternoon. You tell me then."

Mattie nodded and hugged Laney tight.

6 – THE LITTLEST FLOWER

Harley insisted on driving Mattie and Laney home after the service. Laney was asleep on Mattie's lap when they pulled into the yard. Mattie opened her door and grabbed her purse and Bible from the seat between her and Harley, anxious to escape. Before she could lift Laney up and get out, Harley put his big hand on the back of her neck.

Startled, she turned to look at him. He pulled her toward him and kissed her. He smelled of tobacco and his lips were rough. Mattie's stomach coiled into a hard fist and she pressed her lips together. If her hands hadn't been full with Laney, her purse and Bible, she would have wiped her mouth.

"Just to give you a little idee of the fun you're in for." Harley grinned.

Mattie stared at him, seized by the horror of a glimpse of her future. Harley seemed to think he had rendered her speechless with admiration or desire, so he squeezed her neck and leaned toward her again. Mattie practically fell out the open car door, knocking her Bible and purse to the ground, struggling to keep from dropping Laney.

"Tomorrow. Now, you hear. I expect an answer tomorrow," Harley said as he leaned across and closed the car door.

As Harley drove away, Mattie stood rooted to the spot, clutching Laney who was now awake and crying. *Stop time. Right this minute. Don't let there be a tomorrow.*

"Harley seems to pay you a lot of attention," Ma said as they sat around the kitchen table eating their customary bedtime snack of cold cornbread and buttermilk.

26

Mattie dropped her spoon onto the table with a clatter and burst into tears. Laney jumped out of her chair and climbed into Mattie's lap, crying just as loudly.

"Why, whatever is the matter, Mattie?" Ma exclaimed with alarm.

"He asked me to marry him," Mattie sobbed, wiping her eyes with the back of her hand.

"It bears thinkin' on," Pa said, spooning the cornbread mixture into his mouth. "Times is hard. Nobody kin be choosy."

"I don't want to marry him. I can't..." Mattie's voice trailed off. She couldn't tell them she couldn't be a wife anymore.

"You're lucky you got an offer," Pa declared.

"That's a fact," Ma added. "Ain't many unmarried men in these parts."

"You need to be prayin' about it." Pa pushed his chair away from the table.

That was all Mattie knew to do, pray about it. After she had finally gotten Laney to sleep, Mattie knelt on the braided rag rug by her bed and folded her hands. Closing her eyes and leaning her forehead on her hands, Mattie talked to the Lord for a long time.

"Lord, I don't know what to do. You know I have no place to go with my child. This stranger has come offering a way out. Now, I know, Lord, that even the littlest flower don't wilt in the sun without your notice and that you love and take care of your own. Have you sent this man to answer my need? I don't think to know better'n you, Lord, but it just don't feel right. But why is he here if not by your will? You know how it is with me, Lord, so if this is your will, are you going to protect me from childbearing?

"Lord, if my feeling is right, and it's not a good thing to marry this man, then what is your will? What would you have me do? Lord, you'll have to show me. You know I'm just an ignorant country woman. You'll have to make the way plain to me. Open another door for me, Lord. Show me plain as day what I'm to do.

"Now, you know, Lord, I don't have a lot of time but time don't mean nothing to you. You can fix anything in the blink of an eye. I don't want to marry this man, Lord, but I can't live under a tree with Laney. He's offering us a home. I'd do anything for Laney, even marry Harley. He travels a lot, so maybe it wouldn't be so bad if he was gone all the time. So, Lord, if you don't plainly show me another way by the time Harley gets here tomorrow, then I'll take that as a sign I'm supposed to marry him."

7 – HOME SWEET HOME

Two days later, Mattie stood in the Trotters' front room in her Sunday go-to-meeting dress, erect and grim as a tombstone. Harley Faddis, in the same rumpled suit he had been wearing all week, stood beside her, grinning.

There were no guests at the wedding, so Brother Ripley kept the ceremony short. It was just as well because Mattie didn't hear a word he said. She was too busy chanting to herself, *for Laney... for Laney... for Laney.* Laney cried and squirmed on Ma's lap the entire time. *You just go right ahead and cry, dumplin'. I wish I could set right down and bawl with you.*

As soon as Harley drove onto the main road, he said, "I gotta go by the boardin' house and pick up my grip and my truck."

Mattie turned toward him sharply. Was he expecting her to drive the car? "How will you get the truck and car both home, Mr. Faddis? I can't drive."

"Harley. Call me Harley, and don't fret none. This car belongs to the boardin' house lady."

"But..."

"Did I ever say it was my car? I didn't and it ain't." Harley's hand tightened on the steering wheel. "That old biddy charged me five dollars to use her car for a week."

"But, why?"

"I couldn't come courtin' in my old truck, could I? Truth be told, you've cost me a lot of money. I had to buy this here suit and on top of a week's room and board, I lost a week's work." He turned to Mattie and grinned. "But don't worry, I plan to get my money's worth."

Mattie's heart stumbled a beat as she swallowed hard. "You came for me in particular? But, I never knowed you before."

"No, but I been hearin' about this pretty widder and her troubles all over the county. I figgered you needed ole Harley. And if you was pretty as they said, why, I'd just accommodate you."

"But..."

"Now, you don't have to thank me. Truth be told, I purely do need a woman regular like." He winked at her. "You know how hard it is to get a woman when you're only in these little hick towns a day or two? It ain't easy, I tell you. I've had some long dry spells. So I heard about you and the idee came to me to marry you."

He reached across Laney sitting between them and squeezed Mattie's thigh. "That way I don't have to always be lookin' for quickies. You know what I mean?"

Mattie clenched her teeth as she swallowed down a vile taste suddenly filling her mouth. *Lord, what have I done?* Mattie stared at him speechless, but he turned away as he drove into the yard of Opal's boarding house.

"Come on," he said as he took a stack of four handmade quilts and three pillowcases filled with Mattie and Laney's belongings from the trunk of the car. He carried the quilts toward a large, battered flatbed truck parked under a pecan tree. The truck was mostly red with dents and rusty spots and some kind of metal frame attached to the top of the cab. Mattie gripped the door handle as if she could hold it closed. *Just stay right there. Never get out of the car.*

Harley threw the quilts into a large box built onto the back of the truck cab, then made a second trip for the pillowcases.

"Come on," he said, motioning with his hand, but Mattie couldn't move. Harley strode back to the car and jerked the door open. "Don't set there all day. Get a move on." He gripped her arm and yanked her out. She pulled her arm away and turned to help Laney.

"So it's gonna be like that, is it?" Harley said, and something in his voice caused Mattie to turn and look at him. She drew back when she saw his fists clench, but he seized her arm again and pulled her toward the truck. Laney burst into tears and sat on the ground. Harley's fingers bit into Mattie's thin arm, hurting her, but she pulled away again and said, "I have to get Laney."

"Well, get her then and get in the truck. I'm not gonna put up with this kind of foolishness. You hear me?"

Mattie nodded, picked up Laney and lifted her into the truck.

"You wait here. I'll be right back." Harley disappeared into the house and came out again with a battered suitcase in one hand and a pair of boots in the other. He tossed those into the box behind the cab, then crawled in under the steering wheel. He turned to Mattie and, although his eyes focused in two directions, she knew he was giving her a hard look.

"Let's get somethin' straight right here and now. I'm the man. You'll do what I say." He reached across and gripped her chin in his hand. "They'll be no moanin' and groanin'. You hear me?" Mattie nodded. "And shut that bawlin' young'un up." Harley slammed the truck door and started the engine.

Mattie hugged Laney, bent her head and whispered softly in Laney's ear. Laney's sobs subsided into hiccups. Mattie looked up in time to see Harley turn the opposite direction from the town of Junction. She kept her voice meek and asked, "Aren't we going to Junction?"

"Why would be go there?"

"Well, you said you live in Junction."

"No, I never did. I said I was from Junction. And I am, born and raised, but I haven't been back there since I run away from home at sixteen."

Mattie inhaled sharply and fought a ripple of panic that seized her. "But where do we live?"

"You'll see," Harley grinned. "We'll be there directly."

Mattie's heart lifted when Harley turned into the lane to a two-story farmhouse set back from the road. It needed some paint, but it was large and solid with a deep porch across the front. The barn was new and the outbuildings, while older, were well kept.

"Look, Laney," Mattie laughed with relief. "We're home."

Laney stood up and looked out the windshield. "Mama! There's a baby goat."

Just then Harley turned off the lane and followed some recently cut tire tracks in the grass. He stopped beside a tent set near a large oak tree. Mattie closed her eyes. She didn't want to see it, but she knew. The farmhouse was not going to be her new home. She couldn't stop the tears that ran down her face. She bowed her head. *Lord, what have I done?*

"Well, this is it," Harley said as he opened the passenger door. "Get on out. It's gonna be time to get supper on pretty soon."

Mattie stared at him. She couldn't think of a single word to say. She was supposed to fix supper? In a tent?

It was common to see people living in tents in the recent years of the Depression and some still did, but Mattie had never lived in one. How was she supposed to bathe? Wash clothes? Keep Laney and herself clean? And where was the outhouse?

Mattie covered her mouth with her hand and shook her head and kept shaking it like she couldn't stop. "No," she whispered, barely aware of Laney starting to whimper and cry beside her.

Resting one hand on the cab of the truck and the other on the door, Harley leaned in close to Mattie.

"You're my wife now. This is how I live," he said, his lip curling back over his yellowed teeth. "It's how you'll live and be thankful for it. Where would you be if I hadn't taken you on?"

He gripped her arm, yanked her from the truck and dragged her, stumbling, toward the tent. Laney was running beside them, wailing at the top of her lungs.

"Shut that young'un up!" Harley snarled as he raised the flap and pushed Mattie into the tent. Mattie sprawled on the tarp floor. "Stay put while I unload the truck."

"Mama! Mama!" Laney fell on top of her mother, hugging her neck and sobbing.

Mattie's breath came in ragged gasps as her body trembled. She pulled Laney into her arms and held her close. *Calm. Easy. Breathe easy.*

"Shh!" After a minute or two, Mattie sat up. "It's okay, Laney." She looked around as she spoke softly to Laney and quieted her. The fading afternoon sunlight against the canvas lit the interior with a rusty glow. Mattie pushed to her feet and, hugging Laney against her, slowly inspected her new home.

At the end opposite the entry flap, a tarp hung on a sagging rope, like a room divider. A hinged wooden box sat at the end of two surplus army cots shoved side by side against one wall of the tent. A galvanized tub sat under metal legs supporting a two-burner kerosene stove on the opposite wall. There were three wooden boxes with hinged lids shoved under a small table, apparently intended for storage and stools for eating. Other than a kerosene heater and the tarp spread beneath her feet, that was it.

Run. Far and fast. Grab Laney and go. Mattie's heart pounded and her breathing was labored as she started for the flap, pulling Laney after her.

Then she stopped. Where would she go? She had exactly eighty-three cents in her purse. Her shoulders slumped and she hung her head until her chin almost touched her chest. *Lord, help me,* Mattie prayed. *Help me find a way to get away from here.*

The flap opened and Mattie turned, holding Laney close against her, as her new husband walked in carrying the pillowcases filled with all of Laney and Mattie's belongings. He tossed them down on the tarp at the end of the cots.

"So here we are." He grinned. "Home, sweet home."

8 – TRAVELING MAN

"Well, don't just stand there like a post," Harley said. "You need to get some vittles on 'fore it gets dark."

"What should I cook?" Mattie saw no food.

Harley opened the lid of a box by the table. "They's some canned chili in here. We can have that tonight and you can start cookin' proper tomorrow."

"But what about pans?"

"All you need's in them boxes. You get started. I'm gonna get my stuff outta the truck, then walk up to the farmer's house to see if I can buy a few eggs for breakfast. I'll bring some water when I come back." Harley picked up a bucket near the flap and walked out.

Mattie felt numb, like she was moving in a trance as she looked in the boxes. This had to be a bad dream. If she could just wake up, none of this would be true. Laney tugged on Mattie's skirt. "Mama, I'm scared."

Mattie knelt down and put her hands on Laney's shoulders. "I am, too, dumplin'," she whispered, "but we just have to trust the Lord to take care of us. Here, why don't you play with my purse?"

For some reason, Laney loved to play with Mattie's purse. She could entertain herself for an hour or more, taking things out, placing them just so, then putting them all back and doing it again and again.

One of the boxes yielded a small dishpan, two cast-iron skillets, one aluminum pot, two tin plates, two tin cups, one glass, four small bowls, a few knives, forks and spoons, sharp carving and paring knives, a can opener, a worn bar of lye soap, a box of matches and some dirty rags.

Mattie shook her head and took out the can opener and matches.

When she removed the lid from a large cast-iron Dutch oven on the stove, it was so filthy and crusted her stomach slammed up unto her throat with such force she gagged. She swallowed down the dry heaves and carried the pot outside. By the time Harley returned with water, Mattie had the chili in the aluminum pot on the stove but couldn't figure out how to light it.

"I hope you ain't gonna be one of them fancy-dancy women that don't know how to do a damn thing," Harley grumbled as he lit the burner under the pot.

"You only have to show me once," Mattie replied more sharply than she intended. Harley's head snapped around as he fixed his odd gaze on her. She saw his fists clench, so she quickly added, more softly, "It's just that I've never used a kerosene stove before, but I learn fast."

By the time the chili was hot, Mattie had set the table and opened a can of peaches she found in a box along with some crackers. They pulled out the boxes and sat on them around the table. *I've got to make the best of this until I figure a way out. Don't give him any reason to be mad.* Mattie forced herself to look at Harley and smile as she served Laney's plate.

"So how long have you lived here, Harley?"

"I don't live here." Harley crumbled crackers into his chili.

"You don't?" Mattie paused, the spoon halfway to Laney's plate. "Where do you live?"

She put the spoon back in the bowl. Maybe there was some explanation for this. Maybe this was temporary. Maybe there was some hope after all.

"Oh, I live in the tent all right. I set up here a few days before I went over to Menard lookin' for you, but usually I'm in a spot two or three days at the most."

Mattie stood up so fast she banged the table and Laney's water sloshed out of the glass. Mattie gripped the side of the table as hard as she could to stop the trembling of her hands. "I don't understand."

"Set down." Harley flapped his hand at her. "No need to get all a'flutter."

Mattie remained standing. "I don't understand," she repeated.

"Set," Harley said again and Mattie sat. "Here's the thing," he said between bites of food. "I go all over the state findin' old cars, farm machinery, anything metal people want to get rid of. I buy it cheap as I can and move on to the next town. When the truck is loaded up full, I haul it to Dallas or Houston, whichever is closer, and sell it to a junk yard and start over again. Once in a while I get over into Oklahoma or Arkansas, even Louisiana. Always on the move."

He scooped some more chili into his bowl. "So I set up the tent wherever I am for a day or two, then break it down and move on."

Mattie was speechless, but she could see his chest swell and pride gleam in his eyes.

"Yep, I'm a pretty smart businessman, if I do say so myself. I can always find an ole farmer who'll let me pitch my tent on his place for a few dollars and use his well and outhouse. I sometimes buy a few eggs or milk from 'em, so it's good business for them, too. And the missus gets a couple of dollars for herself if she washes my clothes, but now you can do that."

"But what about Laney?" Mattie found her voice. "She can't go to school unless we stay put someplace."

"She's a girl. She don't need no schoolin'."

"Yes, she does," Mattie insisted, and glanced at Laney who was looking back and forth between Mattie and Harley, her bottom lip quivering.

Harley stood up and pushed back his bowl. "I'm just gonna say this once," he said. "Then I don't want to hear another word about it." He put his hands on the table and leaned across, his face inches from Mattie's face. She could smell the chili and tobacco on his breath.

"I'm a travelin' man. You're goin' where I go. I don't care about the girl. If you want her to go to school, give her to somebody who's stayin' put. We'd be better off without her anyhow."

Harley turned and walked out of the tent. Mattie hunched over and threw up into her bowl of chili.

9 – PIG IN A POKE

Harley came back into the tent and sat on a stool watching as Mattie washed and Laney dried the dishes.

"That's good," he nodded. "Teachin' her young. She keeps her mouth shut and stays out of the way, she'll be fine."

Mattie pressed her lips into a hard line to hold in the words she wanted to say. Instead, she began sorting the clothes in the pillowcases, putting her nightgown and Laney's on the cot.

"We better hit the hay." Harley stood, stretched, and walked to the flap. Lifting it, he spat a wad of tobacco into the dirt.

"But it's not dark yet." Stall. Put off bedtime as long as possible. "Where's the outhouse? I need to take Laney."

"Up between the house and the barn, but don't take all night. We gotta be on the road early in the mornin'. Besides," he grinned. "I don't plan on spendin' all my time sleepin'."

Mattie turned away. It wouldn't do for Harley to see the disgust she knew was written all over her face.

"Where's Laney supposed to sleep?" Mattie asked when they returned from the outhouse.

"I made her a nice place."

Harley pulled back the side of the tarp stretched over a rope at the back of the tent, revealing a small space. There was nothing there except another cot covered with a dirty blanket.

Mattie put one of her quilts down on the cot for padding and the other for a cover. Her hands slowly caressed the quilts as she spread them out. They were the last things she had from her mother. Mattie remembered Mama lowering the quilting frame from high in the ceiling of the front room and spending hours working the tiny stitches. Sometimes, when neighbor women came in for a quilting bee, they could make a quilt in a day.

"Come on, Laney. Time for bed." Mattie picked up her nightgown and Laney's and motioned for her daughter, who was sitting on the tarp floor holding Mattie's purse.

"Don't want to." Laney clutched the purse to her chest.

"Maybe so, but you're going to bed."

"No."

Mattie glanced at Harley who was watching them. She picked Laney up and carried her behind the tarp wall. "You can sleep with my purse."

"I want my bed."

"This is your new bed. You'll like it. It'll be like an adventure," Mattie said, then holding Laney close, she whispered in her ear. "Please, Laney. Be a good girl for Mama. It's important."

Mattie pulled Laney's nightgown on and lifted her onto the cot.

"Are you gonna take all night?" Harley called.

"Just a minute," Mattie replied. She heard Harley snort and rushed to remove her own clothes and put on her nightgown. "Now, you stay in bed. Don't get up. I mean it, Laney."

"Okay, Mama."

Mattie kissed Laney and pulled the tarp closed behind her as she stepped out. She inhaled sharply and took a step back, feeling her face go hot. Harley was standing by the shoved-together cots grinning, wearing nothing but his underdrawers.

Mattie had never seen a man other than Calvin in a state of undress and the sight fascinated her in spite of herself. Harley was really hairy and muscular, especially his chest, and not much taller than her. Nothing like Calvin who only had a little patch of blond hair on his chest.

She knew what made the front of his drawers stick out like he was hiding a stick of firewood, even if she wasn't used to near naked men. And she very well knew what it meant for her.

Suddenly she felt that tightening in her chest. She bent forward and put her hands on her knees, fighting for breath, making that awful goose-honking sound.

"What the hell?" Harley grabbed her shoulders, raised her up, and shook her hard. She gulped again and air flowed into her lungs. "What the hell?" Harley said again.

"Mama." Laney ran out from behind the tarp curtain. "You okay, Mama?"

Harley threw up his hands. "Son of a bitch! What have I gotten myself into?"

What have you gotten yourself into? Mattie almost laughed, but she took a deep breath, grabbed Laney and turned her away from near-naked Harley. "It's okay, Laney. Back to bed."

Mattie led Laney behind the tarp curtain and sat her on the cot. She shook Laney harder than she intended. "You listen to me, Laney. You stay in bed. You understand me? I mean it. No matter what, you stay in bed."

Laney nodded, but her lower lip quivered and tears trickled from her eyes as Mattie covered her.

"It'll be better in the morning," Mattie promised, but she knew it wouldn't.

Harley was still standing in the same spot. "What in hell's the matter with you?"

"It's just a little cough. It won't be a problem," Mattie said, but she knew that wasn't true either.

"Well, I hope I haven't bought myself a pig in a poke," Harley grumbled as he removed his drawers. Mattie turned her eyes away. "Get into bed and let's see if you can breathe long enough to have a little fun."

Mattie's back had hardly touched the cot when Harley was on her. He lifted her nightgown and pushed her legs apart. The cots, even pushed together, were small, so one of Mattie's feet rested on the floor. Panting noisily, Harley made a quick and rough entry, then began pounding Mattie like he was a hammer and she was a nail. He had just started snuffling like a horse when there was a loud crack. The wood frames of the cots split apart and Mattie and Harley fell on top of the wreckage.

Laney ran screaming from behind the divider at the same instant Harley jumped up, squealing like a hog on killing day. "I'm hurt! Shit! I'm bleeding."

Harley hopped around on one foot while pressing his hand over a patch of blood oozing from the other leg. Laney hurled herself at Mattie.

"He hurt you, Mama? He hurt you?"

"No, honey. I'm okay." She picked Laney up, keeping the girl's face turned away from the naked Harley.

Harley kept hopping toward the table, moaning and cussing. A crack of one of Harley's toes against a storage box stool brought on louder cussing. He fell onto the floor, let go of his wounded leg and grabbed his other foot, howling and smearing blood everywhere.

"Shit, Mattie! Put that young'un down and help me. I'm bleedin' to death."

Mattie carried Laney behind the divider and plunked her onto the cot. "Stay put, Laney. I mean it. *Don't move until I say so.* You understand me?"

Laney nodded and Mattie turned back to Harley, pulling the divider closed behind her. Harley sat on the floor pressing one hand against his bleeding leg and holding his toe on the opposite foot with the other hand, moaning and cussing loud enough to wake the dead.

"Took you long enough," Harley snarled. "I'm dyin' here."

"No, you're not dying." Mattie knelt in front of him, pulled his hand away from his bloody leg and looked at the wound. "It don't look too bad, but I need to see it better. Set still."

Mattie gathered up a rag and a pan of water and washed Harley's leg. "See," she said. "It's just a deep scratch. Probably when the frame broke. It don't look like any splinters in it. I saw some alcohol and iodine in one of the boxes. I'll fix you right up."

Harley kept up the moaning and groaning while Mattie cleaned the scratch, painted it with iodine, and wrapped it in some strips she tore from her one clean slip. She wrapped the stubbed toe tight against the adjoining toe and tied the bandage securely. Mattie sighed and pushed herself up. At least Harvey's fun was over for that night. Thank the Lord for small blessings.

10 – ON THE ROAD

"Hurry up, Laney." Mattie was grabbing things and stuffing them in the boxes while Laney finished her breakfast of oatmeal with Karo syrup but no milk. "Harley wants us to help."

Harley had been whining, cussing, and hobbling around the tent for the last two days and his mood was no better now that they were finally able to move on. Best not rile him up even more if it could be avoided.

Mattie grabbed the rope handle of a box and dragged it out through the tent flap. She sat on the box for a minute, wiping her face with her sleeve. Sunrise was still just a soft glow behind the farmer's barn, but it was already hot.

"Come on, Mattie," Harley said, standing on the rack on top of the truck. "Hand me up that box. We ain't got all day."

Mattie pushed herself up, put her hand on her lower back and stretched. They had been sleeping on blankets and quilts spread on the tarp floor since Harley broke the cots. She didn't have a muscle or a bone that didn't feel like they were being pounded with a sledgehammer.

She dragged the box to the truck, then couldn't lift it no matter how hard she tried. Shading her eyes and looking up at Harley, she said, "I can't lift it."

"Well, shit on a cracker." Harley stood high above her, hands on his hips. He leaned over and let loose a stream of tobacco juice that splatted on the ground not far from Mattie's shoes. "Can't you do anything?" he muttered.

"I'm sorry," Mattie whispered as she felt the familiar fist beginning to squeeze her chest. In a moment she was leaning against the truck gasping for breath. Harley scrambled down and, grabbing her shoulders, shook her hard. Mattie forced herself to take slow, calm breaths and felt the bands around her lungs beginning to ease.

Harley shook her again. "Why didn't you tell me you was sick before I married you? And don't tell me it's just a little cough. They's somethin' really wrong with you."

"The doctor says I have a little weakness in the chest… a little asthma." Mattie laid her palm flat on her chest and inhaled carefully. "It comes and goes."

"Well, now, ain't that just fine and dandy?" Harley threw both hands up in the air. "A sickly woman and a whiny young'un!" He heaved the box onto the bed of the truck, followed it up and shoved it up onto the rooftop rack, muttering to himself.

"Laney's not whiny," Mattie said under her breath, turning back to the tent. She put her purse, Bible, and Laney into the cab of the truck. "You sit here, Laney, and don't be a bother. You hear me?"

"Yes, Mama." Laney knelt on the floorboard, spilled out the items in Mattie's purse on the seat and began arranging them.

Mattie was amazed that Harley was able to get all their camp equipment stowed in the box behind the cab and the rack above. Covered with the tent canvas and tied down on the rack, the stuff looked like a weary beast hunched on top of the truck, raggedy and dirty. Mattie glanced down at her own dress, which was none too clean. *Lord, don't let us run into anybody I know.*

"We're gonna work our way down towards Fredericksburg," Harley said as he turned onto the road. "Haven't been that way for a while. Should find quite a bit of junk metal. I got to make up for all the time I've lost."

They made two stops in the morning at farms where Harley loaded an old wrecked car onto the truck at one and a rusted piece of machinery at the next. He put staves into slots around the side of the truck bed and tied the metal on.

About noon, Harley pulled into the dusty yard of a crossroads gas station and grocery. He went inside and returned with baloney, bread, a jar of mayonnaise, a plastic knife, and two Royal Crown Colas. They sat on the ground under a shade tree across from the store while Mattie made sandwiches and shared her cola with Laney.

"We should be somewhere around Lockhart by night," Harley said around a mouthful of baloney and bread. "We'll set up there for a few days. If I can find enough in the country 'round there to finish this load by Saturday, we'll head out to Houston on Sunday and be at the junkyard bright and early Monday morning."

Harley made a deal with a farmer named Crofton just outside Lockhart to set up camp. Mattie heated two cans of pork and beans, fried some hot water cornbread and opened a can of fruit cocktail for supper. She took more time than she needed washing the dishes, dreading bedtime. Harley was still whining and limping a little, but Mattie suspected he was well enough for his idea of fun. He disappeared for about an hour and returned with some eggs.

While Harley stripped down to his underdrawers, Mattie got Laney ready for bed, dawdling as much as she could. When she stepped from behind the divider, she was relieved to see Harley sound asleep, snoring lightly with his mouth open. She could see the skin around the bandage on his swollen toe was dark blue. She knew it had to hurt. Maybe the wrapping was doing more harm than good, so she would take it off in the morning. Very quietly and hardly breathing, Mattie slipped onto the floor pallet beside Harley. Thank the Lord for just one more night without Harley's "fun."

The next night, a Saturday, Harley had not returned by supper time. Mattie made a couple of eggs and more hot water cornbread for herself and Laney, putting some aside for Harley. He still hadn't arrived by the time Mattie put Laney to bed, so she put on her gown, blew out the lantern and lay down on the pallet.

Where could he be? What if something happened to him? *She would be free.* But what would she do? Where could she go? There had to be something, someone. There had to be, but who? What?

Mattie heard the truck several minutes before the headlights dimly lit the canvas tent as Harley pulled alongside and parked. She heard him bang into something and swear, then raise the flap and come into the tent.

"Hellooo, little wifey." His words were slurred, and Mattie could hear him stumbling around. *Oh, Lord, he's drunk.*

A small burst of light followed the sound of a match scratching against wood. Harley swayed as he lit the lantern, casting a giant misshapen shadow against the tent walls and roof.

"There you are, little wifey." Harley grinned as he put a hand on the table to support himself. "I got myself a good load of junk and a good little wifey. Come give your man a kiss, honey dove."

A thin line of tobacco juice trickled over his lip and down his chin. As he staggered toward the pallet, Mattie jumped up.

"Here, let me help you undress," she said as she unhooked his overall straps. "You're drunk. You need to lay down and sleep it off."

"Nope," Harley grinned. "No sleep. Been a week and no nooky from my wifey. Tonight's the night and about time, too." He flung his arm up in a big gesture. "You lucky little sweet thang." He reached up and pinched her cheek, giving it a jiggle.

"Sit down, Harley, so I can get your overalls and boots off." Mattie pushed him down on one of the boxes.

"Mama," Laney said, her voice hoarse with sleep. "I need the outhouse."

"Use the slop jar under your bed, Laney. That's what it's for." Mattie removed Harley's boots, pulled off his overalls, and put her arm around him to help him stand. "Come on, Harley. You need to sleep it off."

"No sleep." Harley grinned as she struggled to get him on his feet. "Fun time."

"No fun time. I won't lay with a drunk."

Harley reared back, his head swaying on his neck like bloomers on a clothesline on a windy day. "No nooky?"

"Not while you're drunk." She saw him stiffen, his blurry eyes harden, his grin turning to a snarl.

"It's gonna be tonight." He straightened himself and took a step back.

"No, Harley. Tomorrow night."

It was so fast she didn't see it coming. He drew back his fist and hit her right on the chin. Her head snapped back so hard it felt like it would separate from her neck and she tasted blood, warm and rusty in her mouth. She staggered backward a few feet and fell to the floor.

"Mama! Mama!" Laney came tearing around the divider.

Harley whirled and backhanded Laney across the face. She tumbled across the floor and landed a few feet from Mattie, screaming. Mattie scrambled to her feet and wiped the blood from her own face with the back of her hand. Then she did something she would never have imagined she could do.

Placing herself between Laney and Harley, she grabbed a butcher knife off the table. Her arm extended, the quivering knife pointed at Harley, fighting against the tightening in her chest, Mattie said in a cold voice, "They's plenty I can't do nothing about, but this one thing I can do. If you ever lay a hand on my child again, I will kill you, Harley Faddis. I will kill you in your sleep. *Do you understand me?*"

"Simmer down." Harley spread his arms wide and gave her a sly smirk, like a fox might give a plump chicken just before breaking its neck. "No need to throw a hissy fit."

He took a step toward Mattie, but she didn't lower the knife. "Young'uns need to be corrected," he said, with a smile. "But you're right. You're her mama. Up to you to do it, not me. You keep 'er in line, everything'll be just fine. No need for me to do it."

"Don't ever touch her again," Mattie said, lowering the knife and placing it on the table. She picked up a sobbing Laney, held her close and spoke softly as she carried her back to her bed. Mattie sat Laney on the cot and knelt in front of her, holding her shoulders firmly.

"Now listen to me, Laney." Mattie shook her. "Don't you ever come out unless I tell you, *ever*. No matter what you hear. No matter if you're scared. No matter if you're sick. Call me, but don't come out. I'll come as quick as I can, *but don't come out*. You understand me?"

In the faint light from the lantern glow above the divider, Mattie could see Laney's eyes were large and shimmery with tears and her lower lip trembled, but she nodded. Mattie swallowed and forced her voice to be steady and hard.

"If you do, Laney, I will whip you with a switch. Do you understand?" Laney nodded silently, tears running down her cheeks. Mattie grabbed her and held her tight. "I love you, Laney, but you have to help me. We have to get through this."

"You gonna be all night?" Harley yelled.

"I'm coming."

Mattie covered Laney, stepped from behind the divider and pulled it closed. Harvey was naked and standing just a step or two away. He grabbed her by the arm, dragged her to the floor pallet and shoved her down. He took her brutally and he took his time. Mattie clenched her fists until her ragged nails cut into her palms, but she didn't make a sound. She understood she was being punished for the knife.

11 – THE LORD'S ANGEL

Mattie stood absolutely still, holding a ball of biscuit dough in her hand, until the sound of Harley's truck faded away. She exhaled, relaxed her shoulders and patted the dough into a disk.

"You want one biscuit or two, Laney?"

Laney, sitting at the table, yawned and rubbed the sleep from her eyes. "Two, Mama."

Mattie fried two biscuits in the bacon grease in the cast-iron skillet, put them on a tin plate and gave it to Laney.

"We ain't got no milk, dumplin'. You want some coffee?"

Laney nodded, so Mattie measured a little coffee into a tin cup, adding a lot of hot water. She poured more coffee for herself, then sat at the table watching Laney drench her biscuits with Karo syrup.

Mattie sipped the coffee carefully, trying to use only one side of her mouth. The other side of her lip was still raw where she had cut it against her teeth when Harley had hit her two nights before. She reached up and laid her palm against one cheek. It was throbbing and felt hot. A sneaked look in the little mirror she carried in her purse showed a dark purple cheek and an eye almost swollen shut.

Now she studied her daughter with her good eye. At ten, Laney had lost her baby fat and grown tall for her age, but she still seemed to be all arms and legs. Gone was the chubby baby face, replaced with high, smooth cheekbones, a slightly squared chin, and a full, wide mouth. She still had deep dimples when she smiled, which was seldom.

The white cotton of her baby hair had been replaced with the color of corn silk near harvest time. Gone, too, was the happy little jabber box she had once been. Nowadays, Laney was quiet and reserved, and when Harley was present, she sat with her head down and spoke only when spoken to.

We got to get away… Mattie had tried to think of a way since the day she married Harley almost four years earlier. But now it was all she thought about, every waking moment, since Harley said what he did a couple of weeks ago.

One night Mattie had a coughing spell, worse than usual, and Laney finished putting a supper of collard greens, fried potatoes, and fried cornbread on the table. When Harley finished eating, he sat drinking coffee and watching as Laney cleaned up.

"Mattie," he said, grinning, "I use'ter figure I got snuggered into marryin' a useless sick woman and I was gonna dump you and that young'un faster'n a jackrabbit on moonshine, but then I got to thinkin'…" He tapped a finger against his temple. "Contrary to what some people think, ole Harley has more'n a turnip patch between the ears." He laughed and slapped his palm against his thigh.

"No argument you're sickly and useless about half the time, but I figure puttin' up with all this foolishness is gonna give ole Harley a big payoff. One of these days you'll just turn toes up in one of your coughin' fits and while I'm waitin', I'm raisin' me up a woman to suit me."

He turned and looked at Laney. "Yes, sir. She'll be exactly to my likin', and anybody can see she's gonna be a real looker."

"No!" Mattie had said but it came out as a strangled sound. She struggled to get up from the pallet and made it to her hands and knees. *He's right. My life ain't worth a plugged nickel. Got to get Laney to a safe place before I die.*

Her body trembling and swaying like a porch swing in a high wind, Mattie managed to croak, "You're a purely evil man, Harley Faddis." Then the darkness overtook her and she pitched face down on the pallet. She had come to herself with Laney sitting beside her, washing her face with a cold rag.

Mattie seized Laney's wrist. "Laney," she whispered and then threw up in Laney's lap.

"Well, shit," Harley had said, "that stinks like a dead skunk," and he stomped out of the tent.

Now Mattie was frantic to get Laney away from Harley. But how? She still had the same eighty-three cents she'd had the day she married Harley.

He bought everything and rarely allowed Mattie or Laney to go in a store with him.

So, she and Laney were always with Harley or stuck at the campsite on some farm miles from anywhere, with only their legs to carry them away if they had dared to leave. Harley forbid Mattie and Laney to visit with the farm women and children where they camped.

One time, soon after they were married, Harley came home and found Mattie sitting on a stump visiting with the farmer's wife. Later in the evening, he had beaten her almost senseless.

After that, Mattie and Laney stayed out of sight inside the tent. If women or children occasionally approached them, they just hung their heads and said nothing. The farm women seemed hungry to visit with another woman, but after one or two attempts, they always gave up and kept their kids away, too. Mattie figured the women thought she and Laney were deaf-mutes or just plain unfriendly, maybe even crazy.

Lord, show me the way. There has to be a way. For Laney's sake, Lord.

Mattie sighed and pushed herself up from the table to begin the daily routine. It seldom changed. They cleaned up from breakfast. Then, if there was wood available, Mattie would sometimes build a small fire outside and keep it going all day under the cast-iron Dutch oven filled with pinto beans, water, and bacon grease.

About once a week, if it wasn't raining, she would do the wash. There wasn't much of it. They each had only two sets of clothes, one to wear and one to wash. It had been a long time since Mattie had enough energy to wash the heavy quilts and blankets even with Laney's help.

Still, she and Laney had to carry water from the farmer's well to fill the wash tub, heat it over a wood fire, then scrub the laundry with a rub board and lye soap. The rinse water for the second tub had to be carried, too. Then the heavy wet clothes had to be hung on bushes to dry.

In the wintertime, she didn't wash clothes at all. Mattie had always taken pride in cleanliness and order, so the burden of their slovenly home and appearance was almost more than she could bear. Worst was the pitying looks she received from other women.

Even with the chores they completed every day, there was little real housekeeping, so Mattie and Laney had a lot of time on their hands with nothing to do. Usually they just sat in the tent and talked to each other.

"Mama," Laney said as Mattie cleared away from breakfast, "Can we go to the creek today? It's down by them pecan trees."

"Why, I think we can, dumplin'."

Mattie had just wiped her hands on a dingy dish towel when they heard a woman's voice, close by, outside. "Hallo. Y'all in the tent. Yoo hoo."

Mattie and Laney both froze.

"Hallo. Y'all in here?"

A shaft of sunlight fell across the tarp floor as the tent flap lifted and a butterball with a head, arms, and legs stepped inside. Everything about her was yellow, blue, and sunny. Yellow hair piled in a knot topped a smiling face with big blue eyes and she wore a blue dress with yellow flowers under a yellow apron—clean, no doubt donned for the visit.

"There you are!" Her voice bubbled like spring water splashing over rocks. "I brung you some cool buttermilk."

Mattie and Laney gaped as she marched in, her work boots clomping on the tarp, and put the Mason jar of buttermilk on the table. She pulled up a stool and plopped on it, and Mattie wondered how it could possibly hold her up.

"I'm Mazie," she said, "Mazie Halston, and let me tell you, I'm glad to make your acquaintance. It gets mighty lonesome out here with no womenfolk to talk to for days at a time."

Mattie put her palm up to try to cover her bruised face, but she couldn't think of a word to say. Mazie didn't seem to notice her face or mind that she wasn't talking.

"I wanted to come right over here as soon as y'all set up last night, but Clovis—that's my husband—said I should allow you folks to get settled in a bit."

Mattie glanced at Laney. Her mouth was hanging open as she stared at their visitor.

"That is one purty little gal you've got there, Missus." She turned to Laney and patted her hand "It's just a shame we don't have no young'uns for you to play with."

She turned back to Mattie. "Ole Clovis—his pistol seems to always misfire; you know what I mean?" She cackled and snorted until tears rolled down her cheeks. She reached up and wiped her face with a pudgy hand.

"Well," she said, putting her hands on the table to push herself up off the stool, "I just wanted to stop in and say howdy. Clovis said your man paid for a whole week of camping, so I'm glad we'll get to chew the fat some more. Y'all enjoy the buttermilk, you hear? Toodle-ooo."

With that she was gone, dropping the tent flap behind her.

Mattie and Laney sat in stunned silence for a couple of minutes, staring at each other. Then Laney said, "Who was that woman?"

Mattie put her hand over her mouth and chuckled. "She must be the farmer's wife. Ain't she a whirlwind?"

They drank the buttermilk and hid the jar, saying nothing to Harley that night about their visitor.

The next morning Harley wiped the last of the egg off his tin plate with a piece of biscuit fry-bread and popped it in his mouth. He slurped a gulp of coffee and wiped his chin on his sleeve. Taking a plug of tobacco from his bib overalls pocket, he cut a piece and pushed it into his jaw.

"I'll tell you one thing," he said, "this war sure has been good for business. Everybody's so het up to help out, they practically give me their junk metal and, believe me, the government is paying top dollar. The junkyards take all I can deliver and ask for more."

Mattie said nothing. She wondered why they couldn't live better if money was rolling in. She knew not to ask. As for the war, she knew very little about it except that there was one.

They often passed long military convoys on the road, but the only time she heard the news on a radio was when they were in the truck. She sighed, patted two more balls of biscuit dough into flat disks and put them in the hot bacon fat in the cast-iron skillet.

"I don't have much room left in this load," Harley went on. "Some ole boy told me yesterday they's some good metal to be picked up down around Caldwell and Somerville, so I'm headin' that way."

Still, Mattie said nothing and neither did Laney, who was sitting on a box stool at the table waiting for her breakfast, her eyes on her hands in her lap.

"That should finish my load, so they ain't no use me back-trackin' way back here to Rockdale. I'll just keep on going to Houston. I'll be gone maybe three, four days."

Mattie removed the fried bread to two plates and broke two eggs into the skillet.

"You hear me, Mattie?"

"Yes," she answered without turning to look at him.

"Well, then, dammit! Say somethin'." Harley slammed his fist against the table making his coffee cup jump. "I know I said I don't like a woman jawin' all the time, but I don't like talkin' to a post either."

"Fine. You're going straight on to Houston." Mattie put a plate with the bread and egg in front of Laney. "We'll be here when you get back." *Yes, God help us. We'll be here. Where else would we be?*

"You have enough vittles to last till I get back, so you should be fine."

"We'll make do." Mattie was pretty sure he didn't care whether they had enough to eat or not. He certainly wouldn't give her any money even if she had a place to spend it.

"Well, then, I'll see you when I get back." He stood and pointed a finger at her. "And don't you go jabberin' with the farmer's wife. Ain't no call for them to know our business."

"I won't," Mattie said and put her breakfast plate on the table.

He turned and walked out without another word. Mattie and Laney sat silently looking at each other until the sound of the truck died away. Mattie exhaled with a whoosh and said, "Eat your breakfast, Laney."

Mattie had just sat down for a second cup of coffee when she heard Mazie's voice again.

"Yoo hoo! Y'all here?" The tent flap lifted and Mazie filled the opening. "I saw your man leave and I smell coffee. Sure could use a cup if you have it made." She set a quart jar of canned peaches on the table and plopped herself onto a stool, grinning. "Don't trouble yourself none, if you don't have any made."

"No trouble," Mattie said. "I have some." She poured a cup and put it in front of Mazie. "We don't have no cream."

"Oh, that's alright. Long as it's hot. I brung you some peaches."

"Thank you."

Laney picked up the jar. "Can I have some, Mama?"

"You sure can, dumplin'. Get a bowl." Mattie tried to open the jar.

"Here, let me do that." Mazie took the jar. She opened it in about two turns of the ring. "I thought I never would get done canning peaches last year, we had so many. And we give a bunch away."

"Thank you," Mattie said again as Laney put her head down and shoveled peaches into her mouth. "It's been a spell since we had home-canned peaches."

"I 'spect it has." Mazie studied Mattie so closely that Mattie looked away. "I'll tell you what," Mazie went on, "I'm goin' down to the creek to get some cress. Why don't you and the girl come with me? Do you good. Get some sunshine."

Mattie hesitated. Harley wouldn't like it. He wouldn't like Mazie being here. But Harley was gone, maybe for days, and Mattie never got to talk to anybody but Laney.

"Yes," she said. "A little cress for supper sounds good."

The two women walked to the creek in silence as Laney ran ahead picking wildflowers. It looked to Mattie like Mazie had something on her mind, but she said nothing.

"Can I wade in the creek, Mama?"

"Stay near the edge, dumplin'. Don't get your dress wet."

"It's all shallow," Mazie said as she settled herself on a large flat-topped rock and Mattie sat beside her.

Mattie shaded her eyes with her hand and watched Laney. She shouldn't have come. She had no idea what to say anymore. She felt Mazie studying her like a hungry chicken must study a bug. Mattie's hand started to shake, so she dropped it to her lap.

"Does he beat you a lot?"

Mazie's voice was soft and kind, but the bluntness of the question was like a slap across Mattie's face. She opened her mouth to say… what? No? That lie just wouldn't come out of her mouth, so she hung her head and nodded.

"Does he beat the girl?"

"No! Never!" Mattie's head snapped up, her heart hammering against her chest.

"You protect the girl. Why don't you protect yourself?" Maxie reached over and laid her hand over Mattie's.

"Well, I…"

Why didn't she protect herself? Maybe it was because she was afraid if she fought him, he really would kill her. Maybe she only had enough energy to fight for one of them.

"I guess it's because him beating me is a small price to pay if he leaves Laney alone."

"You know, Mattie, a man like him don't know when to quit. Someday he'll start beating her." Mazie squeezed Mattie's hand.

"He says…" A bitter taste boiled up in Mattie's mouth. "I've got chest problems, sometimes real bad. He says he's training up Laney to take my place when I die." Mattie sobbed the last few words.

"Oh, Lord! Lord!" Mazie slid off the rock and started pacing. "I knowed it! I jist knowed the minute I saw you... I said to myself, Mazie, here's a woman with more trouble than she can handle."

"But what can I do? I've been trying to think how to get away almost since the day I married him."

"Keeps you close, does he? Won't let you talk to anybody? No money of your own? Threatens you?"

"How did you know?"

"Well, I'll tell you how I know... but first, is the girl his?"

"No, her daddy died."

"Well, the Lord done blessed you when he led your man to pitch his tent on Clovis Halston's farm." Maxie came back and sat by Mattie.

"I don't know what you mean," Mattie said. A little jolt of hope made her catch her breath.

"Well, my brother is a preacher up in Memphis. A little time after he took that church to pastor, he married a widow from the congregation. Her husband had just about beat her to death. She never could carry a babe to term; he'd beat them right outta her. He was mean to his livestock, too, and one day a mule up and kicked him in the head, deader'n a doornail."

"Oh, my!" Mattie said, wishing she had such an accommodating mule.

"When Buford—that's my brother—really understood what Pearl's life had been like, he got all fired up, like the Lord give him and Pearl a mission to help other women caught in a trap like that. But they have to be real careful.

"Folks don't take to anybody interfering in a man's family even if he is meaner'n a snake," Mazie continued. "So far, in the last five years, they've helped three women get clean away and start a new life."

"But I don't understand how they could help me. They're in Memphis and I'm here. And then, there's Harley."

"What time will he be back tonight?"

"He won't. He said he'd be gone three or four days."

"Another blessing from the Lord," Mazie exclaimed. "I got me an idea. But first, I have to ask you straight out, Mattie. Do you want to get away from this man for good?"

"*Oh, my Lord, yes!*" Tears streamed down Mattie's face. Was this real?

Could it be?

"Okay. Here's what we'll do. Clovis has to go into town in the morning to get supplies and I have to take my eggs to the general store. I have a friend with a phone. I'll use it to call my brother so he'll know you're coming."

"But how will I get to Memphis? I only have eighty-three cents."

"Don't you fret none. I've been saving up my egg money for some time. I'll buy a bus ticket for you and Laney."

"I can't let you do that."

"You druther your man beat you to death? Besides, it's my own money and this is how I want to spend it."

"I doubt I could ever repay you." Mattie was shaking from excitement and her breathing was raspy. *Easy. Breathe easy.* "I don't know how to thank you."

"No need to repay me and no thanks needed. I wouldn't sleep nights if I didn't do whatever I can to help."

"What will I do when I get there?" Mattie lay her palm on her chest to quiet herself. "I don't think I can make a living for me and Laney."

"You can sort that out with Buford and Pearl when you get there. The Lord will make a way. You just worry about getting yourself ready to go tomorrow. The next morning I'll take you and the girl to town and put you on the bus. You'll be on your way to Memphis way before your man gets back." Mazie laughed, clapping her pudgy hands together.

Mattie slid off the rock. "Is this really happening, Mazie? Am I dreaming it?"

"No dream, girl. Now I got to get up to the house and get ready for town tomorrow. I'll talk to you when I get back. You just make sure you're ready to leave bright and early Wednesday morning."

"God bless you, Mazie Halston," Mattie cried and hugged as much of Mazie as she could.

Mazie patted Mattie on the back then walked toward the farmhouse. Laney ran up to Mattie, squeezing water out of the skirt of her dress.

"Them was good peaches," Laney said as they watched Mazie disappear into the house.

Mattie sat on the rock and, taking Laney's hand, helped her up to sit beside her. "I have to talk to you, Laney." She put her hand on Laney's chin and turned Laney's face toward her. "I want you to listen to me very carefully, you understand? This is probably one of the most important things I'll ever tell you. Are you listening?"

"Yes, Mama."

"You know sometimes we talk about getting away from Harley?"

"I want to, Mama. He's so mean."

"I know and I've been thinking and thinking for a long time how we could get away, but there was just never any way to do it. Now, I think we can."

"We can?" Laney's eyes got big. "For real?"

"I believe so, Laney, for real. Mazie's gonna help us."

"She will?"

"She says she will."

"She sure is a funny lady."

"An angel is what she is." Mattie smiled. "The Lord's very own angel. Just today and one more day and, with Mazie's help, we'll not see Harley ever again. Thank the Lord."

Part Two
Ruby Jo Cassity

May 10, 1930 – July 23, 1933

12 – DISCONTENT

Freeburg, Texas — Thursday, May 8, 1930

Ruby Jo Cassity nudged her book satchel a little further under the table with her foot. She reminded herself there was no way Mama could see the nickel hidden in an inside pocket. But, then, Mama was just like an old hen worrying a worm out of a hole. Once she got hold of something, she never let go.

There was no way Ruby Jo could think of to explain the nickels, so Mama could never, ever know. If she found out, she would beat Ruby Jo within an inch of her life. So, Ruby Jo couldn't help but feel a little itchy until she could hide the nickel in the secret place with the others.

"How was school today?" Mama put a slab of cold cornbread, a bowl, and a glass of buttermilk on the kitchen table in front of Ruby Jo.

"It was Sally Free's birthday. She brought ginger cookies for everybody, and Mr. Teller made us sing Happy Birthday." Ruby Jo, frowning, crumbled the cornbread into the bowl and poured buttermilk over it. "She was prissy as-you-please because her daddy's present was her very own horse to ride to school."

Ruby Jo gave Mama what she thought was a pitiful look, hoping Mama would see in her eyes what she didn't dare say… that the whole thing was not one bit fair. Not to mention really disgusting.

"Well, that was nice." Mama put a pan of potatoes and a knife on the table.

"Nice!" Ruby Jo snorted so hard a bit of cornbread and buttermilk shot up the back of her throat and into her nose, throwing her into a coughing fit. Mama slapped Ruby Jo hard on the back until she caught her breath, then sat down.

"You shouldn't be small-spirited about it." Mama's hands flew around the potatoes, the peels falling in long spiral strips. "Besides, times as hard as they are, he probably gave her a horse he already had."

"No. She was bragging he bought the mare from a Mr. Jacobson over at Junction." Ruby Jo slurped a spoonful of cornbread and buttermilk. "It was his wife's horse before she died."

"Well, then, it's good to know somebody has money for a horse. Lord knows I can't remember the last dollar that passed through my hand."

Ruby Jo bit her tongue and didn't point out that, on her own thirteenth birthday just five days earlier, all she got was the birthday song at school. That was it. There sure wasn't no horse or any other present. Mama didn't even have enough sugar to make a cake and didn't know when she would get any.

"That's not all." Ruby Jo looked at Mama, trying hard to make a couple of tears come into her eyes. Nope, guess not... "Sally had a new store-bought dress."

Mama's hands stilled and rested on the table, holding the knife and a potato. She let out a big breath like she was really tired.

"We've been over this so many times, Ruby Jo. Your daddy is a good, hard-working man and he does the best he can by us. Mr. Free owns the general store, the gristmill, and the cotton gin. I guess you can say he owns just about the whole town, so he's better off than most. Daddy's a farmer, and times are worse than they've ever been right now, what with all that crashing and trouble that's been going on with the big banks and things back East. You know that."

"Well, it ain't fair," Ruby Jo insisted. "Having the town named for her family ought to be enough. She don't need no horse to boot."

"Be thankful for what you have, Ruby Jo," Mama said. "No matter how bad it gets, they's always folks worse off." She began cutting the potatoes into little squares and dropping them back into the pan.

"Well, it looks to me like the Lord could see his way clear to let me have one measly horse." Ruby Jo dropped her spoon and it clattered against the bowl.

"Watch your mouth, Missy. Be careful you don't vex the Lord."

A little twinge of fear twisted around Ruby Jo's belly button. She sure didn't want to get crossways with the Lord, but she wasn't ready to give up just yet. She folded her arms across her chest and slumped back in the chair.

"I ain't trying to vex him. I just don't see what difference one horse makes to the Lord. You're always saying he owns everything anyway."

"You ought to be thankful you ain't walking to school, young lady. If you didn't have your Daddy twisted around your little finger, that mule would have been gone long ago." Mama picked up a pitcher of water, poured it over the potatoes and carried the pan to the big wood stove against the wall.

"Mosey's been too old to work for a long time, and it ain't like your Daddy to feed something that don't earn its keep, especially the way times are. Besides," she said over her shoulder, "a mule is a lot smarter than a horse any day of the week."

"I don't believe that." Ruby Jo kept her arms folded tight against her chest, determined to hold her ground.

"Well, your Daddy believes it and that's all that counts."

"Even if that's true, a horse is a whole lot prettier than a mule."

"Smart is always far better'n pretty." Mama took flour and cornmeal out of a battered Hoosier cabinet and put it on the table. "That's a lesson you need to think hard on, Ruby Jo. Pretty fades like a summer flower, but smart stays with you all your days."

"Mr. Teller says I'm smart. As smart as anybody in the whole school."

"I know that." Mama turned to look at Ruby Jo, taking in a breath and letting it out in a big puff. "But you've got way too much pretty for your own good."

Ruby Jo didn't believe that for a second. Pretty was a lot more useful than smart and there was no such thing as too much of it. Pretty got you what you wanted, like the nickel hidden in her book satchel.

"And don't you go turning them witchy green eyes on your Daddy." Mama gave her a strong look. "They ain't nothing he can do about a horse and you know it. You'll just make him feel less a man than he is. You hear me, Ruby Jo?"

"Yeah, Mama, I hear you." She made her voice as sassy as she dared and picked up her satchel. If she saved enough nickels, she'd just buy her own horse someday. So there.

13 – NICKELS

Ruby Jo sang softly about grabbing her coat and hat and directing her feet to the sunny side of the street as she took her books out of the satchel and put them on the bed. Mama would have a hissy fit if she heard. "Don't be singing them trashy songs, Ruby Jo," she would say. "Good gospel hymns keep the mind where it ought to be." Ruby Jo snorted.

Sally Free knew all the latest songs because her family was the only one in Freeburg who had an RCA Victor phonograph player, and every time she went on a shopping trip to San Angelo with her mother, Sally got a new record. Sally was always singing and showing off at recess and, once in a while, Mr. Teller asked her sing a whole song for the class while he played piano.

No doubt Sally could sing, but she looked like a donkey with big square teeth and more freckles than a speckled puppy. And she wasn't even a redhead. Ruby Jo thanked her lucky stars for, by rights, she should have been the one with the freckles, with her hair so red it looked like it would be hot to touch. But she didn't have a single freckle anywhere on her body that she could see.

Besides, even though they were both in the seventh grade, Sally was a year younger than Ruby Jo. Still a silly child. The only reason they were even in the same class was because Ruby Jo had scarlet fever really bad when she was five and didn't start first grade until she was six. By rights, she should have already been in eighth grade.

Ruby Jo took the nickel out of the little pocket in the satchel, crawled to the back corner under her bed and pulled up a loose floorboard. She added the coin to the others in the quart fruit jar, replaced the lid and put the jar back in its hiding place.

As she scooted out from under the bed, she heard Mama yell, "Ruby Jo, take off your school dress."

"Take off your school dress!" Ruby Jo mimicked and stuck her tongue out at the closed door, but she took the dress off and hung it on a hook on the wall. She only had two school dresses, both made by Mama from flowered flour sacks. She switched them every other day, so she wore the red one twice and the blue one three times each week.

That stupid Sally was the only girl in school who had a different dress for every day of the week and she pranced around like they were real princess dresses instead of out of the Sears and Roebuck catalog, or store-bought in San Angelo.

Well, that was okay. Let her twirl around like a dust devil. Ruby Jo would just keep collecting nickels and someday she would have enough to buy real princess dresses and a whole herd of horses if she wanted them.

"Come help with supper, Ruby Jo."

Ruby Jo trudged to the kitchen. Why did she always have to help with everything? Someday she would have people to do for her, not work herself to death like her Mama.

Nobody said much while they ate. Ruby Jo couldn't figure out why Daddy listened to the news on the little battery-powered radio during supper all the time when he just got upset by what he heard. He was always telling Mama how the new president, Mr. Hoover, was going to run the country into the ground, in spite of the fact he promised a chicken in every pot and a car in every garage.

Who cared about Hoover? As soon as she finished helping Mama clean up the kitchen, Ruby Jo escaped to her room.

Ruby Jo put on her nightgown, pulled a book out of her satchel and lay down on the bed. She tried to concentrate on her reading assignment, but the light from the kerosene lamp on the bedside table was dim, and she really didn't want to read.

What she really wanted was to take the nickels out, count them and feel them, but she didn't dare. She might get caught, then Mama would want to know where they came from and that Ruby Jo could never tell.

It had been about a year ago, around the time of her twelfth birthday in early May, when she got that first nickel. All sixteen students of the one-room school were playing hide-and-seek during morning recess. Ruby Jo ran into the woodshed and quietly closed the door behind her. She was trying to catch her breath when the door opened and Boyce Claypool stepped in and leaned his big frame against the door.

"Go hide someplace else, Boyce," she whispered.

"I want to hide with you," he whispered back. Boyce was fourteen and man-sized, but he was only in the seventh grade because he missed so much school every year from always having to help his Pa on the farm. He smelled sweaty and a little like manure.

"They'll find us quicker with you in here."

"No, they won't. I'm holding the door. They can't open it."

Something about his voice caused Ruby Jo to turn and look at him in the dusky sunlight filtering through the cracks in the wall.

"You sure are pretty, Ruby Jo."

"Shut up, dummy," Ruby Jo hissed. "They'll hear you."

Boyce licked his lips. "Show me your panties," he whispered.

"I'll do no such thing! Are you crazy?"

"I'll give you a nickel."

"You don't have no nickel."

"I do, too. I been helping ole Scroggins with his hogs after chores on Saturdays. He pays me twenty-five cents a week."

A nickel? She'd never had a nickel of her own. "That's all? Just look at my panties?"

"That's all."

Ruby Jo squinted a look through a crack. Nobody was near the wood shed that she could see, so she grabbed her skirt, whipped it up, and put it down. "Now, gimme the nickel." She held out her hand.

"No." Boyce shook his head. "You gotta hold your dress up for a minute or two so I can get a good look."

Ruby Jo looked through the crack again and pulled her dress up. Boyce, breathing a little hard and fast, his lips sagging apart, stared at her panties until she put her dress down and said, "That's it. Somebody's going to find us. Gimme the nickel."

When "it" found her, she was alone in the wood shed with a nickel in her pocket.

Since then, Boyce had been good for ten-to-fifteen cents a week just for staring at her panties. Ruby Jo didn't see a thing wrong with showing him her panties. But she knew everybody else, especially Mama, would have a hissy fit, so they had to be really careful not to get caught.

Ruby Jo couldn't figure out what there was about homemade flour-sack panties that was worth good money to Boyce, but it was always the same. He would stare, his mouth hanging open, and seem awful nervous, because his right hand in his overalls pocket would jerk something awful. Sometimes he would moan funny.

But it didn't hurt her none and it was an easy nickel. And there was something else… something about him staring at her panties that made her feel kind of good, a little tingly. And strong. She always felt so strong watching him stare at her panties, like she could smash the big rock at the crossroads on the way to school with one stomp.

She didn't understand all of it, but she was beginning to get the idea that as long as there were men or boys around, there could be nickels for Ruby Jo. There couldn't be a whole lot wrong with that.

14 – ECONOMIC DOWNTURN

On the last Friday in May, Mr. Teller sat at his desk peering at a piece of paper as he made announcements for the end of term and the class roster for next school year. There were only girls and a couple of really young boys present, because the older boys had already dropped out to help on farms and ranches for the summer.

"The Sparter twins will be starting this fall," Mr. Teller said. "They will be our only first-graders." He rose, picked up some papers and stood in front of his desk. "Now, we'll hand out the certificates of completion and promotion for this term. Please stand and come forward when I call your name."

There was scraping and shuffling as the class stood.

"Our first promotion from first to second grade this year is Martin Tillis and Lucy Bayloft."

Ruby Jo's attention drifted as she thought about summer and how it would be next to impossible to find nickel time with Boyce. She was jolted back at the mention of her name.

"Ruby Jo Cassity, Sally Free, Velma Russell, and Billy Bob Beason all move on to eighth grade. Ruby Jo, Sally, and Velma, come forward for your certificates. Velma, you can give Billy Bob's to him."

Velma blushed and ducked her head as the girls marched up one after the other to accept the certificates and return to stand by their seats. Billy Bob, the preacher's son, and Velma, the daughter of a cotton farmer, had been sweet on each other ever since anyone could remember.

"But what about Boyce?" Ruby Jo blurted.

"I'll see that Boyce gets his certificate for this year, but he won't be back for eighth grade," Mr. Teller replied. "His father decided he's had enough schooling and he's needed on the farm."

Well, shoot a speckled hen. There went Ruby Jo's nickels, not just for the summer, but for good.

15 – SIREN

In early September, Ruby Jo took her seat near the back of the classroom for the first day of eighth grade. She didn't know if she was happy school had started again or not. But at least it would get her away from the house and Mama.

It had been a long, hot, and fretful summer. Day in and day out, except for Sundays, it was the same old thing. Ruby Jo helped her mother pick and can the little they had managed to grow. When they weren't picking and canning, there was still work from daylight until dark.

Clothes had to be washed in an iron pot of water boiling over an outside fire, rinsed, and hung on the line to dry. Then brought in, sprinkled down in a basket, taken out, and ironed with an iron heated on the back of the wood stove. Raw pine floors had to be sprinkled with creek sand, then swept clean. And there was mending, cooking, cleaning, feeding the chickens, gathering the eggs, milking the cow. It was all hot, back-breaking work. The one thing Ruby Jo knew for sure was that it wasn't the way she wanted to live her life. There had to be a better way and she would find it.

It seemed her dress stayed soaked with sweat all summer and she stank so bad she could even smell herself. It wasn't just the work, the heat, and the sweat. Ruby Jo felt odd, kind of itchy and twitchy and out of sorts. Her chest ached in a funny way.

Just about everything made her mad and sometimes she had to pop off and say what she thought even though she knew Mama was going to slap her mouth.

"You'll not talk to me like that, Ruby Jo," Mama would say. "I'll not have it. Your brothers never spoke to me like that and you ain't going to either. I don't know why you have to be such a peevish child."

Ruby Jo had heard it all before—how perfect her brothers were and how she was the contrary one right from the start. How, in spite of all Mama's begging, nothing would do, but her firstborn twins, Avery and Everett, and their younger brother, Luther, just had to join up and fight in the Great War in France a few years back.

During the battle at Belleau Wood on June 6, 1918, Everett was killed with his twin, Avery, standing so close they were almost touching. But Avery was unable to save his brother. The next day, less than a mile away, young Luther was also killed. Avery came home in one piece except for his mind. He had been in the San Antonio Insane Asylum all of Ruby Jo's life.

Mama said all he done after he come home was stare off into space and sing "Humpty Dumpty" over and over. She never went to visit him anymore; said she couldn't bear that her own child didn't even know his own mama.

Ruby Jo hadn't been even a year old when her brothers went to war. Mama said she was a "change baby," born after Mama thought she was done with childbearing, but Mama was way off on that one. She had another girl child four years after Ruby Jo, but it was stillborn.

According to Mama, Ruby Jo was the hardest carry of all and was born after two days of labor so bad Mama thought she would die.

"I wasn't at myself when Granny Jones laid you on my breast," was how Mama told the story, "but I almost jumped out of bed when you clamped down on my nipple. You sucked so hard it was like you was determined to pull the life right out of me. I knew right then you were going to be a testy child."

For once Ruby Jo agreed with Mama. She knew she was being more contrary than usual but didn't know why. She thought maybe it was the loss of the stream of nickels, but it turned out to be more than that. By the end of summer, Ruby Jo had two plump mounds with hard little nipples on her chest and she'd had her first visit from what Mama called a "woman's curse."

"I should'a knowed this was coming on," Mama said. "You been unsettled as a hen with a fox in the coop." Mama pressed her lips together and shook her head. "Best if you could stay a girl, but that ain't the way of things. You're a woman now and you need to start actin' like one."

Mama went on to warn Ruby Jo not to let boys "get too close or touch you" because getting the curse meant she could get babies now. Mama didn't go on to say how boys touching her could make a baby, but Ruby Jo was beginning to have some ideas about how that could happen. She didn't look too favorably on this curse business, but she was right proud of her new titties. She was even prouder the first day of the new school term when she observed that Sally Free was still as flat as a flapjack.

The younger students were already cutting jack-o-lanterns and witches out of construction paper to decorate for Halloween when Billy Bob joined the class late because of his summer work. He took a desk across the aisle from his *true love*, Velma.

Ruby Jo's chest didn't hurt so much anymore but she still felt restless, like ants were crawling all over her. She had trouble concentrating on her school work, especially when Mr. Teller was working with the students in the other grade levels and she was supposed to study on her own. Ruby Jo sat in the last row behind Velma so she could study her and Billy Bob without being noticed.

What was it about Velma that Billy Bob liked so much? She was all little and gray-like, with mousy hair and two front teeth like a gopher. But they were always together and Velma acted like Billy Bob was some kind of king. Everybody said they would marry as soon as Velma turned fifteen.

Now, on the other hand, Ruby Jo could see why Velma liked Billy Bob. He was big-chested and had muscular arms from all the farm work. His golden blond hair curled just over his collar, and he seemed to always have a happy smile. Ruby Jo couldn't quite figure that out. It couldn't be all that wonderful being a preacher's kid, but Billy Bob didn't seem to mind.

The big puzzlement was if he couldn't like Velma for her looks, what was it? What did that little mouse have that Ruby Jo didn't have? There was no question Ruby Jo was much prettier—in fact the prettiest girl in the whole class, the whole town even. Probably the whole county.

Billy Bob must have felt her staring at him because he turned his head and looked at her. His eyes widened when Ruby Jo lowered her lashes a little, gave a small smile, and pressed her back against her chair so her titties stuck out like two ripe and juicy melons about to bust open.

Thank goodness every morning when Ruby Jo went into the barn to get Mosey's bridle, she secretly took off the brassiere Mama had made for her and hid it in the bottom of her satchel. More like a harness, it cut into her rib cage and pinched the skin under her arms. She had to put it back on again when she put Mosey's bridle away every afternoon, but for the school day, her new titties with their hard little nipples were plainly there. The other older girls whispered and frowned, but Ruby Jo didn't care. They were just jealous.

Billy Bob snapped his head around and didn't look at her anymore that day. But every day after that he sneaked more and more looks at her over his shoulder. Ruby Jo began to wonder if maybe she couldn't shake him loose from his precious Velma.

Except for an occasional peck on the cheek during recess games, Ruby Jo had never been properly kissed by a boy and lately it was almost all she thought about. She had taken to kissing her face in the mirror, as well as her forearm and her pillow, but knew there was a lot more to it than that.

Who better than Mr.-Perfect-Preacher's-Kid-in-love-with-Velma to be the first one? She couldn't get the idea out of her mind. That would surely show Ruby Jo was not only the prettiest, but could also make a man like her even if he liked someone else.

Ruby Jo plotted and planned. Every day Billy Bob walked Velma home a quarter mile from school. Then he walked back past the school and down the same dirt road Ruby Jo traveled, a few minutes ahead of him until he reached the fork in the road where he went one way and Ruby Jo the other.

One afternoon she was standing by Mosey waiting for him at the fork in the road. As soon as he saw her, he stopped and looked back down the road he had just walked, then walked slowly on.

"Hi, Billy Bob." Ruby Jo gave him her best smile.

He looked back down the road again, then down the two forks leading off into the trees. Narrowing his eyes, he said, "What's the matter, Ruby Jo?"

"Oh, it's just plain silly," she replied. "I was riding along, not paying attention, you know, daydreaming. Mosey stumbled over something and I fell off."

"You fell? Off Mosey?"

"Yes, and I need help getting back on."

Billy Bob lifted his eyebrows, but he grinned. "Okay," he said, leaning forward to make a stirrup out of his hands.

Ruby Jo put her hands on his shoulders but didn't put her foot in the stirrup. Instead, she leaned hard into him and said, "I was daydreaming about you, Billy Bob."

She felt him tense and he started to pull back, but she put her arms around his neck. "I want you to kiss me," she whispered. "Nobody has ever kissed me and I want you to be the first."

He tipped his head back and stared at her. She closed her eyes and lifted her face, lips slightly parted. "Please."

Billy Bob groaned. She felt his body relax a little, then his arms were around her and his lips were full and warm against her mouth. It felt good but not quite what she had expected. A tickly itch in her stomach demanded *more...more.*

She opened her mouth a little and ran just the tip of her tongue along his lower lip. Dropping his arms, he jumped back like he had been shot. He stared at her, his mouth working like he might pucker up and cry. "Oh, Lord," he moaned and took off running toward home.

Ruby Jo stood on the big rock at the fork and climbed onto Mosey. She burst out laughing several times on the ride home. She felt good.

16 – REVELATION

Billy Bob didn't come back to school the rest of the week. When he came back the following Monday, he stared straight ahead and didn't look at Ruby Jo. During first recess, Ruby Jo gave him her best smile as she walked toward him. A look of panic crossed his face as he turned and ran for the outhouse. After that, he stuck to Velma like pig manure to the bottom of a shoe.

Sitting behind Velma, Ruby Jo scrunched down so she wouldn't be seen by Mr. Teller and stuck her tongue out at Billy Bob's back. She didn't want him anyway. He wasn't going to be anything but a dirt poor farmer like her daddy. Velma could have him and starve while she worked herself to death and had one baby after another. Ruby Jo didn't know what she was going to do, but being Billy Bob's wife wasn't it.

Ruby Jo gritted her teeth, tapped her foot, stared out the window, drew senseless doodles in her notebook, skimmed over her lessons, and got through the days.

She wanted to be through with school and get on with her life so bad, but what was *getting on with her life?* You grew up and got married, sometimes before you hardly graduated eighth grade. Although Ruby Jo had never known one personally, she knew that a few girls went on to college and became schoolteachers or nurses. And she had heard it was possible, in the big towns, for a girl to work in a store or an office.

College was totally out of the question even if she wanted to go, and who wanted to drudge their life away in a dumb store or office? *What did she want?* And why did she feel like she would scream if anybody even looked at

70

her cross-eyed?

Several times during winter break Ruby Jo almost blurted out she wasn't going back to school. But she held back because she knew Daddy wouldn't care and she was pretty sure Mama wouldn't care either. It would just mean more help for Mama and that was worse than school.

In the middle of the first week of the spring term, one of the fourth-graders was reading a lesson aloud and the rest of the class was supposed to be silently studying their own lessons. Ruby Jo noticed Sally, across the aisle and a couple of seats ahead, reading a movie magazine concealed in her open geography book.

Ruby Jo was trying to get a good look at a full-page picture of Mary Pickford and didn't notice Mr. Teller walking quietly down the aisle until he snatched up the movie magazine. Sally's geography book crashed to the floor. Several students jumped and Sally, her face bright red, cried out like somebody had pinched her.

"And what does 'Photoplay' have to do with geography, Miss Free?" Mr. Teller flapped the magazine back and forth.

"Nothing, Mr. Teller," Sally blubbered.

"Exactly." Mr. Teller put the magazine in his desk drawer. "So you will stay in from afternoon recess and write *I will not read movie magazines in class* one hundred times on the blackboard. Understood?"

"Yes, Mr. Teller." As Mr. Teller turned away to the blackboard, Sally glared at Ruby Jo, put her thumb on her nose and waggled her fingers in a donkey salute.

A few minutes before the end of the school day, Mr. Teller looked up from a paper in his hand and said, "Ruby Jo, your history composition about the massacre at the Alamo just won't do."

"What's wrong with it?" Ruby Jo stammered and sat up straighter in her chair. She felt her face go hot when she looked over and saw Sally snickering behind her hand.

"Well, for starters, don't you think it's important to note that even though they all died, one hundred-and-eighty Texans held the mission for thirteen days and killed more than six hundred of Santa Ana's men?" Mr. Teller pushed his spectacles up his thin nose. "Don't you think their uncommon valor deserves at least a paragraph, Ruby Jo?"

"Yes, Mr. Teller."

"I'd like you to stay a few minutes after school and rewrite this," he said. "Class, the rest of you are dismissed for the day."

Ruby Jo slouched in her seat and kept her eyes on her desk as the other students gathered their belongings from the cloakroom and filed out. She knew if she looked up and saw Sally's smirking face, she'd be hard pressed not to slap her.

As soon as all the chatter and noise of leaving died away, Mr. Teller walked to Ruby Jo's desk and laid her composition paper in front of her. She glanced at it, inhaled sharply and looked at it more closely. There was an "A" clearly written in red pencil at the top of the page.

"But... what... why..." she stammered, looking at him.

He smiled. He really did have a nice smile. She hadn't noticed that before. He was thin, not much taller than Ruby Jo, and had brown hair, poorly cut. Now that she thought about it, he probably wasn't too many years older than her. He sat on the desk across the aisle and crossed his legs at the ankles.

"I believe you are ready for some advanced studies, Ruby Jo."

She thought she saw a twinkle in his blue eyes and relaxed a little. "I don't know what you mean, Mr. Teller."

"I know all about you and Boyce," he said.

Ruby Jo felt her face flame as her heart dropped to the bottom of her stomach. A ripple of panic rolled over her whole body. "We didn't really do anything," she mumbled.

He put a finger under her chin and lifted her face. He was still smiling. "I'm aware of that."

"How did you find out?"

"I watch my students. I see more than you think. And you forget I room and board with Boyce's folks. It wasn't hard to get Boyce to admit to the panty viewing. And the nickels. Especially since he isn't coming back to school."

That rat. Ruby Jo should have known she couldn't trust Boyce to keep his mouth shut. "You won't tell my folks?"

"Of course not. I suspect a little something went on between you and Billy Bob, too."

"It wasn't anything."

"I know that, too." Mr. Teller stood and walked toward the cloakroom. "I have something for you. Come with me."

Ruby Jo hesitated, then followed him, curious. He reached up to the top shelf and handed her Sally's "Photoplay" magazine with a picture of Clara Bow on the cover.

"For me?" Ruby Jo wanted her own "Photoplay" almost more than she wanted anything in the whole world. It wasn't that she couldn't buy her own copy, but if she spent the ten cents for it at the general store, it might get back to Mama. First, Mama would make her throw the magazine away, then she'd want to know where Ruby Jo got the ten cents.

"Yes, for you," Mr. Teller said.

"Thank you, Mr. Teller." Ruby Jo pressed the magazine to her chest. She'd have to hide it from Mama.

Mr. Teller reached out, gently removed the magazine from Ruby Jo's hands and put it aside. "Show me your breasts, Ruby Jo," he said softly.

Ruby Jo inhaled sharply. The idea that Mr. Teller wanted to see her titties made her feel all tingly, but *Mr. Teller?* Why would her teacher want to see her titties? When she said nothing, he whispered, "I'll give you ten cents."

"Just to look?"

"Just to look."

Ruby Jo nodded. Mr. Teller slowly unbuttoned the front of her dress all the way past her waist and pushed it back off her shoulders. Ruby Jo leaned against the wall and watched Mr. Teller look at her. He was breathing deeply and smiling. She felt a smile curl her lips, too, and stretched herself one way then the other against the wall, like a kitten waking from a nap.

"May I touch you, Ruby Jo? For another dime, of course." He laughed and she nodded.

She watched his hand as he slowly placed just the tip of his finger on the end of her nipple. Then he bent forward and took her nipple into his mouth, gently tugging and pulling.

A thousand Fourth of July sparklers flashed and burned quick as lightning inside Ruby Jo, then they all balled together into a single rocket that shot straight to her crotch and exploded like a stick of dynamite. She moaned, her legs shook, and she sagged against the wall. She turned inward, curled and coiled around her insides, like she was disappearing into herself.

Suddenly, Mr. Teller stopped. Ruby Jo seized his hair and pulled him back to her, but he shook his head and she heard it too. The creak of a wagon seat, the snuffling and snorting of a horse.

Mr. Teller dashed from the cloakroom. She buttoned her dress as fast as she could as she heard the scrape of his chair on the floor, then the sound of the door opening and her father's voice.

"Passin' by on the way to home from town, Teller. Saw Mosey still waitin' out front. Ruby Jo okay?"

"Yes. Yes, Mr. Cassity. She's just getting her lunch bucket from the cloakroom. I'm afraid I had to keep her a few minutes after school to rework a history composition."

"I'm ready to go, Daddy," Ruby Jo said. "I'm sorry I'm late, but I did get an A." She picked the paper up from the desk as she walked by.

"See you tomorrow, Ruby Jo," Mr. Teller said behind her. "Don't forget to do your arithmetic homework."

"I won't, Mr. Teller." Ruby Jo followed her father out without looking back.

17 – PIANO LESSONS

"Somethin' ailing you, Ruby Jo?" Mama looked up from her plate of green beans and mashed potatoes.

"No, I'm okay."

"You ain't eatin'. That ain't like you." Mama frowned. "Does she looked well to you, Homer?" Mama turned to Daddy.

"Looks fine to me," Daddy said around a mouthful of potatoes. "Can't a man get a piece of meat after working all day?"

"I used the last of the bacon yesterday. Won't be no more meat till hog-killing time." Mama turned back to Ruby Jo. "Eat your supper, girl, and be thankful for it."

"I'm just not very hungry." Ruby Jo took a bite of cornbread and a couple of gulps of buttermilk. Mama was still frowning, so she ate a forkful of green beans. "I was just thinking about my arithmetic homework. I think it's going to be a hard assignment."

What she was really thinking about was how soon she could get to her room and devour her "Photoplay" magazine. She was pretty sure a good grade wouldn't depend on whether or not she did her homework, so she wasn't going to do it.

"Well, finish your supper and git to it then. I'll ready up the kitchen tonight."

* * * *

There was no opportunity the next two days for private time with Mr. Teller and he acted like he always did, like nothing had happened between him and Ruby Jo. She went into the weekend wondering if she had imagined it all, but she could still feel the electric sensations dancing through her veins. She hadn't imagined it. It was real and Ruby Jo was on pins and needles to feel those fireworks again and see what came next.

She was nervous and restless all weekend. She couldn't eat or sleep and thought she would scream being stuck in a pew between Mama and Daddy for over two hours on Sunday morning at the Living Water Pentecostal Holiness Church. She knew Mr. Teller was sitting in a pew a few rows back with Boyce and the Claypool family, but she didn't dare turn around and look at him. Mama would notice.

The only real blessing was that old Sister Farley, the piano player, was out sick and nobody else could play. So they only sang two hymns instead of the usual seven or eight, which would have stretched the service to three hours or more.

On Monday, Mr. Teller took the opportunity to smile and press two dimes into her hand when nobody was looking. After school, Ruby Jo rode Mosey slowly toward home until everyone was out of sight, then rode back to the schoolhouse. Mr. Teller was waiting at the door. They walked to the cloakroom without speaking and repeated exactly the scene from the week before. Twice more that week, Ruby Jo rode back to the schoolhouse after school.

On Friday evening, as she was helping put supper on the table, Mama said, "You were late getting home from school again today. Third time this week."

"I know, Mama. I'm sorry. I've been having trouble with arithmetic and Mr. Teller has been giving me a little extra help after school."

"You're needed here at home as soon as school's out. You have chores to be done before dark."

"I know, Mama. I'll try not to be late anymore."

Now what? She had to have her time with Mr. Teller. Now that she knew what it felt like to have him play with her titties, she couldn't stop. She thought about little else all weekend and by Monday decided she had a safe plan. She could hardly wait for class to be over so she could tell Mr. Teller.

Ruby Jo took a chance on being late to home one more time. Following Mr. Teller into the cloakroom, she said, "Mama don't like me being late to home so much."

"I've been thinking about how we can spend some time together, without anyone being suspicious, but so far I've come up blank," Mr. Teller replied, frowning.

"I think I know how we can make Mama happy that I'm spending extra time at school, and nobody will think a thing of it." Ruby Jo was so excited by her idea she almost jumped up and down.

"I'm all ears."

"Well, you know, Sister Farley at church is old and poorly and she can't always play piano for services. Nobody else can play either. What if you started giving me piano lessons after school two or three days a week?"

Mr. Teller burst out laughing. "Brilliant, Ruby Jo. Absolutely brilliant." He playfully tweaked her nose. "You're as smart as you are beautiful."

That night while she was helping Mama with supper, Ruby Jo said, in what she hoped was a casual voice, "You know, I've been thinking, Mama. It's really too bad Sister Farley being so poorly lately."

"It is," Mama agreed. "I'm afraid she won't be able to play the piano much longer. I don't know what we'll do for a piano player when she's gone."

"That's what I've been thinking about." Ruby Jo made sure her voice was steady. "I'm pretty sure Mr. Teller would give me piano lessons after school two or three days a week. I could learn to play and take Sister Farley's place when needed."

Mama dropped the pot she was carrying to the stove and spilled water all over the floor. She swung around, her eyes wide, mouth open, and gaped at Ruby Jo.

"Well, what do you think, Mama?" Ruby Jo held her breath as she grabbed dish towels and began mopping up the water.

"Ruby Jo, I don't know what's got into you, but that's the best idea I think I ever heard." Mama put her hand on the table and sat down hard in a chair, like her legs wouldn't hold her up.

"Well, I just can't think of anybody else who would do it." Ruby Jo let out her breath and relaxed.

"I declare, girl, I think the Holy Spirit must've been working on you. This is just what you need. Spending time learning good gospel hymns should settle you some. You've been as flighty as a hummingbird in a patch of honeysuckle. Praise the Lord."

"You know," Mr. Teller said when she told him the news the next day, "I really am going to have to give you piano lessons."

Ruby Jo had never thought of playing the piano before, but once she started having lessons three days a week, she was surprised how much she loved it.

"Who would have thought, Ruby Jo? You've taken to the piano like a duck to water." Mr. Teller laughed. "I swear I think you could be a serious musician."

"I don't like learning nothing but hymns. Can't you teach me some real songs?" Ruby Jo begged. So she learned "Puttin' on the Ritz" the first week. It took two weeks to learn "You Do Something to Me" because they could hardly get through half the lesson before Mr. Teller would start kissing the back of her neck and singing the words softly to her. Then they would leave the lesson unfinished and head for the cloakroom for what Ruby called TP for tittie play.

TP was just about the best thing ever invented, even better than a Mason jar full of sweet iced tea on the hottest day. Or licking chocolate frosting off her finger. Better than anything in the whole world.

How could anybody think such a wonderful-feeling was bad? And they would, if they knew, especially Mama. They must all be crazy or maybe none of them had ever had the sparklers shooting off inside them like Ruby Jo. But, regardless, Ruby Jo knew she had to keep the TP secret.

It wasn't just the powerful craving for TP that was a constant clawing inside her; she fiercely craved the intimacy of the time she and Mr. Teller spent just talking. He told her things she was sure he hadn't told any of the other students, about growing up in Philadelphia. About going to school to be a teacher; about his sister; his old dog, Mutt; and his Mama's special bread pudding with whiskey sauce.

And, he truly listened to Ruby Jo. He understood how the other girls were jealous of her, how she couldn't abide the thought of marrying some dirt clod farmer, and how, somehow, she had to get away from Freeburg. He became her friend, her only friend.

Mama was anxious about the piano playing and kept saying just about every lesson day, "Are you learnin' the piano, Ruby Jo? I can't wait to hear you play. Who would have thought? My own Ruby Jo playing piano in church? Praise the Lord."

It wasn't more than four weeks until they showed up for church one morning and Sister Farley wasn't there.

"You go up and play." Mama nudged Ruby Jo.

"I can't do that," Ruby Jo said.

"Why not? You been learning, haven't you?"

"Yes, but it hasn't been that long. It takes a while to play good enough for church."

Sister Farley was absent again three weeks later.

"You ought to be able to play at least one song by now," Mama said. "You been takin' them lessons quite a spell."

Ruby Jo panicked. She couldn't play a single hymn all the way through and she sure couldn't walk up and play "Tea for Two" or "I Got Rhythm."

"Mama, taking lessons isn't enough. Mr. Teller says I'll never be able to play good unless I really practice. He says I need to practice every day for at least an hour."

"How're you gonna do that? We can't buy no piano."

"I don't know, but I'm trying as hard as I can. And I don't want to just give up; I want to keep on."

So there. That fixed having to play hymns for a while. Ruby Jo turned her face away so her mother wouldn't see her grin.

"I know what!" Mama slapped Ruby Jo on the knee. "I'll talk to the preacher and see if you can come over to the church and practice on Saturdays and the days you don't have lessons."

Ruby Jo swallowed hard and it was all she could do not to groan out loud. Mama didn't seem to notice Ruby Jo wasn't joyful about the idea and went on, "I purely do want to see you sitting up there playing the piano for the Lord. I purely do." Mama smiled and fanned herself with a song book.

18 – A CAREER CHOICE

On the first Friday in May, just three days after her fourteenth birthday, Ruby Jo sat on the floor of the cloakroom waiting for Mr. Teller to finish grading papers so they could have a piano lesson and TP. She sucked on Necco wafers and thumbed through a "Photoplay" with Marlene Dietrich on the cover.

In addition to the flow of dimes, Mr. Teller kept her supplied with candy and the latest movie magazines. If Mama found those magazines, Ruby Jo would have more trouble than she could explain, so she only took one at a time home with her. She hid that one down in the floor space with the nickel and dime jar; the rest Mr. Teller kept for her in the bottom drawer of his desk.

Mr. Teller plopped down on the floor beside Ruby Jo, popped a Necco in his mouth and looked at the full-page picture of Gloria Swanson Ruby Jo was studying.

"You know you're every bit as pretty as she is," he said.

"I am?" Ruby Jo looked closely at Mr. Teller, trying to decide if he was telling the truth. "Really and truly?"

"Cross my heart. You're young. When you're her age, you'll be far more beautiful than she could ever be."

"You really think so?"

"I don't think so." He began unbuttoning her dress. "I know it."

That's when it hit her. Why hadn't she thought of it before? That was what she was saving all those nickels and dimes for. She would go to Hollywood and be a movie star. Her picture would be in all the movie magazines. She would be famous. It was perfect.

Her heart pounded so hard it practically made her titties bounce. Ruby Jo wanted to jump up and dance, not that she knew how. Dancing was forbidden, but in that moment she had no doubt she could win a jitterbug contest. Instead, she put her hand behind Mr. Teller's head, pulled his face to her and kissed him.

She felt him stiffen. In all their TP, he had never kissed her on the mouth. She was too happy, too excited to settle for the closed mouth touching of their lips. There was more to kissing; she just knew it. She opened her mouth and ran her tongue along his lower lip. He opened his mouth, moaned, and deepened the kiss. The familiar electric jolt set her limbs to trembling. This was almost as good-feeling as TP.

He pushed her back to the floor and stretched his body on top of hers. They kissed frantically for a few minutes and then, groaning, he rolled off her, putting his elbows on his knees and his face in his hands.

"What's the matter? Did I do it wrong?" Ruby Jo sat up quickly and put her hand on his shoulder.

"You didn't do anything wrong, Ruby Jo." He lifted his face and looked at her. She was startled by the pain she saw in his eyes, then she smiled. Could she really make a man, a full-grown man, hurt that bad?

"But you stopped. I really liked it," she said.

"Oh, Lordy, Ruby Jo." He took both her hands in his. "I want you so much I can't stand it. I've been telling myself our TP would be enough, but it's not. I can't be around you and not go all the way. It's killing me."

"All the way?"

"Yes. Do you know what I mean?"

"I think so."

"But you've never done it before?"

"No."

Mr. Teller lifted one of her hands, turned it, and kissed her palm. "You're every bit a woman, Ruby Jo, but you are a very young woman. It's because you're so young I just can't do what I want to do."

"I don't want to do all of it either," Ruby Jo said. That was a lie. She couldn't wait to find out what "all of it" was, but seeing the intensity of his desire put a thought in her head. Ruby Jo wasn't sure how she knew, but she understood she had something of value. When the time was right, she would trade it for something she wanted more than satisfying her curiosity or a few minutes of feel-good on the floor of the cloakroom with her teacher.

"Then you're smarter and stronger than I am." Mr. Teller stood, took her hand, helped her up and led her out of the cloakroom.

"We're not doing TP today?" Ruby Jo couldn't believe they wouldn't.

He burst out laughing, but it wasn't a happy laugh. It was sad.

"Well, what about my piano lesson?" She pouted and gave him her best "pretty please" look.

"Not today." He took his coat from the back of his chair, picked up a stack of books from the desk and walked to the door.

Turning in the open door with his hand on the knob, he said, "You have no idea how you're killing me, Ruby Jo. You really and truly are killing me. I don't think I can stand being around you and not taking what I want."

Then he was gone.

Ruby Jo smiled. TP on Monday ought to be extra special good with Mr. Teller all stirred up like that.

* * * *

Sunday morning Ruby Jo didn't see Mr. Teller in church and wondered where he could be. As the congregation stood for the final prayer, Brother Bothell, the head of the school board, asked if he could come to the pulpit and make an announcement.

"They won't be any school for the next few days," he said. "Mr. Teller was called away suddenly for a family emergency. I took him to San Angelo yesterday to catch a train to Philadelphia. He doesn't know when he'll be back. School won't take up again till we find a substitute teacher."

The bottom dropped out of Ruby Jo's stomach. She clenched her fists and gritted her teeth. Before she could think, she drew her foot back and kicked the leg of the pew in front of her. Pain exploded up her leg and she collapsed onto the seat, crying. Not from the pain in her toe, not for the loss of TP or the dimes, but from the pain of losing her only friend.

19 – "FROGGY WENT A'COURTIN"

Ruby Jo slammed the door of the mailbox shut. Nothing. She found a reason to check the mailbox herself every day since Mr. Teller had been gone—even when she had to hobble to the road for over two weeks with a really sore toe.

There was never anything for her. What did she expect? A letter saying he was coming back for her so they could be together? She didn't even want that. So what did she want? Well, a little more TP sure wouldn't hurt, but what really made her mad was that he could leave her without saying goodbye.

How could he? She saw in his eyes how he felt about her and yet he could leave—just like that? If she had an address for him, she'd give him a piece of her mind. Ruby Jo stamped her foot on the ground and snorted her disgust. It was stupid to keep checking the mailbox. She wasn't going to hear from him.

The school board had realized right off it would be impossible to find a substitute teacher for the last few weeks of school on such short notice. They voted unanimously to issue passing certificates to all the students and close the school until fall term.

A week later Brother Bothell called a special session and handed out the certificates. The schoolhouse was never locked so Ruby Jo had sneaked back for her movie magazines. She couldn't fit them all in her satchel so she chose her favorites and hid them under her feather mattress.

Ruby Jo sighed as she turned away from the mailbox. It was going to be an even longer summer than usual. She needed to spend her time thinking about how to get to Hollywood instead of some stupid teacher who didn't even say "kiss my foot."

A sound caused Ruby Jo to turn and shade her eyes against the shimmering heat. A man on a mule came riding over the crest of the hill. Curious, she waited.

Boyce Claypool's older brother, Clarence, better known as Boomer for his huge size, reined in his mule and tipped his hat. "Ruby Jo."

"What are you doing in this neck of the woods, Boomer?"

"I come to see your Pa."

"Well, I saw him coming in from the fields, so you should find him in the barn."

"Do you want to ride up to the house?"

"No. I guess I'll just walk."

"It's hot enough to raise a blister on a cactus. Are you sure you don't want to ride?"

She squinted up at him. "No, I'll walk." The sooner she got back to the house the sooner she'd have to help Mama fix supper, and it was hotter in the kitchen than it was outside.

When she looked out the kitchen window as she put a platter of fried potatoes on the table a little while later, she saw Boomer was still standing in the barnyard with Daddy.

"I wonder what in the world Boomer wants." she said, mostly to herself. Mama didn't say anything, so Ruby Jo asked her directly, "What do you think Boomer wants?"

"Lord knows," Mama said, but she turned away to the stove and Ruby Jo got the feeling she did know.

"Mama…" Ruby Jo's stomach shot straight down to her toes, but before she could say more the back door opened. As Daddy walked in, behind him, Ruby Jo could see Boomer riding out of the yard.

"Daddy…"

Daddy held up his hand. "Later, Ruby Jo."

Ruby Jo knew enough to shut up when Daddy used that tone of voice, but she squirmed and fidgeted all through supper. When Daddy finished eating and pushed his plate back, Mama didn't get up and start clearing the table like she usually did. She put a cup and a pot of hot coffee on the table in front of Daddy, then sat in her chair and waited, looking at her folded hands in her lap.

Daddy poured his cup full, lifted it to his mouth, blew on it, then slurped a mouthful. Ruby Jo wanted to scream. *Just say Boomer was here for any reason but me.*

"Ruby Jo." Daddy cleared his throat and looked at her. "Boomer come by asking my blessing to come calling on you and I give it."

Ruby Jo jumped out of her chair so fast it crashed on the floor. "No!" she screamed. "How could you?" She clenched her fists and backed away from the table. "I'm not marrying anybody, especially not some stupid dirt farmer."

Mama flew out of her chair so fast Ruby Jo hardly had time to catch her breath before Mama slapped her across the face with such force she staggered.

"How dare you?" Mama said, her voice as steady and grim, like the whir of a rattlesnake. She righted the toppled chair and pushed it toward the table. "Set," she said.

Ruby Jo sat, cheek burning and heart pounding. She hated it but she knew her chin was quivering, and she swallowed hard, holding back tears.

Mama sat and folded her hands on the table. Daddy picked up his coffee cup and studied its contents like he thought there might be a silver dollar in the bottom.

"Ruby Jo, as long as you live, don't you ever speak such a thing again," Mama said. "Your daddy's a farmer and the finest man who ever lived. Do you understand me?"

"Yes, ma'am." Ruby Jo couldn't keep her voice from shaking. Daddy must have actually seen something in his cup, because he leaned forward and studied it even harder.

"Boomer Claypool comes from a God-fearin', hard workin' family." Mama pushed back a lock of hair that had escaped her bun and fallen forward.

"But, Mama, I don't want to marry anybody." Ruby Jo cringed. *Why do I have to squeak like a mouse?* She cleared her throat. "At least not for a good while." *I'll marry somebody famous in Hollywood.*

Mama pressed her lips together and sighed. "Well, if wishes was horses, beggars would ride."

"Daddy..." Ruby Jo turned to him, but he kept his eyes on his coffee cup.

"You've graduated eighth grade, and you'll be fifteen your next birthday. It's fitting you should start looking for a husband."

"But, Mama, there are other things besides getting married right off the bat."

"Like what? You want to go on to high school? What for? They ain't nothing beyond that except marrying and childbearing, so it's just a waste of another four years."

"But what if I wanted to do something else?" Ruby Jo kept her voice low and even, making sure it was a question. She sure didn't want it to sound like sass.

"What, Ruby Jo? Tell me that." It was clear Mama's patience was being sorely tried. "It takes college schooling to be a teacher and that costs money we ain't got. They ain't much else for a woman. So, you want to be an old maid, living with me and your Daddy till we die?" Mama shook her head. "A good man and a few young'uns'll settle you down. Lord knows you need settling. I see a wildness growing in you like a weed and, to tell you the truth, Ruby Jo, it plumb scares me half to death."

Ruby Jo looked sharply at Mama. She couldn't believe Mama sounded like she was about to cry. Ruby Jo's own throat thickened. There was no way she could tell Mama she wanted to go to Hollywood and be a famous actress, so she said, "But, Mama! Boomer? Boomer Claypool?"

"You could do worse. Besides, they ain't but a handful of single men in these parts, so it's not like you can be choosy." Mama stood and picked up dirty plates from the table. "Boomer will be takin' supper with us tomorrow night. See that you wash your hair and put on your good church dress."

The next afternoon Ruby Jo sat in the porch swing and watched Boomer slowly ride his mule around the bend in the lane from the road.

I wonder if Boyce told him about the panties and the nickels? Ruby Jo felt a moment of panic, then pressed her lips together and shook her head. What if he did? That might be a good thing. She had no intention of marrying Boomer, but while she was figuring out how to get out of it, she might have a little fun with him. She sure hadn't had any fun since Mr. Teller left.

Boomer was a lot bigger than Boyce and his body looked like a lump of yeast bread left too long to rise in his clean overalls and white shirt. He was freshly shaven and his brown hair was slicked so flat to his head it made his large brown eyes look too big for his face.

Why, he looks like a frog. Ruby Jo couldn't help herself; she giggled as a tune popped into her head.

"Froggie went a courtin and he did ride. Mhmm…"

20 – THE BEST LAID PLANS

The heat lay on everything, thick and heavy as a blanket of molasses. Nothing moved. Not a fly, not an ant. Not a bird or a cloud in the sky.

Boomer had given up pushing the porch swing with his big feet. He hadn't said a word for at least half an hour. Not that it mattered much; he never said anything worth hearing. Sometimes Ruby Jo wondered if maybe he wasn't a little slow.

"Let's walk down to the creek, Boomer. It has to be cooler than here." The back of Ruby Jo's dress was so wet with sweat she stuck to the back of the swing.

"Do you think your Mama will let you?" He pulled a big checkered handkerchief out of his pocket and mopped his face. "She's been keepin' watch on us like a flea eyein' a dog's butt."

In the three weeks since she had been walking out with Boomer, they had done nothing but sit together on the porch swing within Mama's sight or hearing, at Mama's supper table or on a church pew with Mama and Daddy. They had been walking out long enough to have a little time alone. She leaned toward the open window and called out, "Mama, me and Boomer are gonna walk down to the creek for a little while."

There were footsteps. Mama held the screen door open and leaned around it. She looked straight at Boomer for a minute then she said, "All right. You behave yourselves, you hear?"

"Yes, ma'am," Boomer nodded. "We'll just cool off a bit and be right back."

"Here." Mama held out a dish towel. "Use this to carry back some cress if you see any."

Ruby Jo grabbed the dish towel and Boomer's hand, dragging him down the porch steps.

"How far is the creek?" Clarence puffed and mopped his face some more before they were hardly past the barn.

"For crying out loud, Boomer! You're slower than the seven-year itch. Come on, you sissie."

Ruby Jo strode ahead and didn't look back. She had her shoes off and her skirt hiked up into her belt, wading in the knee-deep water when Boomer collapsed on the grass in the shade. His face was as red as an overripe tomato and slick with sweat. Ruby Jo wondered if he was going to pass out.

"Take your shoes off and come on in. The water's cool."

"Let me catch my breath just a minute." Clarence lay back and crossed his arms over his mountain of a chest.

Ruby Jo shrugged and splashed down the creek, pulling a little cress along the banks, until she lost her balance and fell. The dish towel and cress floated off around a bend in the creek.

Ruby Jo was already wet to the waist, so she lay back in the water. It was too shallow to really float or swim, but it covered most of her. Her hair came loose and danced in the current around her head like a water ballet of fire serpents.

Her chest was above the water and she felt her nipples hard against the tight, wet fabric of her dress. Without thinking, Ruby Jo lifted a hand and rolled a nipple between her thumb and finger. Suddenly she felt funny, like somebody was watching her. It was Boomer, standing on the bank, grinning. She dropped her hand and pushed herself up.

"What are you grinning about, Boomer?" Ruby Jo slowly unbuttoned the top of her dress as she waded out of the creek. He watched her, his mouth hanging slightly open. She pushed her dress down off her shoulders, exposing her bare chest as she stopped in front of him.

"Dang, Ruby Jo." His voice sounded moist, like he was slobbering a little. "I reckon I figgered you plumb wrong."

"How's that, Boomer?" She looked at him through lowered lashes, but he was staring at her chest.

"Well, you know. Locked up tighter'n a tick on a hound dog till the weddin' bed. Dang."

She cupped a breast with her hand. "Put your mouth on me, Boomer."

His head shot up and he leaned back a little. "Why, I can't do that, Ruby Jo."

"Why not?" She rolled a nipple between her thumb and forefinger and slowly ran her tongue over her lower lip.

"It ain't natural, that's why not." Boomer swung his head back and forth like a bull that saw red in two places and didn't know which way to go."

"You've got to be joking."

"No, I ain't jokin'," he said. "Titties is for babies."

Ruby Jo shook her head. "I'll swear, Boomer, you have to be as dumb as a turkey gobbler in a rainstorm."

"Don't call me dumb, Ruby Jo." He frowned and gave her a hard look. "If I didn't know your Daddy would shoot me dead, I'd throw you down right here on the ground and give you a taste of what's waitin' for you when we get married. You'd see I ain't dumb."

"Who says we're getting married?"

"Well, ain't we?"

"No, Boomer, we ain't!" Ruby Jo quickly buttoned her dress, grabbed her shoes and socks and stalked toward the house.

"You'll be sorry," Boomer called after her.

She was sizzling with the need for some fun, but there wasn't going to be any TP with old Boomer. That made her so mad she could spit enough nails to build a good-size house.

It was dusk when Ruby Jo got back to the house. She raced past Mama and Daddy sitting in rockers on the front porch, slammed the screen door and went straight to her room. Before she was out of her wet clothes, she heard Boomer riding his mule out of the yard.

There was no way around it. She had to say something or Mama would hound her until she did. As soon as she was in dry clothes, she went out to the porch and sat in the swing, thankful the light of day was seeping away, making it just dark enough Mama couldn't clearly see her face.

"I fell in the creek," Ruby Jo said.

"I could see that," Mama replied.

"How come Boomer took off like a scalded cat?" Daddy asked.

"He was all wet from helping me out of the creek. He wanted to get home."

Except for the squeaking of Mama and Daddy's rockers, it was completely quiet for a few minutes.

"Boomer'll probably be coming home with us after church tomorrow, so I reckon I better get up and kill a chicken in the morning." Ruby Jo heard the question in Mama's voice and braced herself.

"You don't need to kill no chicken for Boomer, Mama. He won't be coming home with us."

"Oh, Ruby Jo!"

Ruby Jo didn't have to see Mama's face to feel her disappointment.

"You can't mix kerosene and water, Mama, no matter how much you want to."

21 – BIGGER FISH

Ruby Jo only saw Boomer at church after that. She didn't have to look at him because she played piano for church most of the time now and kept her eyes on the song book. But she could feel his eyes on her. After three or four weeks, he stopped showing up for services.

On the way out of church one Sunday, Old Sister Turner sidled up to Mama, shot a smirky glance at Ruby Jo and said, "I hear tell Boomer is walking out with that youngest Skinner girl over to Knockville."

"That so?" Mama smiled at Sister Turner but grabbed Ruby Jo's arm so hard it hurt and steered her down the church steps to the wagon.

Before Ruby Jo could even settle herself in the back, Mama turned in her seat and mimicked, "*We just don't suit. We're kerosene and water.*" Mama snorted like she was clearing her nose after coming from under water. "I swear, Ruby Jo, you ain't got the sense God give a turnip." She shook her head and turned toward Daddy as he climbed into the wagon.

Ruby Jo said not a word but smiled to herself. There were only two other unmarried men in the neighborhood. Cletus Howard lived with his widowed mother a few miles out of town, raised goats and tried to raise corn. He had bulgy eyes and big lips and never said a single word to anybody. Well, except for an occasional loud "amen" when Brother Brokus preached a real hellfire and brimstone sermon.

Wilbur Marker, a widower, was so old and stooped he shuffled around with a cane. He lived with his daughter and son-in-law and twelve kids back in the woods a few miles from Ruby Jo's folks.

Even Mama wouldn't think of those two as husband material, so Ruby

Jo felt pretty safe. Now she could give all her thinking to how to get to Hollywood instead of worrying about all this walking out business, especially when there was no fun to be had in any of it.

In secret, she counted her nickels and dimes and decided she had a goodly sum of money. She didn't know how much anything cost, but the first big problem was how to get to a real town with a railroad. If she could do that, then she would worry about her fare to Hollywood.

The Frees went to San Angelo pretty often, but everybody knew everybody's business. If Ruby Jo tried to hitch a ride, Mama would know about it before Mr. Free could start the engine on his new Model A Town Sedan. It was way too far to walk. Maybe she could ride Mosey. No, that would take so long they'd be looking all over the country for her before she could get halfway there. There had to be a way and she would find it.

Late on a Friday afternoon, about a week before Halloween, when Ruby Jo rode Mosey into the yard from practicing piano over at the church house, she was surprised to see a Ford Huckster pickup parked under the pecan tree. *Jacobson Mercantile, Junction, Texas. Serving You Since 1895* was painted on the door panels. Who in the world could that be? Jacobson? Junction? Maybe man who sold Sally's daddy the mare? What would he be doing here?

Ruby Jo put Mosey away and tiptoed through the back door into the kitchen, pulling off her sunbonnet and laying it on the table. She could hear voices in the front room.

"I took over management of the store seven years ago when my father died," a man said. "So now, it's just my mother and me and my two little girls, Rose and Pearl."

"I'm so sorry to hear about your wife's passing," Mama said. "I can imagine how hard that must be."

"Well, it's been almost two years now and the Lord does give comfort according to his promises, Mrs. Cassity."

"Amen, to that, Mr. Jacobson. I think I heard Ruby Jo putting Mosey away. She plays piano for our church, you know, and she is so faithful with her practicing."

"Music is a blessing, especially when used for the glory of the Lord."

"Mr. Cassity should be coming in from the field pretty soon and we'd be most honored if you'd take supper with us."

"I don't want to put you out, ma'am, dropping in unexpected like this."

"No trouble, Mr. Jacobson; no trouble a'tall. Now, where is that girl? Ruby Jo!"

Ruby Jo straightened her dress and pushed through the door into the front room. A man leapt to his feet. He was taller than Daddy and thin. He was wearing a clean, pressed gray suit, a white shirt, and a red string tie. Ruby Jo's eyes shot to his feet. He was wearing clean shoes, not dirty boots.

"Mr. Jacobson," Mama said with the biggest smile Ruby Jo had ever seen on her face, "this is my daughter, Ruby Jo."

"Ruby Jo." Mr. Jacobson stepped forward and extended his hand. No calluses or dirty fingernails. "I'm so happy to make your acquaintance. I've heard about you and you're even prettier than they say." His light gray eyes crinkled at the corners when he smiled.

"Thank you, Mr. Jacobson. You've heard about me?" Ruby Jo took his hand, keeping her eyes on his. She didn't need to see Mama frowning at her right now.

"Yes. We get people in the store from around here from time to time and a beautiful woman always stirs up talk."

Ruby Jo couldn't help it. She felt a hot blush creep up her face. Mama cleared her throat and said, "Yes, well, Mr. Jacobson, can we get you some iced tea while we get supper on? It's right pleasant in the shade of the porch."

"Thank you, ma'am. I purely would enjoy that and thank you for the supper invitation."

"Not at all, Mr. Jacobson. Me and Ruby Jo'll just go get that tea for you."

Mama gave Ruby Jo a little push to start her toward the kitchen and followed behind. As soon as the kitchen door closed, Mama put her hands on Ruby Jo's shoulders, turned her around, and said in a low voice, "Ruby Jo Cassity, if you mess this up, I will whip you until you can't stand up. Do you understand me?"

Ruby Jo's heart tripped a beat before she replied, "Yes, Mama."

Before they could chip ice and fill a glass, Daddy walked in the back door, stomping the mud off his boots. "We got company?" he asked as he hung his sweat-stained hat on a peg.

"Yes," Mama said, "and he wants to talk to you. Get washed up and join him on the porch. I'll bring y'all some tea."

The door between the kitchen and front room was closed, so Ruby Jo couldn't hear what Daddy and Mr. Jacobson said. When they sat down to supper, Mr. Jacobson removed his suit coat and hung it on the back of his chair. Ruby Jo could see that he was muscular and hard even if he was thin. He must be as old as Methuselah, at least thirty-five or forty, but he was a good-looking man. And clean. He wasn't even sweating.

This was a full-grown man who had been married. He ought to know everything there was to know about fun. Surely he wouldn't be a stick in the mud like Boomer and he was a lot better to look at. Ruby Jo looked up at him through her lashes and smiled several times during supper. He was watching her and smiled back.

"So, Mr. Jacobson," Ruby Jo said, trying to make her voice sound like she thought Marlene Dietrich's voice would sound, "I think you sold a mare to Mr. Free?"

"I did. A while back." Mr. Jacobson took a sip of iced tea. "I believe he bought it for his daughter."

"Sally. She used to ride the horse to school."

"Pepper. The mare's name was Pepper. My wife loved that horse. She was quite a rider." Mr. Jacobson paused, buttering his biscuit, said nothing for a couple of seconds, then went on. "But in the end, that's how she died. Something spooked Pepper. Mariah was thrown, hit her head on a rock. I just got to where I couldn't bear to have Pepper around."

"How awful." Ruby Jo looked at her plate. "I'm so sorry."

Nobody said anything for a minute, then Mama asked, "So, Mr. Jacobson, do you live near your store?"

"Actually, my wife and I lived in an apartment above the store but, after my father passed, we moved into the house with my mother. It was better for the girls and for Mama."

"I'm sure your mother's been a godsend, taking care of the little ones," Mama said as she passed the biscuits.

"Actually, we have a woman living in who does the cooking and takes care of the girls. A cleaning woman comes in every day to handle the laundry and everything else. Mama works in the store with me, but she says she's tired of it. She wants to quit and go stay with my sister in Omaha."

Ruby Jo saw Mama's eyes go wide and her chest rise and fall real fast at the mention of household help.

"What all kinds of goods do you carry?" Daddy wanted to know as he spooned a big helping of black-eyed peas onto his plate.

"Just about everything, Mr. Cassity. A large line of groceries and staples, soft goods, small tools, some tack and guns and ammunition, a few books. We have a pretty good selection of ready-made clothes and lots of fabric, of course. We don't carry much furniture, but we can order just about anything a person would want."

Ruby Jo glanced at Mama. Her lips were slightly parted and her eyes were glazed as she gazed at Mr. Jacobson. She looked like she could be drunk.

Uh-oh! Mama was going to marry Ruby Jo off to Mr. Jacobson, come hell or high water. Well, Mr. Jacobson was a mighty fine man, but not as fine as Hollywood. Ruby Jo would just have to be smarter than she had ever been and figure a way out of this little trap. Nothing was going to stop her from going to Hollywood.

After serving a quickly made canned berry cobbler for dessert, Mama said, "Why don't we set on the porch for a spell? I'll ready up the kitchen later."

So they all filed out. Mama and Daddy sat in the rocking chairs; Ruby Jo sat in the swing with Mr. Jacobson.

Daddy and Mama rocked. Mr. Jacobson set the swing in motion. Nobody said anything for what seemed a long time, then Daddy said, "Mr. Jacobson here has asked permission to call on you, Ruby Jo, and I've given it."

Mr. Jacobson stopped the swaying of the swing and turned to Ruby Jo. "Is that all right with you, Ruby Jo?"

"Yes, Mr. Jacobson," Ruby Jo smiled and looked at him from under her lashes. It's all right with me." She hoped the look she gave him was as alluring as the look on Mae West's face in the last "Photoplay" Mr. Teller gave her.

"Please, call me Berlin," Mr. Jacobson said. "We're going to be walking out, so I think you can call me by my name."

"Berlin? I haven't heard that name before."

"It's strange, I know, but my grandmother insisted I be named after the city where she was born. My father's family are from Germany."

Mr. Jacobson… Berlin… just kept looking at her, a little smile making tiny dimples in his cheeks.

Mama coughed. "Ruby Jo is very young, Mr. Jacobson, and you're an older man…"

"Berlin," he corrected. "And I'm thirty-seven."

"Berlin. Yes, as I was saying…"

"I understand, Mrs. Cassity. I assure you of my good intentions. My wife has been gone for some time and I desire to marry again. And, even though we have help with Rose and Pearl, they need a mother."

"How old are they?" Ruby Jo asked.

"Rose is five and Pearl is three."

Good heavens! Ruby Jo drew her lower lip between her teeth. What would she do with a couple of young'uns? Well, she wouldn't have to worry about it.

"They're very well-behaved little girls," Berlin was quick to add.

"Ruby Jo won't be fifteen herself until late spring," Mama said.

"I understand," Berlin smiled at Mama. "If we decide we're suited, we can certainly wait until after Ruby Jo's fifteenth birthday."

"That's a spell." Daddy leaned forward in his rocker and fixed a steady look at Berlin.

Berlin put both hands up as if in surrender. "Mr. and Mrs. Cassity, a long, slow courtship will suit me just fine. I am a Christian man, a deacon in Crossroads Baptist Church. I assure you that not only are my intentions toward your daughter honorable, her virtue is as safe with me as if you were present every minute."

Well, shoot a speckled hen! Hopefully that was just a pretty speech for Mama and Daddy and he really didn't mean it.

Daddy cleared his throat, "Well, yes, I'm sure we didn't mean…"

Berlin stood up. "I understand perfectly, Mr. Cassity. I will treat Ruby Jo with the utmost care and concern, and if we choose each other, I will be very good to her. Now, it's getting late and Saturday is a big day in the store."

Mama and Daddy both stood up. Berlin shook their hands as he said, "I have duties at church, so I won't be free Sunday. But, with your permission, I'd like to call on Ruby Jo Monday evening after supper."

"Of course," Mama said.

Berlin turned to Ruby Jo. "Is that suitable to you, Ruby Jo?" She nodded. He extended his hand. "Then would you be so kind as to walk me to the truck?"

22 – A KNIGHT IN SHINING ARMOR

Mama just went plumb crazy. A body would have thought Berlin was courting her. She talked about him every minute.

"I confess, Ruby Jo, I thought you should have married Boomer, but I was dead wrong. Berlin is the perfect man for you," Mama would say. She might stop rolling out biscuit dough and stare off at the kitchen ceiling like there was a painting or something up there.

"Just think. You won't have to stand outside in the heat or the cold, putting your hands in boiling water and washing clothes with lye soap until your skin burns. Dragging heavy overalls sopping wet to the clothesline. Getting so wet yourself that your clothes freeze to you when it's cold...." She would drift off and stand motionless for a few minutes. Then she'd come back to herself and go on.

"No cooking or cleaning, and you'll get to wear store-bought clothes. And work in the store where it's clean and warm. Oh, Ruby Jo, the Lord has blessed you mightily with Berlin Jacobson. Maybe he'll get you a horse like you always wanted."

Ruby Jo heard it over and over and so did the ladies at church at every service.

"You know, Sister Tuner, Ruby Jo's Berlin owns the mercantile over at Junction. I'm just so glad she had the good sense not to marry Boomer Claypool."

"Ruby Jo's Berlin is just the finest gentleman, Sister Martin. He wouldn't think of letting Ruby Jo work herself into the ground. He has full-time help to do all the cooking and cleaning. She'll be working in the store right along with him."

"I just can't get over it, Sister Clark, what a thoughtful man Ruby Jo's Berlin is. Why, just this last week, he brought me a whole bag of walnuts and he gave Ruby Jo that green scarf she's wearing. Said it matched her eyes. He's so sweet to her."

"That Berlin's a mighty fine man, Sister Rafferty, even if he is a Baptist."

"Did I tell you, Sister Calley, Berlin was calling on Ruby Jo Monday, Thursday, and Saturday evenings but that wasn't enough. He hired a man to come to the store at noon on Saturdays to help his Mama so he could spend more time with Ruby Jo. That's a smitten man if I ever saw one."

Mama was right about Berlin being thoughtful. He almost always brought Ruby Jo something—chocolates, ribbons for her hair, a little carved box for holding keepsakes, a book, always something very proper. He brought Mama some little thing about once a week—a box of fine Dutch cocoa, a pair of handkerchiefs, a bit of candy. Once he brought her enough fabric for a new apron. After he saw Daddy using a hammer with a cracked handle to fix something in the kitchen, he brought Daddy a new one.

Sometimes Berlin would drive over in the family car, a Chevrolet sedan, and take all of them for a ride on Saturday afternoon. He would usually hold Ruby Jo's hand or kiss her on the forehead with Mama and Daddy right there, and Mama would grin from ear to ear.

Mama was really beside herself one Sunday when Berlin skipped services at his own church and visited Living Water Pentecostal Church with them. He drove them in his car and Mama sat so straight and proud in the back seat as they parked in the church yard anybody would have thought she was a queen riding in a chauffeured limousine. When she walked down the center aisle of the church, behind Daddy but ahead of Ruby Jo and Berlin, she held her head so high her hat liked to touch the ceiling. It was probably the proudest day of Mama's life.

Ruby Jo couldn't help strutting a little herself as this fine-looking man, wearing a suit and shoes instead of overalls and manured boots, kept his hand lightly on the small of her back as they found their way to the pew. This must be what it felt like to be a movie star, to have all the women looking at you, wishing they were you, and all the men wishing they were the man with his hand on you.

After Berlin dropped them off at home after Sunday evening service, Mama heaved a big sigh, turned to Daddy, and said, "Thank the Lord, the Spirit didn't come on nobody during preaching today. The Baptists don't hold with speaking in tongues and rolling around on the floor."

It seemed that one tizzy after another kept Mama spinning like a top, because the next time Berlin visited, he invited them to spend Thanksgiving with his family in Junction in less than two weeks.

"Just tell me what I'm supposed to wear, Homer," Mama fussed at Daddy. "I ain't got but one Sunday go-to-meeting dress and it's five years old if it's a day. At least Ruby Jo can still wear her school clothes."

"Your dress is fine," Daddy replied around a mouthful of mashed potatoes. "You ain't meeting the queen of England."

"No, but we'll be meeting Berlin's Mama. She's gonna be Ruby Jo's mother-in-law. We have to make a good impression."

"We're good people, Alma." Daddy stopped his spoon halfway to his mouth and looked at Mama. "If Berlin's Mama can't see that through what we're wearing, then she ain't worth knowing."

"I guess I could take my new apron."

"You don't need no apron, Mama," Ruby Jo reminded her. "I doubt you'll spend any time in the kitchen. They have help, remember?"

"Oh, Lord, how'm I supposed to act with nothing to do? I'll probably have to talk to Missus Jacobson. What'll I talk about, Ruby Jo?"

"It'll come to you, Mama," Ruby Jo said, but the truth was she stewed about meeting Mrs. Jacobson herself. Then, as she was dozing off to sleep one night, she thought, *It doesn't matter what she thinks of me. I'm not marrying Berlin anyway.* She didn't worry about it after that.

Mama heated the iron on the back of the wood stove and pressed her dress and Ruby Jo's twice the night before Thanksgiving and made two mincemeat pies. Mama might not have a new dress but nobody could fault her pies.

Mama nervously rattled on about one thing or another in the back seat as Berlin drove them to Junction early Thanksgiving morning. Ruby Jo had never been to Junction. Everything the Cassitys needed they grew or made, bought in Freeburg or ordered from the Sears Roebuck catalog.

She took careful notice as they drove through the town. It was a lot bigger than Freeburg, which was mainly a crossroads with three or four buildings. She didn't see a railroad station but needed to find out if there was one. If so, her escape to Hollywood could be a whole lot easier than trying to get to San Angelo.

"There's my store," Berlin said, his voice swollen with pride, as they drove down the main street. "It's closed today, but maybe next time you'll be able to have a look at it."

It was a big building, taking up almost half the block. There, in big letters right across the front, was *Jacobson Mercantile*. Mama and Daddy oohed and aahed and said they couldn't even imagine all the wonderful things that might be inside. Ruby Jo couldn't stop herself from thinking, *That could be mine.*

Mama said "Lordy" and Ruby Jo's mouth dropped open when Berlin pulled into the driveway of a two-story house sitting back off the street behind a big oak tree and a wide green lawn. It was painted white with black shutters and had a deep front porch. The Cassity's small house hadn't had a coat of paint in Ruby's entire life and the front yard was dirt speckled with chicken droppings.

"Welcome to my home." Berlin, grinning, reached over and patted Ruby Jo's knee.

"You live here?" she gaped. Her heart started jumping around in some kind of crazy dance that drove all thought of Hollywood right out of her head.

"I do," he said, then leaned over and whispered in her ear, "and so will you."

Just as Berlin killed the motor and opened the car door, the front door of the house banged open and two little girls ran like excited puppies down the sidewalk.

"Daddy! Daddy!"

A large-bosomed woman with iron-gray hair and a big smile on a wrinkled face stepped out behind the girls and waited on the porch.

As it turned out, Mama's fretting was wasted because she and Mrs. Jacobson hit it off like they were at least kissing cousins. Mrs. Jacobson hugged Ruby Jo right there on the front porch and said, "You're every bit as pretty as Berlin said you were."

Rose and Pearl each grabbed one of Ruby Jo's hands, jumped up and down and said, "Come see our room, Ruby Jo."

Berlin swooped the littlest one up, swung her around and said, "In a minute, punkin. Give our guests a chance to catch their breath and we'll show them the whole house."

The "whole house" left Daddy, Mama, and Ruby Jo all shaking their heads in wonder and saying,

"My goodness."

"Oh, my."

"Will you just look at that."

"Well, I never seen anything like that before."

The front door opened on a wide, long hall down the middle of the house. Double doors that slid back into the wall opened to a large parlor on one side and a dining room that would seat at least twelve on the other. Behind the living room was a room Berlin called his study.

Across the hall, behind the dining room, two women worked at a big table in the middle of a large kitchen filled with the smell of roasting turkey, apples, and chocolate. Mama put her hand over her heart and said, "Oh!" when she spotted the electric stove and a new-fangled refrigerator.

What really left the Cassity family speechless was a tiny room with an indoor toilet and a small sink with running water tucked under the stairway. They still hadn't recovered from that when Mrs. Jacobson showed them an upstairs room with another toilet and sink and a big claw-foot tub. Mama said, "Oh, Ruby Jo!"

Ruby Jo didn't reply. She was busy imagining sitting in the tub covered with bubbles and reading a "Photoplay."

There were four large bedrooms upstairs, each with real bedsteads and coverlets, not quilts. Everything was color-matched—the coverlets, the drapes, the rugs on the polished floors.

Rose and Pearl's room was all pink and white with a tiny rose-patterned wallpaper. Ruby Jo ran her hand over a bookcase full of books, dolls, and stuffed toys. She sure never had anything like that growing up… but her young'uns could… hers and Berlin's. Ruby Jo shook herself like she had walked into a big spider web. *No. Stop it.* She was going to be a famous actress. She didn't think movie stars had babies.

Back in the parlor, as they were about to sit down, Berlin walked up behind Ruby Jo, right there in front of everybody, put his arms around her waist and whispered in her ear, "I hope you like it."

She turned to face him and said, "I've never seen anything like it. I can't hardly take it in."

"Well, you better get used to it." He grinned and tapped the end of her nose with his finger.

The Saturday after Thanksgiving, Mama didn't say a word when Berlin showed up just after noon and suggested he take Ruby Jo for a drive and an early supper at a little café in Mason a few miles away, just the two of them.

Finally! Totally alone. Ruby Jo was almost beside herself. It was sunny but cold, so Ruby Jo bundled up in a coat, her neck wrapped in her new scarf. She sat in the middle of the seat, cuddled against Berlin. When he shifted gears, his hand brushed her knee.

"You always smell so good." Ruby Jo giggled.

"I'm glad you like it." Berlin laughed. "It's bay rum."

Ruby Jo had never eaten in a café before. She sat straight in her chair and glanced around at the other diners. She imagined she was in a restaurant in Hollywood with a famous actor, maybe Gary Cooper. She had read all about him and Marlene Dietrich in "Morocco" in the last "Photoplay" magazine Mr. Teller gave her. She didn't know where Morocco was but she knew it was a place she wanted to go someday.

Berlin ordered a steak for himself and chicken for Ruby Jo. They had peach cobbler with ice cream for dessert. All though supper, Ruby Jo was very careful of her manners and carried on a conversation she figured was worthy of a star, maybe Jean Harlow or Loretta Young. Berlin laughed a lot and reached across the table to squeeze her hand a few times.

The sun hung low in the sky, but it was still full daylight when they left Mason. That familiar sizzle raced through her veins and made a tingle bounce around at the bottom of her stomach and tickle her crotch in a funny way. She snuggled as close to Berlin as she could and put her head on his shoulder as he drove.

"Oh, look," she said. "There's an old schoolhouse. Pull over. Let's get out and look at it."

"Are you sure? It's cold."

"I'll warm up walking around. Besides, I like old buildings." Good things could happen in a schoolhouse.

They walked all around the building, wading through weeds, peeking in windows.

"It's definitely abandoned," Berlin said.

"It looks like they just walked off and left some books and stuff. Let's see if we can get in." Ruby Jo raced around the corner and up the steps.

The door swung open with a squeal and she stepped inside, Berlin right behind her. Dust lay heavy on the desks and floor and the place smelled musty. A world globe sat on a table in the corner and an arithmetic problem was still clear on the blackboard.

"It's almost exactly like my school." Ruby Jo spun around and laughed. "It even looks like it has a cloakroom behind the teacher's desk just like we did." She disappeared through the open cloakroom door and Berlin followed her.

"I keep forgetting you haven't been out of…" he began.

She strode toward him, put her arms around his neck and kissed him right on the mouth, cutting off whatever he had been about to say. He stood very still for a moment, then his arms slid around her and pulled her against him.

He kissed her back and, at last, Ruby Jo was properly kissed. The feel of his lips moving expertly on hers and his tongue exploring her mouth, set her heart to banging against her ribs like a prisoner trying to bust out of a jail cell. The sizzle that had been dancing around inside her for so long burst into a roaring inferno.

She put her hands in his hair and held him hard to her. She wanted to bite him, lick him, crawl inside him. Just when she began to moan, he put his hands on her shoulders and held her away from him. She tried to wiggle back but he held her firm.

"My Lord, Ruby Jo! I took one look at you and knew you were going to be passionate, but you're… you're a fireball!" His eyes had turned from light gray to the color of dark smoke and his face was flushed. She could see his pulse beating against the skin of his neck like a woodpecker at a tree.

"Kiss me again, Berlin," she whispered and closed her eyes.

"Just hold on, you little firecracker." Berlin laughed and she opened her eyes as he took her hand and led her out of the cloakroom. He picked her up and sat her on the teacher's desk. Standing in front of her, he took both her hands in his.

"We have to slow down, Ruby Jo. Do you know what you would be getting yourself into? I mean, have you ever… been with a man?"

"No." She shook her head. "Not like that." She looked straight at him. "But I want to."

But not right now. Right now she wanted TP, wanted it so bad she felt like her flesh was crawling around on her bones.

He put his finger under her chin, tipped her face up and kissed her lightly on the lips. "I'm going to love loving you, Ruby Jo. And you're going to love it, too, but we have to wait. I just can't go against my word to your folks."

"No." She put her hand behind his head to pull his face to hers, but he took her hand and held it back in her lap. He shook his head, a smile playing at the corner of his lips. "You're such a fascinating contradiction, you know that?"

"What do you mean?"

"I mean you're young but you're old. You're a woman, all woman, so much so that sparks practically fly off you, and I don't mean just your hair. But just like that..." he snapped his fingers, "in an instant you can be all child and all the time, woman or child, you're a starry-eyed dreamer."

"If I'm a child, why are you walking out with me?" Ruby Jo lifted her chin as she pushed her lower lip into a pout.

"Because of the woman. That's what really counts. The child part of you I can raise up to match the woman, then you'll be something else, Ruby Jo Cassity. Lord help us all, but you'll really be something else." He kissed her lightly again and squeezed her hands.

Well, shoot. Mama was right. Berlin was a man of his word and a gentleman. Weren't there any more men like Mr. Teller out there anywhere?

23 – THE TENDER TRAP

On Christmas morning, Ruby Jo stretched against the cool smooth sheets and wiggled her toes. She wanted to make sure she really was lying on a real mattress and not her lumpy feather bed at home. Opening her eyes slowly, she saw sunlight slicing through a slit in the drapes and falling like a smear of soft butter across the polished hardwood floor and the white chenille bedspread. Ruby Jo grinned and hugged herself.

She threw back the covers, jumped out of bed and, holding her arms out, spun around two or three times. Covering her mouth with her hands, she giggled. This was so much fun. It was how real people lived. She always knew she didn't belong on a run-down farm (sorry, Mama) in Nowhere Freeburg, Texas.

Ruby Jo wandered around the room touching things, the wallpaper with sprays of pale daffodils, the gleaming furniture made of some kind of dark wood that was not pine, the soft fabric with more yellow daffodils on the chair by the window with real drapes, not curtains.

Ruby Jo had never been in Sally Free's house, but she would bet all her nickels and dimes this was every bit as nice and it could all be hers. That would show Sally and her horse a thing or two.

Ruby Jo opened the drapes, and sat in the chair by the window. She rubbed her bare feet against the carpet, so smooth, not like the knobby hand-braided rugs on the floor at home. Resting her chin in her palm, she gazed out at the real honest-to-goodness town, and thought about how fast everything happened after their Thanksgiving visit with the Jacobsens.

It seemed there had hardly been enough time for Ruby Jo to turn around in those few weeks, much less think about Hollywood. Every time she thought she might have a minute to herself, Mama had her embroidering pillowcases or crocheting a doily to take to her new home, or making a new nightgown for her wedding night.

It seemed Berlin was always underfoot, taking supper with them, driving Ruby Jo about the countryside on Saturday afternoon, or just sitting by the fire in the front room talking with Mama and Daddy. Berlin had attended church with the Cassitys again and they had visited the Crossroads Baptist Church and taken dinner after with the Jacobsons.

"Them Baptists sure are a dry bunch," Mama said to Daddy a few days later. "A little toe-tapping and hand-clapping would liven things up a bit, but I reckon Ruby Jo'll get used to their ways."

Then it had gotten jumpier than a bullfrog in a hailstorm when Berlin announced he wanted Ruby Jo and her parents to spend Christmas Eve and Christmas Day with his family, returning home the day after Christmas. The thought of that was almost enough to send Mama to her bed.

"That's two nights staying at their house, Homer," she fussed. "I don't even have a nightgown without holes and I sure don't have a wrapper. What if I have to go to the necessary in the middle of the night?"

"We'll make do with what we have, Alma."

"But, Homer, I can't wear my one good dress two days in a row. The Jacobsons are high-tone folks. It's bad enough I already wore it at Thanksgiving."

"The Jacobsons already know who we are," Daddy said. "Another dress ain't gonna change anything now."

"Well," Mama sniffed, "I've been saving them lilac-print flour sacks for something special. I reckon I could use them to make up a new dress."

The idea of the Christmas visit even made Ruby Jo uneasy. It was one thing to eat supper with somebody, but how did you act when you slept at their house? What if you were seen in your faded old nightgown? Well, how would Loretta Young act? That's how she would act, Ruby Jo decided, and she didn't worry about it anymore.

The next morning at breakfast, Mama was still fretful. "And what about presents, Homer? You know they'll be something for us under the tree, being there both days. What are we gonna give them?"

Daddy just shook his head, put on his coat and hat and went to the barn. Mama turned to Ruby Jo. "Well, what are we gonna' give 'em? You're school-educated. You have any ideas?"

That did worry Ruby Jo, but Berlin solved the problem.

"We're awful busy during the holidays," he said. "How would you like to come stay with us a couple of days early and help out in the store? I have to pay extra help during the holidays anyway. It might as well be you, and that way you could earn some Christmas money."

Following Berlin's suggestions, Ruby Jo bought hair ribbons for Rose and Pearl and a tin of lavender bath salts for his mother. She selected a new apron for Mama and a bag of hard Christmas candy for Daddy, but she couldn't think what to buy for Berlin. Finally, she decided on a book, "The Illiterate Digest," by Will Rogers. Even after she picked presents for Mama and Daddy to give the Jacobsons, there was a little money left to add to her hoard of nickels and dimes.

So now it was Christmas morning and the Cassitys had done themselves proud. There were presents under the tree for everyone from the Cassitys. Mama had not only survived Christmas Eve but had a bath with orange flower salts in the big claw-foot tub.

"No Christmas present could top that," Mama whispered when she said goodnight, but Ruby Jo had seen Mama peeking at the labels on the packages under the tree.

Ruby Jo was surprised everyone was still asleep on Christmas morning, until she glanced at the clock and saw it wasn't even six o'clock yet. She washed up in the bathroom and dressed quickly in a new store-bought dress, an early gift from Mother Jacobson.

She tiptoed down the stairs and settled into a soft chair near the tree decorated with big red balls, paper snowflakes, and popcorn strings. Ruby Jo just wanted to quietly look at the tree and the pretty packages labeled with her name for a little while. She was really excited about those packages, but she reminded herself not to get carried away. There wasn't a present in the world as exciting as being a famous movie star.

* * * *

All the presents had been opened and the torn wrapping paper cleared away. Dinner was over and dessert had been served. Berlin and Daddy sat in the big chairs in front of the fire. Mother Jacobson and Mama, side-by-side on the sofa, looked like they were about to nod off any minute while Rose and Pearl played with their new dolls on the floor by the Christmas tree.

Ruby Jo sat on a low stool in front of the fire between Daddy and Berlin, watching all of them. It was quiet for a change, everyone seemingly lost in their own thoughts, the only sound the crackling of the fire. All of a sudden a big knot filled Ruby Jo's throat and her eyes filled with tears. It was all so perfect, just like out of a movie magazine, and she felt good, like her insides were filling up with hot, sweet cocoa.

"I'll tell you what!" Berlin slapped his hands on his knees and stood. "I'm not normally a drinking man, but I just happen to have a bottle of fine sherry tucked away. I've been saving it for a special occasion since before those fools in Washington passed Prohibition." He walked to his desk and took a fancy bottle out of the bottom drawer. "I believe this qualifies as a special occasion."

When they were holding small glasses of the rusty-colored liquid, Berlin stood in front of his chair.

"Here's to Ruby Jo, the beautiful woman who has brought happiness back into my life." He raised his glass and took a sip.

Mother Jacobson and Daddy did the same, but Mama held her glass with both hands on her knee. Ruby Jo knew it was because Mama wasn't at all sure the Holy Spirit would be happy with her drinking liquor even if it was a special occasion. Ruby Jo took a small sip and coughed. It burned, so she put her glass on a side table.

Berlin set his glass down and held his hand out to Ruby Jo. "Come sit with me." He pulled her into his lap. Ruby Jo quickly looked at Mama but Mama was smiling.

Berlin hugged her and kissed her forehead, then twisted around to reach into the pocket of his jacket hanging on the back of the chair. He took out a small gift-wrapped box and handed it to her. "One more present, Ruby Jo. Open it."

It was the prettiest wrapped present of all. Ruby Jo took it and carefully removed the ribbon and paper. Berlin's grin practically filled up his whole face. He took the black velvet box from her and snapped it open. There were two rings in the box, side by side. One was a plain gold band. The other had a big shiny stone on it with two smaller stones on each side.

Berlin slipped the ring with the stones on her finger and said, "This one is for now. The other one is for later. Will you marry me, Ruby Jo?"

Ruby Jo looked at him then around the room. They were all looking at her and grinning. She looked back at Berlin. He pulled her to him and kissed her quickly right on the lips.

"I've talked to your folks, Ruby Jo. I don't want to wait any longer. I thought we could be married February fourteenth, Valentine's Day."

Ruby Jo looked at the ring on her finger, then back at Berlin.

"Everything will be okay," Berlin whispered. "I love you, Ruby Jo. I'll take good care of you."

In the background, Mama and Mother Jacobson were talking and crying all at once, saying where to have the wedding, who to invite, what Ruby Jo would wear.

No! It's too soon for this. I need more time. Ruby Jo intended to say it out loud, to scream it, but she knew she hadn't said a word. The chunk of ice in her chest had frozen her mouth shut.

24 – TIME RUNS OUT

Ruby Jo wiped away the sweat that trickled into her eyes, trying to see, but she slammed head-on into iron bars. Backing away, she turned and stumbled in the opposite direction, only to bang into iron bars again. With tears running down her face and dripping from her chin, she swung her head wildly from side to side. *Get out! Get out now!*

Then she saw it. The door of the cell was standing slightly ajar. She ran for it, her breath hot and searing in her lungs. She reached for the door to push it open—*escape! Safety!* Then suddenly they were there, blocking her way, all of them grinning like crazy people. Mama, Daddy, Berlin, Mother Jacobson.

Berlin put out his hand to close the door and lock her in. "I love you, Ruby Jo. You'll be happy with me."

No! You're just a storekeeper in a nothing town. I have to get to Hollywood. I have to!

Ruby Jo slammed her body against the closing door as hard as she could, knocking Berlin and Mama down. She jumped over them and flew out of the cage, through the bedroom door and down the hall, running as fast as she could, her sweat-soaked gown cold and clammy on her skin.

Yes. There were the stairs. Get down them and out the front door. *Free.*

She flew down the stairs, taking them two at a time, barely seeing where she was going. Just as her bare feet touched the hall floor, she crashed into something solid and smelling of bay rum.

"Ruby Jo! What in the world?" Berlin pulled her into his arms.

"Get away," Ruby Jo mumbled and struggled against him. "Free."

"You're soaking wet and shaking like a leaf, sweetheart." He cupped her head and held it gently against his shoulder. "You must've had a bad dream." He picked her up and carried her down the hall to his study. She lay limp against him, too tired to fight anymore.

Berlin stood her on the floor and held her upright with one hand as he took a lap robe off the back of the sofa and wrapped her in it. Pulling her onto his lap, he picked up her unfinished sherry. "Here, drink a little of this. It'll settle your nerves."

Ruby Jo shook her head. "I don't like it." Her throat was raw and the words hurt.

"It gets better after a couple of sips." He held the glass to her mouth and she sipped, then again. He was right. The burn actually felt kind of good.

"Now, tell me, sweetheart," he said, holding her against him, "what is it?"

"I'm scared, Berlin. I don't want to get married." She didn't look at him.

"Well, I understand that. You're young, and I know I said we'd wait until after your birthday. But I just don't want to wait that long, Ruby Jo. I don't think I *can* wait that long." He slipped his hand under the lap robe and laid it on her thigh. "I talked to your Mama and she agreed there was no reason to wait. You do want me, don't you?" He kissed her ear and down the side of her neck.

The cold seeped out of Ruby Jo like he was drawing it out with his hand and his lips. She nodded. She did want him. He was a good-looking man and he smelled good. And his body was hot and hard beneath her. She just didn't want to marry him.

"I'm not ready to get married yet," she whispered.

"Well, you have almost two whole months. That'll give you time to get used to everything." His hand moved up and down her thigh. "I know what. Why don't you and your Mama stay here with us for another week or so and you ladies can have a great time making plans for the wedding together. How does that sound?"

No! I'll never get away. Ruby Jo grabbed the front of Berlin's shirt and gripped it in her fist. "No, please, Berlin. I want to go home. At least for a week or two."

"Okay, sweetheart, if that'll make you happy." Berlin spoke the words against her hair as his hand slid up her thigh and over her ribs. "You're still as cold as a chunk of ice," he said. His hot hand cupped her tittie and rubbed gently. Ruby Jo sighed and leaned in to him.

* * * *

The men sat in the best chairs near the stove as Mama and Ruby Jo came in from the kitchen with Berlin's special treats. He wasn't staying until midnight, but he had brought cider and cake to celebrate New Year's Eve.

"Well, that bunch is long gone from here, Homer," Berlin was saying. "I don't think we have to worry about them. I heard the law thinks they've hightailed it north. Probably trying to make Fort Worth. Ah! Here are the ladies." Berlin stood, took the cake from Ruby Jo and put it on the table.

Ruby Jo knew they had been talking about a Christmas Eve bank robbery over in San Angelo. It was all anybody had talked about for days afterward. She took her cake and cider from Mama and sat on a chair near Berlin.

"Besides, we have more important things to talk about." Berlin reached over and patted Ruby Jo on the knee. "We have a wedding coming up."

"I been tellin' Ruby Jo we need to get busy doing something about a dress." Mama stopped a forkful of cake on the way to her mouth long enough to give Ruby Jo a hard look. "She says we have time."

"Now, Ruby Jo…" Berlin began.

Suddenly Daddy sat straight up in his chair and put his plate down on the table with a clatter. "Listen!" he said and turned up the volume on the radio playing in the background.

This is an alert from the Mason County Sheriff's Department, the announcer said. *The Bennett gang has been sighted twice near Brady today. They are now believed headed toward Austin or San Antonio. They are armed and very dangerous. As you all know, these are the crooks that robbed the Farmers & Merchants Exchange Bank in San Angelo on Christmas Eve, leaving one bank clerk seriously wounded and one of the gang, Clovis Holder, dead. It's believed another one of the gang was seriously wounded and they may be seeking medical assistance.*

Last July, the four men—Clovis Holder; T.C. Bangs; Desmond, also known as 'Horse' Dillon; and their leader, Wick Bennett—split off from the notorious Barker Gang after a bloody dispute that left one of the Barker bunch dead. Wick Bennett was paroled eighteen months ago from the McAlester, Oklahoma, State Penitentiary after serving six years for armed robbery.

Mason, Llano, Gillespie, Kerr, and surrounding county law are on high alert. I repeat, these men are armed and dangerous. Lock your doors, folks. Keep your eyes open. If you see these men, do not approach or engage them. Notify your local sheriff as quickly as possible.

Daddy got up and locked the front door. Mama headed for the kitchen. There was no lock on the back door, but Ruby Jo heard Mama sliding a chair under the knob.

"Well, I guess the law was wrong about them heading north," Daddy said.

"Apparently so," Berlin agreed.

"Now, you be careful going home tonight, Berlin. Don't you go stopping for anybody or picking up hitchhikers."

"I won't, Mother Cassity." Berlin smiled. "I doubt they're still around here anyway. I'll bet they're traveling fast."

"A terrible thing." Daddy shook his head. "But you got to admit they was pretty slick."

"Well, I think it's a disgrace." Mama snorted to show her disgust. "It's bad enough to try to take people's money, but to dress up like Santa Claus to do it! Well, I never!"

"You do have to hand it to them," Berlin said. "Nobody thought a thing of Bennett walking down the street in a Santa suit and beard, handing out candy to the kids on Christmas Eve."

Ruby Jo had heard the account several times on the radio. When Bennett strolled into the bank, dropped the candy bag and pulled his gun, two of his men, Bangs and Holder, were already inside, posing as customers. Horse Desmond had the car running at the curb outside. The bank wouldn't say how much money the gang took.

"I heard he even gave one of the deputies a piece of candy." Daddy chuckled. "I know that ain't funny, but still…"

"I heard that, too," Berlin replied.

Good golly, Molly! This was exciting. Terrible, but exciting. It was just like a book or a movie. What role would she play? Maybe a good-hearted bad girl who saves Wick Bennett from himself and his bad ways. She would be so beautiful…

Ruby Jo jumped when Mama spoke sharply, "Ruby Jo! You ain't paying attention."

"Sorry," she mumbled and sat straighter.

"Berlin was just saying he thinks we ought to go home with him for a few days when he comes on Saturday."

Berlin took Ruby Jo's hand. "Mother is so excited about helping you and your Mama with the wedding plans."

"It's barely six weeks away, Ruby Jo," Mama said. "We need to get started. I think we should go with Berlin on Saturday."

They were all looking at her. She wondered if this was how that poor butterfly felt when Mr. Teller stuck a pin through him and put him on the cork board for the class to study.

25 – A DESPERATE CHOICE

Ruby Jo pushed her scrambled eggs around on the plate. If she hadn't tossed and turned so much on her lumpy bed all night long, she would have frozen to death. She was still cold and her head was pounding.

"What's ailing you, girl?" Daddy shoved his breakfast plate away and stood.

"It's just nerves," Mama answered. "It's not every day a girl gets married. Especially to a man like Berlin."

"It's not nerves," Ruby Jo snapped. Mama gave her a hard look so she added, "I about froze last night. I didn't sleep much."

"Nerves," Mama said again.

Ruby Jo took two big swallows of hot coffee to stop herself from answering something sassy. Daddy shook his head, plopped on his hat, and walked out the back door.

"Berlin'll be picking us up tomorrow, so after you tend to the chickens and pigs, you better get all your things together. Maybe you can lay down a little after that."

Ruby Jo's feet felt heavy as anvils as she dragged herself through getting dressed and the morning chores. When she opened her suitcase, a Christmas gift from Berlin, and put it on the bed, she just stood staring at it. She couldn't think what to put in it.

What was she going to do? There was no way out. It was too late to make plans now. Why hadn't she done something sooner?

Because you actually liked playing footsies with Berlin. Admit it.

I never said he wasn't nice.

And good-looking. And he smells good.

He's an old man.

He's in his prime and you know it.

Oh, shut up.

And he has a really nice house. His mother likes you.

It's not his mother or his house that wants to marry me.

He wants you.

Yeah. I'd probably be old and gray by the time he warmed up. The other night when I was half-naked on his lap, all he could do was give me a little squeeze.

Oh, Ruby Jo! Grow up and stop whining. Marry the man.

"No!" Ruby Jo said aloud and slammed the suitcase closed. She had to get out of here for a while. She couldn't think. Mama had been watching her like a hawk all morning.

She grabbed her coat and scarf and raced downstairs before she could change her mind.

"Mama, I'm going to ride Mosey over to the schoolhouse and practice the piano for a while."

Mama looked up from the bread dough she was kneading. "It's way too cold to be out if you don't have to."

"I haven't practiced at all lately."

"I don't see the need right this minute seeing somebody else will be playing at Berlin's church."

"But he has a piano at home. I can play there."

"Well, why don't you go practice at the church? It's way closer."

"I can't practice on that piano. There's a stuck key. It's bad enough to have to play it that way for service."

"Preacher said he was getting that fixed."

"I don't want to ride over there and find out it isn't. I'll just go to the schoolhouse." Ruby Jo wrapped the scarf around her neck and buttoned her coat. "It'll be unlocked and there won't be anybody there. School doesn't start up again until next week."

"It's awful cold for Mosey."

"I won't be long. I'll put him in the woodshed while I'm there." Ruby Jo stopped buttoning her coat and looked at Mama. "Are you telling me I can't go, Mama?"

Mama plopped the dough into a greased bowl and covered it with a dish towel. "You're about to be a married woman, Ruby Jo, so I'm not saying you can't go. I'm saying I don't want you to go."

"Oh, Mama!" Ruby Jo buttoned the last button and grabbed one of Daddy's old hats from the peg by the door. "If you're worried about what they said on the radio last night, forget about it. Like Berlin said, those men are long gone from these parts. Who would want to stick around a nothing place like Freeburg?"

"Still, I wisht you wouldn't go, Ruby Jo."

"I promise I won't be long. I'll be back way before dark."

Ruby Jo bridled Mosey, jumped on his bareback, and rode out of the yard as fast as he would go. No use giving Mama any more chance to talk her out of getting away from the house for a little while.

It was cold. No doubt about that. Ruby Jo scrunched down into her coat as much as she could, put her hands in her pockets, and hugged the mule with her legs for the warmth. She gave Mosey his head to find the familiar way to the school and settled easily into the rhythm of his gait.

She wasn't going to Hollywood and be a famous movie star. There was just no way she could see. In a few short weeks she would be married and her life would be over.

Don't be silly. Your life will just begin.

It'll be dull, dull, dull. I want excitement. I want to go places and do things. I want to ride in fast cars. I want to be with smart, beautiful people, not work in a dumb mercantile in a hick town in the middle of nowhere.

Berlin is a good man. You'll have a good life.

It's not the life I want.

You're stupid, you know that? Do you know how many girls would kill to marry Berlin? Live in that house? Not work their fingers to the bone until they dropped?

Then let somebody else have him.

Ruby Jo, you are going to marry Berlin Jacobson and you're going to like it.

I am going to marry him. Looks like there's no way out of it, but I'm not going to like it. I guarantee you that right here and now.

Mosey jolted to a stop and Ruby Jo looked up to see they were in the school yard. She slid off Mosey's back, led him into the wood shed and tied him securely.

Shoulders hunched, head hanging down, Ruby Jo trudged across the icy yard. She was so frozen with disappointment and despair on the inside she hardly noticed the cold anymore or her footsteps crunching the icy mud. *It was over. She had lost. Mama and Berlin won.*

The door wasn't locked but it seemed swollen in the frame, so she had to put her weight against it. The door scraped across the floor as it swung abruptly, pulling her off balance.

Before she could fall, someone grabbed her and slapped a gloved hand over her mouth. The more Ruby Jo struggled against him, the tighter he squeezed her. And he was big. She knew he could squeeze the breath right out of her and she would pass out, so she quit struggling. The man swung her around and kicked the door closed. The first thing she saw was a man lying on the floor with blood all over his clothes. He looked dead.

Another man sat on Mr. Teller's desk, his long legs stretched out in front of him and crossed at the ankles.

Ruby Jo's heart slammed against her ribs so hard she heard it in her ears like gunshots, and a hard knot was growing big as a baseball right at the base of her throat. She tried hard to stop it, but a trickle of warm pee dampened her panties. For the first time in her life, Ruby Jo understood fear. She tasted it in her mouth like a rotten egg and felt it turn the muscles of her legs to jelly so that she sagged against her captor.

"So what do we do with her?" the man said and tightened his hold. His voice was so deep and booming it sounded like he was yelling down a well.

The other man sat, unmoving, studying Ruby Jo with a steady, unblinking stare, like a snake watching a mouse.

Even in all the pictures of Hollywood movie stars, Ruby Jo had never seen such a beautiful man. Black hair fell in loose curls on his forehead. Dark eyebrows looked like an artist had drawn them above blue eyes so pale and cold, Ruby Jo shivered. His face was so perfect it could have been sculpted by the hand of God.

The Perfect Man pushed himself off the desk and stood. His dark gray suit moved a little loosely on his tall frame as he walked across the room. Ruby Jo knew if she saw him naked, his body would be as beautiful as his face. Something else ignited in her and twisted and coiled along with the fear. The new dampness in her panties was not pee.

He stopped very close in front of her and cupped her chin in his hand, his thumb gently rubbing her lower lip. Ruby Jo knew this man could kill her and, for some reason, that excited her more than anything else in her entire life. Her hands shook with wanting to touch him.

"Let her go, Horse," the Perfect Man said and his voice flowed over her like soft music in the still of the night.

Her captor dropped his arms and Ruby Jo would have fallen to the floor, but the Perfect Man caught her. He helped her sit at one of the desks, then sat on top of one opposite her.

"What's your name, honey bee?"

"Ruby Jo." She sounded like a bullfrog.

"Well, Ruby Jo, I don't know what brought you here today, but we have ourselves a little problem."

"The piano."

"The piano?" He lifted a perfect eyebrow.

"I came to practice."

"So, a piano player, are you?"

Ruby Jo nodded. She glanced out the window over the Perfect Man's shoulder and saw a big, black Packard parked close behind the schoolhouse.

"Well, little piano player, what are we going to do with you?" He crossed his arms, rested his chin in his palm and tapped one slim finger against his jaw. "What do you think, Horse?"

Horse stood at the back of the room, the bulk of his body bigger than the closed door behind him. "You know what I think, Wick."

"Yeah, but we haven't taken up with killing innocent girls just yet. We'll have to think of something else." He grinned and said it like a joke, but Ruby Jo knew as if her life depended on it that there was nothing funny in it.

"Whatever you're gonna do, you better do it fast," Horse grumbled. "No tellin' who'll sashay in here next."

This is my one chance to get away from here… from Berlin. From Mama. From Freeburg. Ruby Jo made an instant decision, one she knew would change her life forever. "I know a place."

"Do you now?" Wick stood, towering over her so she had to tilt her head back to look at him.

"Yes. It's not too far from here. An abandoned farmhouse. It's all falling down and overgrown. Nobody goes there." A shiver ran through Ruby Jo. The die was cast. There was, for sure, no going back now

"We need a place to look after Bangs for a day or two," Wick said to Horse. Then he asked Ruby Jo, "Can you get us some medical supplies? Anything?"

"Maybe some carbolic salve, some iodine. We don't have much. I think we have Epsom salts and alcohol."

"How about shine?" Horse asked. "Your old man got any?"

"Bangs could really use some," Wick said.

"We don't have anything like that."

"Do you know of any bootleggers hereabouts?"

Ruby Jo did, but she shook her head. Everybody knew the Snelton boys had a still in an old barn a few miles up in the sand hills, but she knew better than to tell any stranger about it, no matter what.

"How about food?"

"It won't be a lot, but some."

"And then what, honey bee?" Wick cupped her chin in his hand again. "What will I do with you then?"

"I want to go with you when you go. You can drop me at any train station."

"Oh, piss in a bucket!" Horse snorted and slapped his palm against his broad forehead.

Wick glanced at Horse, then back to Ruby Jo. "Don't worry, Horse. This little lady's going to help us. Aren't you, honey bee?"

He squeezed her chin lightly, then slowly, ever so slowly, leaned forward and kissed her on the mouth. Quick, but it was like striking a match to a dynamite fuse. The blood in Ruby Jo's veins bubbled and danced and the breath she exhaled in a whoosh was hot in her mouth.

"Are you out of your mind, Wick?" Horse stomped back and forth across the front of the school room. "She's a kid. You can do the hot squat in the chair for kidnapping a kid.."

"You dumb sap. You won't live long enough to worry about the hot squat." Wick's lip curled but it wasn't a smile and Ruby Jo thought if the sound he made was supposed to be a laugh, it missed the mark. "Besides, she doesn't look like a kid to me." He turned to Ruby Jo and grinned. "Are you a kid, honey bee?"

"No." Her heart thumped harder. "I'm no kid."

"That little twist won't get out the door before she's lookin' for a copper," Horse insisted.

"Have a little faith, Horse. We can trust... what's your name again, honey bee?"

"Ruby Jo."

"We can trust Ruby Jo." Wick fisted his hand and tapped Ruby Jo gently on the chin. "But, if it'll make you feel better, go with her, Horse. Stay out of sight and get back fast."

"I can't get stuff and leave until my folks are asleep," Ruby Jo said.

"Well, make it as fast as you can. Horse, see if you can find some rope while you're waiting around."

26 – THE TWIST

Ruby Jo held her Christmas suitcase, resting on the floorboard of the back seat, tight between her knees. It didn't hold much except her nickels and dimes, her two favorite Photoplays, and her new Christmas dress.

She held with both hands to the strap above the car window to keep from being thrown from side to side as the car jounced and jerked along the deep ruts of a road so overgrown it was little more than a trail. Close tree limbs and shrubs scraped along the side of the car with squeaky mouse shrieks.

Ruby Jo couldn't help it. She kept seeing Mama's face in the morning when they found out Ruby Jo was gone. Tears stung her eyes. She wanted to throw open the door, jump out and run back home. But, no matter how bad she wanted to, how bad she felt for Mama and Daddy, too, she couldn't. She was on her way. She was going to Hollywood just like she dreamed.

The wounded man crumpled in the opposite corner groaned. He had started bleeding again. Ruby Jo couldn't see the blood, but she smelled it.

At the end of the road, the headlights illuminated a small clearing littered with an old bedstead, a rotting wagon, some other unidentifiable junk, and an outhouse leaning crazily backwards. The house was still standing but a big part of the roof was missing shingles, a couple of windows were shattered, and the front door sagged on one hinge.

Horse snorted and Wick said, "Damn, honey bee. You weren't joshing when you said this place is abandoned."

"Nobody ever comes here," Ruby Jo replied. "The kids say it's haunted. I thought it was what you wanted."

"It'll do for now."

Horse carried Bangs inside and laid him on a rickety table in what was once the kitchen. Ruby Jo carried her own suitcase and put it under the kitchen table by her feet while she held a flashlight for Wick. He removed Bang's jacket, then tore the bloody shirt off him. Bangs flopped around like a rag doll and moaned.

A small black hole in Bangs' upper chest oozed blood. The skin around the wound was an angry red. Ruby Jo knew infection when she saw it. The little bit of cornbread and buttermilk she had managed to swallow at supper jumped up in her throat. She gagged and her hand shook.

"Hold that light steady, honey bee."

Ruby Jo gripped the flashlight with both hands. She wanted to look away but she couldn't. Bangs screamed when Wick poured pure alcohol on his chest and into the hole, then swabbed it with one of the clean rags Ruby Jo had brought. Horse stood just outside the circle of light.

"He needs a sawbones."

"I can see that," Wick snapped.

"Somebody's gonna walk in anytime and see all that blood in the schoolhouse," Horse said.

"I know but we have to stay here tonight."

"It ain't safe," Horse insisted. "By morning they'll know the twist is missing."

"Well, hell, Horse, we both have to get a little sleep and Bangs needs some rest before we move him again."

"I'm just saying…"

"Plus, we need gas before we go too far. We'll take a chance on laying low here tomorrow. The next day's Sunday. Everything'll be closed, but we'll get up real early and find us a gas station where we can borrow a little gas."

"And then what?" Horse insisted. "What are you gonna do about Bangs?" Ruby Jo couldn't see Horse's face in the shadows but she felt him looking at her. "And what about the twist? What're you gonna do about her?"

Wick painted iodine on Bangs' chest. "Let me worry about the honey bee. Here, lift Bangs up for me."

Bangs moaned as Horse raised his shoulders and Wick bandaged him with torn strips of one of Mama's old sheets.

"As for Bangs, I know a fella, a chicken farmer, over in Kendalia, not too far from Kerrville."

"So what're you gonna do? Throw eggs at ole Bangs?" Horse's rough laughed echoed in the darkness of the empty house.

"Don't be such a dumb futz," Wick snapped. "I met Wilbur before I was paroled out of Big Mac. He was a for-sure doctor up in Oklahoma City, but he lost his license over some kind of business. He never said exactly what." Wick eased Bangs back on the table. "I heard he's running a chicken farm down here as a front for a place for bad boys to get patched up and lay low for a while. It's the best shot we have."

Bangs groaned and jerked his legs on the table. "Wick," he whispered. Ruby Jo swung the flashlight full on his face. He was so young! Probably not a lot older than she was.

"What is it, T.C.?" Wick bent over the boy and put his hand on his forehead.

"I'm thirsty."

Wick turned to Ruby Jo. "Did you bring any water?"

She shook her head. "There's probably an old well somewhere out back."

"We'll get you some water," Wick promised. "Are you hungry? What did you bring to eat, honey bee?"

"Some cold corn bread and bacon. A jar of buttermilk and a jar of pinto beans."

"Want some buttermilk, boy?"

T.C. shook his head. "I hurt bad, Wick. And I'm cold."

"I know you hurt, boy, and I wish I could do something about it." Wick took off his jacket and put it over T.C.'s chest. "You have to hold on just through tomorrow, then I'll take you to a doctor I know. Can you do that?" The boy's eyes fluttered closed.

"We need to be findin' that doc tonight," Horse said.

"You heard what that fool said on the radio last night," Wick replied "Every copper in three counties is looking for us. One more day and they'll figure we've passed on through even if they find the blood in the schoolhouse."

'Not when they find the twist missing," Horse muttered.

"Even with her missing, they'll figure we're long gone," Wick said.

"You just take your flashlight and see if you can find some kind of well out back."

Horse flicked on his flashlight and disappeared through the back door. Wick turned, smiled, and walked very slowly toward Ruby Jo. She backed up until she was against the wall, the flashlight hanging from her hand, illuminating the floor. In the dim fringe of light, Wick's teeth were square, white, and perfect, his eyes now a deeper blue.

"What am I going to do with you, honey bee?" He pushed his hard body against hers, pinning her to the wall. She tilted her head back and looked up at him. His face was very close to hers. She wanted to say something, but her tongue seemed too big for her mouth.

He could hurt her, but something told her he wouldn't. *You better be right. You're betting your life on it.* She shivered.

Wick raised his arms and braced his hands against the wall, then lowered his head so slowly it seemed like an hour before his lips touched hers. He didn't kiss her. He put his lips to hers lightly, like a feather, and stood still. Her heart was hammering her chest so hard, he had to feel it.

Dimly, like it was far off, she heard the squeaking of a pump handle from outside, then the creaking of a step on the back porch. Wick stepped away and turned toward the sound.

"I found an old pump," Horse said, carrying a dented blue dipper.

"Let's try to give T.C. some water." Wick lifted the boy's head. T.C. groaned but didn't drink when Horse tipped the dipper to his mouth.

Wick looked intently at the boy for a minute or two, then lowered his head back to the table.

"We need to eat. Did you bring the food in?"

"Yeah." Horse sat on the floor next to a pillowcase, untied the knot in the top, and set out the jars of beans and buttermilk. Wick slid down beside him and they sat with their backs against the wall, devouring the food fast like a pair of hungry wolves.

Wiping his hands and mouth on the pillowcase, Wick stood and said to Horse, "Wash these jars and fill them with water." To Ruby Jo, he said, "Come on. Let's check out the rest of this place."

He took one of the flashlights and led the way through a door at the back of the front room. A shaft of moonlight fell through a hole in the roof and lay on the floor like a circle of frost. A sweep of the flashlight revealed nothing in the room except some small animal droppings and a soggy-looking torn mattress on the floor.

"Well, well," Wick laughed. "It's not the Ritz, but it'll do. Wait here."

He came back with a lap robe and spread it on the mattress. "It'll be cold, but I think I can warm you up," he whispered as he pulled her to him.

Wick's mouth closed over hers as his hands worked at her clothes. When she was naked, he picked her up and lay her on the makeshift bed. She shivered with the cold and the mattress felt damp through the lap robe. When he covered her with his naked body, his heat engulfed her, and she thought she could smell steam rising from the moldy bed under her back.

Everywhere Wick touched her came alive and danced with little sparks. It felt like many hands were on her, not just his two. And as her hands moved over him, the smooth, hot, hardness of his body was like nothing she had ever felt before. She couldn't feel him fast enough and she wished for more hands, enough to feel all of him at once.

Why had she waited for this? She should have done it long ago. With who? Mr. Teller? Boomer? Berlin? No. It had to be Wick. Only Wick.

Ruby Jo realized the itching heat that had picked and nagged at her before had been nothing more than a tiny ember. What Wick set loose in her was a wild, raging thing and the vision that overwhelmed Ruby Jo's mind as Wick consumed her was of a dragon in a school story book long ago.

She clearly saw the beast unleashed inside her, fierce in its beauty, moving through all of her body—every muscle, every nerve, every fiber of her hair. It moved fast for such a big thing, swaying its massive head from side to side, fire blasting from its nostrils. Wherever the flame touched, it ignited and burned. The fire licked at her nipples, coiled and twisted in her stomach, and clutched her crotch in a blistering grip of such exquisite pleasure she wanted to put her arms around it and hold on to it forever.

Then there was an instant of real pain as Ruby Jo felt Wick's penetration. Ruby Jo cried out. Wick covered her mouth with his. She was consumed. She saw herself, all burning flames, whirl and twist together into one red, gold, and white pillar of fire dancing before the dragon.

It opened its big mouth and inhaled, and she was plunged into the belly of the beast. She became the dragon, embraced its power—a power thousands of times greater than she had felt that day on the road with Billy Bob. Yes. *Yes!*

It didn't matter what Wick did or didn't do, or even if he was there anymore. She was in the claws of the dragon and the fire from his mouth burned her so that every fiber of her being, everything she was, pulsated with a white hot brilliance, blinding in its glory.

Ruby Jo awoke so sore she could hardly move. Only the fierce cold, hunger, and the need to see if the outhouse was useable had brought her from the depths of the soundest sleep of her life.

Where was Wick? Even as sore as she was, she wanted him. The dragon was not gone. It waited inside, trembling, smoke from its nostrils curling round and round, poking at the tenderness between her legs.

Horse was sitting on the floor, back against the wall, his chin resting on his chest when Ruby Jo walked into the front room.

There was a pile of guns on the floor next to him. Most of them she recognized. A sawed-off shotgun, a couple of rifles. and several pistols. There was one piece she knew was a gun, but it was the strangest looking thing she had ever seen. She glanced at Horse as she walked by. He was studying her.

"What's the matter, girlie?" he sneered. "Ain't you seen a Chicago typewriter before?"

"Knock it off, Horse." Wick walked up beside her. "You know she hasn't." To Ruby Jo he said, "It's a Thompson submachine gun. Nasty piece of business."

Ruby Jo didn't answer. Her eyes had moved to a large black satchel near the guns. Wick's glance followed hers. "Money to burn." He laughed. "And I can't even buy you breakfast. Are you hungry?"

Ruby Jo nodded. Her stomach growled and tumbled. She was hungrier than she ever had been in her life. "I'm sorry, honey bee. I'm afraid there's no way we can get food until tonight."

"That's okay," Ruby Jo said, surprised at how hoarse her voice was.

Wick reached out and gave her nose a gentle tweak. "I think I know how to keep your mind off food a good part of the day."

Horse snorted. "You're thinking with your damn dong, Wick, and you're getting us in deeper trouble ever minute. We need to get Bangs to a doctor."

Wick whirled toward Horse, his hands clenched into fists at his side. "Anytime you figure you're smart enough to run this outfit, speak up, Horse."

Horse lowered his head and looked at his shoes.

"That's what I thought," Wick said.

"The twist is big trouble," Horse muttered.

"What did you say?"

"Nothin'."

27 – ON THE RUN

Even lying snuggled against Wick's hot naked body, it was still bone-chilling cold. It was just turning dusk outside. They had been on and off the mattress two or three times during the day, much to Horse's snorted disgust.

"Couple of rabbits," Ruby Jo heard him mutter once as Wick led her to the back room.

"You're just mad because you aren't getting any." Wick had laughed.

Ruby Jo shivered and put her arm across Wick's chest. "I've been thinking, Wick," she said.

"And what would you be thinking about, honey bee?"

"I don't want you to drop me at a train station. I want to stay with you."

Wick rolled onto his side to face her. "I know what you're thinking and you wouldn't be the first."

"What am I thinking?"

"You think mean parents or a poor childhood or some such thing turned me bad and you're the one woman who can save me from myself." He grinned and tapped her nose with a slim finger. "You think you could have me sitting on a church pew singing "When the Roll is Called Up Yonder" in no time."

"I'm not thinking any such thing." It was very close to what she was thinking.

"Let me set your little mind straight." His face was washed by a kind of bronze blush in the falling twilight. She wanted to lay her hand on his cheek, but she didn't. "I am the youngest of three sons of a very old, very rich, and well-known New York banking family. I had everything I could possibly want growing up and I guarantee you I never missed a meal. Well, not until lately. I even went one year to Harvard."

"Harvard?"

"A really expensive college for rich kids."

"But why are you robbing banks if you don't need the money?" And here she had been worried about them taking her little hoard of nickels and dimes.

"For fun. For excitement." He cupped her chin in his hand. "For a reason to get up in the morning. So you see, honey bee, there's nothing you can do for me. I've got a mean streak a mile wide running right through me."

Ruby Jo thought about how he had put his coat over T.C. and gently laid his hand on the boy's forehead. "I don't think you're mean at all."

"You haven't been looking at me from the other end of a gun barrel." He laughed and there was something chilling about the sound. "If you asked somebody who has, you'd get a whole different picture."

"But don't you want to get married some day? Have a family?"

"No. There's no time for it and even if there was, I wouldn't."

"Why?"

"Because there's already a bullet out there with my name on it. It's just a matter of time."

Ruby Jo climbed on top of him and lay flat against his body, her face against his cheek, her tears trickling down the side of his neck. "Please don't talk like that, Wick. I don't want anything to happen to you."

"You're so sweet to care about me." Wick put his arms around her. "But you live hard and fast you die hard and fast. That's the truth."

"But you could change."

"It's too late. And I don't want to change."

"But, why? Surely you don't want to die."

"No, but everybody does. To my mind it's a lot better to live fast, have fun, and die young." He gave her a squeeze and kissed her on the temple. "So, don't cry for me, honey bee. Save your tears for the poor slob that stumbles around for seventy or eighty years waiting for death to put him out of his misery."

"What about your mama and daddy? They must be out of their minds with worry." *Like my mama and daddy are worried about me.* Ruby Jo shivered again and tried to swallow down a knot that suddenly filled her throat.

Wick's body went tense and still under her and he seemed to hold his breath a second or two. Then he swatted her on the behind and said, "Come on, you little pest, we need to start getting things together. I want to get out of this dump about midnight."

* * * *

It was well after midnight when Horse carried Bangs, moaning, his limbs twitching and jerking, out to the car and started to put him in the back seat.

"Put him in the front seat and tie him in with the rope," Wick said. "I don't want him falling all over me if I have to do any fancy driving."

"Then he oughta go in the back seat," Horse argued.

"No. I want you in the back seat right behind me so you can give us the best cover in case anybody gets too close and curious."

While Horse tied Bangs in the front seat, Ruby Jo climbed behind the passenger seat and put her suitcase between her feet. Wick leaned in, gave her a light kiss and took her suitcase. She grabbed for it. He pulled it away. "This goes in the trunk, honey bee"

"But I want to keep it with me."

"Can't have it getting Horse's way. Sorry, but we'll be easier to spot traveling in daylight later on."

Ruby Jo pulled her coat tight around her and flopped back against the seat. Well, shoot. She didn't like being separated from her nickels and dimes one bit.

Wick stopped the car at the main road, the headlights shining across into the dense trees on the other side. The car trembled gently as the motor idled. "Where's the nearest filling station, honey bee?"

"There's one at the crossroads about five miles past Freeburg."

"Will there be any food there?"

"They have a very small store but there might be some stuff. Soda pop and candy for sure."

"Anything else around?"

"No, that's all."

"Where's the owner live?"

"He has a house out back."

"Okay, that's it then," Wick said, his face hard in the faint light.

* * * *

Wick turned off the headlights, parked, and killed the engine about a quarter mile from the store. They sat in silence studying the two buildings. The Texaco star sign hung on a tall post, cold and still in the night, like a soldier on sentry duty. There were no lights except for a neon Havoline sign flickering in the window. The owner's house, visible a few yards behind the station, was completely dark.

"Horse, get on up there. See if we can get into the pumps. And see if there's anything to eat."

Horse slid silently out of the car, stepped across a ditch, and disappeared into the brush along the road. Ruby Jo pulled her coat tight around her, a chill rippling over her body.

This wasn't a movie or a book. Anything could go wrong. Somebody could get hurt. It could be her. She shoved her hands in her coat pockets and slouched down in the seat. She could still plainly see the buildings at the crossroads. Wick didn't speak.

After what seemed a long time, Horse appeared at the edge of the road and waved them forward. Wick drove very slowly with the lights off and stopped by an old gas pump. Horse pushed the last of a candy bar into his mouth and handed a bag through the window to Wick.

"Dumb country hicks," Horse said. "Nothing's locked up."

Horse grabbed the long handle on the side of the pump and pushed it hard, back and forth. In the dim light, gasoline gurgled into the glass tank at the top. Wick passed the bag to Ruby Jo then got out and leaned against the car, facing the station and the house. His arms hung loosely at his sides, a pistol gripped in one hand.

Ruby Jo dug into the bag to find three bottles of Nehi Root Beer, a loaf of bread, a hunk of cheese, a bottle of milk, and what looked like about two dozen candy bars. Looking back and forth between Wick and the station and praying Old Man Crouse would sleep soundly, she ripped open a Baby Ruth and a Milky Way. Hands shaking with hunger, she shoved them down as fast as she could, barely chewing.

When the glass tank was almost full, Horse stopped pumping and grabbed the hose. The yellow gas in the glass cylinder gurgled and bubbled as it flowed into the car's tank. Ruby Jo opened a Butterfinger and a Hershey bar.

Wick took what looked like a wad of bills out of his pocket and stuck it between the hose nozzle and the tank. Wick and Horse pushed the car onto the road, the gravel crunching under the tires. Once they were rolling on the paved road, they jumped in. Wick started the motor and they sped off toward Kendalia and Wilbur's chicken farm.

* * * *

Ruby Jo felt sick. She had never eaten so much candy in her life. The Nehi pop, two slices of bread, a piece of the cheese, and several big gulps of milk all mixed together in a vile soup that sloshed up into her throat and stung the back of her nose. The chocolate, so sweet going down, now tasted like a mixture of blood and mud.

Wick drove in silence. Horse rested his head against the back of the seat, eyes closed. Bangs hadn't made a sound in a long time. Ruby Jo wondered if he was still alive.

The sun was a faint glow below the rim of the world to the east when Wick sped around a curve and into the glare of oncoming headlights. The car whizzed by. Horse jerked up and turned to watch the taillights disappear as they cleared the curve. Wick stomped on the gas and the rear of the car fishtailed, then recovered.

"Shit! Shit!" Wick said. "One damn car on the road all night and it's got to be coppers."

"You sure?" Horse asked.

"Pretty damn sure, but I'm not pulling off to see if they come back to check us out, you dumb shit."

Horse rolled down his window and picked up the submachine gun from between his feet.

Oh, God. *Oh, God!* Ruby Jo retched and her mouth filled with slime. She vomited into her lap. *What was she doing here?* This was no movie. She could be killed for real.

"I think they've turned around," Wick said. "They'll be coming up fast."

"We can't get caught with the twist!" Horse yelled.

"What?"

"I ain't sittin' in no hot seat for kidnapping a kid!"

"You're right." Wick slowed the car and steered to the edge of the road.

"Don't stop!" Horse yelled. He reached past Ruby Jo, opened her car door, put one foot against her hip, his hand on her shoulder, and pushed hard.

There was a second, while she was suspended in the cold air, when she yelled, "My money!" Then she slammed into gravel and slid, tearing her face and hands. She rolled through high grass into a ditch. A car careened around the curve, its headlights sweeping a swath of brilliance several feet above where she lay. A blinding white pain shot up her leg and everything faded to black.

28 – TULLY

"Knob, you're the dumbest dog I ever seen," Tully French said as he put the small rubber ball, slimy with dog spit, in his pocket. "I swear you'd chase a ball till you dropped dead."

Knob barked, jumped around and pushed his wet nose against the pocket hiding the ball. He wagged his tail, his pink tongue hanging out.

"No more, you idiot." Tully patted the dog on the head. The dog ran ahead, then came trotting back, looking up at Tully as if to say, "Are you sure?"

Tully laughed and broke into a run. It was plenty cold, but he started back to school tomorrow, so he wanted to do some squirrel hunting today with his new Christmas slingshot. There were a lot of squirrels in the big oak trees across the road from their mailbox, so Papa said surely he could get enough for a good mess for supper. Him and Papa sure liked fried squirrel.

Knob ran ahead, got to the mailbox first, circled the post a couple of times, then peed on it. Tully grinned. He reckoned what was good for Knob was good for him. He sure didn't want to wait until he got all the way back to the outhouse, so he looked up and down the road and peed on the post, too.

Knob trotted down the side of the road a ways, his nose to the ground. Tully looked around for some good rocks. You couldn't use just any old rock. Being a good squirrel hunter was as much about choosing the right ammunition as it was being a good shot.

Suddenly Knob stopped. His tail went stiff and the hair rose up on his back.

"What's the matter, boy? You found a dead coon? Leave it alone. Come on now, Knob."

Knob stayed put and kept barking, an odd sound Tully hadn't heard before.

Tully walked to a stand of tall grass where Knob was going crazy. Something, probably hit by a car, had knocked down some of the grass and dragged itself off the road to die. But maybe it wasn't dead. Whatever it was, a badly hurt animal could be real dangerous and this looked like a good-sized one. Probably a big dog.

Tully carefully parted the grass. He gave a loud yelp in spite of himself, then took off running as fast as he could, yelling "Papa!" at the top of his lungs, with Knob right on his heels.

Tully ran the half mile from the road to the house like the demons of hell were in hot pursuit. His chest burned as he raced around the barn to where Papa was moving hogs out of a pen into a pasture.

"Papa! Papa!" He bent over, put his hands on his knees, and gulped air.

"Good heavens, Tully. What in the world lit a fire in your britches?"

"It's a girl! Down by the road." The words tumbled out. "She's all bloody. I think she's dead."

Papa broke into a run, with Tully and Knob right behind him.

"Thank the Lord she's not dead," Papa said as he dropped to his knees beside the girl. She moaned and tossed her head from side to side. "She's busted up pretty bad, though." Papa put his hand on the girl's forehead.

"She's awful cold. We have to get her up to the house. Stay with her while I get the wagon." Papa took off his coat and put it over the girl, then took off running again.

Tully sat on the cold ground, Knob beside him, and studied this stranger. *Oh, boy! A real honest to goodness mystery, just like on Sherlock Holmes, and right here on the French farm.* Papa and Tully never missed a radio broadcast of Sherlock Holmes if they could help it, but nothing like the stories on the show ever happened around here.

Well, nothing but that big, fancy black car that had been driving ever so slowly past their house about once a month all his life. Papa and Mama, when she was alive, always found a way to ignore his questions, but there was something about that car that had made Mama fighting mad.

About a week after Mama died, Tully walked way up the hill behind the house. He said he was going squirrel hunting but he really just wanted to be by himself. While he was sitting up there, staring at nothing, that big car drove into the yard. A man in a suit and a funny cap got out and opened the back door. Another man in a suit got out. He stood talking to Papa for several minutes, then he got back in the car and it drove away. When Tully asked about it, Papa said it was nothing for him to worry about.

Tully was going to solve that mystery someday, but right now there was a new one to figure out.

The girl began thrashing about and Tully jumped.

"It's okay," he said. "Papa'll be right back." He didn't think she heard him.

The gravel had torn up her face pretty good and blood was matted in her red hair. He couldn't tell how old she might be, but he thought she looked pretty young. What was she doing out here in the middle of nowhere, on a cold winter morning, all bunged up? Who was she?

The wagon wheels crunched in the gravel and the mules snorted and stamped their feet in the cold as Papa pulled the wagon to a halt.

"This is gonna be mighty tricky," Papa said. "She's got a broken leg, but we have to get her to the house before she dies from the cold." He handed Tully a quilt.

"I'm going to ease her up a little at a time. You work the quilt so it's flat under her. We'll use it to drag her the best we can up to the wagon."

Sweat was dripping off Papa's face by the time they got her in place just below the open tailgate. The girl continued to moan but didn't wake up. Papa wiped his face with his shirt sleeve, stretched his back and looked up and down the empty road. He shook his head.

"We'll just do the best we can. I'm gonna pick her up, Tully, and I'm afraid it'll hurt pretty bad. You have to hold her hurt leg. Try not to move it. Just hold it like it is."

The girl screamed when Papa lifted her and slid her on the quilt into the wagon. She screamed again when Papa took her into the house and lay her on the bed in Tully's room. They both jumped when the girl opened her eyes and spoke.

"What'd she say?" Papa asked Tully.

Tully shrugged his shoulders. "I couldn't understand her."

Papa leaned over the girl and brushed some bloody strands of hair off her face. "I'm going to get a doctor for you. He'll fix you right up, then we can get hold of your family."

"No! Please. No doctor. Don't get anybody."

What in the world? Papa and Tully looked at each other. Why wouldn't somebody hurt like that want a doctor to fix them up? This was going to be a real super-duper mystery.

"You have a broken leg. It has to be fixed."

"No. No. Please don't tell anybody I'm here!" The girl started crying hard and rolling her head back and forth like a wild animal cornered by a pack of dogs.

Papa put his hands on her shoulders to still her. She gripped him hard on both arms and looked right at him, her eyes kind of crazy.

"Please."

The two of them stared at each other for a good long minute, then Papa said, "All right. I don't know what this is about yet, but I'll do as you ask for now." She relaxed her grip and he went on, "I know someone I can trust. He's not a doctor but he can help you, and he won't talk. I promise.'

Turning to Tully, Papa said, "Ride the mule and get your Uncle Jube."

"But he's…"

"I know, but he can help her and he'll keep quiet. Don't you tell him anything, you hear? Not a word. Just tell him I need him to come quick."

* * * *

Tully huddled down in his coat and kicked the mule in the flanks. It didn't do any good. Rain or shine, cold or hot, the mule had just one speed and that was whatever he felt like. Right now he felt like slow.

Tully could understand why Papa would send for Uncle Jube. Jubal Parnell wasn't really Tully's uncle but he was as close as Tully would ever get to having one. Uncle Jube and Papa had been best friends all of their lives, growing up on neighboring farms.

Tully had heard the story many times… how Papa and Uncle Jube, being young and foolish, had thought it would be a fine adventure to fight in the Great War. So, with visions of heroism clouding their good sense and over the protests of their folks, they went with Pershing to the Western

Front, in France, the summer of 1918. They were both plain old dog faces, until one day they were commandeered as stretcher bearers to carry a wounded captain back to the medical tent.

When they walked in, a surgeon was working on a man on a table. He took one look at them, pointed a finger, and said, "You. Get over here and hold this man down. I'm out of anesthetic and I have to sew up his ass."

Uncle Jube stepped forward and was the surgeon's assistant from then on. Papa went back to the trenches, until he was shot at the Battle of the Argonne Forest and sent home. He still had a big scar on his back where they had dug out the bullet. Papa always said Uncle Jube had a lot more scars than him but you just couldn't see them.

Anyhow, Uncle Jube found a some way to go on to school to become a horse doctor before coming back home to settle down. Papa just became a pig farmer like his papa before him. They were still best friends and Papa said Jubal Parnell was the only man on the whole earth he would trust with his life.

Tully started yelling as soon as the mule trudged into Uncle Jube's yard. He came out on the porch and said, "What in the world is the matter, Tully?"

"Come quick, Uncle Jube. Right now. Papa needs you bad."

"What's the matter?"

"Papa said not a word, ceptin' come quick. Right now."

"Put the mule in the barn. You can ride back in the car with me," Uncle Jube said as he opened the door and ran into the clinic.

* * * *

Uncle Jube asked no questions. He threw back the covers and said, "What have we here, young lady?"

She was awake and looked at him, wide-eyed, her lips pressed so hard together they were white around the edges. He raised her skirt above the knee and unrolled her torn cotton stocking down her leg.

Tully got close enough he could see the girl's leg was all bulgy below the knee and covered with big black splotches.

Turning to Papa, Uncle Jube said, "Her leg is broken, Milo. She needs a doctor."

"No!" the girl said.

"She's dead set against it," Papa said.

"I haven't worked on a human in a long time. And I was just an assistant."

"Well, you helped set a lot of legs. And I know you'll keep this to yourself until I can figure out what it's all about."

"I don't have any anesthetic." Uncle Jube turned from Papa to the girl. "You understand what I'm saying? That leg has to be set. Then I'll have to see what I can do about your face and hands. That won't be any fun either and I don't have anything for the pain."

The girl looked white as a porcelain doorknob but she nodded.

"Fortunately, it's about mid-point between the knee and ankle. That's a lot easier to set than a break in the upper leg," Uncle Jube said to Papa. "Still, you and Tully will have to help me."

Tully's stomach rolled over and he could taste the flapjacks he'd had for breakfast in this throat. He had helped Papa birth a calf one time but the cow didn't scream or anything.

"You got any shine?" Uncle Jube asked.

"Some," Papa replied.

"You get the shine, Milo. Tully, you get me two of the wooden paddles off that big butter churn in the kitchen. And I'll need your bottle of rubbing alcohol and a sheet I can tear up. A couple of clean towels, too. I don't suppose you have any ice? No? Didn't think so."

When Tully brought the stuff back, Uncle Jube was pouring moonshine out of a quart jar into a glass. He handed the glass to Papa and folded a pillow under the girl's head. "You drink as much of this as you can," he said, then to Papa, "It probably won't take a lot."

Papa tipped a little shine into the girl's mouth. She sputtered and sprayed the liquid all over the place.

"Come on, now," Papa said. "You have to drink some of this so Doc Parnell here can fix your leg."

"You said you wouldn't get a doctor." She pushed the glass away.

"Don't worry. He's a horse doctor."

Her eyes got big. "And he's going to doctor me?"

"You're in good hands, believe me." Papa held the glass to her mouth again, as Uncle Jube poured alcohol all over the butter paddles and wrapped them in strips of torn sheet. "It gets better after a couple of sips," Papa coaxed.

She took a small swallow and scrunched up her nose. Tully didn't blame her. He had done the same thing when he had stolen a sip one time while Papa was busy in the barn.

She took two or three more sips, then she gave Papa a little grin. "You're right. It gets better and it makes me warm in my belly."

"I reckon you might like it right well before we're done here." Papa laughed and gave her more.

The emptier the glass got, the happier the girl got. She didn't seem to mind her leg so much anymore. She hiccupped, then looked first at Papa, then at Uncle Jube.

"You know," she said and giggled, "y'all are pretty swell looking. All three of you."

Tully ducked his head and blushed.

"You're mighty pretty yourself, young lady," Papa said. "Now, drink just a little more."

"You think I'm pretty? Well…" She hiccupped again. "I am pretty and I'm going to Hollywood and be a movie star." She seemed to have trouble with her tongue being too big for her mouth.

"So, what's your name? We'd like to come see you in the movies."

"Honey Bee." Her words were thick and slurred. "Honey Bee Wick. Thaasss my name."

"Honey Bee Wick?" Papa raised an eyebrow at Uncle Jube who just shrugged and laughed. Papa turned back to the girl and tipped the glass again, but she was passed out cold.

Uncle Jube pulled the pillow out from under the girl's head. "Let's get her flat," he said, straightening her arms by her side. He soaked a corner of a towel with the alcohol and gently cleaned the girl's leg.

"This is going to hurt like hell," he said. "She's gonna feel it even if she doesn't know it. Lay across her chest, Milo, enough to hold her down, just in case, but don't squash the poor girl."

Uncle Jube took her ankle in both hands and pulled and kind of twisted a little very slowly. There was a faint crunch sound, and the girl screamed like there were two million ghosts after her. Tully squeezed his eyes tight and clamped his jaws together.

Papa scrambled up. The girl was very pale and still as a fence post, but

Tully could see the gentle rise and fall of her chest.

"Will she be okay, Uncle Jube?"

"Oh, sure. She's young and it was a clean break." To Papa he said, "She'll have to stay off that leg for about six weeks. It'll probably be six or seven months before she's back to normal."

Tully wanted to pat the girl on the head and tell her "good job," but he didn't touch her.

"You better get a bucket in here," Uncle Jube said. "She's gonna be sick as hell when she wakes up." He put his hand on his back and stretched. "I could use a little shine myself,"

"Well, come on in the kitchen and set a spell," Papa replied. "Tully, I think Bessie wandered down in the lower pasture. Take Knob and get that old cow up to the barn. It'll be milking time soon."

Tully knew that meant they wanted him out of the way for some man talk. He wanted to stay but knew better than to talk back to Papa, so he headed for the pasture.

Oh boy! What a day. It felt good to help somebody in need. Tully puffed out his chest. Maybe he would change his plans and be a doctor or a vet like Uncle Jube instead of a detective.

29 – MILO

"Thanks for coming so quick, Jube." Milo handed his friend a glass with a small splash of shine

Jube nodded and took a sip. "Who is she and what's she doing here?"

"You heard her." Milo grinned. "She's Honey Bee Wick."

"Yeah, and I'm Mickey Rooney."

"I don't know who she is." Milo poured shine into his own glass. "All I know is Tully and Knob found her in the ditch down on the road about froze to death and bloody as all get-out."

"Well, she didn't trip over her own feet. It's my guess she jumped or was thrown from a moving car."

"Surely she wouldn't be crazy enough to jump." Milo shook his head. "And who would be mean enough to throw her out?"

"Hell, a lot of people, these days." Jube splashed some more shine into his glass. "Hard times, people get desperate. They do things they wouldn't normally do."

"Yeah, you're right." Milo tipped his chair back on two legs and leaned against the wall. "It's one thing for a man to go on the bum, but I'm seeing whole families pass by every day."

He took a swallow of the moonshine, wanting to feel the burn going down. He didn't want to think about the families that camped from time to time in ragged tents in the pecan grove down by the road. Sometimes they didn't have a tent and just huddled under a dirty quilt strung between the trees. Worse was how he felt when he gave what little he could to families who came to the back door, gaunt and gray, with hollow eyes.

Milo pinched his nose hard between his thumb and forefinger to force back the tears that stung his eyes. With the drought and the shape the country was in, it was getting mighty close to that being him and Tully out there living under a tree.

"I see the same thing at the clinic," Jube said, clearing his throat. "I give them what I can."

"Do you see any end to it, Jube? Is it going to be this way forever?"

"I don't know, Milo. Hoover keeps saying the Depression is about over, but I don't see it." He poured into Milo's glass again and his own. "Even if it is, it's going to be a long time before this part of the country recovers."

"You know I can't pay you." Milo ground his jaw teeth together and slammed the chair legs to the floor.

"I know. Nobody can these days. I'll take a pound or two of bacon if you have any left in the smokehouse."

"Yeah, I do." Milo laughed and it left a bitter taste in his mouth. "About all I have is pork. Nobody can buy hogs. I didn't even breed the last time around. All I've got now is my brood sows. I'll have to slaughter them if I can't find a way to keep feeding them."

"You know Tully could have a different life if you let them take him."

Milo frowned. "I know that and it eats me alive, believe me. But, he's my son, Jube. I just can't do it. Besides, Laura would raise right up from her grave and kill me while I sleep."

"That gal probably would." Jube chuckled, then, "Do the Oakleys still drive by?"

"Regular as clockwork."

"I don't reckon the Depression has hurt Old Man Oakley much."

"Nope. That old fool has so much money he could live like a king for a thousand years and still have a lot leftover."

They sat without speaking for a few minutes, then Jube said, "This girl could be big trouble for you."

"I know."

"I'm not just talking about feeding her and taking care of her and who she might be and all that kind of trouble."

Milo looked at the liquid in the bottom of the glass and swirled it around before tossing it back in one gulp. "I know."

"If you tear a scab off a near-healed sore, it can be much worse than it was to begin with." Jube tapped a big finger against the table. "Can you bear to have another woman in the house? Can Tully?"

Milo met Jube's direct gaze. "I don't know, Jube, but I guess we're about to find out. I can't very well turn her out unless you want to take her home with you."

"Nope."

"I'll find her folks as fast as I can."

"That may not be easy. I don't think she wants anybody to know who she is."

"I'll do the best I can," Milo replied and picked up the Mason jar. "Might as well kill this." He divided the last of the moonshine between their glasses.

30 – WOMAN IN THE HOUSE

The girl sat up in bed, elbows on bent knees, head in her hands, as Milo walked into the room.

"It's not fancy but it'll fill you up," he said, holding out a cup of coffee and a plate with a split biscuit covered with milk gravy.

The girl moaned into her hands and shook her head. "I can't eat."

"Do you need the bucket again?"

"No. I can't throw up anymore."

"Then you need to eat." Milo pulled up a chair and sat down.

She raised her head and looked at him. Her face was pale and a little greenish. Milo couldn't help himself and laughed. "I could probably find another swallow or two of shine."

She retched and put her hand over her mouth, shaking her head.

"You'll feel better if you eat something,"

"You promise?"

"I promise."

Her hand trembled a little as she took the plate from him. She ate a small bite, then another, and then really began eating. "You're right," she said. "I am feeling better. I didn't realize I'm starving."

He watched her silently. The early morning winter sun fell across the bed, isolating her from the rest of the room in a circle of pale radiance. Her red hair seemed to flicker and shimmer like a wood flame burning in the dark.

An urge to reach out and touch her hair niggled at him. *What was that?* He hadn't felt anything like that since Laura and he had never expected to again.

He shook his head. Enough of that foolishness; she was just a child. No, that wasn't true. She was young but she was no child. And she was a beauty. No doubt she could be a movie star. It would be a shame if her face didn't heal right. Jube had cleaned it up but it still looked raw. Jube said to put bag balm on her face a couple of times a day—good as anything—he said, so Milo brought the green can in from the barn.

"That was good." She held out the empty plate and leaned to look over his shoulder toward the open door. "Did your wife make it?"

Milo cleared his throat. "No. I made it." He took the plate. "My wife died. I'll bring you some more coffee."

* * * *

Milo stood looking out the kitchen window several minutes before he took the coffee to her. When he entered the room, her head was tipped back against the headboard and her eyes were closed.

"What's your name?" he asked.

She opened her eyes. They were a luminous green, like where the creek ran deep at the swimming hole, a stunning contrast to her hair. For a minute she just looked at him, then she shook her head.

"Sooner or later you'll have to tell me. We'll have to get hold of your folks."

"No! I can't go back."

"Sometimes things aren't as bad as we think they are."

"I can't go back. If I go back, I'll never leave again."

"They must be worried."

She looked down at her hands in her lap. "I'll write to them."

"I'll get you a pencil and paper."

"No. When I get to where I'm going."

"Where is that?"

"Hollywood."

"Hollywood?"

"Yes."

"Oh." He sat in the chair, leaned forward and rested his elbows on his knees. "When you were drunk yesterday, you said your name was Honey Bee Wick."

She jerked like he had poked her, and her mouth dropped open. "I did?"

"You did. So, I guess for now you'll just be Honey Bee."

She hesitated, a small frown wrinkling her forehead, then said, "Okay." A small smile played at the corners of her mouth. "What's your name?"

"Milo," he replied. "Milo French."

"And the boy?"

"Tully."

"Where is he?"

"School."

Her eyes widened. "Won't he…"

"He won't say a word," Milo assured her. "It'll mighty near kill him but he'll mind me."

"Thank you." She slumped back against the bed. "Is this his room?"

"Yeah."

"I don't want to take his bed."

"He'll sleep on a pallet by the cook stove. It'll give him an excuse to sleep with Knob."

"Knob?"

"His dog."

"That's a funny name."

"Yeah, it is. When he was a puppy, Tully's Mama said he was as little as a doorknob." Milo pushed himself up. "Well, work's waiting, so I better get to it. You be okay for a while?"

Her face flushed red as she frowned and rocked her body a little in the bed. "Well, I…" She bit her lip.

"What?"

"I have to use the outhouse," she blurted.

"Oh, my word!" He slapped his forehead with his palm. "I'm sorry. I didn't think about that." He felt his face redden, too. "I guess I'll have to carry you."

He turned back the covers. What was he thinking? The girl was still in her torn and dirty dress from yesterday and she smelled a little like the rotting stump in the barnyard when it got wet. Something had to be done about that but, first, the outhouse.

And how was he supposed to handle that little problem? Go in with her? Milo shook his head, muttering, "Damn, damn, damn." He slid his arms under her back and legs and picked her up as easy as he could and carried her out.

He opened the outhouse door with one hand, then looked at her.

"I can do it," she said.

"You can't put any weight on that leg."

"I won't."

"Okay." He set her down inside. She stood on one foot, balancing herself with her hands against the wall. "Are you sure?"

"I can do it," she repeated so he closed the door.

By the time he got her back to the bed, both their faces were covered with a sheen of sweat. He lay her down as gently as he could, but saw her clench her teeth.

Are you in pain?" he asked. "I can get you some aspirin."

"Please."

"Okay, I'll get some and we need to get those clothes off and wash you up a bit."

She nodded.

All Laura's clothes were exactly as she had left them, so he easily found a nightgown. He held it against his nose and inhaled deeply. After all this time, it still smelled like her. It would be big on the girl, but it was the best he could do. He put a pan of warm water, soap, a wash rag, and a towel on a table by the bed.

"I can do it," she said.

"Okay. I have work to do, but I'll wait outside the door for a bit to see if you need help. Just call me."

He eased the door closed behind him and leaned against the wall. He listened but didn't hear anything for several minutes. Then she cried out and he heard a thump just as he pushed away from the wall to head for the barn.

She was sitting on the floor, her splinted leg straight out, her good leg curled under her. She was hanging onto the side of the bed.

"I couldn't keep my balance and get the dress off at the same time."

"Are you okay?"

"I think so."

"Well, the easiest thing I can think of is just to cut the dress off you.

It's ruined anyway."

"Okay."

He helped her stand with her back to him, both her hands on the bedstead. "Hold on and don't let that foot touch the floor." He pulled out his pocket knife. "And be still so I don't cut you."

He grasped the back hem and pulled the dress out from her body a little. He slid the sharp blade straight up to the neckline in one quick movement. The dress fell away and she grabbed it with one hand and held it to the front of her body.

"One more," he said and did the same to her cotton shift. Her white cotton bloomers were torn and dirty. He hesitated.

"I think I can do it from here," she said.

"You sure?"

"Yes. Thank you, Mr. French." She looked at him over her shoulder.

"Milo," he said. "Call me Milo."

"Thank you, Milo." She smiled.

"You're welcome, Honey Bee."

No. This was no girl. This one was too sure of herself. His glance slid quickly over her shoulders, the gentle curve of her back, her long legs, her skin smooth and pale as ivory.

He nodded and turned away. His hands trembled as he strode down the hall. Jube was right. This girl spelled trouble and it was only beginning.

31 – BREAKING NEWS

Tully tried to be quiet in case Honey Bee was asleep, but Knob would have none of it. He raced past Tully, almost knocking him down and slamming the door into the wall. The dog spun around in two or three circles on the floor in front of the bed.

"Are you awake, Honey Bee?" Tully asked, but the answer was obvious as she sat up in bed, looking out the window.

"Yes, I am," she said. Knob put his front paws on the side of the bed and leaned in to be petted.

'Papa said it was okay for Knob and me to visit."

"I'm glad for the company, Tully. This bed sure gets tiresome."

"Papa's getting supper on."

"I can smell it."

"It's ham. And turnips. And biscuits. Just like yesterday."

"Well, it was good yesterday. I reckon it'll be good today."

"Is that your new crutches?"

"Yes. Your papa just made them for me today. We've tried them out already."

Tully walked over and looked at the long sticks with a padded piece across the top and a hand-hold nailed on one side. Honey Bee had been with them five days and Papa said tonight she could use her crutches and come sit at the supper table. Tully had never seen crutches before. He didn't even know Papa could make something like that. But then, Papa was mighty smart.

Look how he'd figured out an inside outhouse for Honey Bee. He had cut a circle in an old chair just big enough to hold Tully's night pot. Then he put it in the corner and hung a blanket in front of it.

Last summer Papa said Tully was too old for a night pot, so now he had to go to the outhouse if he got up in the night. Winters could get to freezing and in the summer there were rattlesnakes to worry about. And a monster could pop up anytime. He sure would like to keep that inside outhouse when Honey Bee left.

"How was school, Tully?"

"Okay. Our teacher's kinda grouchy, though. Papa says it's because she's getting way too old to teach anymore."

"You haven't said anything about me, have you?"

"No. Papa said if I did, he'd whup me within an inch of my life."

"That's good." She smiled at him. "Not that you'd get a whuppin', but that you didn't say anything. Thanks."

What was all this business? Why couldn't anybody know about Honey Bee? Why did Papa get Uncle Jube instead of a real doctor? This was going to be a Real Big Mystery. He could feel it in his bones.

After supper tonight he would get out his secret tablet with "Clues" written on the cover. He'd write down every single thing about Honey Bee from the beginning. Maybe he should think about being a mystery writer instead of a doctor or a detective. He could call his first book "The Honey Bee Mystery."

* * * *

Honey Bee's leg might be hurt but there was nothing wrong with her belly. She ate almost as much ham and biscuits and turnips as Papa.

"I'd like to help ready up," she said, taking hold of her crutches.

"No. No. Tully's a good helper—aren't you, Tully?"

Tully nodded. Sometimes he thought Papa said things like that just to get him to do stuff he really didn't want to do. How could you fuss about doing something when somebody just said how good you were?

Honey Bee watched quietly as Papa readied up, then opened the back door and slung the dirty dishwater into the darkness.

"Tully and me generally read for a bit in the evening. You feel good enough to set with us a spell?"

"I really do." Honey Bee laughed. "I'm so tired of that bed."

Papa slapped his forehead with the heel of his hand. "Well, damn me! I should have offered you something to read. We're not totally ignorant around here. We do have a couple of books."

"I like to read, but I haven't felt much like it the last few days. Maybe I can take a book tomorrow?"

Papa took the lamp and led the way into the front room. He put the lamp on the table by his chair and sat down. Tully nudged Knob over and flopped down on the quilt folded up on the floor by Papa's chair. He always sat there while Papa read.

Honey Bee stood in the door. She looked around the room, then walked past the sofa toward another chair near Papa's. Tully scrambled up. Papa raised his head and they both said at the same time, "Honey Bee!"

She stopped. "What?"

"That's..." Tully began but Papa looked at him and shook his head.

"Nothing," Papa said. "Please, sit down." He cleared his throat, picked up the book from the table and opened it to the marked page. "We're trying to read our way through Jube's library and I'm afraid he favors mysteries. Right now we're on Ellery Queen's "Roman Hat Mystery." I hope that's okay."

"Yes." Honey Bee smiled. "I like a mystery."

Papa began reading aloud. Tully's heart was bouncing like the rocks he skipped across the stock pond. He absently scratched Knob's head, looking from Papa to Honey Bee, hardly hearing what Papa was reading. He just couldn't believe it. Nobody sat in Mama's chair. *Nobody*, not since the day she died.

* * * *

Ruby Jo propped the crutches against what she had come to think of as "her chair" and lowered herself into the soft cushions. Milo brought her a cup of coffee and put it on the table beside her, then disappeared back in the kitchen.

Sipping her coffee, Ruby Jo looked through the open curtains down the narrow lane that joined the main road about a half mile away. It had been just two weeks and one day since Tully and Knob found her in the ditch.

She could understand Horse doing what he did but why would Wick let him? How could he? After what they had done together? Didn't it mean anything to him? How could it not? Wasn't he consumed by the same fire that seized her or was it different for a man?

Their coupling had meant everything to her. It scratched an itch she knew she had but didn't know how to scratch. It fanned the ember that had come alive with TP into a roaring inferno and awakened in her a restless need that knew no peace.

She had done little but think about Wick when she was awake and dream about him when she slept. Twice, during the first few days, when she had been confined to bed in Tully's room, she thought she heard Wick's name while Milo listened to the morning news and farm report in the front room. She had pushed up on her elbows and listened hard, but she couldn't be sure. Since then, she hadn't heard anything.

During the day, she stared at the main road for hours, her heart pounding every time a car came around the curve. They all sped on by, except the big black one that had stopped on the road by the mailbox one day. It sat there for at least five minutes before it drove slowly away.

Nobody in this part of the country had a car like that. And, who would just sit there? And, what were they doing if they weren't watching the house? It had to be Wick. She had waited, holding her breath for the car to drive up the lane, for Wick to rush in, pick her up and take her away with him.

But how could he know she was in *this* house? It had still been near dark and Wick was paying attention to driving when Horse threw her out. But if it wasn't Wick in that big car, who could it be? And if Wick didn't come for her, what would she do? She would go to Hollywood just like she planned. She would become a rich, famous actress and Wick would be sorry. But she had no money. Well, she would find a way.

Milo came in carrying his coffee cup. "I got Tully off to school. I'll tell you, that boy can be a regular whirlwind." He laughed and lowered himself into his chair.

Ruby Jo sipped her coffee and studied him over the rim of her cup. Milo French was a good man and she had learned in her short time there that he wasn't just a simple pig farmer.

Laura's Bible rested on the table by his chair and he often read it silently for a few minutes before going out to do chores in the morning. Ruby Jo had read what was written in a soft hand on the fancy family records pages in the front.

Laura Elizabeth Oakley, b. 15 October 1897, Dallas, Texas

Milo Althus French, b. 17 August 1889, Kendalia, Texas, to Sarah Jane (Moore) French & Samuel Althus French,

Laura E. Oakley & Milo A. French, m., 27 December 1918, Boerne, Texas,

Tully Althus French, b. 13 December 1922, Kendalia, Texas, to Laura (Oakley) French & Milo French.

Then, in a different, stronger hand, *Laura Elizabeth Oakley French, d., 23 July 1929, Kendalia, Texas*

Ruby Jo had put her palm softly on the open page and wondered why Laura's parents weren't named. She counted up on her fingers and determined that Tully had been only six when his mother died. He was now nine and Milo was forty-two.

Sometimes, when sitting quietly, Milo would get a faraway look and rub something hidden under his shirt between his thumb and forefinger. One day he leaned over to help her out of bed and a plain gold ring on a chain had fallen out of his shirt.

Being nosy, Ruby Jo had found Laura's clothes, all clean and neatly folded in a couple of drawers in Milo's room, like she would come back and wear them any day. Instead, Ruby Jo was wearing them now.

Then there were the three worn books of poetry on the bottom shelf under the table by Milo's chair. A number of passages were underlined in pencil and, in several places, *Laura* was written in the margin. In one place, the penciled inscription read: *my love, love.* On a back page in one of the books, he had written: *In your smile—the glory of the morning sun. In your whisper—the song of my soul. In your touch…* The sentence wasn't finished.

If… when… if Wick came for her, she wouldn't let him or Horse hurt Milo or Tully.

Milo glanced at her and smiled. "Hey, you were a million miles away."

"Wool gathering, I guess."

Milo switched on the radio. "I think I'll catch a little of the news and farm report, then I've got to get to work." He leaned back in his chair and crossed his legs.

Ruby Jo sat holding her coffee and gazing down the lane toward the road, paying little attention to the announcer. Then she turned her head sharply toward the radio as the announcer said:

We interrupt our regular morning report to bring you breaking news. The Bexar County Sheriff now confirms that Wick Bennett has been killed in a bloody shootout with sheriff's deputies and special assignment Texas Rangers.

Ruby Jo's hand jerked and she spilled her coffee in her lap. Milo jumped up and started toward her but she put her hand up, palm toward him, and he stopped.

Bennett and Desmond, also known as Horse, Dillon, were cornered in a vacant house on the outskirts of San Antonio. Lawmen surrounded the hideout and demanded the outlaws lay down their guns and surrender. Bennett's answer was to come out shooting with a Thompson sub-machine gun. Two deputies were wounded before Bennett fell, riddled by a hail of bullets.

Ruby Jo sat frozen, her mouth open. She could not feel the beat of her heart. She was aware Milo was staring at her, but she didn't look at him as the announcer continued.

Horse Dillon was found on the floor in a back room, face down, spread-eagled with his hands clasped behind his head when officers stormed the place.

There was no sign of P.C. Bangs, nor was there any sign of a missing Mason County girl, Ruby Jo Cassity. It was originally thought the girl had been kidnapped by the Bennett gang, but Dillon denied knowing anything about her and there was no indication she had ever been with them. Officials now conclude Ruby Jo Cassity is a runaway.

Milo switched off the radio. A howl, like an animal dying, tore from Ruby Jo as she buried her face in her hands. Milo knelt by her chair and put his arms around her. "Ruby Jo?"

Wick? Gone? No. She pretended it was no big deal; she would just go on to Hollywood. But, in her heart, she really believed Wick would find her and take her away.

She put her head against Milo's shoulder and folded into him, tears pouring from her like a waterfall in flood time. Ruby Jo cried and howled until she was limp and empty. She didn't pass out; she simply slid down into the emptiness and gave herself to it.

32 – LAURA

"Can you hear me, Ruby Jo?" Milo looked at the girl lying on the bed, a shaft of winter sun falling across her face, making her look pale and cold. He reached over and placed his palm on her forehead, then tucked the quilt more closely around her.

He had held her on his lap for hours the day before, then sat in a chair by her bed during the night. He talked; he offered her coffee, water, food, and shine. He rubbed her hands and arms and put a warm cloth on her forehead.

Tully and Knob came in and made a lot of noise, the dog jumping around and barking, and Tully wanting to know what had happened. Nothing, Milo had said. She just isn't feeling well. Still, she had not stirred but lay as one dead. But she wasn't. He knew that because her breathing was regular.

"You have to wake up sooner or later," he said, easing himself into the chair by the bed. "You're gonna have to tell your story and, Lord help us, whatever it is, we're right in the middle of it. What happened to you, girl? Why were you with them outlaws? Did they throw you out of the car or did you jump?"

She didn't move.

"And what about your family? They must be crazy with worry. You're gonna have to get hold of them, Ruby Jo."

He sat studying her, drumming his fingers on the arm of the chair. Maybe she had good reason to run away from home, but with those men? Was she that desperate? Shouldn't she be happy they were caught?

"You're a puzzle, girl, and I don't know what I'm going to do with you."

More, he didn't know what to do with himself. This girl gave him a gnawing ache in his groin and stirred feelings in him he hadn't felt since Laura... feelings he wanted to reach out and hold tightly to himself. At the same time, he wanted to push them away. He wanted to embrace the heat in his blood and feel alive again, but his head told him: *not with this girl; this girl is dangerous.*

But that very glow of danger that she wore like a dress had been keeping him awake at night, tossing in his bed. He was burning with wanting her and frozen with the fear of wanting her.

Laura. Think about Laura. Talk about Laura. Keep her in the front of your mind until you can get this girl, this Ruby Jo, out of here before she ruins your life. Yours and Tully's.

Milo stared at Ruby Jo, trying to determine if she was awake. She didn't seem to be. He began slowly rocking the chair.

"I don't know if you can hear me, Ruby Jo, but as soon as you're awake and able, I'm going to take you home or someplace else. We just can't have this and you know very well what I'm talking about." The chair creaked as he rocked.

"I'm a married man. I know, I know; Laura's dead, but I'm still very much a married man. I just don't want to give her up, not yet. Someday maybe, but not now."

Milo looked closely at Ruby Jo. She looked like she was still asleep. Good. He needed to, had to talk about Laura. Bring her face, her laugh, her voice, her love sharp into his mind. Now. Because, lately, she had been fading from his memory, pushed into the background by Milo's lust for this red-haired girl.

"I know it's been three years and Jube keeps telling me I need to move on. But he knew Laura and he knows why I haven't.

"Laura was not a beauty like you, Ruby Jo, but she was beautiful in a different way."

Milo stopped rocking, stretched his legs and chuckled. "That was one determined woman. At first, when I was lying in that hospital in Dallas, shot up from the war in France, I thought she was just being nice to me like she was to all the men.

"I knew I felt something special, but I never thought a fine, educated, and rich girl like her could fall for a pig farmer. But she did. Even then, I didn't think anything could come of it. You see, Ruby Jo, what I didn't credit was how fierce she truly did love me. She stood up to her daddy, gave up everything and never looked back.

"There was only two things that troubled her, troubled both of us, all those years. The first was that it took a long time for Tully to be born and she never did have any more babies no matter how bad we both wanted them. It was the greatest wish of her heart and mine.

"The second was that her father did forgive her after a time, probably a lot of her mother's doing, but Laura never forgave them. They wrote, but she sent the letters back unopened. They came to the house a few times but she wouldn't see them. They left envelopes with money in them in the mailbox. She sent it back. They kept leaving it until she wrote and said she was going to start giving it to the Pentecostal Holiness Church over in Boerne, so they stopped.

"They came to Laura's funeral, sat in the back and left without a word. But they came about a week later when Tully was out hunting one day. They wanted Tully. He's the only kin they have left.

"They shamed me by saying how I was cheating him out of a good life and a good education, but I just couldn't let him go. He's all I have, too. And, I'm his Papa. That's worth more than a big house and money. Laura thought so, too. She made me promise to keep him away from them.

"I do my best, but they still drive real slow down on the road about once a month. Can't stop'em from doing that.

"But one thing I can't figure. Seems like they know as much about what goes on around this place as I do. Like when Tully was born. It wasn't a week before they sent a big box of baby stuff. Laura did keep that. And when she died. They knew. I think they must pay a neighbor or somebody to keep an eye out and tell them what goes on. That's all I can figure." Milo set the chair to rocking again.

"Laura was the kindest woman I ever knew, but she was also the strongest and the stubbornest. But we were happy. I loved her the best I could and better than I ever expected of myself until that day three years ago when nothing would do but we have a jar of peaches for supper.

"I was just coming in from evening milking. She was getting supper on the table. 'Peaches sound good,' she said. 'I think I'll run down in the cellar and get a jar.'

"'Take a lantern,' I said. It was still daylight but it would be dark in the cellar. It was summertime and hot. Snakes like cool dark places. 'It'll only take a minute,' she said. 'I know right where they are, first shelf inside the door, so I'll only go to the bottom step.' She kissed me on my nose. 'You old worrywart.' And she was out the door, crossing the yard to the cellar.

"I was just setting the milk pail on the kitchen table when I heard her scream. I dropped the pail. Milk went all over. I slipped and fell and hit my head on the floor. 'Bout knocked me out but I jumped up and ran, Tully right behind me.

"Laura was still standing on the bottom step. She was holding her right arm with her left hand, holding it kind of out in front of her, just looking at it. Then she looked up at me and she looked so surprised. 'It bit me,' she said.

"The evening sun was shining right down on her, like she was standing in a spotlight in the shadow of the cellar steps. It made her hair shimmer and her skin look golden. I had never seen her look more beautiful. My heart shriveled up inside me to about the size of a pecan.

"I carried her into the house, pushed all the dishes and stuff off the table and laid her there. There were two puncture holes just above her wrist. By the space between the holes, I figured it to be a young rattler, the worst kind for getting bitten. A bright red color was already spreading out around the bite.

"I took my pocket knife and quick as I could, I cut an X right between the holes. Laura didn't even scream when I cut her. She just stared at me like she was watching all this happen to somebody else. I started sucking on her arm hard, sucking and spitting, trying to get all the poison out. Gagging on the blood and the rottenness in my mouth.

"Tully was screaming and crying so hard I could hardly think, but I didn't have time for him. Laura held out her good arm and hugged him to her. 'It'll be okay, Tully,' she said. 'While Papa doctors me, tell me about the mystery story on the radio last night.' So, Tully started the telling but he was hiccupping so bad you could hardly understand a word.

"When I had done all I thought I could do, sucking the bite, I found a plug of chewing tobacco left over from Papa. It was hard, but I chewed until my jaws ached to get it soft. Then I spread it over the bite and tied a clean rag around her arm to hold it on. Mama always said chewed tobacco could draw out most anything. I didn't know about snake bites but I knew for a fact it worked on bee stings.

"Tully had stopped talking and was lying against his mother, his head on her breast. When I put my hand on her forehead, she opened her eyes and smiled. 'It's bad, Milo,' she said.

"I put my hand on her chest. Her heart was fluttering fast, like a bird beating its wings against a cage, trying to get out. 'I'll get you to Jube,' I told her, but she shook her head and I remembered Jube had gone to San Antonio to some kind of meeting.

"We both knew the closest doctor was twenty miles away in Boerne. There was no way I could send for him; I would have to take Laura there.

"I hitched the mules to the wagon, cussing myself, God and everything I could think of that I was so dirt poor I couldn't afford a car.

"I wrapped her in a quilt I pulled off Tully's bed. Her eyes were closed. Her arm was darker red and now mixed with some black and purple, but it was real yellow right around the bite when I lifted the poultice and looked. She opened her eyes and they looked a little glassy. 'I love you, Milo,' she said and she spoke like her tongue was swollen. 'I love you, too, Laura.' I carried her out to the wagon and kissed her on the lips. 'I'll get you to the doctor as fast as I can.'

"I prayed a car would come along to help us, but nobody came by. I could hear Laura talking in the back, but I couldn't stop. I couldn't understand what she said either. It sounded foolish, like some young'un's nonsense rhyme.

"I whipped them mules without mercy. Finally, they balked and wouldn't take another step no matter how much I whipped them. It didn't matter. Laura was dead."

Milo passed his hand over his face and stopped rocking. He inhaled deeply, then, with a tremble in his voice, said, "So, you see, Ruby Jo, I still love my wife and that's why…"

He shook his head, then stood and walked to the window. He stared out for several minutes, his eyes passing over the barren yard where chickens pecked in the dirt, the gray barn that was starting to lean, the main road down by the mailbox where the big black car passed by, regular as clockwork.

Truth. The truth was that love that had killed Laura, her love for him that brought her to this poor excuse for a pig farm and his love for her, so great, but not great enough to make her stay away.

Milo turned and looked at Ruby Jo, lying so still, her eyes closed. Was she asleep? Had she heard a word he said? It didn't matter. He was the one who needed the telling, to bring Laura sharp into his mind, sharp into this room.

He stood by Ruby Jo's bed, his fists clenching and unclenching at his side. "No," he said. "I was about to say a falsehood. It is true I still love Laura, maybe more than ever, but the truth is, Ruby Jo, you make me burn in a way that scares hell out of me. That's why you have to go."

33 – THE NIGHT VISITOR

Ruby Jo didn't know if it was the same day or days later. But she knew it was daytime because she could feel the faint warmth of a winter sun falling across her face and see the glow behind closed eyelids.

She heard a voice, like somebody talking in a paper sack at first, then stronger, and she knew it was Milo. She did not want to talk. She did not want to answer questions, so she lay still and kept her eyes closed and listened as he talked about his wife, Laura.

Ruby Jo didn't move or hardly breathe until she heard the door close. She still waited a minute or two before opening her eyes. She had started hearing Milo's story of Laura while she was asleep and thought she was dreaming. As she slowly came awake and fully understood what he was saying, she was careful to let him think she was still sleeping. She realized he was talking more to himself than to her, but she didn't want him to stop.

There were parts of the story that made Ruby Jo's heart jump around in her chest. Some parts gave her a lump in her throat and made tears seep into the corners of her eyes. She had to be careful not to sob or make a sound. She swallowed hard once or twice and hoped Milo wouldn't notice.

Jumpin' jeepers. What a story. It was terrible, exciting, wonderful, sad. Just like the movie stories she had read in "Photoplay."

Ruby Jo had a lot to think about. Mainly, he was going to make her leave. Where would she go? Not back home, that was for sure. But, how could she stop him from taking her there? Now he knew her name and that she was from Mason County, the rest wouldn't be all that hard. She had no money. What happened to that satchel full of money she saw in the old house? What happened to her nickels and dimes? If she just had some money, she could figure out how to get away and get to Hollywood.

The door eased open and Milo stuck his head in. "You're awake. How you feeling?

"I'm okay. A little hungry."

"You should be. You slept through the night and most of the day." Milo walked in and sat in the chair. "Ruby Jo…"

Just then Tully and Knob rushed into the room like twin dust devils. Knob spun round and round and Tully said, "Are you sick, Honey Bee?"

Ruby Jo glanced at Milo, then said to Tully, "My name isn't Honey Bee. It's Ruby Jo."

Tully looked at her, then at his Papa, then back to her. "Well, are you sick? Is it catching?"

"No, I'm not catching. Just a little worn out, I guess."

"Supper'll be on the table in a few minutes," Milo said. "Can you come and eat?"

"Sure," Ruby Jo replied. "I'll be right along."

As soon as Milo, Tully, and Knob left, Ruby Jo worked her way out of bed. She used the indoor outhouse, washed up with the pitcher of water and basin on the washstand and went out to supper.

* * * *

Tully chattered away, doing most of the talking all evening. After clearing up from supper, they listened to Sherlock Holmes on the radio, then played dominoes until Milo said, "It's bedtime, Tully." Then he turned to Ruby Jo. "I'm tuckered out myself, so I'm gonna turn in. Are you staying up?"

"No. I'll go to bed."

As she pushed herself up and slipped the crutches under her arms, Milo said, "Well, good night then." He picked up the lamp to light their way, hesitated, then said, "Ruby Jo, we have to talk. Tomorrow morning, as soon as Tully leaves for school."

* * * *

Ruby Jo settled in bed but she was wide awake, going back over everything Milo had said when he thought she was sleeping. She smiled to herself in the dark, remembering how he said she made him burn.

When he said it then and remembering it now, it made her feel strong like she had felt with Billy Bob, Mr. Teller, and Wick... like she had the power to make men do things. She liked the feeling, but it was nowhere near as wild and mighty as when she was with Wick.

Wick had... what? Begat a dragon in her like Adam begat Cain and Abel? Or, had the dragon been there all along and Wick just woke him up and gave him fire?

The dragon was always with her now and she could see him in her mind, sometimes lying still, chin resting on his crossed paws but ever watchful. The tip of one long claw touched dead center in that electric spot deep inside just above her crotch. He slyly moved that one claw back and forth, back and forth, back and forth, day and night, tickling, tickling, giving her a deep itch that made her wildly restless.

With the splint on her leg, she couldn't pace or toss and turn in bed, but she did sometimes sweat at night and grit her teeth, so big was the hunger. In the daytime it was not as strong, but the tickly itch was there—always, at that deep place that trembled with the need to burn.

Now she rolled her head on the pillow and felt the itch grow into a throb. She needed Wick. But Wick was dead. She sat straight up in bed. Did that mean the dragon could die, too? Would he go to sleep and not wake up anymore?

She couldn't let that happen. She couldn't live without the dragon and his fire that burned her, not to death, but electrified her with a radiance that made her disappear into herself. Never to feel it again? No. She had to have it. She had to keep the dragon alive.

Milo. Milo was a swell-looking man. He didn't have to say he burned for her. She knew it, felt it already, and had almost from the first. He could light the dragon's fire.

Ruby Jo's hand trembled as she threw back the quilt and pulled herself out of bed. She was careful to be quiet with her crutches as she moved down the hall toward Milo's room. The door creaked a little as she pushed it open. Ruby Jo stopped, held her breath, listening. All she heard was the sound of Milo's even breathing, so she slowly pushed the door all the way open.

The winter moon gave enough light through the closed curtain that she could see Milo lying on his side, one arm curled under his pillow, his brown hair curly and falling on his forehead. Very quietly she eased to the other side of the bed and leaned her crutches in the corner. Balancing herself against the bedstead, she pulled her nightgown over her head and dropped it to the floor. A strong shiver rippled from the bottom of her feet to the top of her head, but it wasn't from the cold.

Ruby Jo eased into the bed the best she could with the splinted leg, then spooned herself against Milo's back, her arm around him, her palm spread across his chest. She felt him stir, then his whole body went rigid and he groaned, "Oh, God." Then again, "Oh, God."

34 – A CHANGE OF PLANS

"What the hell?" Jube let the screen door slam behind him. "You look like something the cat dragged in and couldn't eat."

"That good, huh?" Milo closed the front door against the cold. The truth was Milo had been a little startled when he looked in the mirror while washing his face earlier. His eyes looked sunken and stared back at him with the look of the hunted.

"I don't think you're sick." Jube grinned. "So, the little movie star must be giving you a run for your money."

"How'd you guess?" Milo couldn't quite manage to grin back.

"Well, since she puts Mae West to shame in the vamp department, it wasn't hard to figure. Did you find out who she is?"

"Yep. Name's Ruby Jo Cassity."

"And?"

"And, what?"

"I'm taking the splints off today. So when are you taking her back to her mama and daddy?"

"I asked her to marry me." Milo wiped his hand across his forehead but he wasn't sweating.

"You didn't!" Jube flopped into a chair, dropped his doctor's satchel on the floor and looked up at Milo with his mouth open.

"I'm afraid I did."

"And what did the little lady say?"

"She said no."

"Well, then, you can take her on home."

"I'm hoping she'll change her mind."

* * * *

Milo leaned against the bedroom wall half listening as Jube talked to Ruby Jo while removing the splint. His head told him marrying this girl, if he could convince her, was the worst idea he'd ever had. Loving her was nothing like loving Laura. Laura had been soft and easy, warm and gentle, a whisper on a summer evening. Loving Ruby Jo was like trying to dog paddle and keep his head above the surface of a pot full of boiling water.

Every night it was more, faster, harder, until he could hardly drag himself out of bed in the morning. Oh, it wasn't that he didn't like it. He was hungry for her with an appetite he didn't know was possible, but he was terrified of how much he liked it. It was like a demon was chasing him while he was pursuing some beautiful thing out in front of him, something he couldn't see or touch, or wasn't quite sure what it was, but that Ruby Jo demanded of him.

And, it wasn't just him. Tully had become quieter, more thoughtful, not his usual rowdy self. Did he know what was going on? Did he understand? How would he feel about Ruby Jo as a mother? He seemed to like her well enough.

Ruby Jo *would* be Tully's mother. Milo had to convince her one way or another. He had lost Laura. He couldn't lose Ruby Jo, too. As much as it scared him, he couldn't just let her walk out of his life.

"Milo!"

"What?" Milo jumped and straightened from the wall.

"I said Ruby Jo's going to have to get used to walking on this leg again," Jube said. "She needs to ease out of using her crutches."

Jube picked up his doctor's satchel and said to Ruby Jo, "You behave, young lady. It'll take a little time, so don't overdo."

"And, you," Jube said as Milo followed him to the front door, "you might try it yourself."

"What?"

"Slowing down. Taking it a little easier."

* * * *

Ruby Jo shoved back her breakfast plate, picked up her coffee cup and looked again at the Watkins calendar hanging on the kitchen wall. February fourteenth, the day she was supposed to be marrying Berlin Jacobson. What would have happened if she had stayed and married Berlin? Would he have lit fire to the dragon like Wick did but Milo couldn't?

She tasted her breakfast pancakes in the back of her throat and took a sip of coffee. Milo sat at the other end of the table, his head tipped forward, staring into his coffee cup. He had been sitting that way for several minutes.

It was Sunday and freezing, a sheet of ice on the ground. Milo would be limited to absolutely necessary chores and Tully couldn't play outside. Ruby Jo could hear him laughing and rolling around with Knob on the living room floor.

It had been two days since Jube removed the splint from her leg and she had been practicing walking for a few minutes several times a day. She had to get out of here. With no money, she wasn't quite sure how, but she knew the first step was to be able to walk without crutches.

Ruby Jo wasn't worried about Milo taking her back to Freeburg anymore. Unlike Wick, who let Horse throw her out of the car, Milo wasn't about to let her go. And that might be a problem. She could probably find a way to manage about the money, but how to get far enough away before Milo missed her and came after her?

There was no way she would marry Milo French. A pig farmer's wife? That was worse than being a storekeeper's wife. She wasn't going to be anybody's wife. She was going to make it to Hollywood if it killed her.

Ruby Jo liked her power over Milo. He did things for her she knew he had never done for anyone else, not even his precious Laura. She laughed to herself and took another sip of coffee.

Milo hadn't lit the dragon's fire yet but he was trying awful hard and she liked being with him. Even as Milo made her feel good, Ruby Jo could see the dragon behind her closed eyes. He would raise his head once in a while and let out a snort of hot smoke when Milo did something especially nice. So, who knew? Maybe Milo would fire up that old dragon one of these days. She had to have the fire. She couldn't wait much longer.

It happened so fast Ruby Jo didn't even have time to stand up. She barely had time to turn away from the table before she threw up all over the floor.

* * * *

Fifteen days it had been going on. Her throat was raw from so much vomiting.

She felt half-starved most of the time and sometimes she would just gobble food, but she couldn't keep it down. She was so tired and had a constant headache. Couldn't she just die and get it over with?

Milo carried the night jar back into the room and put it by the bed. She couldn't make it to the indoor outhouse to throw up because she was so weak and the vomit came out so fast.

She didn't lift her head as Milo sat on the bed beside her and took her hand in his. Although she was still anxious about people knowing where she was, she knew she needed a doctor. Something was really wrong with her.

"I think I need to see a doctor, Milo."

"No." Milo grinned. "I don't think so."

Why was that fool grinning when she was so sick? "Please, Milo. I'm really sick."

"I know you are, honey. But you don't need a doctor, at least not for a few months."

"But, Milo, I really don't feel good."

"You'll feel better in a while. We're going to have a baby."

Ruby Jo's heart stopped beating for a minute, then it started hammering against her ribs so hard it hurt. She jerked up in the bed.

"No!" she cried. "I don't want a baby. I can't have a baby." Tears spilled down her face. "I'm going to Hollywood. I'm going to be a famous actress."

"What you're going to be is a mother." Milo took both her hands in his. "Oh, Ruby Jo, you've made me so happy. I wanted more children so bad. I just never thought it could be. Tully'll be so excited."

"No, Milo, please. I don't want a baby."

"You'll love it. You'll see." He leaned over and kissed her on the forehead. "We're going to get married right away."

"No! No!" Ruby Jo screeched. "No, Milo, please."

"Hush now, Ruby Jo." Milo pushed a strand of hair off her face. "No child of mine is going to be born a bastard. Jube is driving us to Boerne in his car tomorrow. We'll be married by the justice of the peace."

Ruby Jo fell back on her pillow. She was too tired to fight him. What difference did it make anyway? As sick as she was, she'd be dead long before she could have any baby.

35 – LITTLE MOTHER

Ruby Jo was dying. For real this time. Her body was being ripped apart by this thing she did not want. Screaming didn't help. Neither did cussing or crying. She hated Milo.

Right now he was waiting out in the hall, waiting for this thing to kill her so it could be born. That's all he wanted anyway. It was all he talked about for months. He wouldn't even care that she was dead, just so he could have the baby he wanted so bad. Well, he could have it.

Two neighbor women fussed over her but they couldn't stop the pain. She was dimly aware the doctor had arrived, but it didn't matter. He couldn't make this thing go away and give her body back to her, the body she needed to be a movie star.

Just then somebody took an ax and split her in half right down her spine. With a final, fierce scream, she felt the thing leave her body and she fell back against the pillow. There was a faint, squeaky cry and the doctor said, "It's a girl. She's little but appears to be sound."

Ruby Jo didn't care. She fell into a deep darkness and heard no more.

* * * *

Ruby Jo did not want to wake up but something kept pestering her. She opened her eyes. Milo was fumbling with the front of her nightgown, pulling it back so her tittie was uncovered. He picked up a squalling bundle from the foot of the bed and brought it up to lay on her chest. He put it so the thing could nuzzle her nipple.

"No! No!" She tried to scoot away, but the pain in her belly gripped her so hard she couldn't move. The thing's sucking little mouth clamped down on her nipple and Ruby Jo screamed. It felt like her nipple had just been slammed between a hammer and an anvil.

"Now, stop it, Ruby Jo!" Ruby Jo had never heard Milo's voice so rough before.

"Please, don't make me, Milo," she whimpered.

"Stop this nonsense. You are going to feed this baby. What is the matter with you?" Milo picked up her arms and put them around the baby. "Now, hold her."

He sat down in the chair beside the bed and watched as tears trickled down Ruby Jo's face. She wasn't dead but she might as well be. Nursing this baby would just ruin her titties. She had seen the sagging sacks on a few of the older women over the years.

"Would it help if your Mama came for a little while?"

"No!"

"You really should get in touch with them, Ruby Jo."

"No. Not yet." They would just add to the trap closing around her. And how could she face Mama after Mama had been so dead set on Ruby Jo marrying Berlin? Mama just might kill her for sure.

"It's a girl," Milo said. "She needs a name. What do you want to call her?"

Ruby Jo glared at him. "I don't care. You name her."

Milo pressed his lips together and shook his head. "I just don't understand you, Ruby Jo. This is your baby."

"No. It's your baby. I told you. I never wanted it."

"Well, she's here and she needs a name."

"Then you name her."

The tugging on Ruby Jo's nipple shot a quivering jolt right into the depths of her stomach. It was not unpleasant once she got past the blistering pain to her nipple. In fact, it felt kind of good. Except she just couldn't have this thing ruining her titties.

Milo sat staring at her until she felt jittery. She didn't like the way he was looking at her, so she looked at the thing he had forced into her arms and onto her nipple.

It was kind of cute, she guessed, as babies go. There was a light honey-colored fuzz on its head and its skin looked as soft and pale as cotton. Its little cheeks moved in and out as it sucked.

"Mercy Grace," Milo said.

"What?"

"Mercy Grace. You said name her. That's her name." Milo reached over and gently ran the back of a finger along the baby's cheek. "Because it is only by the mercy and grace of God that I have another child. I never thought I would. Mercy Grace. Our little girl."

* * * *

A light April rain pecked at the window panes as Ruby Jo cleared the dishes off the breakfast table. Milo held Mercy Grace in one arm and tickled under her chin, making her gurgle.

"Put on your coat and hat before you leave for school," Milo said to Tully. "It's wet out there."

"Okay." Tully gulped down the last of his milk, then raced out of the room, Knob right behind him. A few minutes later he raced back in, kissed Mercy Grace on the forehead, grabbed his lunch pail off the table, and raced out the back door. Mercy Grace jumped and started crying as the door slammed.

Knob bounced around and barked at the closed door until Milo said, "Stop it, Knob. Go lay down."

The dog flopped down on an old blanket by the cook stove as Milo put Mercy Grace to his shoulder and rubbed her back, softly singing, *Rock-a-bye baby in the tree top...*

When Mercy Grace stopped crying, he put her on the kitchen table and held her in a sitting position. "She should be sitting up by herself by now," Milo said. "Tully was sitting up by himself when he was four months old."

"She's really little, so maybe it'll just take her longer."

"It's worrisome. If she doesn't show some signs pretty soon, I'm gonna take her to the doctor over in Boerne."

Ruby Jo sat down at the opposite end of the table. "I been thinking,

Milo. We ought to wean her to cow's milk." However she finally got out of here, the first step was to get Mercy Grace to stop nursing.

Milo looked up. "Why?"

"You said yourself she's way too little, and she spits up as much milk as she keeps down. Maybe that's why she's not growing like she ought to." Ruby Jo took a sip of coffee. "I think she'll do better on cow's milk." Ruby Jo held her breath.

"You might be right. Mrs. Willis, on the next farm over, she had to put her last baby on cow's milk almost from the start. I'll bet she even has some baby bottles we can borrow. I'll ride over there after chores and see."

* * * *

Ruby Jo's luck took a big turn for the better a little more than a month later. Mercy Grace was doing as well on cow's milk as she had nursing, and Ruby Jo was finally past the pain of her milk drying up. One night, as they were getting into bed, Milo said, "I have to get rid of a couple more brood sows. I can't keep feeding all of 'em."

"Are you going to slaughter them?"

"No. Jube has to drive over to Boerne tomorrow and I'm going with him. He knows a feller he thinks will buy two or three of the sows." The bed creaked under Milo's weight. "Jube has business to tend to, so we'll be gone all day. Don't wait supper. Just leave something on the back of the stove."

Ruby Jo hardly dared to breathe. Tully was out of school. *Please, please take Tully.*

"Tully is beside himself wanting to go, so I'll take him along."

Ruby Jo exhaled but didn't say anything.

"You and Mercy Grace be okay here on your own?"

"Oh, sure," Ruby Jo replied. "We've got Knob to take care of us."

* * * *

Ruby Jo waited a full hour after Jube picked up Milo and Tully. She wanted to be sure they were good and gone. She didn't take much, only one dress and a change of underwear. The clothes really didn't fit her all that well anyway.

She filled a jar with milk and wrapped some cold corn bread in a dish towel. All of it hardly made a lump in the bottom of the pillowcase. Mercy Grace followed her with eyes too big for her face as Ruby Jo gave her a bottle, changed her diaper and put on a clean wrapper. She put the baby in her bed in a dresser drawer on the floor and put a light blanket over her.

It was a warm sunny day, but Ruby Jo added one of Milo's heavier shirts to the pillowcase, then tied it so there was a loop to put her arm through. She put the pillowcase and one of Milo's old hats by the front door.

That was it then. She could hardly believe it. She was really going to get away. How she would get to Hollywood she didn't know, but one step at a time. Ruby Jo tiptoed into the bedroom and looked at Mercy Grace. Good. She was sleeping.

Ruby Jo walked as quietly as she could to the door, picked up the pillowcase and the hat and let herself out. It was still early but already warm. She plopped the hat on her head and walked fast down the lane toward the main road.

About halfway there, she turned and looked back at the house. Everything looked okay. Knob wasn't barking. There wasn't any smoke coming out of the house or anything.

Jeepers creepers. What if the house caught on fire before Milo got home? Or what if some stranger came with nobody home and took Mercy Grace? She really was a cute little thing. No, Knob would throw a fit. He wouldn't let a stranger in. But houses caught on fire all the time.

Well, shoot a speckled hen! Ruby Jo snorted. She looked down the lane toward the main road, then back at the house, then down the lane again. She puffed out her cheeks as she blew out a big whoosh of air.

She sure couldn't wait around for Milo to get back. She didn't want to do it, but she trudged back to the house. It didn't take long to gather up Mercy Grace's clothes and clean diapers. Ruby Jo made up the three baby bottles full of milk and wrapped them in a dish towel. Then she added another jar of milk to the pillowcase and retied the knot. It was heavier now. The last thing Ruby Jo did was open the top dresser drawer, take out

Mercy Grace's birth certificate and add it to the pillowcase.

Mercy Grace didn't even wake up when Ruby Jo picked her up, wrapped her loosely in the light blanket and put her over her shoulder. Lucky she wasn't even as heavy as the pillowcase.

Ruby Jo didn't have to walk very far. The first car that came along picked up the two of them. Ruby Jo didn't even have to stick out her thumb.

Part Three
Laney Belle Hawkins

May 24, 1943 – July 16, 1951

36 – MAMA'S BAD FEELING
Rockford, Texas — Monday, May 24, 1943

"Are we really getting away from Harley?" Laney sat at the table finishing the last of her cornbread and beans as she watched Mama hustle around gathering up their few clothes. She had asked the same question a dozen times during the day and always got the same answer but she just wanted to be sure.

"Praise the Lord, I believe we are." Mama tried to smile, then groaned and put her hand along the side of her black-and-blue cheek.

Laney hated Harley for hitting her mama. She wanted to come out and fight him when he did it, but Mama, said, "No, stay in bed, stay quiet as a mouse. That's the best way to help me." Laney did as she was told, but it didn't stop her from wanting to take a gun and shoot old Harley for what he did to her mama.

"Tomorrow morning?"

"That's what Mazie says." Mama folded the clothes and put them in a pillowcase.

"What if Harley comes back?" Laney shivered and goosebumps popped up on her arms.

"Lord, I pray he don't." The box of dominoes and Mama's Bible went in on top of the clothes. "Well, I think that's about it." Mama sat on the mattress on the floor and curled her legs under her. "Just leave your dishes, Laney. Come set with me. I want to talk to you."

Laney sat beside Mama. "I have to tell you something and it's important you remember it." Mama cupped Laney's face in her palm and looked hard into her eyes. "If anything happens and we don't get away and if anything, *anything at all,* happens to me, whatever you do, *do not let Harley touch you, ever.* Do you understand me? *Don't let him touch you anywhere. And I mean don't let him hug you or hold your hand or kiss you. Nothing.* Do you understand what I'm talking about?"

Laney would as soon eat worms as let nasty old Harley touch her. Why would he even want to touch her? "I think so, Mama."

"I didn't plan on telling you all this until you're older, but Lord knows what can happen from one day to another, so you have to know this. In another year or two, you'll be a woman and able to have a baby."

No way! She was never gonna have babies. She'd like to have a puppy but no baby. She had seen how the babies at church squalled and threw up and smelled like a pigpen. "I'm not gonna have any babies, Mama."

"Well, you may not, but you need to hear this." Mama took her time and was real careful to tell all about how, at a certain age, a girl got the curse and from then on she could get a baby. Mama was real strong about not letting any men or boys anywhere close until Laney was married. She explained exactly how the curse worked and how Laney should take care of herself. As far as Laney knew, Mama had never told a lie, but Laney didn't know what to think about all of this business. She would just as soon not have this old curse, thank you very much.

Mama was really stirred up and nervous. Laney shivered hard like she did when she thought a monster was under the bed. Mama said again, real strong, *"If we don't get away, and if anything happens to me,* you have to find a way to get away from Harley. Up to now, I didn't think you'd be able to do it alone, but you're ten now and smart. I think you could do it if you had to. *If I'm not here, get away. Run. Find a way. Run. Promise me.* Do you understand, Laney?"

"I promise, Mama, but nothing's gonna happen to you, is it?" Tears ran down Laney's face.

"Lord, I hope not, not till you're grown and married. But Laney, I have a jittery feeling. I won't rest easy till we're in Memphis. Now, let's ready up and get to bed. Tomorrow's the big day and we need to be up early."

Laney had barely closed her eyes when the sound of the truck motor and the sweep of the headlights across the canvas snapped her right up in bed. In the darkness, she heard Mama say, "Oh, no. Lord, no."

The truck door slammed, then there was the sound of Harley's boots shuffling on the tarp floor.

"Get up, Mattie." His voice was thick and slurred. "That summabitch plain lied to me. They wasn't no metal where he said. Wasted the whole damn day."

Laney could hear the sounds of Mama getting up. "Why don't I make you some coffee, Harley?"

"Don't want no damn coffee. Got me some Wild Turkey." It sounded like Harley fell onto a stool and banged into the table.

"There's leftover beans and cornbread."

"No, siree, no vittles. Little woman. That's what I'm hungry for. Come'ere. Come set on old Harley's lap."

"You need to get some sleep, Harley. You'll feel better tomorrow." Mama sounded like she was about to cry and Laney knew she was thinking about Memphis.

Laney wanted to crawl under her cot, lift the tarp curtain and peek, but Mama had told her a thousand times, "Don't ever get up, Laney. No matter what you hear, stay in bed." So Laney lay as stiff and quiet as a fence post, but her heart was pounding.

"Dammit to hell, Mattie! Can't you just do what you're damn told one damn time?" There was the sharp crack of a slap. Mama cried out, then there was a smooshy sound like a watermelon dropped on the ground.

"What the hell? Get up from there, Mattie." It was real quiet for a minute, then Harley said, "Mattie? *Mattie!*" His voice wasn't slurred anymore and he sounded scared. "Shit. *Oh, shit!*"

Laney heard him walk toward her little cubbyhole. She held her breath and kept her eyes closed. She could feel him standing there for what seemed like forever. Just when she thought she couldn't hold her breath anymore, she heard him stepping away.

What was wrong with Mama? Why wasn't she answering? Laney threw the covers back and started for the opening. No. Mama said *NEVER*, no matter what. A thousand times she said it. Why wasn't Mama talking or crying or begging like she sometimes did?

Laney lay still, trembling so hard the cot shook, but she stayed put and listened. There was a lot of moving around, but neither Mama or Harley said a single word. Then she heard Harley grunt and the sound of him shuffling across the tarp floor. A couple of minutes later the truck started up, the headlights came on, and he drove away.

As soon as Laney was sure the truck was gone, she jumped up. She had to see if Mama was okay and help her if she wasn't. It was dark, but Harley had left the tent flap open and enough moonlight came in for Laney to see she was alone.

Where was Mama? Had she gone somewhere with Harley? No. Mama would never leave her, ever. She had promised. Maybe they just went somewhere and would be back. She would wait. But, what if they didn't come back? What if they had truly left her? Laney's heart beat so hard in her throat she could hardly breathe. Tears ran down her face and seeped into the corners of her mouth. What could she do?

Mazie. She would go to Mazie. But she was getting scared for nothing. They would be back. She would wait until sunup. If they weren't back, then she would go to Mazie.

Laney curled up on Mama's pallet, holding Mama's purse close. She sniffed. Something smelled funny, like wet wood. She ran her hand over the purse; it felt damp and sticky. Looking at it closely in the dim light, she could see a big, dark splotch on the side. Laney put the purse on the floor, wiped her hand on a quilt, and lay back down to wait.

Why didn't Mama take her purse? *Mama never went anywhere without her purse.*

37 – THE FIRE

It was near daylight when Harley's truck rolled up outside the tent again. All that worry was for nothing. Mama was back!

Laney jumped up and ran to the tent flap. Only Harley got out of the truck.

"Where's Mama?" Laney intended to scream the words but they came out like a bullfrog croak.

"Get on back in there, girl. Set down. I need to talk to you." He pointed at a stool in the dusky light. Laney sat.

"Now, your Mama done decided she didn't want ole Harley anymore. I dropped her off at the bus station so she could go back to that place you come from." Harley sat on a stool across from Laney. "Seems she figures to find you a place to live. She said you have to stay with me until she comes back for you."

"But Mama wouldn't leave me." Laney's chin quivered.

"Well, it looks like she did." Harley snorted. "There ain't no accountin' for what a woman might do."

"When will she be back?" Laney tasted the salt of the tears that rolled down her cheeks.

"As soon as she finds a place. Could be a week. Could be a month. Important thing is she said you should stay put with me." He narrowed his eyes and looked hard at Laney. "She'd never find you if you go running off someplace. You understand me, girl?"

Laney nodded. Could it be? Mama did want to get away and she probably would go back home. But why wouldn't Mama take Laney with her? Well, because she had to find a place to live first. That made sense. But she had said, *"Get away! Run."*

Laney couldn't very well run with Harley watching her like a hound dog guarding his bone. Wait. Wait a little. See if Mama comes back.

Laney jumped when Harley said, "Get your clothes on and be quick about it."

Laney went behind the divider and put on the clothes Mama had laid out for her for the day. When she came out, Harley was carrying his suitcase out through the flap. "Gather up just your clothes. Leave everything else."

Laney glanced at the two pillowcases Mama had packed, one with Laney's things and the other with her own. "What about Mana's things?"

"I reckon she took what she wanted, so leave the rest." Harley called over his shoulder.

Mama didn't want her clothes? That didn't sound right. Laney shifted uneasily from foot to foot. She really should take Mama's stuff. She jumped when Harley gave her a shove and snapped, "Get a move on. Now. We don't got all day."

As Harley carried out his toolbox, Laney grabbed Mama's purse and shoved it to the bottom of the pillowcase under her clothes. Just as she picked up Mama's Bible, Harley snatched it from her hand and threw it on the floor.

"You don't need that foolishness," he said. "Get in the truck."

Harley grabbed an armload of Mama's quilts, carried them out and put them behind the seat. As Laney climbed in and put her pillowcase on top of the quilts, she noticed Harley pick up a can of kerosene sitting by the tent flap and go inside.

In a minute or two, Harley came out, climbed in, started the motor and then got out again, leaving the truck door open. What in the world was he doing? Wasn't he going to pack up the rest of their stuff like usual?

Harley walked to the open flap, stood there for a minute, then turned and ran back to the truck. Before he could slam the door, there was a huge sucking sound and in one second the entire tent was blazing. It lit up everything like a noontime sun. Harley rammed the truck into reverse and backed away.

Laney jumped up so quickly she hit her head on the top of the truck. There was too much strangeness going on. Nothing had ever scared her like this—not monsters, not when Daddy died, nothing. Her teeth clacked together from her shaking.

"*Mama!*" she screamed. "I want Mama."

Harley backhanded her across the face so hard she fell into the seat. "You set there and keep your trap shut. You understand?"

Laney nodded and, whimpering, put her palm against her cheek.

"Stop sniveling or I'll give you something to cry about."

Laney swallowed her sobs and curled up against the truck door as far away from Harley as she could get. Through all the smoke, she could barely see Mazie and Clovis Halston standing on their porch as Harley drove out of the pasture.

"Stay here and don't say nothing, you hear?" Harley said as he got out of the truck and walked toward the couple.

They were too far away for Laney to hear what Harley said, but he was back in a couple of minutes. As they drove away, Laney looked out the back window. Mazie stood on the porch until Harley drove around a bend in the road and Laney couldn't see the farmhouse anymore.

"Now, you listen to me, girl," Harley said as the truck rattled down the road, "I've got enough money coming in, so we'll be able to stay in tourist cabins. They's plenty of them along the roads. I was plumb tired of living in that tent anyways."

Laney looked at her hands clenched in her lap and said nothing. She couldn't stop shaking and her head was pounding.

"You'll be going with me on my rounds, so I'm telling you now, keep your mouth shut. If you know what's good for you, you'll let people think you're a dummy. You got that?"

Laney nodded. Harley glanced at her. "Answer when I speak to you, girl."

"Yes," Laney said, barely above a whisper.

"Good." Harley grinned. "We understand each other; we'll get on just fine." He steered the truck into the parking lot of a small café. "I need me some vittles."

When they were settled at a table, he ordered flapjacks and coffee for both of them, plus eggs and sausage for himself. As the waitress took their order, she frowned and glanced at Laney. Laney looked away.

When the waitress brought the bill, she said, "Are you okay, honey?"

Laney nodded.

The waitress said again, "Are you sure you're okay?"

Laney nodded again and Harley said in a hard voice, "She's just fine."

Somewhere along the road that afternoon, Harley stopped at a secondhand store. He went in by himself and came out with a sack. That night, after they had supper and checked in to a cabin in a tourist court, Harley opened the sack and took out two boy's shirts and two pairs of overalls and put them on the table. Pulling out a chair, he said, "Set here."

As soon as she sat down, Harley took out his pocket knife and started whacking off her hair. 'No!" She tried to duck away but his fingers bit into her shoulder so hard she cried out.

"Set still."

Laney did as she was told.

"From now on," Harley said, "you'll wear the boy's clothes. You keep your mouth shut, everybody'll think you're my boy. Less trouble that way. You understand me?"

Laney nodded.

"Dump all your girl clothes in the garbage before we leave in the morning. No use carrying that useless stuff around. You hear me?"

Laney slumped in the chair and didn't answer.

"You hear me, girl?"

"Yes, sir."

"Well, hear this, too, while you're at it." Harley sat on the bed and drew back his lips in a grin that made his yellow teeth fill half his face. "You got to stay with me till your mama comes back. She'll never find you if you go running off. You understand?"

Laney nodded.

"You know what happens to little girls running around alone with nobody to look out for 'em?" Harley reached inside his overalls and scratched his crotch. "Well, that's what you call an orphan. First off, the sheriff picks you up. Then you have to stay in jail while they talk around and find out if you really are an orphan.

"If you are, then they start looking for somebody to take you in—adopting, they call it. Now mind you, people don't take in orphans because they want a young'un. They take 'em because they want a slave. You'd have to work day and night, doing the nastiest jobs, and they wouldn't hardly feed you, and you'd just wear rags. Probably have to sleep in a barn or something like that. You might as well be an animal. You understand?"

Harley pushed his chaw further back in his cheek with his tongue and a little tobacco juice dribbled down his chin.

"Now, if nobody wants you, and I doubt anybody would, you being such a scrawny little thing... well, in that case, they just put you right in prison. You ever hear about that?"

Laney shook her head, so terrorized she couldn't speak.

"Well, prison's a whole different story. Nothing them murderers and criminals like better than young girls with nobody to protect 'em. What they would do to you is worse than torture. Yes, siree, you are a far sight better off with ole Harley. I'll take care of you and protect you till your mama comes back. We understand each other?"

Laney nodded.

After dark, Laney lay on a pallet of Mama's quilts on the floor and using the pillowcase of her belongings as a pillow, covered her shaggy head with her arms. She didn't cry aloud because Harley wouldn't like it, but her insides filled with so many tears she thought she would drown. *Where was Mama? Would she come back?*

* * * *

Laney's life became a routine of silence. She spoke to no one except Harley and then only when Harley spoke first and demanded an answer. He left her in the truck when he made his calls and never took her in a store with him. And Harley was right; when she was exposed to people, mostly when they stopped in a café to eat, people assumed she was a deaf-mute and didn't talk to her.

Harley repeated his warning every day. If she ran away she would most likely be picked up and put in prison. Mama would never find her in prison, he said.

But Harley couldn't stop her from thinking. In the silence, her thoughts went around and around, pounding so hard it made her head hurt.

Laney remembered the sound of the slap followed by the wet, smooshy sound, then not a word from Mama. But did that mean for sure something had happened to Mama or did she go away like Harley said? Harley was right. As long as there was any chance Mama could come back,

Laney should wait.

She would be a lot worse off if she was an orphan or adopted or put in prison. Mama would never find her then.

But Mama had said, "If anything happens to me, *run.*" How could she run with Harley watching her every second? If she ran from Harley, where could she go and be safe? Harley took care of her, fed her and gave her a warm, dry place to sleep.

Get away from Harley. Wait for Mama. Don't let him touch you. Orphan. Adopted. Prison. Harley takes care of you. Around and around, and Mama always whispering, *Run, Laney, run.*

38 – THE ESCAPE

Brady, Texas – Wednesday, April 25, 1945

Laney had to act fast because Harley never let her lock the bathroom door.

He had just gone out to the truck to get a new supply of his precious peaches and would be back any minute. He loved canned peaches better than anybody she ever saw. Every night he opened a can, stabbed the slices one at a time with his pocket knife and slurped them down. Then he drank the juice. He always kept at least a half a dozen unopened cans under his bed.

The curse her Mama had talked about had started about a week ago. Thank the Lord, Mama had told her about it or she would have been scared to death. Without quite understanding why, she knew it best not to let Harley know about it. But how was she supposed to take care of herself?

She had managed by tearing up two boys shirts she had outgrown and folding them to make pads to fasten to her panties with a safety pin. There were no more shirts to tear up, so she had no idea what she would do next month.

So far, she had been able to dispose of the soiled pads in filling station restrooms or by wrapping them in toilet paper and burying them in the bottom of the bathroom trash at night. Now, it was the last one and it was hardly soiled at all, so she knew she was at the end of the curse for this time. As usual, she wrapped the pad really good in toilet paper and buried it in the bottom of the wastepaper basket under the discarded wrappings from the hamburgers Harley had bought for supper.

She pulled on her nightgown and carried her overalls and shirt back into the main room where she folded them and placed them neatly by the foot of her pallet.

Although Harley still kept her hair chopped off, it was getting harder and harder for her to pass for a boy. Not only had she gotten the curse, but over the last two years she had grown taller and filled out in the chest. She was as full grown as a woman and Harley tried to hide it by buying really big men's shirts for her to wear over the top of her overalls.

Harley came in, took a can of peaches out of a sack and slid the sack under the bed. Laney sat on her pallet, saying nothing, as Harley opened the can and ate the peaches. She watched him out of the corner of her eye. She didn't look directly at him because he always wanted to know what her problem was.

Well, he was her problem. It had been the same ever since the day Mama went away and the tent burned. They ate hamburgers and sandwiches out of sacks, or in greasy cafes. Every night was spent in some rundown cabin in a tourist court on a main road with traffic roaring by nonstop. She was never out of his sight except to go to the bathroom.

He had rigged up some kind of contraption out of scrap metal that he called his trick lock for the door at night. He said there was no way she could open it without knowing the trick.

When he was gone for several hours in the evening once or twice a week, he put the trick lock on the outside of the door. He told her she better hope the place didn't catch on fire because nobody but him could open that lock. Laney would lie rigid on her pallet, wide awake with heart hammering, sniffing every few minutes to see if she smelled smoke, until he returned.

The last few months he had kept even closer watch on her. She would glance up to find him studying her and he'd ask, "How're you feeling, girl? You alright?"

Once in a while he would actually sniff her just like she'd seen male dogs sniff female dogs. He made her skin quiver like red ants were crawling on her.

Harley wiped his mouth on his sleeve and carried the empty peach can into the bathroom. Laney exhaled in relief and lay back on her pallet.

Harley came out of the bathroom, as he usually did, wearing only his drawers. He sat on the edge of the bed and grinned at her without saying a word. What was the matter with him? He was acting more like a lunatic than usual. She closed her eyes but could still feel him studying her.

"I'll bet you wasn't gonna tell me." He chuckled and she opened her eyes. He was scratching himself under his arm. "You wasn't, was you?"

"Tell you what?" Laney was very careful of how she spoke. Wouldn't do to make him mad.

"That you're finally a woman."

"What do you mean?" She sat up and crossed her arms across her chest.

"Don't play possum with me, girl. I done saw the proof in the bathroom."

Laney chilled, like she had been plunged into ice water. "Why would you want to know?"

"Are you shittin' me?" Harley sputtered. "Here, I been waitin' like a patient man, first puttin' up with your sickly mama, then taking care of you all this time. You think I did that for my health?"

Laney said nothing. He was a crazy man but surely he wouldn't do anything to her.

"I just been waitin' and waitin' and it weren't easy, I tell you, but I ain't no monster. I don't have no truck with little girls." Harley flicked his tongue over his lips. "But you ain't a little girl no more and now Harley gets his payoff. You and me are gonna have lots of good times."

With that he dropped his drawers. Bile rose up in Laney's throat. She scooted backward until her back touched the wall.

"Don't be skeered, Laney," Harley said in a sing-song voice. "You're gonna like this. You're just lucky ole Harley's your first. You could do a lot worse." He laughed and pulled her up by an arm, dragging her toward the bed.

She kicked and thrashed, sending her pillowcase of belongings flying, the contents spilling out on the floor. He pulled the nightgown over her head and threw it aside.

"Whooo-eee!" Harley held her still for a minute, looking her up and down and laughing. "I told your mama I was gonna raise you up to suit me and, honey, you suit me just fine."

He pushed her down and was on top of her before she could think. She turned her head away as he tried to kiss her.

Do not let Harley touch you, ever. And I mean, don't let him hug you, or hold your hand, or kiss you. Nothing. Do you understand what I'm talking about?"

"Don't be contrary." Harley grabbed her chin to hold her face still. "Be nice to ole Harley and I'll be nice to you."

His mouth came down on hers, his whiskers scratching her face and his breath so foul she gagged. She pushed against his chest. *Don't let him touch you!* How? *Lord, help me.* She felt him hard against her leg. *Please, no.*

She knew better than to scream for help. She had to help herself. He was trying to stick his tongue in her mouth so she bit it, hard.

Harley yelled like a cat with its tail caught under a rocking chair. He reared back and punched her in the face twice and she saw an explosion of white light. She tried to kick him and he hit her in the face again. Then he put his knee between her knees and forced her legs apart.

She shook her head once, twice. "No!"

Heart pounding, vomit rising in her throat, she felt around on the floor for something—anything—then her hand closed on a can of peaches. Before she could even think about it, she slammed the end of the heavy can into the side of his head. He grunted and went tense, so she slammed his head twice more as hard as she could and he slumped down on her, his weight pressing her to the bed. She lay still for a minute, disoriented, eyes closed, panting, and gagging, not even sure she was alive.

She forced one eye open, the other being swollen shut, thinking to see hell for she was not expecting heaven. Not after she had just killed a man.

What she did see, only a breath away from her own face, was one glassy, sightless eye under a shaggy eyebrow and Harley's mouth, slack-lipped and drooling something thick and yellowish.

The dark brown and muddy taste of his blood was sticky on her lips, the coppery odor bringing a surge of blistering bile high in her throat and into her nose. People didn't puke in hell did they? Her heart slammed against her ribs. She must be alive.

That was when she really started shaking. She pushed Harley off her and onto the bed. As soon as her feet hit the floor she made a dash for the door. She was lucky Harley had forgotten to put on his trick lock.

Just as she flung the door open, she realized she was naked. She quickly closed the door and, trying not to look at Harley's body, pulled on her overalls, a shirt, and her shoes. She didn't take time for underwear and socks or to wash off Harley's blood.

Rushing to the door, Laney stumbled over Mama's purse. She grabbed it and stuffed it down the front of her overalls.

She wouldn't have to worry about being an orphan or adopted or even spending her life in prison anymore. If you kill somebody, you go to the electric chair. Laney had heard about several executions on the radio. Just last week there was the story about a woman who had killed her husband over in Alabama. But, she didn't get the chair. They hung her.

Laney threw open the door and, hugging Mama's purse against her body, she ran.

39 THE GOAT TRAIN

Laney ran around the corner of the cabin and into the darkness of a field she had seen from the bathroom window earlier in the evening. Bushes and tree branches grabbed at her as she ran blindly.

She stumbled and fell to her knees more than once. The sound of her own breathing was loud in her ears, so she ran right into shallow water before she heard the ripple and flow of a river in the dark.

Turning, she walked out of the water, leaned over and pressed her hand to her side, trying to ease a pain that felt like it was going to tear her leg from her body. Her face throbbed and one eye felt swollen.

She could see the lights of the cabins about a mile away. Everything appeared to be quiet. No sirens. No flashing red lights.

In the moonlight, she could see the river was wide but there was no telling how deep it was. She was not a strong swimmer, and the water filling her shoes had been cold. To her left, the river disappeared into trees and a dense darkness. To her right, was a well-lit rail yard with box cars on several switching tracks.

She stood panting, head hanging down, trembling, trying to think. There was a limit to how far and fast she could go on her own two legs, and she had no money.

Why didn't she think to take Harley's money? He always had some. Too late now. Even if she had money, she wouldn't dare be seen. She was covered in Harley's blood. The rank and raw smell of it mixed with her own sweat and fear burned her nose.

She stood up and studied the rail yard. It was night, so there probably wouldn't be many people around. If she could find an open car, she could climb in and hide, go wherever it was going. The cops would probably just be looking around here for her once somebody found Harley's body.

But, ride the rails? How hard could it be? She could; she knew she could. People did it all the time during the Depression, but not so much anymore. What choice did she have? She couldn't go out to the highway and stick her thumb out.

Laney bent low and ran into the dim light at the outskirts of the rail yard. She squatted and studied the dozens of box cars. There was one with the doors open and there didn't seem to be anybody around.

Staying low, she ran from shadow to shadow until she was just one box car away from the open door. She ducked under the end of the box car and, gasping to catch her breath, shaking with cold and fear, she studied the open door. From what she could see, it was empty, so it might be hard to hide inside. But it was the only one with an open door and a ramp to make it easy to get up inside.

Laney took another quick look around and then, holding her breath and ready to make a run for the darkness if anyone saw her, she ran toward the ramp. Nobody yelled or came running. She ducked inside.

It was empty except for a galvanized livestock water trough, full of water, not quite shoved against the front wall. The space behind it provided the only possible hiding place. She cupped her hands and splashed water on her throbbing face, then climbed into the trough and waded to the back. She would have to lay on her side but it would hide her. Splinters from the rough wall dug into her back as she wiggled and contorted and forced her body into the narrow space.

Her nose practically touched the cold metal and she couldn't move or change positions. Not even five minutes in hiding and already her body ached and cramped. She shivered in the cold night air and wiggled her toes in her soggy shoes. No matter how miserable, she had to do it. She had to get away... or be hung or strapped in an electric chair.

She waited, listening for sirens, expecting to see light from searcher's flashlights flooding her hiding place, but it remained quiet and dark. In spite of her fear and the pain of her face and body, she dozed from plain exhaustion.

The first hint of light barely paled the darkness when the rumble and rattle of a truck driving up to the ramp startled her awake. *Harley!* She tried to jerk herself up but was wedged firmly in the small spot and stiff as a block of ice from lying in one position for so long. No, not Harley. Harley was dead. She had killed him.

Laney heard the sound of a tailgate being lowered, then a couple of men yelling and cussing. She smelled them before she heard their bleating or the clickety-clack of their hooves on the loading ramp. Goats.

The goats streamed into the box car. Laney couldn't tell how many from the sound. She glanced at the side wall of the car. Slatted. A livestock car. She hadn't noticed in the dark and her rush to hide. Another reason it was so cold. Plus, it made her hiding place easier to spot if anybody was looking. She shrunk herself down as small as possible and tried not to breathe.

It seemed like forever, but finally the door slid shut. The box car jolted like it was slammed with a giant sledgehammer as it coupled to the main train, and they were rolling. Slowly at first, then picking up speed until the clicking of the wheels against the rails was a steady hum. The goats were restless, moving back and forth and bleating a steady conversation among themselves

Laney waited until she was sure the train was really underway, then she wedged herself out of her cubbyhole and waded across the trough again. Her legs were so numb she had to hold on to the sides to keep from falling.

The place stunk so bad she gagged even though she tried to barely breathe. She swung her legs over the side of the trough, nudging aside goats and stood. Her feet flew right out from under her and she sprawled flat on the slippery floor. Goat shit pebbles had been made slick by trampling and water sloshed from the tank.

Laney scooted up until her back was against the trough. She put her elbows on her bent knees, her face in her hands, and cried. Goat mess was everywhere. On her clothes, in her hair, on her hands and now on her face.

The goats crowded around, bleating and nudging her with their wet noses, like they were trying to comfort her. Laney put her arms around the neck of the nanny closest to her, buried her face in the goat's smelly hair and howled her fear and pain. The goat bleated and cried right along with her, or so it seemed to Laney.

What to do? There was no way she was crawling behind the trough again and she couldn't wait for them to herd her out with the goats when the train stopped. Laney dried her tears and tried to think. There really was only one thing to do.

* * * *

The heat from the sun, now high in the sky and filtering through the box car slats, added to the body heat of the goats as the train finally began slowing down. The hard fist of hunger clutched Laney's stomach and she thought it had to be at least the middle of the day.

She made her way to the door, then sat to the side and waited. When the box car came to a complete stop, Laney stood and flattened herself against the wall at the edge of the door. She didn't know what she would see when the door opened, but she had just one chance and she had to act fast.

As soon as the door opened wide enough for her to get through, Laney jumped onto the loading platform, then to the ground. She hit the dirt running. The two men on the loading platform were so surprised they didn't even yell until Laney had disappeared around the end of the car.

Where was she? Not a rail yard… a siding with some corrals and sheds and what looked like a small depot or office. A few houses scattered about.

Laney glanced back. Nobody was chasing her—yet. But she couldn't take a chance, so Laney ran as fast as she could, darting around the last shed and into a thicket of trees. Keeping low, she prayed she wouldn't run up on a rattlesnake.

The thicket became so dense she couldn't run anymore, so she stopped and leaned against a tree to catch her breath. There was no sound except the goats being herded out of the box car back at the siding and a dog barking someplace. Nothing unusual, like somebody running through the brush after her.

Laney slid to the ground and sat with her back against a tree trunk. She stunk to high heaven and even gagged herself. She was thirsty on top of being hungry.

She had to move on; she couldn't stay there forever. So after a few minutes, she pushed herself up. Which way to go? Not the way she had just come for sure. She listened hard, but still no unusual sounds, so she sighed with relief.

A narrow small animal trail curved back into the brush ahead. She bent over, putting her arms over her head to shield her face from limbs, and pushed through. The brush poked and slapped at her with every step until she suddenly emerged out of it and stood on the top of a low hill. Just a mound really, at back fence of a pig pen.

Dried mud and no sign of fresh water or slop told Laney no pigs had been in the pen for some time. The back of the pen was a wall of a shed with a half-door cut into it.

Laney slid down the grass and bending low, eased her way around the side of the pen and into the shade of the shed. A full-size door was cracked open. She peeked inside. No pigs. Nothing except some kind of dirty old box with gunny sacks stacked on top. Laney slipped inside, pulled the gunny sacks onto the dirt and hunkered down behind the box as best she could. She had to catch her breath. She had to think.

She curled up with her arm under her head. The thumping of her heart and her breathing slowed. In spite of the flies buzzing all around, she dozed.

It was the smell of apple pie that had her jerking straight up like a Jack-in-the-box. She sniffed deeply, scrambled up and crept to the door. Nobody in sight. She slipped out and edged along to the corner of the shed.

There was a small barn to the right and straight ahead across the barnyard was the back porch of a house. A window into the house was propped open with a Mason jar and a pie sat cooling on the sill.

Laney didn't think. Bending low, she ran across the yard and tiptoed up on the porch. Taking care to stay below the level of the window, she reached up and touched the pie pan. It was too hot to handle. She took the chance to slowly stand up and peek through the window. It was a kitchen but nobody was in it.

Laney folded the sides of her shirt as padding and lifted the pan off the sill. As fast as she dared, she made a run for the shed. She sank onto the gunny sacks and put the pie down on the box in front of her. It was still hot but she dug in with both hands, filth and all. She blew on the apple filling, then crammed it into her mouth as fast as she could.

The apples were soft and she swallowed almost without chewing. When the pie was all gone, she licked the pan and burped. All of a sudden she gagged and it all came back up. She leaned over, braced herself against the box, and vomited until she had the dry heaves.

Laney put her arms on the box, buried her face and cried a flood of tears with great gulps and sobs, sounding like a honking goose. When she could cry no more, giant hiccups shook her body. She sat still. Maybe if she just lay there quietly she would die. That would be best for everybody and it sure would beat hanging or getting electrocuted.

40 – MISS FAIRYDEANE

"I wouldn't make any sudden moves if I were you, sonny."

Laney jerked her head up and scooted across the dirt until her back was against the shed wall.

Standing in the door was the smallest woman Laney had ever seen, holding a pitchfork a lot taller than she was. She looked like she meant business.

"How was the pie?" the woman asked in her mouse-squeak voice.

Laney gaped at her but didn't answer.

The woman, wearing a housedress and an apron, looked like she would come about to Laney's shoulder. Row after row of tight little gray curls hunkered down on her pink scalp like they were under tornado warning. Her bright blue eyes and narrow face reminded Laney of a sparrow.

"Must not have set too well." The little woman looked at the vomit as she walked over, sat on the box, and put the pitchfork across her lap. "I hope you held your own with whoever gave you that shiner." She leaned forward and peered more closely at Laney's face.

"What's your name, sonny?" She didn't sound mean, but she still had a good grip on the pitchfork.

Laney couldn't have spoken if she wanted to, and she didn't want to.

"So, you don't want to tell me your name?"

Laney shook her head.

"Well, that's okay, young man. I don't put a lot of stock in names myself. Who would, with a name like Fairydeane Tinkel?" The old woman shook her head and chuckled. "That's what you can call me, Miss Fairydeane."

"Fairydeane?" Laney blurted. She couldn't help herself.

"I'll be jiggered! You're a girl!"

Laney nodded.

"I thought there was something off about you. If that don't beat all." Miss Fairydeane smiled. "Well, whatever your name is, I hope it isn't as burdensome as mine.

"It was my Mama's doing. That woman loved fairy tales better than anybody I ever knew, even until the day she died. I'll bet she read 'Grimm's Fairy Tales' hundreds of times. Why, I could recite every story by memory by the time I was four."

Miss Fairydeane stood and leaned the pitchfork against the wall. "Well, come along, girl with no name. You stink to high heaven. We'll get you cleaned up, then you can have some real food. How's that?"

Food. Laney scrambled up and followed Miss Fairydeane out of the shed. As they walked toward the back porch, Laney looked around quickly but didn't see anybody else.

"Wait here," Miss Fairydeane said. "You can't come in the house smelling like that." She disappeared inside and came back with a bucket of water, soap, and some rags. "What you need is a real bath, but this will have to do for now. Take your clothes off and throw them into the back yard. We'll burn them later."

Laney stared at her.

"Go ahead; nobody's going to see you back here. Do as I say."

Miss Fairydeane disappeared into the house again and returned with a teakettle of boiling water, which she poured into the cold water in the bucket. "Best I can do," she said. "Now get on with it."

Laney put Mama's purse on a shelf and threw everything else, including her shoes, into the yard. As she was washing, Miss Fairydeane came out again and spread a towel over the porch railing.

"Wrap yourself in this and come inside. My clothes won't fit you, but I think there might still be a dress or two of Mama's in a back closet. Maybe I can find a pair of slippers that'll work for now. We'll make do."

Laney ducked her head in the bucket to get the soap out of her hair, poured the water over her body to rinse and dried off.

She pulled the dress, smelling of musty lavender, over her bare body.

It was big enough to be shared with company and hung almost to the floor. Clutching Mama's purse to her chest, she followed the smell of frying eggs into the kitchen.

"Well, you're a sight, that's for sure." Miss Fairydeane laughed and it was a tiny sound, kind of like a bird, not singing, but coughing. "What's that you have there?"

"My mama's purse."

Fairydeane paused and studied Laney for a couple of seconds, but she didn't ask any questions. "Here. Eat slowly. You don't want to make yourself sick again." She put some cold biscuits, butter, and a glass of milk by the plate of eggs. Laney dug in.

"When's the last time you ate?"

Laney tried to think. Was it just yesterday? Supper? But she had thrown all that up after Harley. She shivered. "Yesterday, I think," she replied.

Laney finished the food and sat hunched in the chair, staring at her plate. What now? Would this Miss Fairydeane turn her in to the law? Should she jump up and run right now? She was pretty sure she could outrun this little bird of a woman.

"How about we have some coffee? You drink coffee?" Miss Fairydeane asked.

Laney nodded.

"Cream and sugar?"

Laney nodded again. The old woman poured two cups of coffee and put them on the table along with cream and sugar, then sat in a chair across from Laney.

"Well, young lady, what are we going to do with you?"

"Where am I?" Laney took a sip of the hot, sweet coffee. It felt so good going down.

"You don't know where you are?" Miss Fairydeane raised her white eyebrows.

"No, ma'am."

Miss Fairydeane put her small fingers across her lips and studied Laney. "You're in Ardmore, Oklahoma. In my home, Miss Fairydeane Tinkel, retired schoolteacher. And who are you?"

Laney's hand shook so bad she had to put the coffee cup down, but she didn't speak.

"It seems to me you might have yourself a bit of trouble."

Laney nodded.

"Well, you're going to have to talk to me. I can't help if I don't know the problem."

"You'll turn me in to the law!" Laney blurted.

Miss Fairydeane's eyebrows shot up again. "Now, what in the Lord's name could a youngster like you have done to have the law after you?"

"I killed a man." Laney had no intention of saying it. It just jumped out of her mouth and, once it was out, she couldn't take it back.

41 – SHELTER

Fairydeane put her coffee cup down so quickly it thunked against the table and sloshed a little coffee on the red-and-white-checkered oil cloth. She studied the girl sitting across from her, head bowed, trembling in Mama's dress that hung on her as big and loose as a sheet on a Halloween trick-or-treater.

If there was one thing Fairydeane knew, it was youngsters. She had spent almost every day of her life with all ages, sizes, and kinds for over fifty years and she would bet her bottom dollar this girl didn't kill anybody.

And if she did, Fairydeane hoped it was the low-life who battered the poor girl's face and blackened her eye. But whatever the problem was, Fairydeane could see the girl was terrified and exhausted.

"I doubt that." Fairydeane picked up the coffee cup and wiped the spill with a dish towel.

The girl's head snapped up. "I did. The law's after me." Her voice was low and it shook. "They'll send me to the chair or hang me."

Fairydeane resisted the urge to snort. "Well, why don't you just tell me all about it? Let's see if we can sort this out."

The girl looked quickly at the door and moved on the chair as if preparing to flee.

"You can trust me. I'll help you." Fairydeane tried to make her voice calm and reassuring. Why did she always sound so squeaky instead of confident and authoritative?

The girl looked at Fairydeane, then at the door again. Fairydeane said again, "You can trust me. I promise."

Fairydeane could see the moment of surrender as the girl seemed to shrink down into Mama's dress, like somebody let air out of a balloon.

"Why don't we just have ourselves some fresh coffee?" Fairydeane quickly bustled about, refilling the cups.

When she was settled at the table, she said, "You know who I am. Why don't you tell me who you are?"

The girl's eyes got big and she swallowed hard, but then she said, "Laney. Laney Belle Hawkins."

"Well, Laney Belle Hawkins, why don't you just start at the beginning and tell me how all this happened and how I can help you?"

Laney nodded, straightened in the chair and began speaking low and slowly. As she talked, she seemed to make a decision to fully trust Fairydeane and the words came tumbling out as though Laney couldn't tell it fast enough. She revealed everything from the day Daddy died until the night she killed Harley Faddis.

Fairydeane listened carefully. She sometimes nodded, muttered to herself, wiped tears from her eyes, or ground her teeth together and clenched her fists in her lap, but she didn't speak or interrupt.

"So I killed him with a can of peaches and I ran. I hid in a box car full of goats and when the train stopped here, I jumped out and ran before they could stop me."

"I see," Fairydeane said.

It had turned to dusk while Laney talked. Fairydeane pulled the long string hanging over the table to turn on the single electric bulb. "First, Laney, I'm pretty sure you didn't kill that man."

"But I did. There was a lot of blood all over the place. He looked dead."

"People think a head wound wouldn't bleed much because the head is so bony, but a head wound bleeds a lot worse than the wound actually is." Fairydeane picked up their coffee cups and put them in the sink. "It's my guess you clobbered him good, and he probably had a powerful headache for a few days, that's all."

"No." Laney shook her head. "I killed him all right."

"Okay," Fairydeane said, "Let's say you did. Do you know what I think?"

Laney shook her head again.

"I say good riddance. An oaf who preys on little girls doesn't deserve to live anyway. That's what I think."

"So you won't call the law on me?"

Fairydeane could see Laney was holding her breath. "Absolutely not. The first thing we're going to do is fix some supper and you're going to help me. After supper, we'll see if we can figure out what we're going to do with you."

Fairydeane could hear the whoosh of Laney's exhale as the girl nodded and, for the first time, smiled.

Fairydeane thought and talked as she prepared a supper of fried sweet potatoes, chicken and dumplings, and canned green beans, giving Laney instructions on helping.

"So, how old are you, Laney?"

"I was twelve April second."

"That would make you in the eighth grade?"

"No, ma'am." Laney hung her head and mumbled, "I only finished first grade."

"What! Didn't you get some schooling along the way?"

"No, ma'am. We only stayed in one place a couple of days at a time."

"Well, this just won't do." Fairydeane felt her blood pressure rise and throb in her temples. This had to be fixed. "Let's get supper over and done with, then we'll sit down and make a plan. That sound okay with you?"

"Oh, yes, ma'am."

"So, in all this moving around, it was just you, your Mama, and this Harley person? You never had any friends your own age?"

"No, ma'am. Not regular anyway. I had one friend one time for one day." Laney stopped setting the table, hugged a plate against her chest, and gazed into the darkness beyond the screen on the open back door.

"We camped outside a town called Zenith. Her name was Cazzie and she had an old dog named Shirley. Cazzie came by the tent one Saturday morning while Harley was gone and we played all day."

"Why just one day?"

"When Harley came back and found me playing with Cazzie, he got real mad. He beat Mama terrible that night. I never made any friends anywhere after that even if kids did try to talk to me."

Fairydeane said something she made sure Laney didn't hear and slammed a skillet down on the stove so hard Laney jumped and almost dropped the plate.

As Fairydeane put the last bowl of food on the table, she said, "You start helping yourself, Laney. I have to make a plate of food to take to Horace next door."

"Horace?" Laney glanced toward the door.

"Don't worry about him. He's just an old fool who can't take care of himself since his wife died, so I take him supper every night."

"Oh."

"Unfortunately, you're bound to meet the old coot sooner or later. He comes across mean and crotchety, but don't let him scare you. It's all an act." Fairydeane put a dish towel over the heaping plate and started for the door. "I'll be right back."

In the darkness of the back yard, Fairydeane hesitated and looked back at the girl sitting at the table, heaping fried sweet potatoes onto her plate. Would she make a break for it and disappear into the night now that she was alone for a few minutes? Fairydeane grinned. She didn't think so.

42 – THE WEENIE TRUTH

Laney stopped spooning food onto her plate and looked toward the door that had just slammed behind Miss Fairydeane. For one second she thought about running, then shook her head.

Where would she go? Miss Fairydeane already knew who she was and what she had done. If the old woman told the law, they'd catch Laney sooner or later. But, for some reason, Laney didn't think Miss Fairydeane was going to snitch on her, and she had to trust somebody. She couldn't run forever.

Miss Fairydeane came in the back door just as Laney finished loading her plate with chicken and dumplings.

"Let me fill my plate, then we'll say the blessing," Miss Fairydeane said. As soon as her plate had a little dab of everything on it, she bowed her head and folded her hands. Laney did the same.

"Lord, thank you for this day and your many blessings. Thank you for bringing Laney Belle Hawkins safely to my home. Guide us, Lord, in your wisdom as we decide what is best for Laney Belle. Thank you for this food. Amen."

After the kitchen was cleared up from supper, Miss Fairydeane said, "I'm afraid there's no pie tonight."

Laney felt her face go hot and hung her head. "I'm sorry."

"Oh, posh, girl." Miss Fairydeane laughed her little chirpy bird laugh. "I'm just joshing you a little. No harm done. Now let's sit down and decide what's to be done with you."

Laney sat at one end of the table and folded her hands in her lap.

"Do you have any relatives at all? Anywhere?"

Laney shook her head.

"Well, neither do I," Miss Fairydeane said.

"You don't have a husband?" Laney hadn't seen any sign of a man about the place, but she wanted to be sure.

"No. Oh, I had a chance or two when I was younger, but you want to know why I didn't marry? It was because of their names." Miss Fairydeane patted her tight little curls with her tiny hand.

"Their names?"

"Yes. The first one was Patrick Malarkey. He came calling the first year I was teaching at the schoolhouse at Lone Grove. Two years later, it was Martin Funkel." Miss Fairydeane chucked. "Can you imagine Fairydeane Malarkey or Fairydeane Funkel? At least I was used to Fairydeane Tinkel."

"There wasn't ever anybody else?"

"No. If somebody with a decent name, like Smith or Jones, had come along, I might have married. Of course, Horace asked me a couple of years after his wife died, but I'm too old for that foolishness now. I wouldn't marry that old fool anyway."

"How old are you?" Laney blurted. Miss Fairydeane really looked old.

"I'm seventy-five." Miss Fairydeane sat up straighter in her chair and she still wasn't a whole lot taller than the table. "But don't let that fool you, Laney. I'm a tough old bird."

"Have you always lived alone?"

"I lived in this house with my parents until I went to teacher's college for a year when I was seventeen. In those days, that's all it took to get a certificate to be a grade school teacher, so as soon as I had certificate in hand, I took the teaching job at the one-room school in Lone Grove.

"I boarded with one of the families out there until their kids were all out of school, then moved on to another family. I lived with four or five families around Lone Grove until I took a job teaching sixth grade here in Ardmore and moved back home."

"I don't remember my first-grade teacher," Laney said, "but I think she was young."

"It wasn't easy being a young teacher." Miss Fairydeane got up and put a pot on the stove. Laney was fascinated by the stove. It wasn't a big, black wood-burner like she remembered Mama having when Daddy was still alive. It was small and white and Miss Fairydeane said it burned gas.

"Especially for me." Miss Fairydeane went on as she took some milk out of the refrigerator, another wonder, and poured it in the pan. "Just about all the youngsters were bigger than me, especially the boys. And rough as a cob, let me tell you, those big old country boys. Would you like a cup of cocoa, Laney?"

"Yes, ma'am." Laney couldn't even remember the last time she'd had a cup of cocoa and her mouth started to water.

"Anyway, the very first week," Miss Fairydeane said as she took the sugar bowl off the table, "I gave the three eighth-grade students an assignment and Toby Gustave said he wasn't going to do it. Said he didn't need to know anything more about geography than how to get around Carter County."

If there was one thing Laney knew, it was that you didn't talk back to a grown-up, no matter what size they were, and she couldn't wait to hear this story. "What happened?"

"Well, I'll tell you what happened. That Toby was big, a lot bigger than my Daddy, and Daddy was a big man. But I took the paddle off the hook on the wall and gave Toby a good spanking."

Looking at the tiny Miss Fairydeane and imagining a giant Toby, Laney's mouth dropped open. Miss Fairydeane mixed cocoa and sugar together and stirred it into the hot milk.

"I told him to go to the front of the room and lean over the desk. He looked at me for a minute like I was crazy, then solemn as a preacher, he said, 'Yes, ma'am.' He went right to the front, bent over, and I gave him four or five wallops as hard as I could.

"I doubt he even felt it, but from then on, I never had any trouble with a student." Miss Fairydeane laughed. "That story was told around the county for years."

She slid a steaming cup of cocoa across the table to Laney. "Toby and I became good friends. He went on to become principal of the elementary school here in Ardmore. I asked him one time why he did it. He said because it was the bravest thing he had ever seen."

Laney blew on her cocoa and took a sip. "Do you still teach?"

"Oh, my heavens, no," Miss Fairydeane said. "I would if they'd let me, but they ran me off when I turned sixty and I didn't go easy, I'll tell you. I didn't know what to do with myself for the longest time, then I kind of accidentally got started running a secondhand store in town and I've been doing that ever since. Keeps me busy and, surprisingly, it brings in a good income, but enough of all that. What are we going to do with you?"

Laney tried to sit still and not squirm as Miss Fairydeane studied her. She certainly didn't know what was to be done with her, so she said nothing.

"Here's what I think, Laney Belle Hawkins." Miss Fairydeane drummed her little fingers on the table. "You don't have a family and I don't have a family. I think we should stick together and be our own family. What do you think of that?"

Laney felt tears rush into her eyes. She swallowed hard and nodded.

"Okay." Miss Fairydeane slapped her hand against the oil cloth. "Here's how it's going to be. You can't just pop out of nowhere. This is a small town. People ask questions.

"So here's our story. You can't be a relative because everybody knows I don't have any. You're the granddaughter of a dear friend of mine from teacher's college. She can't be from around here, so let's say she lived in Hot Springs, Arkansas. Your parents died in a car accident and my friend took you to raise, but she recently passed away. With no other relatives to turn to, she asked me to take you when she knew how sick she was. Can you remember that?"

Laney nodded. "I think so, but what if people ask me questions?"

"We'll work out the details for you to memorize. You'll know the story so well you can recite it in your sleep, and don't look at me like that, Missy." Miss Fairydeane's little hand fluttered like a bird taking flight. "I'll bet your mama drummed into you that lying's a sin so you think grown-ups don't do it. Well, let me tell you, they do it all the time."

Miss Fairydeane blew on her cocoa, took a sip and continued. "Besides, our little story about where you come from isn't really a lie."

"It isn't?" It sounded like it a whopper to Laney.

"No, it isn't. It's the weenie truth."

"What's that?" Mama sure hadn't known anything about weenie truths.

Miss Fairydeane grinned, showing little teeth so perfect they could only be false. "It's the thin skin of necessity stuffed with a lie just like weenie meat is stuffed in a flimsy little casing.

"See, when you wrap the lie in necessity, it gets people off the hook for lying. Being necessary makes it okay. You understand?"

"I think so." Actually, Laney did understand. It made sense.

"Now, as to your schooling…"

Laney stood up quickly. "I'm too old to go to second grade!"

"Hold your horses. That's not what I had in mind. Five days a week we'll get up at six o'clock and have school until eight. From eight to nine-thirty, we'll have breakfast and do chores.

"Then you'll work with me at the store from ten until four and all day Saturday. I'll teach you how to be a businesswoman. On Sundays, we'll have school for three hours in the afternoon. You want to learn don't you?"

"Oh, yes ma'am!" Laney wanted to learn almost more than she wanted anything except to go back to when it was just her, Mama, and Daddy.

"Well, I can teach you to use your head for something besides a hat rack. So, do we have a deal? Are we family?"

"Oh, yes, ma'am!" Laney wanted to hug Miss Fairydeane but she stood very still.

"Well, then, I think you should call me Auntie Fairy now."

43 – EIGHTEENTH BIRTHDAY

Laney locked the envelope of cash receipts for the day in the bottom drawer of the old desk shoved against the wall in the small office at the back of the store. She switched off the radio, cutting off Patti Page halfway through the "Tennessee Waltz."

At eighty-one, Auntie Fairy still insisted on coming in to the store from one to four every day. Except today. Auntie was home baking Laney's eighteenth birthday cake, Laney's favorite—devil's food with cocoa frosting.

Laney smiled to herself as she turned on the night light and locked the door. She would like to walk down to Woolworth's and have an ice cream soda, but she wouldn't, not with Auntie's devil food cake waiting.

She couldn't arrive home too early and spoil Auntie's "surprise", so she slipped her purse strap over her shoulder and strolled along the main street.

"Afternoon, Laney." Mr. Swartz was replenishing the bin of potatoes and onions under the front window of his grocery store. "How's Miss Fairydeane doing these days?"

"Doing well. How's your family?" Laney chatted a few minutes and moved on, visiting a moment with everyone she met along the street.

Going up the steps of the library, she passed Marcus Gustave, grandson of the Toby Gustave of the infamous eighth-grade spanking.

Marcus was now principal of the grammar school and, with some convincing by Auntie Fairy, had administered an equivalency test and issued an eighth-grade graduation certificate to Laney one year after she arrived in

214

Ardmore.

Two years after that, Auntie Fairy had worked her magic on the high school principal and Laney had passed that equivalency test as well. Laney didn't know what exactly Auntie Fairy had told the principals as to why she tutored Laney at home, but whatever it was, it worked and Laney had her high school diploma.

Laney loved learning but the education she got in operating the secondhand business was a lot more useful than what she learned in school.

"You have to buy as low as you can and sell as high as you can," Auntie Fairy said when she first took Laney into the store. "And know when to cut your losses and take what you can or you won't stay in business long."

Apparently, Auntie was satisfied Laney had learned her lesson well because Laney had pretty much been running the store since she was sixteen. Recently, Auntie had said, "You're a natural businesswoman. You can haggle and bargain better than anyone I ever saw and I've haggled with some of the best around here."

Laney browsed the library shelves, finally checking out "The Roman Spring of Mrs. Stone" by Tennessee Williams and "From Here to Eternity," by James Jones.

At the last minute, she selected "The Thirteen Clocks" by James Thurber for Auntie Fairy. Most of their evenings were spent dissecting and arguing about the books they read. It was the most fun they had.

"Better than watching the idiot box," Auntie Fairy said, but in spite of her disdain, she never missed an episode of "The Milton Berle Show" if she could help it.

"I'm home," Laney called as she opened the front door and deeply inhaled the smell of chocolate.

"In the kitchen."

Laney pushed open the kitchen door and, just as she expected, a perfect chocolate cake sat in the middle of the table.

"*Happy birthday to you,*" Auntie Fairy sang. "*Happy birthday, dear Laney. Happy birthday to you.*" Auntie clapped her hands and grinned ear to ear.

"Oh, Auntie, what a surprise," Laney said, even though her birthday routine was the same every year. Except this year, there was no wrapped present sitting beside the cake. Laney pretended not to notice. "You know how I love chocolate cake."

"I know." Auntie laughed. "You can have all you want after supper."

All through supper Auntie was fidgety and jumpy as popcorn in a hot pot. As soon as supper dishes were cleared away, she said, "Sit down a minute, Laney."

Laney sat and folded her hands on the table. Auntie came to stand beside her and Laney was surprised to see tears gathering in the old woman's eyes. Her hand shook as she removed an envelope from her apron pocket and handed it to Laney. "Open it," she said.

What in the world? Laney removed a single sheet of paper from the envelope and unfolded it. The letterhead gave the name and address of a local lawyer. Laney looked quickly at Auntie. "What is this?"

"Read it." Auntie Fairy's lower lip trembled.

Laney quickly read the three or four paragraphs. She thought she knew what she was reading but she wasn't sure. "What is this?" she asked again.

Auntie put her hand on Laney's shoulder. "It's a legal agreement giving you fifty-percent ownership in the business. All you have to do is sign it."

Laney burst into tears. Auntie threw her arms around Laney's neck and cried right along with her.

"But why?" Laney sniffed and wiped her nose on the back of her hand.

"Because you're family. All of it will be yours someday, but I wanted you to have this now."

"I don't know what to say, Auntie, except thank you, thank you."

"Don't thank me, Laney. You've earned it. You can take it in to the lawyer tomorrow, sign it and it's done."

"Again, thank you. You've already done so much for me." Tears ran down Laney's cheeks. "I never expected anything like this."

"Oh, pshaw!" Auntie waved her little hand like she was trying to get rid of a fly. "Let's stop this sniveling and take some birthday cake to Horace. We'll never hear the end of it if he doesn't get at least two pieces."

44 – UNCLE HORACE

"It's about time," Horace Greer grumbled as Laney held the screen door to his kitchen open for Auntie Fairy.

"It isn't even dark yet, you old goat," Auntie said as she filled the coffee pot with water, added grounds to the basket, and put it on the stove to perk.

Laney picked up the empty plate from the supper she had delivered to the old man earlier and put a plate with two slices of cake on the table in front of him. She kissed the half dozen strands of gray hair spread across his bald spot. Horace ducked his head and said, "Stop that nonsense, girl."

He knew her name but he never called her anything but "girl." Horace was grizzled and hunchbacked and missing his teeth. He had false teeth but he wouldn't wear them.

"I'm eighteen today, Uncle Horace," Laney said as she rummaged in a drawer for a clean fork. He snorted when she called him uncle. She had done so from the beginning and, in spite of his snorts, she knew he liked it.

"Don't go thinking that makes you grown-up because it don't." He took the fork and dug into the cake. "You're still wet behind the ears."

"It's her birthday, Horace," Auntie scolded, "so just try to act like a decent human being for fifteen minutes."

Horace harrumphed and shoveled cake into his mouth. Laney poured coffee for the three of them, then sat at the table opposite Auntie while they watched Uncle Horace eat cake.

He scraped the plate with the side of the fork, licked the fork, and pushed the plate back. "It's passable as chocolate cake goes."

"You're welcome, Horace." Auntie grinned at him.

"Stop grinning like a monkey," Uncle Horace said, "I got a business proposition I want to put to you and I don't do business with monkeys."

He glanced at Laney and pointed at his coffee cup, so she got up and filled it, then added coffee to hers and Auntie's.

"What business could you possibly have?" Auntie asked.

"That's what I'm trying to tell you if you'll stop blathering for just one minute."

"Okay, Mr. Tycoon Business Man. I'm listening."

"Now you see, that's what I mean." Horace shook his head. "You always think you have a smart answer. Just listen for a change."

"Okay."

"I'm not getting any younger," he said. Laney knew for a fact that Uncle Horace was eighty-nine. "I been thinking I should settle up my affairs the best I can and go into that Shady Pines Rest Home they just opened on the other side of town."

Laney glanced quickly at Auntie and saw the surprise on her face.

"Now, I know what you're thinking," Horace went on. "You're wondering why the need since I'm still able to take care of myself."

Laney almost burst out laughing and she didn't dare even look at Auntie. Horace hadn't taken care of himself in years. He had a woman come in every day to do laundry, a little cleaning, and prepare his morning and noon meals since his wife died, and Auntie had been bringing him his supper every night.

"Well, of course, that's your decision, Horace," Auntie said. "I can see how it could be a good thing, but why is that a business proposition for me?"

"I've got a lot of valuable stuff." He waved his hand generally toward the rest of the house. Mostly a lot of junk was closer to the truth. "I thought you could sort through everything and see what you could buy for the store. It could be a money-maker for both of us."

Laney was proud of Auntie; she didn't laugh.

"Do you know how long it would take to sort through this house, Horace?" Auntie asked. "You've still got the first newspaper you bought sixty or seventy years ago."

"I don't expect you to do it for nothing, Fairydeane. We could figure a fair wage for the work and deduct it from whatever we settle on as a price for my goods." He gave Auntie a hard look. "I pay my way. Always have."

"There's no way I could take on this job," Auntie said and turned to Laney. "You'd have to do it. I could take care of the store afternoons and you could work on clearing out here. You have as much say in whether we take it on as I do."

Laney pressed her palm to her chest and inhaled deeply. She had seen the clutter in most of the rooms of the old house and really didn't want to do it, but looking at the frayed old man hunched in his chair, she knew she would. Like Auntie was family to her, she and Auntie were family to Uncle Horace. They were all he had.

* * * *

The following Monday, just after noon, Laney showed up to begin the job she dreaded.

"Here you are, Uncle Horace." Laney handed him two of his favorite candy bars, Bit O' Honey. He would suck on the little pieces for hours.

When he just grunted, Laney said, "You're welcome." She sighed and added, "I guess I'd better get started or you won't be in Shady Pines by Christmas. Do you want me to start down here or upstairs?"

"I'd like you to start by setting down."

Laney sat in a chair and waited to see what the old man had on his mind.

"I'll not be going to Shady Pines." Uncle Horace looked right at Laney, hard.

"Well, where will you go?" Surely he couldn't be thinking of moving in with her and Auntie.

"Rose Hill Cemetery."

"What?" Laney's heart skipped a beat. "What are you talking about?"

"Just what I said. Something's been wrong with me for a while and I been hearing the Lord calling my name." He folded his hands across his paunchy stomach.

"How long has it been since you've seen a doctor?"

"I don't need no doctor to tell me what's wrong, girl." He snorted. "I'm kissing ninety years old. I've lived long and hard and my body's telling me it's time for us to part ways—him to Rose Hill and me on up yonder to see Vera and the Lord."

A baseball-size knot fisted low in Laney's throat and her chin quivered. "Please don't talk like that, Uncle Horace."

"Don't be silly, girl. My time's about up and I'm glad for it. I'm telling you now because there's something you can do for me."

"Anything." Tears trickled down Laney's cheeks. "You know that."

"First off, stop blubbering. I tell you because I don't want you dawdling and taking forever to get this job done. I don't want to leave this world with my affairs at loose ends. You know what I mean?" He picked up a candy bar, looked at it, and lay it back down.

"I think so." Laney was trying so hard not to cry she hiccupped.

"Next, there are things needing done and you're the one to do them, like making arrangements with the undertaker and the cemetery and getting that shyster lawyer out here to talk to me."

Laney bit down on her lip and nodded.

"Understand this, girl. I don't want Fairydeane knowing anything about this. She acts like a tough old bird, but on the inside she's as soft as banana pudding and I don't want her blubbering over me for the next days and weeks. I can't abide a blubbering woman."

Laney was doing her best not to blubber.

"You promise not to tell her, girl? I want your promise."

"I promise, Uncle Horace." How was she going to do that? She had never lied to Auntie or kept anything from her.

Uncle must have seen her hesitation, because he said again, "I want your solemn promise."

Laney held up her hand, palm toward the old man, and said, "I solemnly promise."

"You'll be a comfort to Fairydeane." Laney could tell he was trying to make his voice gruff and strong, then his Adam's apple jumped as he swallowed hard. His voice broke as he went on.

"She acts like she doesn't like me, but that old woman, she loves me. Since the day Vera died, Fairydeane's the one who looks in to be sure I'm here every morning and brings me supper every night. She's a fine woman." His voice trembled and tears trickled from his eyes.

Laney jumped up, put her arms around the old man, and hugged his head against her breast, not even pretending she wasn't crying.

They clung together for a couple of minutes, then Laney felt when the old man got hold of himself. He loosened his arms from around her waist, cleared his throat, and then said in a gravelly voice, "You're a good girl, Laney Belle."

It was the only time Uncle Horace ever called her by her name.

"Don't just stand here," he said, pushing her away, "Get to work before you turn old and gray."

45 – OLD PICTURES

Laney walked into the front room, now bare except for Uncle Horace's easy chair, a side table and lamp, and a console television set. The old man hunkered in the chair by the window, reading his Bible

"Everything I can do is done downstairs, Uncle Horace, so I'm going to work on the back bedroom upstairs for a while. You need anything before I start?"

He shooed her away with his hand without looking up. It was late April and already hot. A furnace blast almost knocked her over when she pushed open the stubborn door to the back bedroom.

It smelled like a rat's nest, so Laney carefully made her way between boxes, stacks of books and magazines, and stuff she didn't even want to identify. She knew there was a bed in there somewhere but she couldn't see it.

Laney forced open the stuck window, leaned out, and inhaled deeply. Two weeks into this disaster and, looking at this room, she felt she had hardly started.

Sweat and grime slicked her skin and the dust made her sneeze. Her scalp itched under the bandana tied around her head. Why had she agreed to do this? What a mess. It looked like the upstairs was going to be the worst, especially this back room, because over the years it had become the dumping place for everything Uncle Horace thought he might need sometime and never did.

Laney sighed, looked around and decided the best place to start was by the door. She would sort things as she moved them into the hall—a pile for the store, a pile for the junk yard, and a pile to discuss with Uncle Horace. She zeroed in on a box sitting on top of an old Singer treadle sewing machine.

The box looked like it was full of more junk papers for the burn barrel, but on the top was a well-worn Bible. Uncle Horace might want that. It could have belonged to Vera. Laney wouldn't put it in the burn barrel in any case, that was for sure.

When Laney picked up the Bible, half a dozen old pictures fell out. She carried them to the window to get a good look. One was obviously a wedding picture. The inscription on the back was *Wedding day — Homer Roman Cassity and Alma June Greer, July 10, 1894.*

Greer? Maybe Uncle Horace's sister? There was a picture of twin boys, then one of them with a younger boy. Next was a picture of the man and woman, much older, with the three boys and the woman holding a baby, then two pictures of three young men in World War I uniforms.

Laney read all the fading penciled inscriptions: *Avery and Everett, two years. Avery and Everett, four, Luther, two. Me, Albert, the boys, and Ruby Jo. Avery, Everett, and Luther in uniform. Going to France. God keep them.*

The picture that really captured Laney's attention was of Homer and Alma with a girl Laney guessed to be about fifteen or sixteen. The man was wearing overalls, the woman, a homemade dress that hung just above worn shoes. The couple looked stoic and tired, and there was a faint hint of fear or distress about the woman's eyes.

The girl had the turn-around-and-look-twice kind of beauty. It wasn't just her appearance that was so captivating; it was an attitude that projected right out of the picture. The girl was wearing an obviously homemade dress but by the pose—and it was a pose—you would think she was wearing a movie star evening gown. Her head was tipped back a little and the look in her eyes was far too adult. "Sultry" Laney supposed it would be called from the books she had read and the movies she had seen. Who *was* this girl?

On the back was written: *1930 — Homer, Alma, and Ruby Jo, 13.*

Thirteen? Laney turned the picture back over, studied the girl for a minute, then shook her head. She set the pictures on the sewing machine and rummaged in the box for more. She'd like to see what this Ruby Jo looked like when she was older.

There were no more pictures. Besides the Bible, there were only letters, all still in their original envelopes. Laney picked up an envelope from on top and removed the letter.

3 Jan 1932

Dear brother,

It is with heavy heart I put my hand to paper to write you this day. Two days ago, on the night of New Year's, Ruby Jo disappeared. I don't know if you heard up in Ardmore or not but on Christmas Eve four men robbed a bank in San Angelo. One of them dressed up as Santa Claus of all things. One of them was killed and one was hurt bad. Everybody thought they had lit out from these parts fast as they could.

Turns out they was hid out round here—one place was the schoolhouse—it was still closed for Christmas. Anyway, Ruby Jo went over to the school to practice piano—I told you she had learned real good and had been playing for church. I guess she stumbled on that bunch. The law thinks they kidnapped her.

She did come back to the house and, after dark, she sneaked out with some vittles and doctoring stuff. But the law found a man's tracks—not Homer's—in the yard and outside Ruby Jo's window, so they think these outlaws made her do it and now she's kidnapped. The law is looking everywhere for her.

To tell you the truth, brother, I jist don't know if she was kidnapped. I wudn't say that to nobody else. But you jist think on what I have wrote about my worries for Ruby Jo before and tell me what you think.

But if she is kidnapped or no, I pray to God she comes home in one piece. Homer is real tore up. He don't show it, but he puts a lot of store in that girl. As fer me, I pray the Lord for strength. I jist don't know how I can bear up to this and how could the Lord bring it on me after the boys and all. Pray for us, brother, and Ruby Jo in particular that she come back to us safe. I will write again as soon as I know more. Your sister. Alma.

Laney didn't know why, but her hand was shaking when she finished reading the letter. Good golly! She stood staring through the door into the empty hallway for several minutes.

Was Ruby Jo kidnapped or did she run off with those criminals? Did she come home or did they kill her? Laney had to know. But not now. She shook herself like she was awakening from a daydream and put the letter and the pictures back in the box.

Laney put Alma's box off to the side so it wouldn't get mixed up with the other stuff and turned back to cleaning and sorting the room. When she was done for the day, she carried Alma's box downstairs to the front room. Uncle Horace was still in his chair, head back, mouth open, dozing. He jerked awake when she walked across the room.

"Sakes alive, girl. Scare a body to death."

"I'm sorry, Uncle Horace, but I'm through for today." She stood holding the box in front of her. "You know how you said at the first that I could have anything I wanted going through all this stuff?"

"Well, I shouldn't have to say it twice."

"I'd like to have this box."

"Then take it. Don't bother me with it."

"But you might want to keep it. It seems to be your sister's Bible and some pictures and letters." Laney would have crossed her fingers for luck but she was holding the box.

"No use for any of that stuff where I'm going." He leaned his head back against the chair. "Take it. If you find any of Vera's stuff like that, the historical society might want it if you don't."

"Thank you, Uncle Horace, but I think this is all I want." She leaned over, kissed the top of his head, and noticed he didn't shrink away like he usually did. "I'll be back in a little while with your supper. I think Auntie's making ham and sweet potatoes"

He just nodded and picked up his Bible.

When Laney walked through the back door an hour-and-a-half later with a dish towel-covered plate of food, Uncle Horace was sitting at the kitchen table with a knife in one hand and a fork in the other. He was staring at her in a funny way as she carried the plate. Laney stopped, looked at him closely, then burst into tears. Uncle Horace wouldn't be eating supper that night or any other night. He was dead.

46 – AUNTIE

The lawyer, Malcom Udell, came to call on Monday morning following Horace Greer's funeral. Malcom was pencil thin in his black suit, his shock of red hair the eraser on top. His face was skeletal and his teeth really big, but he spoke kindly.

Sitting at the kitchen table with a stack of papers in front of him, he said, "It's simple, Fairydeane. Horace left all his worldly possessions to you."

"That old fool." Fairydeane sniffed and took a quick swipe at her eyes with her knuckle.

"Well, despite appearances to the contrary, that old fool left a sizeable estate." Malcom shuffled some papers and peered at them.

"I knew he was comfortable from the sale of the hardware store, but…"

"Apparently he had the proceeds from that in a savings account and he had modest checking account. Then there's the value of the seventeen acres with the house. It adds up."

"Oh, my," Auntie said. "I guess we should think about selling his place. What would we do with it?"

"I've been giving that some thought." Malcom held up his coffee cup as Laney offered a refill. "A developer from Oklahoma City has been buying up properties in this neighborhood. Name of Watson. It seems he wants to build one of those tract house subdivisions. I handled a couple of transactions for him.

"I know he talked to Horace a couple of weeks ago, but nothing came of it. I'm pretty sure I can get you a good price and a fast sale on Horace's property."

"Then let's do that," Auntie said. She turned to Laney. "How close are you to having Horace's place cleaned out?"

"Probably a few days, a week at the most."

"See what you can do, Malcom."

"I'll get right on it," Malcom replied.

After Malcom was gone, Laney said, "I don't think I can finish cleaning out Uncle Horace's place now that he's gone."

"Hire somebody to do it then."

* * * *

Something happened to Auntie Fairy after Horace died. It was like she just gave up. She stopped coming to the store altogether and Laney usually came home to find her in her easy chair in the front room, staring off into space, instead of bustling about preparing supper.

Auntie quit reading—she said her eyes bothered her—so Laney read to her most nights, but the old woman seemed to pay little attention. She didn't notice when "The Milton Berle Show" came on either.

About six weeks after the lawyer's first visit, he came by with a check for a substantial amount of money.

"You did all right on Horace's property," Malcom said. "That Watson fellow is really interested in tying up everything in this neighborhood. He has a vision of a big development. Could be a good thing for Ardmore."

Auntie sat staring at her hands. Malcom glanced at Laney and continued, "Maybe you should consider selling this place, Fairydeane. Watson wants to buy up everything. You could get a good price."

Auntie's head snapped up. "No. I'll spend my days here. Laney can do what she wants when I'm gone."

"You're not going any place, Auntie, not for a long time," Laney said quickly.

Auntie picked up a doily from the side table, turned it over, put it down, and patted it in place. "Did you offer Malcom some coffee, Laney?" she asked.

* * * *

Auntie Fairy ate less and less and Laney finally insisted she see the doctor. Laney was surprised she went without protest. The nurse visited with Auntie in the examination room for a few minutes while Laney talked with the doctor in his office.

"What's wrong with her, Doctor Flynn?"

"Nothing I can find but old age, Laney."

"But she seemed fine until Uncle Horace died. Now she just sits and stares and lately she's not eating enough to stay alive."

"The elderly often react this way to the death of a spouse or loved one." The doctor pushed his glasses up his nose. "It's not uncommon for one to follow the other in a short time."

"But Uncle Horace wasn't her spouse."

"He was the closest thing to it. Despite their bickering, they were great friends for years. And, remember, just about all her friends are gone now."

"But she's got me." Laney choked on the words and tears filled her eyes.

"Laney, she's old. Her body is slowing down. That doesn't mean she wants to leave you but that's what her mind and body are preparing her to do."

"Isn't there anything you can do?"

"Not unless there comes a point where she's in pain. There are things we can do then."

* * * *

Laney pulled down the shade against the darkness outside and collapsed into the chair by her bedroom window. She had settled Auntie in bed and now that she was alone, Laney leaned down, put her face in her hands and cried.

Couldn't the doctor be wrong for once? Auntie could get well and bounce back to her old self. No matter how much she wanted to believe that, Laney had to admit it probably was a matter of time, a short time at that.

When Laney was finally drained and exhausted, she stood and took her nightgown out of the top dresser drawer. She glanced at Alma's box still sitting on top of the dresser where she had put it the day she brought it home from Uncle Horace's. She had thought about Ruby Jo and wondered what happened to her almost every day, but she had been too busy and tired to read the letters. Maybe one day.

Laney turned off the light and climbed into bed. She slept little.

* * * *

Fourteen days later, on the evening of the fourth of July, Laney looked up from reading aloud to Auntie from Irving Stone's "The President's Lady." Auntie's head was tipped forward, her chin almost resting on her chest, her hands relaxed in her lap.

At first Laney thought Auntie was dozing. Then, slowly, with great effort, like she was lifting a massive stone, Laney pushed herself up and walked the few steps to Auntie. She knelt, pulled the old woman into her arms and held her, soaking Auntie's tight little gray curls with her tears.

47 – MEMORIES

Laney heard the knock on the door. It was the third one that morning, but she didn't want to—couldn't—talk to anybody. What was there to talk about? That she was all alone now? No doubt the friends and neighbors coming to the door wanted to comfort her and offer their help. Laney didn't want to be comforted or helped.

She wanted to scream her grief and roll around on the floor, banging her head and clutching her stomach. The pain filled her like a massive ball of angry snakes with razor fangs—striking, striking—the pain so relentless and sharp that it took her breath away.

It seemed the whole town of Ardmore had turned out for Auntie's funeral yesterday. The church was too small for the expected crowd, so the service was held in the elementary school auditorium. People came by the small house in waves afterward and Laney smiled, shook hands and thanked people until she was ready to drop. Many took food back home when they discovered there was no place left to put any more. Still, there was enough food in the house to feed several people for at least a week.

Sometime in the afternoon, Malcom had pulled her aside in a back bedroom for a moment.

"I have to be out of town for the next few days, but I wanted you to have this before I go." He pressed a sealed envelope into her hand.

"It's pretty simple," Malcom said, "Fairydeane left everything to you. Review the will while I'm gone and we can discuss the details when I get back." Malcom patted her on the shoulder.

"Everything should go quickly. You're already a signer on the bank accounts, so we'll just need to take Fairydeane's name off and transfer title to the store property and the house."

Laney nodded and Malcom went on, "Between Horace and Fairydeane, you are a very well-off young lady. If you need any financial advice or anything like that, you know I'll help all I can."

Laney put the envelope in a dresser drawer. She didn't want a will. She wanted Auntie Fairy.

Now Laney sat in Auntie's chair, lost in that vast canyon of disbelief she had fallen into the day Auntie died. She pressed her body into the chair, running her hands over the arms, wanting to feel Auntie, be embraced by where Auntie had last sat.

The shades were drawn against the hot summer sun and the doors were closed, so it was sweltering in the little house. Laney made no move to open doors and windows to get fresh air or a breeze. Sweat plastered her dress to her body and she itched.

Laney sat, sometimes moaning, sometimes mumbling to herself, but she didn't cry. She wanted to, she felt like it, but her body was so dried out even her mouth was parched.

There were a few more knocks on the door but Laney didn't answer. Surely by tomorrow, everyone would take the hint and stay away. The light in the room dimmed, then turned to total darkness. Still Laney sat.

She laid her head against the back of the chair. Her nose felt big and swollen, like it was packed with old rags, and her throat was raw from all the crying. A dull pain hammered the back of her head. All she wanted was not to feel for a little while, not to think for a few minutes, but thoughts and images and remembered snatches of conversations whirled round and around in her brain, all tumbling over each other.

How could Auntie leave her? No, that wasn't fair. Auntie would never leave her if she had a choice, not like Mama had left her. Now, where did that come from? She hadn't thought about Mama in a long time.

It wasn't that Laney wanted to forget about Mama. She frequently took the old purse off the top shelf and went through its meager contents—a wrinkled handkerchief embroidered with purple violets, a small mirror, half a spool of black thread with a needle stuck in it, a small tin of Carter's Little Liver Pills with one pill still in it and eighty-three cents.

It was just that no matter how hard Laney tried, no matter how much she hugged the purse and touched its contents, Mama's face kept getting dimmer and dimmer. Now Laney could hardly remember what she looked like.

Would Auntie Fairy's face grow dim with time? No. Laney would work hard to make sure that didn't happen. She had a good number of pictures of Auntie to help her remember.

Laney couldn't remember Daddy's face either, but she could still remember how she had felt when he was killed... like somebody had killed her... and scared. Mama had been scared, too, and looking back, Mama had plenty of reason to feel afraid.

There were times Laney was so mad at Mama for leaving, she could have spit. But all the time she missed Mama and kept waiting for her to come back. That was why Laney had never felt the same awful pain she had felt for Daddy and was now feeling for Auntie. Laney had never grieved for Mama, because even now, Laney realized with a start, deep inside, she was still waiting for the door to open and Mama to walk in.

Laney sat in the darkness and silence, gripping the arms of the chair as she forced herself to go back and think about that night. Harley had been drunk and nasty. Mama had said, "You need to get some sleep, Harley. You'll feel better tomorrow."

For some reason, that made Harley really mad and Laney heard him hit Mama, like he did all the time. Mama had made a hurt noise, then there was that strangely sickening smooshy sound and Mama never said another word. *Mama never said another word.* Not *I'm leaving. I'll come back for Laney.* Nothing.

Laney listened intently as that smooshy sound played over and over in her mind. *Mama never said another word.*

But Harley did and he had sounded really scared and suddenly sober. "What the hell?" he had said. "Git up from there, Mattie. Mattie? *Mattie!* "Shit. *Oh, shit!*"

Laney had huddled in her bed like a coward because she promised Mama never to get up. The next morning Harley had rushed Laney to gather her things and get in the truck, but Laney had noticed Mama's favorite quilt was missing from the top of her bed and there were some funny dark reddish brown stains on one of the stools and the floor. Then Harley set the tent on fire.

At the last minute, Laney had grabbed Mama's purse. *Mama never went anywhere without her purse.*

Laney jerked like she had been slammed in the chest by a sledgehammer in the hands of a giant. Oh, God. *Oh, God!* Why hadn't she seen it before? Because she didn't want to see it, didn't want to know. Laney wanted to believe Mama would come back someday, but she would never come back. *Mama was dead.* Harley had killed her!

Laney leaned over and retched but nothing came up. She hadn't eaten since supper with Auntie the night she died. Laney fell out of the chair and stretched herself full out on her stomach on the floor, her cheek against the rough hand-braided rag rug. She wailed and shrieked even as she gave herself to the massive red beast of pain that devoured her.

48 – THE CASSITY FAMILY BIBLE

Laney stirred when the garbage collection truck rattled down the street. She shifted her body ever so slowly. Every muscle screamed with stiffness as she carefully stretched. Even with the shades down, she could tell it was well past daylight by the heat and the sunlight slipping through the crack between the shade and window.

She groaned as she rolled to her hands and knees and, holding on to Auntie's chair, pulled herself up. She needed the bathroom and water.

The face that stared back at Laney from the mirror was a stranger. Her hair looked like a blonde rat, greasy and dead; her lips were cracked and there were dark smears under her eyes. She shrugged. She didn't care.

Gnawing hunger pangs led her to the kitchen where she made a pot of coffee. Laney ate but really couldn't have said what it was. She sat at the table all day, drinking coffee, going to the bathroom, then sitting again, hands cradling her coffee cup, willing herself not to think or feel. At dark she fell into bed with her clothes on.

Laney tossed and turned all night and finally swung her feet out of bed shortly after daybreak. As she walked toward the door to go to the bathroom, her glance fell on Alma's box. When Laney came back from the bathroom, she picked up the box and set it in the middle of her bed. She crawled onto the bed, sat cross-legged and opened the flaps.

When Laney picked up the Bible, a piece of paper fell out. It was a birth certificate.

Mercy Grace French born to Milo Althus French and Ruby Jo Cassity, Kendalia, Texas, October 26, 1932. Rolf Adams, M.D. There was a woman's signature as witness.

Ruby Jo? How did she go from being kidnapped to having a baby? And October, 1932? That meant the baby was only five months older than Laney, so Mercy Grace would be eighteen, too. Where was she now?

Laney opened the Bible and turned to the family records page where, neatly written, all in the same hand, was a record of Homer and Alma's family. The page listed the dates of their marriage, the birthdates of their three boys and Ruby Jo, the death of two of the boys, and near the bottom of the page, two more death records.

The last one was *Homer Roman Cassity, age 59 yrs 11 mos. d. March 3, 1935, Gazely Creek, Calif.*

Just above Homer's death was another one, *Mercy Grace French, age 5 mos 24 days d. April 19, 1933, somewhere in the Arizona desert.*

Laney laid the Bible in her lap and stared at the bare wall across the room. *What?* Her bottom lip quivered. It was like this baby meant something to her, but that was ridiculous. She'd never heard of the family before Uncle Horace gave her the box.

She had to know what happened to Ruby Jo and Mercy Grace, so she dumped all the letters onto the bed, hoping they would reveal the story. She sorted all the envelopes by the postal dates and read the first one, squinting at the faded writing and stumbling over the misspellings.

3 Jul 1918

Dear brother,

I know it's some time since I wrote but I been so tore up over the boys goin to war I haven't been at myself. Now the worst has come true. Everett and Luther were killed just a day apart at a place called Belleau Wood in France in early June. My boys. They tell us nothing of Avery, so pray, brother, and request prayer at yur church there he will come home safe.

And pray for Homer and me. This is near more than we can bear and sometimes my faith fails me. If it wasn't for baby Ruby Jo, I don't think I could go on. That and the hope Avery will come home in one piece. Pray, pray, brother. Your sister, Alma

The next dozen letters were about Avery coming home with his mind gone, Ruby Jo catching scarlet fever and being held back a year in school, crops, church gossip, and routine family news. Laney scanned them quickly, then went to the kitchen, made a pot of coffee and cut a piece of apple pie, which she took back to her room and settled down again with the letters.

15 Nov 1929

Dear brother Horace,

I am sorry to hear of Vera's passing. She was a good woman and I know you'll miss her. Take comfort in knowing she's home with the Lord and at peace. Knowing I'll see Everett and Luther again helps me keep my right mind. Poor Avery is still in the insane asylum. I'm afraid he'll never git out. Sometimes I wonder why the Lord puts us on this earth when every day is so hard. Preacher Upton says trials are to teach us lessons we need to learn to git fit for heaven.

I think I've had enough trials. I was fit to pass on a long time ago. Most mornings I wake so weary I can hardly lift my head much less git out of bed. But the work goes on and so do trials. Right at the top of the list is Ruby Jo. I don't hardly know how to tell it, but that girl keeps me on my knees prayin more'n the boys ever did. I don't understand why she can't be like all the other girls her age but she ain't. It's like she's full of a wildness she don't know what to do with and she's likely to explode anytime. And she's got a sassy mouth on her but she knows better'n to back talk me or her daddy. So, keep prayin for us, brother, as we keep prayin for you. You know I would come to you and stay a while if I could. Your sister, Alma.

20 Sept 1930

Dear brother,

I have in hand your letter of 15 Aug and thank the Lord you at least have a good neighbor lady to help you some. We as always labor to keep body and soul together. It was a trying summer. Ruby Jo just shot up overnight it seems and is full growed, taller'n me. She thinks she's a woman now and struts around like Jezebel but let me tell you she has a long way to go. She has been more jittery than usual and she makes me a nervous wreck. But most of all, brother, she scares me. I don't know why but I fear for her. And for Homer and me. We don't need no more heartbreak. It won't be too much longer before she'll be of an age to marry. I know that's what she needs, a good man and young'uns to ground her. Keep prayin for all of us and specially pray for Ruby Jo to stay steady until she can settle in to her own family and for me that I won't pull my hair out waiting fer that to happen. Your loving sister, Alma.

Laney glanced through another page of mundane news and comments, took a quick bathroom break, then hurried back to pore through more of Alma's heartbreaking notes to her brother.

What exactly was wrong with Ruby Jo? Why was her mama so fearful for her? She skimmed through the next five or six letters containing little of importance before she got to more letters of real interest.

14 Apr 1931

Thank the Lord Ruby Jo has taken up the piano and is playing quite a bit in church. I pray the Holy Spirit will use these precious hymns to work on her heart so she'll accept the Lord and settle down. She's still jumpy as a turkey gobbler at Thanksgiving but she'll be fourteen in a couple of weeks. Maybe gettin older will help. With love, Alma.

Next was just a paragraph in a long letter dated July 15, 1931, about church gossip and hard times on the farm.

I think Ruby Jo is finally goin in the right direction. She's walkin out with a boy from a good family. We'll see but I think it could work out. I pray it does.

1 Dec 1931

Well, brother, the Lord knows what he's doin and we are truly blessed. I could have yanked Ruby Jo's hair out when she run off Boomer. I don't know what happened but she did run him off. Turns out it was for the best. She's been walkin out for some time now with Berlin Jacobson, a fine man who owns a big mercantile over in Junction. He's much better for Ruby Jo and thinks the sun rises and sets on her. I think we'll be havin a wedding soon. Times is gittin harder fer ever body by the day and Berlin says its slow fer him too but at least he'll be able to provide fer Ruby Jo. She'll have a much easier life than I've had I can tell you. So I give the glory fer this blessing to the Lord. Alma

The next letter was the first one Laney had read earlier about Ruby Jo being kidnapped, so she skipped it and went to the next one.

15 Jan 1932

Dear brother,

The law has told us they killed Wick Bennett. One of them is still missing but they caught that Dillion feller alive. He says he never heard of Ruby Jo so now the law says Ruby Jo is a runaway and even if them men did kidnap and kill her theys no way the law can prove it. I always had a hard time understandin that girl but now I think I never knew her at all. I found a whole bunch of trashy movie magazines under her bed after she was gone so who knows what all she was hidin from me. I just can't believe she wudn't get hold of us if she was alive. She must know me and her daddy's heart is broke. I don't know where she would go so, brother, I have to believe she's dead. I think my baby girl is dead, Horace. Alma

49 – ANSWERS

What? Ruby Jo couldn't be dead. Mercy Grace wasn't born yet. Laney snatched up the next five or six letters from the stack. They were all dated over the next year. In the first two, Alma said how she prayed Ruby Jo would be found. Then, in the third one dated in April of '32, she wrote:

I just have to let Ruby Jo be dead, brother. I can't go on living with this hope.

The rest of that letter and the others were mainly about how desperate the times were and her fear they would lose the farm. And, in one dated in December, Alma wrote:

Two more of our neighbors have been put out of their place because they couldn't make their mortgage. One of them went to California and wrote back they are doin good there. The other family we took in for two weeks until their son come down from somewhere up north to git them. We can hardly feed ourselves but we had to do it. Bums and even whole families knock on our door for food every day. They are on the road with no place to go. Homer says we'll likely be next unless the Lord sends us a miracle. If Ruby Jo had married Berlin Jacobson, we wouldn't be so bad off.

I thank you, brother, more than you know fer yur kind offer to send us money or for us to come to you. I know times is hard for you too and business must be down in the hardware store. Homer is a proud man and wants to stand on his own two feet, but you know it's more than that. He's never forgive you for that business when you didn't want me to marry him. Pride is a hurtful burden but his heart is hard against you. There ain't no way I can take money from you behind his back but thank you and God bless you.

In March, 1933, Alma wrote:

This is a good piece of land and has been in his family for many years, so it is killing Homer but he's going to try to sell it for whatever he can git before the bank forecloses. Berlin mentioned what a good piece he thought it was, so Homer will try him. Everything we hear is they's plenty of work in the crops in Santa Clara County in California. A neighbor went and has done real good out there, so our hope is to sell the farm and everything we have to git enough for some kind of truck and git us there. Homer is a hard worker and he will make it if he has a chance to work. You know that. Keep prayin for us as we pray for you and I will let you know what happens. Alma.

Ruby Jo's name didn't come up again until a letter dated April 14, 1933:

Dear brother,

Well, you're not going to believe what I'm about to tell you. Two days ago two men and a boy drove up in the yard. One of the men come to the door and said his name was Milo something or other and he was looking for Ruby Jo. I about fell on the floor. He said he was Ruby Jo's husband. And that wasn't all. He said Ruby Jo had run off from his house the day before and took their baby. He looked like a nice enough feller and we didn't see no reason he would lie but it was awful hard to take in. Ruby Jo would marry and have a baby and not tell us? But at least she was alive, and now she had a baby and had run off again. Lord have mercy, why? How could a child of mine do something like this?

We promised this Milo feller we hadn't heard from Ruby Jo for over a year and thought she was dead. He said he tried to get Ruby Jo to write us but she wudn't. He didn't know why. He said he would be back in a couple of days to see if she turned up and if she did to tell her she could go to Hollywood or wherever she pleased but he wanted his baby.

He was so fuming mad he stomped off the porch and was gone before we had a chance to tell him we were leaving for California in a couple of days and in all the confusion we didn't think to ask where he lived. I really didn't think it made any difference because I was thinking there was no way Ruby Jo would show up after the way she was acting and how she had treated us. I just might slap her face if she did turn up but I told Homer I sure would like to see that baby.

Well, lo and behold, Ruby Jo did turn up the next day and she looked like something that had been drug through a knot hole backwards. No matter how mad I was I grabbed her and hugged her till she made me let her go. We asked her where she had been since she left this Milo's place and she said she got a ride from a couple but then Mercy Grace got real sick so the couple took her and the baby to their house, then when she was better they brought them on home. At least that was her story but who knows?

We told her how she just missed Milo and how he wanted the baby. She wudn't say nothing about how she come to marry Milo or why she left him and she pretended she didn't know anything about that Bennett bunch but I think she did. I guess we'll never know. I was happy to have her back and get my hands on that precious little Mercy Grace.

I told Ruby Jo how we were about to leave for California and how the right thing was go back to her husband. She would have none of it, so I said she should come to this place we were going in California, Gazely Creek, and she acted like she didn't care one way or the other.

I didn't sleep much that night because I couldn't feel easy about Ruby Jo, so I got up at good light. I knew in my heart she wudn't be there when I opened her door and she wasn't. The bed hadn't been slept in. Mercy Grace was asleep in a dresser drawer on the floor.

So, brother, this is all I can tell you. I don't know where Ruby Jo has gone, maybe she has gone to Hollywood but at least she left Mercy Grace. I'll know this baby is taken care of because I'll do it myself. I don't know nothing about that Milo feller. Maybe Ruby Jo left him for a reason, so I'll just keep Mercy Grace.

Ruby Jo left all the baby's stuff and her birth certificate so I don't think she's coming back. If she does, we won't be here because we leave tomorrow for Gazely Creek. I'll write when we get there. Sometimes I just don't know, brother, how Homer and me could have such a child. We tried so hard. I am so mad at her but I want her back so bad. I don't think she'll come back. Alma.

The next letter was from Gazely Creek, California, dated June 1, 1933.

Dear brother Horace,

I am remiss in waiting so long to let you know we arrived in Gazely Creek but it seems before I can get my feet under me from one bad thing the Lord slaps me down again.

We left the home place on April 15. The truck Homer bought was so old I was afraid to start out with a baby but Homer said it had to be done and to just pray the Lord would hold that truck together all the way to California. It was hard.

The truck kept getting vapor lock and shutting down on us and we had to carry water. We didn't have no money to stay in tourist cabins or eat in cafes, so Homer put some staves around the truck bed and tied on a tarp and we put our mattress back there. We bought a bucket of Karo syrup and some white bread along the way and that's what we ate.

Except we bought milk for Mercy Grace. But she was real sickly and didn't want her bottle. She fussed all the time. We finally got somewhere over in Arizona out in the middle of nowhere. Homer pulled off to the side of the road and we settled in for the night. Mercy Grace fussed for a while then she seemed to settle down and I got the first good night's sleep I'd had for a quite a spell. I felt pretty good when I first woke up but when I picked up Mercy Grace she was dead.

I begged Homer to get to the next town and find a doctor but he said no doctor was going to bring a baby back to life. I said we should take the baby into town and get her buried and Homer said he wasn't sure we had enough gas money to get to Gazely Creek, so we sure didn't have enough to pay an undertaker to bury Mercy Grace. So I said, well, let's at least stop and let the law know so theys a record of her passing and Homer said if you get the law in on it no telling what kind of trouble they'll be. What'll we do if they find something to fine us for or say we done somethin wrong. I knew Homer was right.

It was still first light so Homer drove off down a side road into the desert a long way. We cudn't even see the highway anymore and they was nothin at all out there. He dug a grave in the sand with his hands by a great big cactus. We put that poor baby in the sand wrapped in nothing but her baby blanket.

I never seen it before and probably will never see it again but Homer bawled like a baby while he buried Mercy Grace. I can't help it, Horace. I know Mercy Grace was dead but I can't help but wonder, with no doctor to check her, was she maybe in some kind of coma and we might have buried that poor baby alive. It haunts me and I can't sleep.

Laney leaned low over her knees, put her hands over her eyes and wept for Alma and baby Mercy Grace.

50 – A RED TRUCK

Laney wiped her tears, sniffled, and made her way to the bathroom to wash her face. She quickly ate some potato salad and a cold chicken leg while the coffee perked. Cup in hand, she then hurried back to the letters.

10 Mar 1935

Dear Horace,

One more time I set my hand to bring you hard news. On Saturday 3 Mar this Lord's year, Homer was run over by a car here in town and killed.

The police said it was an accident. It was raining and they said the driver didn't see Homer and Homer was drunk and not paying attention. Yes, brother, Homer was drunk. He took up drinking a while after we got here. I don't hold with drinking but I know why he done it. Living just got to be too much for him without help.

Nobody but Homer and the Lord knows for sure but I don't think it was an accident. I think Homer stepped out in front of that car on purpose. He was just plain through with this life. He never was a man to show his feelings, but he put a lot of stock in Ruby Jo and he was never the same after all that business with her and Mercy Grace. It was too much after losing the boys. So Homer is dead and buried here in this California, so far from home.

I know I haven't wrote like I should these past months but I got me a job in the cafeteria in the grammar school here and in the summer I worked the fields along with Homer picking whatever there is during harvest until school starts again. Apricots, peaches, cherries, strawberries, brokoli, peppers, anything that comes to hand.

They have food out here you never heard of, funny stuff they call artiechokes and spareagus and olives. They's no end to it. In the fall I help pick walnuts on the weekends. Yes, Sunday, too. We kind of stopped going to church after Mercy Grace.

For making a living this was a good move. We've had money for things we never had before. They don't know about hard times here like we had back home. I hope things have eased up for you some and that business is up in the hardware store.

I haven't been feeling all that good myself lately. I missed a couple of days work last week so I guess I'll have to see the doctor. I'm just tired I think and weary.

So, brother, pray for me as I pray for you. I so want to see you again and talk about old times, mama and daddy and all that. Who knows, just me now. Maybe I'll come see you and spend this coming summer. I don't know if I'd know you walking down the street. Such a shame.

It's something to think about. I think I'll look into how much a bus ticket would cost and how long it would take to get there. Wudn't that be something, brother?

It was the last letter Alma wrote. The next one was from one of her neighbors.

May 21, 1935

Dear Mr. Greer,

I am sorry to be the bearer of bad news but it falls to me to tell you that your sister, Alma Cassity, passed away ten days ago. She had cancer.

Toward the end when she knew she wouldn't get well, she asked that you not be notified until she was buried and everything was settled because she knew you would try to come and thought it would be too hard for you.

Alma didn't have much. The house was rented so there was no property to worry about. She asked me to sell or give away what furniture and other goods she had and send whatever there was after my expenses to you. I am sending all there was with this letter, a money order for $75.96, as I don't want to take anything for helping a neighbor in need.

Alma asked me to send a box of her personal effects to you as well. She said someday her daughter might show up and maybe she would want it.

I am sorry about Alma and Homer. They were good decent people.

Mrs. Elsie Pinter
157 Costa Ave
Gazely Creek, Calif.

* * * *

Over the next three days, Laney reread every word of every letter three more times. On Monday morning she got up early, took a bath and got dressed. A dress that had fit her perfectly just a few days before hung on her like she had shrunk to a skeleton.

Laney got into the little 1948 Ford Coupe Auntie had bought for her sixteenth birthday. Auntie never learned to drive. She was too short to see over the dashboard but she loved riding around town with Laney.

Laney drove the familiar route to the store without paying a lot of attention. Her mind was on the Cassity letters she now knew almost by memory. What was it about that family that tugged at Laney's heart? Of course, she loved Uncle Horace but, still, she never knew his sister and her family. Why should she care so much? Laney shook her head and sighed as she parked in the alley behind the store. She didn't know why, but she did care.

The store smelled stale and fusty after being locked up for over a week and it was muggy hot. Laney hurried to open the front door to let some air in. She had swung the door open just a few inches when she saw, almost out of the corner of her eye, an old red truck rattle down the street right in front of the store.

Legs shaking so hard they were slapping against each other, she slammed the door shut, turned the bolt lock and slid down to the floor. She leaned back, gasping for breath, her heart pounding so hard she could feel it thumping against the door through her back.

Harley. Harley Faddis. Come for her. He would kill her for sure. Just like he had killed Mama. Laney scrambled to her hands and knees and crawled down the center aisle of the store as fast as she could to the little office in the back. She quickly locked the back door and fell, trembling, into the chair in front of the desk.

Laney gripped the chair arms and breathed deeply. *Wait a minute. Think. Harley was dead.* She *had* killed him. But what if Auntie was right? What if Laney had only given him bloody clothes and a bad headache?

Okay, suppose Harley was alive. He had mentioned a few times he got as far north as Ardmore looking for metal. But Harley's truck was old when Laney had been with him. Surely by now it was chopped up in some junkyard. But this looked like the same truck. It was the same color and had the same dent in the right front fender.

But Harley wouldn't still be in the metal business, would he? The end of the war had changed everything. So if he wasn't still in the metal business, what would he be doing in Ardmore?

Laney pressed a palm against her chest trying so slow her heart rate. Okay. Say that wasn't Harley's truck. Say she had killed him. The law never stopped looking for a murderer.

Reality slammed her like she had been slapped by a giant. Although it was sweltering in the little closet of an office, a sudden freezing chill popped goose bumps on Laney's arms and she hugged herself. How could she have been so careless these last few years? Openly using her own name. Flitting about all over the place. Even if Laney had been too young to take precautions, Auntie was smart; she should have understood the risk.

The truth was that as long as Laney Belle Hawkins lived, whether Harley Faddis was dead or alive, Laney was in serious danger.

The cold fist of fear clutched Laney hard and kept her hunkered down in the office, sweating and shivering, all day. Thoughts went around and around. He was dead; he was alive. The law could come for her at any time. There was nobody to protect her. *Run, Laney, run.*

No. She couldn't live in fear all her life, hiding like a rat in a hole every time a red truck went by. What kind of life was that… but what could she do? There had to be some way…

By the time Laney scurried out the back door to her car after dark, she knew exactly what she was going to do. Now to figure out how to do it.

51 – PLANS

Laney sat in the car in the dark in the driveway for a few minutes and waited until no cars were passing before dashing into the house and locking the door behind her. She dished up some cold ham and pinto beans, poured a glass of milk, and brought a ruled tablet and pencil to the table.

She had to be very careful. This must be done right the first time. It couldn't be done again. Auntie Fairy had said she was a naturally good businesswoman—smart and a clear thinker. Well, Auntie, this is the time for clear thinking.

While eating, Laney wrote page after page of notes and ideas, only to rip them off and tear them up. There had to be a way.

The one absolute was that Laney Belle Hawkins had to disappear forever. However it was done, there had to be a dead end, a place where Laney Belle dropped off the face of the earth, with no way to trace what happened to her.

After supper, Laney made a pot of coffee and continued to scribble notes until three o'clock in the morning. She finally went to bed, satisfied she had a workable plan. The first thing she did when she got up was gather all her notes, including the shredded pages, put them in a wastebasket and burn them in the back yard.

Instead of opening the store, Laney went to see Malcolm Udell. She got right to the point.

"Malcom, I just don't have the heart to keep running the store without Auntie."

"We shouldn't have a problem finding a buyer," Malcom replied. "The store has a sound financial history."

"It's not just the store. It's too hard being in the house without her, so I'd like to sell out completely."

Malcom raised his eyebrows and said, "Watkins ought to snap up the property in a heartbeat. He's bought just about everything else on Turner Road and he's already laying out lots at the east end."

"I actually have some thoughts about that." Laney crossed her legs and leaned back in her chair. "I'll sell the Turner Road property to Watkins providing he also buys the store and all the inventory."

Malcom steepled his fingers under his chin and studied Laney. She went on, "I have almost fifteen acres out there. That could be a lot of tract houses."

Laney uncrossed her legs and leaned forward. "The store is a prime downtown location. He can't do anything but make money on it. He can sell the business and lease the building to the buyer or sell the whole kit and caboodle, or wholesale the inventory and lease the building to a different business. However he goes, it's a good business deal."

"He's definitely your prime prospect for the Turner Road property," Malcom said. "Your timing is actually good. He came to see me a couple of days ago. It seems he stopped by to talk to you a day or two after the funeral, but nobody answered the door. He wanted to know if I'd approach you on his behalf, so I had planned to talk to you this week. I just don't know if he'd be interested in the downtown property."

"Here's the thing, Malcom. I need the freedom to make some serious decisions about my life and I don't want to fiddle around forever." Laney kept her voice steady. "If Watkins will buy both properties, I'll take a package price."

"And if he won't buy the store property?"

"The price on the fifteen acres goes up, way up. If he wants it bad enough, he'll go one way or the other," Laney said.

"What if he digs in his heels and won't buy either way?"

"Then I'll just have to bide my time and find other buyers for both properties." Laney smiled. "I can't help but think there are other developers that would see the potential for tract houses on my fifteen acres."

Malcom grinned and replied, "I'll talk to him."

* * * *

Three days later Malcom called Laney to his office to review an offer for both properties from Watkins. She accepted with minor revisions.

"How long before this will go to escrow for closing?" Laney asked.

"I'd say ten days or so. I'll call you when the papers are ready to sign."

"That's perfect. I think I'll take a few days and just get away for a while. You know, I've never had a vacation."

"Well, then you should take one." Malcom smiled. "You can certainly afford it."

Yes, she certainly could. With a respectable amount of money in the store operating account plus the business savings account Auntie Fairy had accumulated over the years, money was not the problem. Even without the recent infusion of the cash from the sale of all of Horace's property, she could implement her plan and still have enough money left to be labeled "very well off".

"I'll probably leave tomorrow and drive over to Hot Springs. You can reach me at the Arlington Hotel if you need me," Laney said, rising from her chair.

"You think you'll be all right driving all that way by yourself?"

"I'm sure I will. I guess I have to start doing a lot of things on my own now."

"Well, the Arlington is a lovely old hotel," Malcom said. "I know you'll enjoy it. Let me know when you're back and if anything comes up, I'll call you there."

* * * *

Hallelujah! Laney sailed down the highway with the windows open, singing at the top of her voice. She wasn't one-hundred percent safe yet but she soon would be. Her plan would work; she just knew it.

This was the first step. Auntie Fairy would be proud of her plan. She swung her shoulders and wiggled her body in the car seat like a puppy rolling in warm summer grass.

For the next week, Laney soaked in the hot mineral waters at the Arlington, and relaxed with massages and a facial. She walked around town, bought a few new clothes, went to the movies, read, and napped a lot.

A young waiter in the dining room one evening seemed to take extra notice of her. He hovered around much more than necessary. The one thing Laney didn't need or want was some man showing interest, so she started going out for supper, once to Hamilton House at the lake and a couple of times to a place serving fried catfish and hush puppies.

A glowing, confident face looked back at Laney at the end of the week. She arrived in Ardmore feeling powerful and strong like Wonder Woman. If Harley really did show up, maybe she'd just poke him in the eye. No. She wouldn't. That thought sobered her instantly, like she had been slapped, and she was relieved when Malcom called to say the closing papers were ready for signing.

"You're sitting on quite a bit of cash, young lady." Malcom handed her the check for the proceeds. "My offer still stands to give you some financial guidance."

"I appreciate all your help, Malcom, and I actually have an idea I'm kicking around, but I want to give it some more thought." Laney stood and extended her hand. "If you'll send me your bill, I'd like to settle up in the next few days."

"I'll do that." Malcom stood and shook her hand. "You know I'm here if you need me."

Laney went directly to the bank and deposited the check. Although she knew she had a lot of money, still she reared back in her chair with a little jolt of disbelief when she saw the total amount written in black and white on the summary of accounts the banker handed her.

Mama… Mama who never had a store-bought dress. Mama, who only had eighty-three cents. If only…

Laney blinked back the tears flooding her eyes, stood, and quickly left the bank.

She had negotiated for ten days after closing to remove personal possessions from the store office and vacate the house. She put the furnishings and everything salable from the house into the inventory of the store.

All of Auntie's clothes and other items unsuitable for store inventory went to the West Side Baptist Church Women's Missionary Society for their annual rummage sale. Besides her own clothing and personal things, Laney only kept Auntie's picture albums and Bible, Alma's Bible, pictures, and letters, and Mama's purse. Everything fit into two large suitcases and a big shoulder bag.

Seven days after close of escrow, on the sixth of August, she loaded everything into her car early in the morning, ate breakfast at a café and was waiting when the bank opened.

"Well, young lady, what can I do for you this morning?" Finlay Wattell, the banker, smiled as Laney took a seat in his office. She had inherited a longtime preferred customer status from her Auntie, reinforced by her own now healthy bank balance, so she dealt with the banker himself.

That suited her purposes to a T. If anybody asked, they'd get the story from the horse's mouth.

"I'm sure you heard I sold the Turner Road property and the store," Laney said.

"I did hear that."

Time to plant the weenie truth that would eventually spread around town.

"While I was on vacation in Hot Springs, I happened to visit a nice secondhand store there and turns out the owner wants to sell out and retire." Laney smiled. "We were able to come to terms and the deal is ready to close."

"Well, my, my, Laney, we sure hate to lose you." Mr. Wattell's smile collapsed.

"I know, but it just isn't the same around here without Auntie, and I feel this is the best move for me." Laney leaned back in the chair and crossed her arms.

"Yes, well, how can I help you?"

"I would like to close my accounts. I want a cashier's check made out to the seller of the Hot Springs property and then I want the balance of the accounts in large bills."

Laney thought Mr. Wattell was going to cry. His mouth turned down and he swallowed two or three times.

"What amount for the cashier's check?" He looked so pained, Laney actually felt sorry for him.

Laney told him the amount. He looked startled. "That's an absurd amount of money to pay for a second hand store. Don't you think you should get some professional advice? I'd be glad to…"

"It's not just for the store. I'm also buying her house, some accounts receivable, and reimbursing her for a substantial business account balance." Laney smiled and held the banker's gaze. "I don't know the final amounts on those accounts yet. In addition, she has a couple of downtown properties I'm considering and we haven't negotiated a price, so one check keeps it simple. Escrow will refund me any overage."

"Still, Laney, I don't think…" Mr. Wattell frowned. "You should… "

"Please make the cashier's check payable to Mercy Grace French, Mr. Wattell."

52 – DISAPPEARING ACT

Before leaving the bank, Laney went into the restroom and took the envelope with the cash and the check out of her purse. She put two hundred dollars into her wallet.

She spread the rest of the cash, a little over five thousand dollars, flat in a pair of nylon stockings she had sewn together to make a long tube. She lifted her blouse, tied the money tube around her waist, then safety-pinned it to her skirt for good measure. Satisfied it didn't show with her blouse back in place, Laney put the check back in the envelope and safety-pinned the envelope into a zippered compartment of her purse.

Now for the next step in the disappearance of Laney Belle Hawkins.

Laney arrived in Hot Springs in the late afternoon. She checked into a plain, but clean, small hotel a couple of streets away from the Arlington. The next morning, she called on the local banker.

"I'm looking at a couple of business properties and hope to relocate here," she said. "I'd like to open an account."

"Of course," the banker replied. "How much will you be depositing, Miss…?"

"French," she replied. "Mercy Grace French."

She slid the check across the desk to him. He glanced at it, then up at her, eyes wide. Mercy Grace saw his Adam's apple jump up so fast it almost hit the bottom of his chin as he swallowed hard.

"Of course, Miss French. If you'll just fill out these forms."

She completed the information quickly, giving her address as the hotel, and slid the papers back to him. She could tell he was fairly quivering with the urge to grill her.

"I wasn't aware of any large business properties for sale in town. Usually I know about these things. Which properties are you interested in?"

"We're still in negotiations so I'm not at liberty to say."

"Of course, of course. And where are you coming from, Miss French?"

Laney managed to control her urge to laugh. The poor man was almost groveling for a bit of gossip. "How long will it take these funds to clear, Mr. Franklin?"

"Oh, cashier's check... not long a few days."

"Good. I'm looking for a couple of sound investments. If these properties in Hot Springs don't work out, I'll be looking elsewhere so I want to be sure my funds are readily available." Mercy Grace stood and pulled on her gloves.

"Oh, absolutely, Miss French. And I'm sure if these properties don't work for you there are others that would suit your purpose. Hot Springs is a lovely town, and growing. Lot's of opportunities for a smart investor."

"We'll see. Thank you for your time, Mr. Franklin."

* * * *

Laney waited ten days and called on the banker again.

"I'm sorry to say, Mr. Franklin, I was unable to negotiate acceptable terms and I haven't found anything else of interest. Will there be any trouble transferring my funds when I decide on a permanent location?"

"Oh, no. Your new bank can handle it. Pretty simple process." He stood as she stood. "We're so sorry to lose you as a customer."

He looked so deflated Laney actually felt sorry for him.

She drove out of Hot Springs in the direction of Dallas, reasonably confident she had closed the door on any connection between Laney and the bank in Ardmore.

Her plan almost failed when it came time to sell her little Ford. Laney sat in the car in front of a used car lot not far from the Dallas Greyhound station and cried for over an hour. Finally, with swollen eyes and hiccups, she dragged herself into the office and made the deal. A taxi took her to the bus station, where she bought a ticket to Albuquerque, New Mexico.

She arrived in Albuquerque late the next day and asked one of the ticket agents, who looked like somebody's grandmother, to recommend a reasonable boarding house or small hotel that would be safe for a single woman.

A taxi dropped her on a side street near downtown at a three-story, light-colored stucco building that looked more like a church than a hotel. Laney was relieved to see a few respectable looking people in the lobby and a middle-aged woman behind the desk. She checked in as Mercy Grace French.

The next day Laney picked up a New Mexico driver's license test booklet, then went to the post office. Using Mercy Grace's birth certificate and giving the hotel as her address, she filled out an application for a Social Security number. The post office clerk said cards usually arrived in about four weeks.

The hotel was clean and quiet and the staff and other guests minded their own business, which suited Laney just fine. She left the hotel every morning by nine and returned after four, five days a week, to give the appearance she was employed nearby.

The first two days Laney sat in the library and studied the driver's test manual until she felt confident she could pass, then she looked up a driving school in the phone book. When the teacher arrived with a car, Laney explained she didn't need driving lessons. She wanted a ride to the DMV and the use of the car for a driving test.

After making Laney drive around the block twice to be sure she could drive, the teacher took her to the DMV. Laney walked out with a temporary license in the name of Mercy Grace French, with the promise a permanent one would arrive in about ten days.

Laney spent the time reading at the library, shopping, walking around town, and going to movie matinees. After dinner, she stayed in her room writing *Mercy Grace French*, covering page after page of a ruled tablet. Or she would stand in front of the mirror and say *Mercy Grace French* aloud, over and over. She ripped the tablet sheets to shreds and flushed them down the toilet every night.

On Tuesday, September 18, the morning after the Social Security card arrived a little over three weeks later, Laney took a taxi to a Ford dealership and paid $1,465 in cash for a year-end closeout on a dark blue Country

Squire Estate Wagon with wood paneling on the sides.

Laney drove back to the hotel and carefully went through her purse and all her belongings, removing anything with her name or any reference to Oklahoma. She shredded everything, including her Oklahoma driver's license, and flushed it all down the toilet.

Laney Belle Hawkins no longer existed. Mercy Grace French checked out of the hotel, loaded her luggage and headed west out of Albuquerque. She never looked back.

Part Four
Mercy Grace French

September 18, 1951 – July 2, 1962

53 – GAZELY CREEK

Mercy Grace spent an extra day in Tucson and found a beauty shop that would take her without an appointment.

"I want it cut and colored," Mercy Grace told the beautician, who introduced herself as Selma.

Selma raised her eyebrows. "Do you have any idea how many women come in here wanting me to give them blonde hair like this out of a bottle?"

"No," Mercy Grace responded, "but I want mine red. Not blazing red but kind of soft light auburn. And I want a poodle cut."

"Okay." The woman shrugged and put a cape over Mercy Grace, snugging it around her neck.

Mercy Grace's hair had not been cut since she was twelve and hung almost to her hips. She closed her eyes when the woman picked up the scissors and began snipping.

"You'd never know it," Selma said, "because your hair was so long and heavy, but you have a lot of natural curl. You'll really see it with this short cut."

When Selma, looking very pleased with herself, spun Mercy Grace around to face the mirror to see the finished style, Mercy Grace gasped. She hardly recognized herself.

"You make a great redhead." Selma grinned. "You know who you look like? Rita Hayworth. I'll bet you could pass for her twin."

Mercy Grace couldn't help it. For the next couple of days, she kept checking her reflection in the rearview mirror and every other mirror she passed.

As she sped across the country to a new life, she felt powerful and strong, even more than she had coming back from Hot Springs, like she could rock the world. She was free, truly free. No more worry about the law or Harley, even if that mean old so-and-so was still alive. He had nothing to do with Mercy Grace French. Laney Belle Hawkins was gone for good. Mercy Grace French had enough money for a new start and she could be anything she wanted to be.

* * * *

On Sunday morning, September 23, Mercy Grace checked into the only hotel in Gazely Creek, California, a two-story brick-fronted building on Main Street with a small lobby and café on the ground floor. She unpacked, showered and changed clothes. Before leaving her room, she looked in the phone book for Elsie Pinter, Alma Cassity's neighbor, and found no listing at all for Pinter.

After lunch, Mercy Grace asked directions to the local cemetery and found it on a lower slope of a small mountain that towered over the town. It only took thirty minutes to find the graves of Homer and Alma Cassity in the shade of a large walnut tree.

It was weird. Mercy Grace actually felt a pang of sorrow for these "grandparents" she never knew. It was like they really did belong to her. She stood for several minutes trying to imagine what they would have been like. What would Ruby Jo, her "mother," have been like? Mercy Grace shook her head and walked through nearby tombstones.

She breathed a sigh of relief when, a few yards away, she saw a tombstone for Elsie Pinter. Hopefully, all the loopholes were closed and no living person could possibly know the infant Mercy Grace French was dead and buried somewhere in the Arizona desert.

On Monday morning, Mercy Grace walked across the street to the Gazely Creek Bank and asked to speak to the manager. A tall young man rose from his chair and looked at her curiously as she was guided into his office. The name plate on the desk identified him as Lucas J. Symon.

"How can I help you, Miss?" He extended his hand.

"French," Mercy Grace replied. "Mercy Grace French, and I'd like to open an account and have funds transferred from another bank."

"Of course." He took a form from a desk drawer and pushed it across the desk to her with a pen.

Mercy Grace completed the form and handed it to him. He glanced at it, then his head jerked up, eyes widening with obvious surprise, but he just nodded.

Handing the form and the endorsed check back to him, Mercy Grace said, "I'm afraid I don't have an address at the moment, Mr. Symon. I'm staying at the hotel for the time being."

"Please call me Luke. Everybody does." His smile punched dimples in both cheeks. "May I call you Mercy Grace?"

"Yes, of course," Mercy Grace blushed. Luke was sure a few steps up from pudgy old Finlay Wattell at the bank in Ardmore.

"You can give us an address when you have one." Luke picked up the phone and called a teller to complete the deposit. "What brings you to our little town, Mercy Grace?"

She had her weenie truth polished and ready.

"I was raised by my paternal grandparents in Hot Springs, Arkansas. Grandpa died when I was a young teen and Grandma died a few months ago. I really didn't want to stay in Hot Springs with them gone. Fortunately, they left me with the means to make a change."

"Yes, they certainly did. Why Gazely Creek? We're a long way from Hot Springs."

Now for the tricky part.

"My maternal grandparents lived here. I was about two when they died, so I never knew them. I always felt bad about that. Grandma French used to read me letters she had gotten from Grandma Cassity. Her letters made Gazely Creek sound like such a special place. I don't know; it sounds silly. Somehow I felt like coming here—being where they lived—could make up a little for me not knowing them. Does that make sense?"

"I can understand that. Their name was Cassity?"

"Homer and Alma. They died in 1935." Mercy Grace tensed; every muscle in her body went hard, locked and loaded, in case she needed to catapult out of there. "I visited their graves yesterday morning."

"The name isn't familiar to me, but I was only about ten back then." Luke smiled. "So how long do you plan to stay with us?"

Mercy Grace exhaled and willed her muscles to relax. "Indefinitely. I hope to buy some property."

"What are you looking for?"

"Well, a place to live, obviously, and I need a business location."

"That's what I like to hear—a new business coming to town. What do you have in mind?"

"Basically a high-end secondhand store, mostly home furnishings, but good quality, nothing junky. Is there anything like that here?" Mercy Grace asked. "I did a quick drive around. I didn't see anything."

The banker steepled his index fingers and touched them to his chin. "No, there isn't, and your timing couldn't be better."

"Oh?" Mercy's heart beat quickened and she leaned forward in her chair.

"I don't know if you noticed the old Gazely place on the north end of town? You could hardly miss it if you drove by."

"You mean that beautiful old two-story that sits on a really big lot by itself?"

Mercy Grace had seen it just that morning. It was a large Craftsman, set much further back from the street than nearby homes, like it was in the midst of a private park. "Does it have a wrought-iron fence with spikes on top along the sidewalk and some really big trees in the front?"

"That's the one," Luke said. "Those are English walnut trees. They're a lot older than I am."

"I didn't see a sign on it. Is it for sale?" Mercy Grace loved that house on sight and she held her breath.

"It will be very soon." Luke glanced at his watch. "It has a lot of history." His dimples winked at her again as she slowly exhaled. "Hey, why don't we grab a bite of lunch and I'll tell you all about it."

* * * *

"No kid graduates from high school here without knowing the history of the Gazely family." Luke laughed. "The Gazelys are kind of the town treasure—a little weird, but ours. You know what I mean?"

Mercy Grace nodded.

Over a lunch of grilled tuna sandwiches and cherry cokes, Luke related the Gazely story.

"Alistair Gazely was with the first party of pioneers to cross the Sierra Nevada, and he arrived in the Santa Clara valley in 1845." Luke took a sip of Coke and continued. "Rumor says he was shirttail royalty in Scotland and had to get out of town after some questionable business involving a lady."

Mercy Grace laughed. "I'll bet that's not in the local history books."

"No, but whoever he was, he didn't arrive broke. He almost immediately married the dark-eyed daughter of the local patrón and came into possession of more than seven thousand acres of prime valley real estate. He called it Rancho del Gato de la Montaña."

"Goodness. What a lovely name. What does it mean?"

Luke turned and pointed out the window. "See that little mountain over there? If you look at it just right, it looks like a crouching cat. The name means 'the ranch of the mountain cat.'"

Luke signaled the waitress to refill their Cokes.

"The creek that runs behind the Gazely house and angles to the east, south of town, came to be called Gazely Creek. So when the town grew up, it was naturally called Gazely Creek."

"So what happened to old Alistair?" Mercy Grace put her elbow on the table and rested her chin in her palm.

"He planted vast orchards of apricots, almonds, walnuts, and some vineyards, but mainly prunes. In fact, he came to be known as the Prune King.

"He married an Englishwoman he met in San Francisco, Eudora Harcourt, not long after his young Mexican bride and baby died in childbirth."

Luke leaned back in his chair, obviously enjoying his role as storyteller.

"They had five boys. Not one of them ever worked a day in his life. After the old man died, they sold off the property bit by bit and lived very well."

"So when did he build the Craftsman?"

"He didn't. The oldest boy was the only one to marry and he had only one child, a girl, also named Eudora. She never married. By the time she turned thirty-five, she was the only Gazely left. She sold the rest of the property, except for the four acres the house sits on, and had Greene & Greene Architects build the Craftsman."

"That big place just for her?"

"Yep. She rattled around in it by herself, except for a housekeeper and a gardener, until about three months ago when she died at eighty. She lived quite grandly on the proceeds from the last large tract of her granddaddy's ranch."

"That's really sad in a way." Mercy Grace sighed.

"They were all quite eccentric. It's said one of the things the first Eudora brought to the marriage was a silver tea set and, come hell or high water, nothing kept her from her afternoon tea."

"How funny," Mercy Grace said. "I wonder what ever happened to the tea set?"

"Oh, it's still in the house. I don't know about the first Eudora, but our Eudora served tea in the parlor every afternoon until three days before she died. She liked to invite two or three of the high school girls to join her. Said they weren't learning any manners in school. I'm sure you'll find the tea set there along with all the other furnishings. Everything is probably still like new."

Mercy Grace leaned forward. "And the house is going to be for sale?"

"Yes. My brother's the only lawyer in town and he's handling the estate, so I know the house is ready to go on the market."

"What about the furnishings?" Mercy Grace crossed her fingers under the table. Built-in inventory? She would love to expand into antiques if the furnishings were antique quality. Could she be so lucky?

"Included. The whole kit and caboodle."

"When can I meet with your brother?"

54 – EUDORA'S PARLOUR

"The Gazely property is perfectly suited to your purpose," Tom Symon, the lawyer, said. "Our main street is actually Highway 101 and all the traffic between San Francisco to the north and Salinas, Monterey, and Los Angeles to the south passes right through here. I would think an antique store, especially one in such a unique and historic property, would do very well."

"I'm counting on it," Mercy Grace replied. "When can I look at it?"

"I'm tied up for a couple of days, but my wife would love to show you. She's in love with the Gazely place and looks for any excuse to get inside and look around. She wanted me to buy it."

"Why didn't you?"

"She was an architecture student from England when she dropped out of college and married me, so she has all kinds of visions of what she would do with it." Tom opened a drawer and removed a manila file. "But, I'm too busy to get hooked into one of her projects. Besides, I'm still working on paying off the mortgage on the house she couldn't live without seven years ago." He grinned, looking very much like his brother, Luke.

Mercy Grace laughed and said, "So, the big question. What's the asking price?"

She couldn't stop her eyes from widening when he named the amount. Tom noticed.

"I think you'll find prices on all property higher here than in Arkansas."

"It's just that I need to buy a house to live in, too, and I want to reserve substantial operating capital."

"The Gazely place offers a couple of options that might eliminate the need for a second property." Tom handed her the file. "You'll find all the pertinent details in here. Take a look and see what you think."

* * * *

"So, you have a couple of options for living quarters," Linda Symon said as she led the way up the stairs of the Gazely house. "One is to turn the upstairs into a private apartment."

"It's certainly big enough," Mercy Grace agreed, "but I don't want to do that. I think part of the appeal of turning this into an antique store would be people being able to wander from room to room."

"I couldn't agree with you more."

Mercy Grace had to have this house. It was a small mansion, like nothing she had ever seen, and she had no idea of the value of the furnishings. They were, as Luke said, for the most part like new. Her instincts told her they were authentic and tasteful.

She tried to conceal her true excitement from Linda, but Mercy Grace couldn't help touching the woodwork, the stained glass windows, the furniture. Her heart pounded in her chest and she worked at keeping her breathing even.

"Let me show you the alternative to living upstairs." Linda led the way out the kitchen door into a back yard that sloped slightly toward a creek in a line of trees at the back of the property. There were two other buildings, one a barn and the other a smaller two-story, also in the Craftsman style.

The barn was clean but dusty and huge, with a second space upstairs.

"This was used mainly for farm machinery, not animals, so it would be easy to clean up and use however you want," Linda explained as they did a quick walk-through. "But this is what I really want to show you." She led Mercy Grace out of the barn and to the second building. "It's the old carriage house."

Linda guided the way up some outside stairs and opened a door. "The housekeeper and gardener were a married couple. They lived here until Eudora passed away."

It was definitely nicer than any place she had ever lived, Mercy Grace thought, as she followed Linda through the two-bedroom, one-bath apartment.

"You could live here just as it is," Linda said, "but I'll tell you what I would do." Mercy Grace could hear the excitement in the other woman's voice.

"What?"

"The two bedrooms and bath only need some fresh paint and sprucing up, but I would remodel the living-dining area and the kitchenette into a really big master suite and bath." Linda waved her arm in a wide arc. "Except for this one window where you can just see the street light on the corner, your entire view from this part of the house is the grounds, the trees and the creek. We could even give you a balcony."

Linda's excitement was catching and Mercy Grace could easily imagine what she was suggesting. "A balcony would be great."

"We'd knock down the outside stairs, put in a new staircase inside, and remodel the downstairs into the main living area with a parlor, small dining room, kitchen, and guest bath." Linda chattered as she led Mercy Grace down into the garage. "It's just a big open space now but it could be spectacular. We could make the front reflect the big house front porch and entry. On the side, off the kitchen door we'll put a porte-cochere you can use as a carport. It'll all harmonize with the main house, like it was always here."

Linda turned to Mercy Grace. "I was an architectural student, you know. I could help you." She laughed. "Hell, I'd almost pay you to let me help you. So what do you think?"

Mercy Grace could tell Linda was holding her breath. "I love it. I absolutely love it."

"So we're going to do it?"

"By golly, I think we are. I even have a name for the store—Eudora's Parlor." Mercy Grace knew when she spoke the name it was perfect. "That will be for antiques and fine furnishings. And I have some ideas for the barn."

"What?"

"The upstairs can be used for storage and the very back I'll set up as a workshop for repairs and such. The front will be a second store for regular used furniture, nice stuff, just not antiques. I'll call that Eudora's Attic."

* * * *

"So, Linda said you liked the Gazely property." Tom motioned Mercy Grace to a chair in his office and settled behind his desk.

"I do, and I want to make an offer. You said earlier the seller is Eudora's only living relative, an elderly gentleman still living in Scotland?"

"Yes. He has no desire to travel and has instructed me to sell the property as is, including furnishings."

"Okay, here's what I'm willing to pay." Mercy Grace named a figure twenty percent below the price Tom had quoted. He raised his eyebrows but said nothing, so Mercy Grace continued.

"You said yourself this is a unique property, so it would have to be a unique buyer to be a match. I wouldn't think that kind comes along every day, so it could take a while to find the right person. Second, I think this is a pricey property even for this area. Another reason it could take a while."

Well, even so, I don't think your offer will fly with the seller. It's too low."

Mercy Grace leaned back in her chair and crossed her legs. "Okay. You and I both know the property is overpriced by at least ten percent."

Tom just listened so she pressed on, deliberately keeping her voice calm even though her heart was slamming her ribs. "I'm willing to make a firm deal right now, all cash, quick close, no contingencies, no hassles, property as is. That's worth another five percent. So let's say fifteen percent below asking. If this gentleman's old as you say, he might like to have his money sooner than later."

"I think you'll do all right in business, young lady." Tom laughed. "I'll present your offer. The gentleman just might take it. The least he'll do is counter back.'"

Tom called Mercy Grace the next afternoon to say the offer was accepted and that he already had the seller's power of attorney to act in his behalf so the sale could close quickly.

Mercy Grace danced around the hotel room, wishing Auntie Fairy could be with her. Then she called Linda and told her to start drawing the plans for the carriage house remodel.

* * * *

While Linda supervised the remodeling of the carriage house, Mercy Grace traveled throughout the area. She took roll after roll of pictures of the furnishings in the main house to every antique store she could find, from San Francisco to Monterey, and even into the little shops in the gold country, Grass Valley, Nevada City, and Sonora. She bought every book she could find on antiques. By the time she moved into the carriage house, Mercy Grace was confident she knew the value of her inventory.

Mercy Grace stored all the inventory she acquired for Eudora's Attic on the upper floor of the barn and left the downstairs, now cleaned up and remodeled, completely bare.

She took out a full-page ad in the local paper inviting the adults of the town to a New Year's Eve party on the last evening of December, 1952, as her grand opening.

"Brilliant!" Linda declared. "But you know just about the whole town will turn out, don't you?"

"That's the idea." Mercy Grace laughed.

She and Linda, with some of Linda's friends, decorated the barn with colored lights and streamers. They found a rental company in San Jose to deliver and place chairs and tables, a local restaurant to cater food and a small band from Gilroy to play music.

The entire town did turn out. It was the biggest, most glamourous event to ever hit Gazely Creek. Women had their hair and nails done and bought new cocktail dresses and men wore their best suits. The dance floor was a wild display of the latest bop and swing dance steps by younger couples and the jitterbug and Lindy by older dancers. The party didn't wind down until almost three in the morning.

Just before midnight, Mercy Grace was chatting with Tom and Linda and the mayor when Luke snaked his way through the crowd and joined them. He leaned over and whispered in Mercy Grace's ear. "When you come to town, lady, you *really* come to town."

55 – LUKE

Luke strode into the country club's Nineteenth Hole Bar & Grill and slid into a chair at the table where Tom was already nursing a Beefeater martini and reviewing his golf scorecard.

"Sorry I'm late," Luke said. "Old Mr. Ambrose wanted to see me at the last minute and you know how long-winded he is."

"No, problem, brother. It was slow play this morning, so I just got here myself."

Luke signaled a waiter and ordered a Dewar's scotch and soda. "That was some New Year's party Mercy Grace threw, wasn't it?" he said as the waiter walked away.

"It certainly was," Tom agreed. "A smart way to get acquainted with the whole town and kick off a new business all at once."

"Yeah, I think she'll be a real shot in the arm for the community. Maybe shake things up a bit." Luke's chest swelled a little. It was kind of like Mercy Grace French was his own personal discovery. He picked up the menu as the waiter delivered his drink. "You order yet?"

"No," replied Tom, "but I'll have the French onion soup and a roast beef sandwich."

"I'll have the same," Luke said, handing the menu to the waiter.

"So what's up with Little Miss Whirlwind? Have you asked her out yet?" Tom grinned and took a sip of his martini.

"No."

Tom's eyebrows shot up. "No? I thought you'd be all over that one like bark on a tree."

271

"I was going to ask her out before I realized how young she is. I was shocked. I actually thought she was four or five years older."

"Well, how old is she?"

"Nineteen."

"*Nineteen?* Are you sure? Did you ask her?"

Luke laughed at Tom's stunned expression. "No, I didn't ask her, you idiot. It just kind of came up in a conversation. I almost fell off my chair." He moved his drink aside so the waiter could put his soup on the table.

"She obviously knows what she's doing," Tom said and chuckled. "She knows how to bargain and she's good at it. How did she get her business experience?"

"I don't know. She'll talk all day about business, but when it comes to her history, she's evasive."

"Well, a lot of people are very private. Nothing wrong with that," Tom picked up half a sandwich. "But nineteen's old enough to date. So what else, brother?"

"I don't know exactly. It's puzzling. On the one hand, she's this confident, smart, obviously successful ..."

"And beautiful..." Tom grinned.

"And beautiful businesswoman, but on the other hand, I get the feeling she's very inexperienced—even fearful—of a personal relationship."

Luke tapped the rim of his glass with a forefinger, then picked it up and took a drink. "She seems really vulnerable, even fragile."

"Nothing ventured, nothing gained, Luke. You should ask her out."

"I will, but I want to take it slow. I have a feeling about Mercy Grace. I think she could be really special and I don't want to blow it before I even get started."

* * * *

Mercy Grace eased into dating Luke so naturally she hardly noticed. They quickly became fast friends and shared lunch together at least twice a week. She asked his advice on a couple of financial matters and he talked her and Linda into helping him remodel and decorate the abandoned second floor of the bank building into a stunning bachelor apartment.

Luke's social circle readily embraced Mercy Grace, so she, Luke, Tom and Linda and their friends, the chief of police, Johnny Costello and his wife, Karen, bowled together every Thursday night. There were frequent barbecues, picnics, or other outings. Occasionally, they went to the movies as a group, but sometimes it was just Luke and Mercy Grace.

About seven or eight months after her arrival in Gazely Creek, Luke stopped by Eudora's Parlor late in the day on a Friday, just as Mercy Grace was closing. He seemed nervous.

"You busy tonight?" he asked.

"No. Is everybody getting together?"

"No. It'll just be us. I want to take you to dinner in San Jose."

"Wow and it isn't even my birthday." She grinned at him. "Is it your birthday?" She poked his arm. "And you didn't tell me?"

"Nope. Not my birthday either; just dinner. How about it?"

"Okay."

* * * *

In the flicker of the candlelight, Luke reached across the white tablecloth, took Mercy Grace's hand, and said, "I get the feeling you haven't dated a lot."

"No."

"Why?" He spoke softly. "I'd expect a beautiful woman like you to already have a man in her life."

Why? She turned her head and looked at their reflection in the darkness of the window. *Because a man in Mama's life got her killed. A man meant pain, terror. He could hold you down and force your legs apart. Run, Laney, run.*

The old tremor of fear clawed at her insides and her heartbeat shifted into overdrive. But, wait… *She wasn't Laney anymore, and Luke wasn't Harley.* Mercy Grace was safe and Luke was her kind and gentle friend.

"Mercy Grace?" His hand was warm and strong on hers.

She turned and looked at him. "Why? I don't know. Always busy, I guess. Other things to do."

"Do you think we could let this dinner be our first real date?" His smile was small, hesitant.

Still, her hand trembled a little under his as she said. "Yes, I think we could."

56 – A PROPOSAL
October 25, 1961

Mercy Grace had just returned from San Jose, thirty miles away, from her twice-monthly hair trim and color touch-up appointment, and was stopping to pick up the mail.

"Hey, Mercy Grace," Johnny Costello said as they ran into each other in the post office parking lot. "Or should I say Miss Councilwoman?"

"You're jumping the gun, Johnny. I'm not running." Mercy Grace laughed and tipped her head back to look up at the six-foot-four police chief.

"You've made a lot of friends in this town in the last ten years," Johnny insisted. "You could win."

"I'm too young."

"So, what are you? Eleven? Twelve?" He grinned.

"You know very well my birthday's tomorrow and I'll be twenty-nine," Mercy Grace replied.

"So you could be our youngest councilwoman ever."

"It's not going to happen."

"That's a shame. You'd do a good job."

"It's just too much." Mercy Grace brushed a strand of hair away from her eyes. "I'm gone on buying trips several times a year, plus Eudora's Spring Tea and the New Year's Eve party. I'm stretched tight as a tick on a hound dog. Even with managers for the Parlor and the Attic, I'm on overload."

"Well, I wish you'd think about it. I'd vote for you."

"Nope, not going to happen."

"Okay, I'll stop nagging, but just for now," Johnny replied. "We'll see you at the party tomorrow night." He pulled her into a hug that smooshed her face against his shirt not too far above his belt buckle.

Every year Johnny and his wife, Karen, along with Linda, Tom, and Luke, hosted a party for Mercy Grace, but, after the first year, it was no longer a surprise.

"Tell Karen I'll bring the scarf I borrowed from her tomorrow night."

"You bet."

Karen Costello was one of Mercy Grace's best friends and, together with Linda Symon, largely responsible for the success of the annual Eudora's Spring Tea. Mercy Grace had been unable to part with Eudora's tea set and kept it on a beautiful old sideboard, which she also couldn't let go, in the dining room of the main house.

"It's a shame Eudora's tea set just sits there," Linda had said one day. "It's so beautiful; it should be used."

"I love it, but I'm afraid I'm not much of a tea drinker," Mercy Grace replied. "Unless it's iced sweet tea."

"Oh, I know all about tea." Linda laughed. "English, you know."

"You've just given me an idea, Linda. I'd love an excuse to use the set and I've been trying to think of a way to help some of the less fortunate local kids."

"What do you have in mind?"

"The churches and other organizations do a good job at Thanksgiving and Christmas, but I'm thinking of back-to-school. You know, maybe coats and school supplies, that sort of thing."

"Good idea," Linda said. "You have a plan for raising money?"

"I think so. How about if every year—around Mother's Day—we have a tea? It would give Eudora's tea set some use."

"We could call it Eudora's Spring Tea." Linda clapped her hands; she was always excitable.

"Do you think the town women would support something like that?"

"You bet. They'd jump at the chance to attend an event like that."

"Would you take charge of the tea party?" Mercy Grace grinned. "So it's done proper and all that?"

So every year Eudora's Spring Tea raised money and every fall, three weeks before the start of school, Mercy Grace and her close friends hosted a hot dog and soda pop picnic under the shade trees by the creek and passed out coats, book satchels, lunch boxes, and school supplies to the kids who showed up.

Mercy Grace's New Year's Eve party had also become an annual fixture, but in the last couple of years she had begun sending out invitations instead of printing an open invitation in the paper. With the town's growing population, the number of guests was becoming unmanageable for the space, but some people still showed up without an invitation.

Mercy Grace waved goodbye to Johnny and went into the post office to get the mail from her box. She sorted through the envelopes and magazines, discarding the junk. There were a lot of smaller envelopes she knew were birthday cards from various people in town.

She strode out of the post office and across the parking lot to her new Monte Carlo Red Ford Thunderbird convertible. She was so happy she would have skipped, but people would think she was crazy, or worse, drunk in the middle of the day.

Mercy Grace giggled in spite of herself. How did her life get to be so perfect? So happy? There were times, when she was alone, she became so overcome with joy and gratitude she hugged herself and danced around the room.

Mercy Grace French had a good life. She could barely remember Laney Belle Hawkins and the terror that had been so much a part of that girl's life. Mercy Grace French had nothing at all to fear. The world belonged to her.

* * * *

"Hey, birthday girl," Luke said as they were the last to leave the party at Linda and Tom's house. "How about let's pop into my place for a nightcap? I haven't had you to myself a minute all evening." He snugged her light jacket around her shoulders and kissed her on the nose. "Besides I have a little something for you."

"Luke, you spoil me and I love it." Mercy Grace linked her arm in his as they walked the three blocks to a side door on the bank building and up the stairs to Luke's apartment.

Luke draped Mercy Grace's jacket over a chair and headed for the kitchen. "Have a seat," he called over his shoulder. "I'll be right back."

Mercy Grace had just kicked off her shoes and settled in the plush cushions of the couch when Luke came back with two glasses and a bottle of champagne.

"Wow! Champagne. I really feel special."

"You are special to me," Luke said, "every day. Not just on your birthday." He handed her a glass of champagne, leaned over and kissed her lightly on the lips. "Happy twenty-ninth birthday, baby." He clinked his glass to hers and sat beside her on the couch.

"Thank you. And thank you for helping with the party."

"It's no big deal. Linda and Karen do most of the work."

"I know, but I do appreciate it. You've made me feel like I've come home since the day I arrived." Mercy Grace took a sip of champagne. "It seems like it was just yesterday. I can't believe it's been ten years."

"The day you walked into the bank was the best day of my life." Luke rested a hand on her shoulder. "So far."

"For me, too." Mercy Grace reached up and covered Luke's hand with her own.

Luke put his glass on the table, then took Mercy Grace's glass from her hand and set it on the table beside his. She leaned into him as he pulled her into his arms and kissed her. It was a familiar, comfortable embrace and Mercy Grace sighed as Luke deepened the kiss. She turned to press her body closer to his as the tingle of desire began a little tap dance in the pit of her stomach.

Suddenly he loosened his arms and leaned away from her. He put his finger under her chin and tipped her face so he could look directly into her eyes. She tensed and inhaled sharply. *Uh-oh. Here it comes again.*

"We've talked about marriage several times," he said. "At least I've talked about it. You always change the subject."

"No, I don't!" *That wasn't true, was it? Yes, it was.*

"You do, Mercy Grace. I've always let it go because I thought you needed a little more time." He reached into his pocket and took out a small velvet box. "But this time I'm making it official." He slid off the couch onto one knee and flipped open the little box.

Mercy Grace placed her fingers across her lips as she looked at the solitaire diamond gleaming against the black velvet. "Oh, Luke," she said, but she was thinking *no, no.*

"I love you, Mercy Grace French. Will you marry me?" He grinned the funny lopsided grin that punched a dimple in his left cheek and delivered a sucker punch to her heart.

"Luke…"

"It's time we marry, Mercy Grace," Luke interrupted and Mercy Grace heard the edge of doubt in his voice. "I've loved you since the day you walked into my office and we've been dating for at least five or six years. Everybody knows we practically live together as it is."

"Luke…"

"No, just listen a minute. At first I didn't realize how young you really were and when I did, I knew you'd need some time." His words were rushed like he had to get them out before she could stop him. "But, Mercy Grace, you're twenty-nine now. I'm thirty-six and I want a family. If I'm going to have one, I have to start soon."

"Luke." Mercy Grace put her palms against his cheeks. "I do love you. I have for a long time. You know that."

"But?" He gripped her wrists and removed her hands from his face then slid up on the couch beside her.

"I don't know! Getting married just doesn't feel right… at least not right now."

How could she even say that? Luke was a good man and he loved her. He was more than she had ever hoped for. What was wrong with her?

"If not now, then when, Mercy Grace?" Luke stood and began to pace. He pushed a hand through his thick dark hair. "Or is it me that's not right?"

"Luke, it's not you. I couldn't ask for a better husband. It's me." Mercy Grace clenched her hands in her lap. *What was wrong with her? Why didn't marriage to Luke feel right?* She didn't know.

"I think it is me, Mercy Grace." He was like a dog with a bone and he wasn't going to give it up. "I could wake up ten years down the road, close to fifty, too old for a family and be in the same boat… still not right.'"

Mercy Grace stood and walked to him, putting her hands on his shoulders to stop his pacing. "I do love you, Luke. You've always been so good to me."

He put his hands on top of hers on his shoulders. "But you won't marry me?"

Mercy Grace forced herself to look steadily into his eyes. The pain she saw there took her breath away. How could she hurt him like this? *I do love him. Just say yes.*

"Not now, Luke. I can't. What else can I say?"

"You can say there'll be a time in the near future when you will be ready." His voice trembled and Mercy Grace saw tears shimmering in his eyes.

She swallowed hard; her tongue feeling too big and getting in the way, but she said, "You know I can't promise that."

Luke exhaled deeply and hung his head so she couldn't clearly see his face. They stood without speaking for a minute or two. Then he lifted his head, gave a half smile, and said, "I'll take you home."

Neither of them spoke on the short drive. At the door, Luke said, "I love you, Mercy Grace, but I want a family and I need to move on." He pulled her to him and kissed her on the forehead. "I hope you find someone who feels right and makes you happy."

"Oh, Luke, you make me happy!" *What am I doing?*

Luke shook his head and turned toward his car, his shoulders slumped, his steps sluggish. Mercy Grace closed the door behind her, slid to the floor, and put her hands over her face. *Did I just break up with Luke? What am I doing? I must be crazy.*

57 – A SIMPLE QUESTION

Mercy Grace strode along the sidewalk, her parka hood pulled close around her face, partly against the early cold spell, and partly to avoid stopping to chat if she could. Her feet found their way on auto-pilot as her mind simmered and bubbled like a witch's cauldron.

She wanted to run into Luke but, at the same time, she dreaded it. She had seen him for just a minute in the post office parking lot on Friday He had waved and smiled before he got in the car and drove away, leaving her feeling shaken, as if something was unfinished. She had hurt him; she should at least try to do something about that, try to make him understand. How could she when she didn't understand herself?

Had she done right thing? She did love Luke, so what was missing? He was a respected, hard-working man, kind and gentle, and he loved her. He had never pushed or pressured her. A strong friendship had grown between them. Then, after months, he had eased her into dating and, after more months, into his bed. It had been—was—lovely and easy.

Maybe that was the problem. Maybe it all felt too easy. But that was crazy. Why wouldn't she want easy? There were several young women in town who would be glad to take her place. *Ouch.* That thought gave her a quick, sharp jab to the heart.

What was holding her back? What was wrong with her? Why couldn't she feel confident about her decision to let the relationship go? Why was she doubting?

The warm air of the coffee shop wrapped around Mercy Grace, pulling her in, as soon as she opened the door. She shed her coat as she strode across the room and slid into a booth across from Linda.

"So, when were you going to tell me?" Linda demanded before Mercy Grace could even plant her bottom on the seat.

"Tell you what?"

"That you and Luke broke up. What else?"

Mercy Grace lifted her index finger as a signal for her friend to wait as the waitress approached. "Just coffee," she said and they waited while Marie filled their cups.

"How'd you know?" Mercy Grace asked as soon as the waitress walked away.

"Luke told Tom." Linda dumped sugar and cream into her coffee and stirred so vigorously a little coffee sloshed out. "You know I'm mad at you. I'm your best friend. I shouldn't have to hear news like this from the grapevine."

"Luke told his brother and Tom told you," Mercy Grace said. "That's hardly the grapevine."

"Well, I should have heard it from you. Is it for real?"

"Yes, I think so." Mercy Grace heard the doubt in her own voice.

"You *think* so?" Linda raised her perfectly plucked eyebrows.

"It's complicated. I keep beating myself up and doubting my sanity, but I just don't know…"

"I know break-ups are hard, but you're a lot more messed up than just that."

Linda paused as Marie refilled their cups and moved on to a table across the room. It was mid-morning and there were only two other customers besides Linda and Mercy Grace. "You look like you haven't slept in a week. So what is it?"

"I don't know!" Mercy Grace spoke more sharply than she intended and noticed Marie glance up from filling salt shakers behind the counter. Mercy Grace repeated in a softer voice, "I don't know."

"Yes, you do." Linda reached across the table and covered Mercy Grace's hand with her own. "You know. You just have to dig it out and have a look at it."

"Okay. Okay." Mercy Grace slid her hand out from under Linda's and watched her fingers slowly twirl her coffee cup as if it was an event of great importance. Linda sat quietly, waiting.

Mercy Grace swallowed around what felt like a hot stone growing bigger and bigger in her throat, sighed deeply, and said, "I feel guilty. I took up so many years of Luke's life, close to ten altogether. He could be married to someone else and have a family by now. That's what he wants."

Linda shook her head. "No, you didn't take up all those years of Luke's life. He chose to give them to you."

"But…"

"No buts. He could have walked away anytime. He stayed because there was something in it for him."

"Yeah. Hope. He trusted me. I let him believe he wasn't wasting his time." Mercy Grace felt tears film her eyes. "I took advantage of him."

"It's impossible to take advantage of a person without his cooperation and from where I sit, Luke was plenty cooperative. It goes back to the same thing. He could have walked away."

Linda took a sip of coffee and continued, "If there's any guilt, then you're both guilty. So what else?"

"I hurt him. I really care about him but I still hurt him."

"Sometimes you hurt people. Sometimes they hurt you." Linda shrugged. "That's life. It's not like you set out to do him intentional harm. What else?"

"I really do love him. I don't want him to hate me." Mercy Grace dabbed her eyes with a napkin.

"Mercy Grace, you know better than that. It may take Luke a while to sort things out, but can you look me in the eye and tell me you really believe he could ever hate you?"

Mercy Grace shook her head and whispered, "No."

"So, let's get it all out. What else?" Linda patted Mercy Grace's hand.

"Luke's the only man I've ever dated, so how can I be sure he's the one? What if I married him and it was a mistake?"

"My friend," Linda said, "We can talk this to death but in the end, there's only one question. It's a simple question and there are only two answers. If you answer honestly, you'll know the right path to take and you'll find peace with your choice."

If only I could decide for sure, without doubt, and be at peace with it. Mercy Grace sighed and said, "What's the question?"

"What scares you the most… I mean scares you right into your bones—marrying Luke or not marrying him?"

Mercy Grace caught her breath and held it for a second, meeting her friend's steady gaze. She was surprised how calm and sure her voice sounded when she answered.

"Marrying him. As much as I do care for him, the idea of marrying Luke scares the hell out of me. Not marrying him—the thought makes me sad because I hurt him, but it doesn't scare me."

58 – A NEW FACE IN TOWN

On the last day of November, Mercy Grace stopped at the drugstore to pick up a couple of items before making a run to San Jose to buy Christmas decorations. When she took her place in line at the cash register, Gloria Helmsted turned and gave Mercy Grace a smile that had all the friendliness of frostbite.

Gloria owned a small beauty shop in town and had let Mercy Grace know she was a traitor for driving to San Jose twice a month to get her hair done. The last thing Mercy Grace needed was for the talkative Gloria to know Mercy Grace's natural hair color was pale blonde.

"So, Mercy Grace," Gloria said, "have you met Kelsey Clark, the new second-grade schoolteacher yet?"

"Can't say I have." Mercy Grace kept her voice civil.

"From someplace up around Seattle. She came in to get her hair done after school yesterday. Really pretty. I mean, *really* pretty."

"That's nice." Mercy Grace looked over Gloria's shoulder see what was holding up the line. Old Mr. Ambrose arguing about the cost of his prescription. That figured.

"I thought you might know her, seeing she seems to be good friends with Luke already."

Gloria peered at Mercy Grace like she was studying a lunch menu and couldn't decide what to have. Mercy Grace forced herself to smile but said nothing. After a month, gossip about her break-up with Luke was old news, but Gloria was sure to find something snide to say.

"Yeah, Kelsey came in to get all gussied up because Luke was her date

285

for the PTA dance last night."

Mercy Grace's hands tightened on the handle of her shopping cart as she braced for a jolt of pain at the news, but it didn't come. Instead, there was a flush of real relief that Luke was moving on. She gave Gloria her biggest, most sincere smile and said, "That's just wonderful. Luke's a great guy. I'll have to make it a point to get acquainted with Kelsey."

Gloria squinted her eyes and her mouth dropped open. Before she could comment further, the clerk called "Next" and Gloria moved up to the cash register.

Mercy Grace paid for her purchases and went to the door, still smiling to herself. Her hand was on the knob and she was about to walk out when, not three feet away, on the other side of the front window, a man passed by.

Harley. *Harley!* No. *It couldn't be.* Harley was dead. *She had killed him.*

But she knew, with the surety of a lighting strike, it *was* Harley. Older, meaner, thinner. Her heart pounded so hard she reached up and clutched her chest. She could not breathe.

Mercy Grace put her hand out to brace herself against the door as she felt herself dissolving into, not black oblivion, but a hot cauldron of rusty red that filled her nose with the smell of blood. She barely felt the pain or heard the crack as her head hit the edge of a shelf and she fell headlong onto the floor and into the old terror.

Mercy Grace blinked her eyes several times to clear her vision as she felt a strong hand slip under her head. The first face she saw was the new young doctor in town. Behind him was the druggist and a couple of people she knew vaguely.

"Take it easy, Mercy Grace," Doctor Thorne said. "Just be still a minute."

"I think I fainted," she mumbled. *Harley!* She tried to twist her neck to see the front window.

"Be still! Let me have a look at you." The doctor examined her briefly and said, "You're going to have quite a headache from this goose egg on the back of your head, but I don't see anything else significant. I'm sending you to the hospital in Gilroy anyway just so they can check you out."

"No." Mercy Grace struggled to sit up.

The doctor pressed her back to the floor. "Just be quiet now. I've already called the ambulance. "It'll only be a day or two, just to be sure."

"But, I can't..." Wait. *Wait!* Yes. *Yes!* A couple of days tucked away out of sight... a chance to think. She lay back and relaxed. "Okay," she said.

* * * *

As much as Mercy Grace wanted some peace and quiet to think clearly, a constant flow of doctors, nurses, technicians, and now visitors, had surged in and out of her room since she had settled into the hospital bed a little before noon. She was relieved when a nurse stuck her head in the door and said, "Sorry, folks, visiting hours are over."

Linda and Karen each leaned over the bed, squeezed Mercy Grace's hand and kissed her forehead. "I'll pick you up and drive you home as soon as they check you out tomorrow," Linda said. "Call me when the doctor gives you the okay."

"I will," Mercy Grace promised.

The two women fluttered their fingers in a goodbye wave at Luke and walked out the door. Luke pushed off from leaning against the window frame and came to stand beside the bed.

"I'm sure glad you're okay," he said.

"Me, too. Silly thing, fainting."

"Well, at least you've had a good checkup and know you have a clean bill of health."

"It was sweet of you to come, Luke. I do appreciate it."

"What are friends for?" He turned toward the door. "I'll let you get some rest."

"Luke." He turned back and she held out her hand. He walked to the bed and took her hand in both his. They looked at each other for a moment and then she said, "Are you all right?"

He smiled. "Getting there. Thanks for asking."

"I heard you're seeing Kelsey, the new teacher in town?"

"I've taken her out once or twice."

"I heard she's pretty. And really nice."

"She is."

"I'm so happy for you, Luke."

"Thanks." He released her hand. "Gotta run. I'll be seeing you." He waved over his shoulder as he walked out the door.

The nurse brought in water and a little white cup containing a couple of pills.

"These'll help you get through the night," she said. Mercy Grace swallowed them. "You want the TV on?"

"No, thanks. I just want to rest."

The nurse adjusted Mercy Grace's bed and dimmed the lights as she left the room. Mercy Grace lay back on the pillow with a deep sigh. Her head throbbed dully even over the barrier of the pain meds.

She had to think. What to do?

It was Harley, no question. Thank God she had seen him first. What would have happened if she hadn't? What if he had been in the drugstore, saw her walk by, then walked up behind her and shouted *Laney*! What would she have done? The possibilities slicked her body with sweat and made her heart thump in time with the throbbing of her head.

But she had seen him first, so now what?

She could have a talk with Johnny Costello, turn Harley over to the law. For what? Being a mean, miserable excuse for a human being? She couldn't accuse him of killing her mother. It had been almost twenty years and she had no proof.

Harley would just say Mama ran off and he'd done his best to raise the young'un she left behind. And, accusing Harley would explode her world, expose her as a fraud. Could she go to jail for assuming a dead baby's identity?

Maybe she could say he was just some stranger who was stalking her. Johnny would at least run him out of town. But, no, Harley wouldn't take that lying down. He'd do plenty of talking of his own, telling Johnny who-knew-what? He would expose her, maybe say she assaulted him. Even if Johnny didn't believe him, it would undoubtedly open the door to some questions she couldn't afford to answer.

So, she couldn't sic the law on Harley without great risk to herself. But, as long as Harley was here, she was in danger. She knew Harley well enough to know he would do whatever it took to get what he thought was due him or die trying. He would find a way to do something terrible to her, maybe kill her, like he had killed her mother.

She could run, just pack a few things and disappear in the night. Where would she go? What would she do? *Who would she be?*

No! Laney Belle Hawkins was dead. *Mercy Grace French was not a fraud.* Mercy Grace French had a life, a good life. She would not run. She would fight for the life she had built. But how?

Thoughts and ideas raced through her mind at rocket speed. She discarded most as soon as they occurred to her. A few she slowed down and turned this way and that, trying to see all the angles. Finally, about two o'clock in the morning, she knew what she had to do.

There was only one solution. She had to run a bluff on Harley and she had to make it stick.

59 – THE MEETING

Mercy Grace stayed inside her house through the weekend and the following week, telling friends who called she was going to rest a few days. Every minute of the day and late into the night, she plotted how to engineer a seemingly random face-to-face with Harley.

She had to make absolutely certain she controlled the when and where of that first confrontation. She role-played over and over what she would do, what she would say, and how she would act. And especially how to control and hide what she was sure to feel—anger, and surely, fear.

When she was as ready as she could be, she went to town for an hour or so every day at different times, walking the streets, window shopping, wandering into shops, covertly looking for Harley. She was as obsessed with confronting him as she had been with her preparation. She just wanted to get it over with and let the chips fall.

Toward the end of the second week, with no sight of Harley, Mercy Grace was beginning to think he had moved on and she had worried for nothing. Then she saw him.

It was Friday, three days before Christmas. Mercy Grace was sitting in a booth toward the back of the hotel café warming up with a cup of coffee when she saw him enter the bar and grill across the street.

Her hand shook so badly she sloshed coffee out of her cup. She gripped the wrist of the shaking hand with her other hand and steadied herself enough to put the cup down. She inhaled deeply and closed her eyes. *Lord, help me.*

Mercy Grace rose, steadied her legs and paid her bill. At the corner, she crossed the street at the signal light. She pushed her fur-trimmed hood back off her head, then walked slowly past the tavern's large plate glass window, looking straight ahead. Counting off the shop windows, she stopped at the fifth one and pretended to study the display while watching the door of the tavern out of the corner of her eye.

Harley came out of the tavern so fast that he stumbled and almost fell. Mercy Grace turned and casually walked toward him. She returned the wave of an acquaintance crossing the street, then, forced herself to stroll, glancing at the window displays. As she drew near Harley, Mercy Grace directed her attention down the street, past Harley, bringing him into her field of vision, but forcing herself not to look directly at him.

Harley stood like a concrete post, staring at her. She allowed her glance to sweep over him and slide past, taking in the look of puzzlement on his face. Her heart froze but she made herself walk at an unhurried pace. He was so close she smelled an odor like a dead animal.

Just then, Larson Cole, a high school senior and football player who worked part-time at the butcher shop, loped up from behind her. "Hey, Miss French!"

"Oh, hi, Larson. I was just on my way to the butcher shop. I'll walk with you." As they walked away, Mercy Grace did not look over her shoulder, but she could feel Harley's eyes following her and she shivered.

As soon as they entered the butcher shop, Mercy Grace dashed for the restroom in the back. She didn't just vomit. The meager contents of her stomach shot from her mouth like buckshot out of a double-barrel shotgun and left her weak and trembling.

When she walked back into the shop, Mac, the butcher, said, "Are you okay, Mercy Grace? You don't look so good."

"I think I may have overdone it a bit, Mac. Do you think you could walk me to my car?"

"You bet." The big, burly butcher took her arm and walked her out.

"Can you make it home okay?" he asked as put her in the car. "I could drive you."

"I'll be fine, Mac. Really." She closed the door and started the motor. "Thank you so much."

She carefully scanned the streets and checked her review mirror as she drove. Harley was nowhere to be seen.

60 – THE CAT AND MOUSE GAME

Mercy Grace resumed her normal routine as much as possible. She went into town if necessary but didn't go deliberately looking for Harley. She was hoping he would decide she wasn't who he thought she was and leave her alone. But, she was uneasy and knew she would be as long as Harley Faddis was in town.

On Christmas Eve, she made a run to the liquor store for last-minute supplies for the cocktail party she was hosting for friends that evening. Harley was nowhere to be seen as she held the door for the store clerk to carry the box of liquor to the car.

Mercy Grace surrendered to the relief that washed over her and rested her head on her hands on the steering wheel for a minute. When she looked up, Harley stepped out of a doorway two stores down, grinned and waggled his fingers at her in a wave. She nodded, as she would to anyone who greeted her, and was thankful he couldn't see her shaking hand as she made two attempts before she could insert the key in the ignition, start the car, and drive away.

The third encounter happened on the Friday after Christmas. In spite of her role-playing and resolve, Mercy Grace was jittery. She had a strong urge to drive away when she parked in front of the bank and saw him leaning against the building near the door. No. She couldn't give any indication he was anything at all to her. She gritted her teeth and got out of the car.

"So, Miz French, is it?" Harley said as Mercy Grace reached for the door.

Mercy Grace did not allow herself to shudder. Instead, she reached deep inside herself, stood as tall as she could and said, as indignantly as she could, "Yes. Do I know you?"

Just then a customer coming out of the bank pushed the door open and held it for Mercy Grace. She nodded her thanks and stepped inside. She took as long as possible with her transaction, chatting with the teller and a couple of other people she knew. When she came out of the bank, Harley was gone.

* * * *

"What in the world is wrong with you?" Linda asked as she collapsed into a chair across the table from Mercy Grace. Mercy Grace had to lean forward to hear Linda over the din of people laughing and talking and the band loudly playing, "Hit the Road Jack."

"Nothing's wrong with me. Why?" Mercy Grace practically had to shout.

"Don't give me that malarkey, Mercy Grace. I know you always get in a tizzy putting this New Year's Eve party together." Linda picked up her Tom Collins and took a sip. "But you're the only one not having a good time."

"I am having a good time." Mercy Grace picked up her champagne glass and saluted her friend. "Happy New Year," she said, but she was concentrating on not allowing her chin to quiver. She wanted to throw herself into Linda's arms and spill the whole sordid story. She wanted to sit down in the middle of the floor at her own party and bawl her eyes out. But she wouldn't. Couldn't. She couldn't tell anyone about Harley, not even her best friend.

"You haven't been yourself since you went to the hospital. What are you keeping from me?"

Mercy Grace could see Linda was not going to let it go. What to say? She needed one of Auntie's weenie truths. "Okay! Okay. I'm feeling fine. I've just been a little distracted."

"What about? Luke?"

"No." Mercy Grace took a deep breath and plunged ahead. "A good friend of mine in Little Rock is getting a divorce." Where did that come from? Well, it would have to do. "I always thought theirs was a fairy-tale, happily-ever--after-marriage. I think I'm more upset than she is."

"You should invite her out for a visit. Probably do you both good."

"I'll have to think about that." Mercy Grace hated lying to Linda and was relieved when Tom walked up, grabbed Linda and pulled her onto the dance floor.

* * * *

During the first week of January, Mercy Grace encountered Harley twice. The first time she felt a hard jolt right to her gut when Harley walked into the hotel café and sat down just two tables away from where she was having lunch with Linda and Karen. Mercy Grace couldn't help it. She inhaled sharply and clenched her shaking hands under the table. The bastard would be able to hear everything they said.

Tears rose like a flood. *She couldn't keep this up. The pressure and uncertainty was too much. Just get it over with. Walk over there and hit him as hard as you can right in his rotten teeth. Get in one good punch before your life blows up.* Mercy Grace tensed her muscles and pushed her hands against the booth seat, ready to rise.

"What the hell is the matter with you, Mercy Grace, and don't give me any crap," Linda snapped. "You look like you're going to pass out."

Mercy Grace turned her head toward her two friends sitting across from her, all blurry like she was looking at them underwater. She shook her head, clearing her vision, and saw the concern, even near panic, on their faces. Karen reached across and took Mercy Grace's hand.

They both stared at her, waiting. Waiting for her to say something.

She couldn't give up her life, her friends. To hell with Harley. She *would* outwit him in this cat and mouse game. He would not win. She *could* do it. She covered her eyes with her hands for a minute, then looked directly at her friends. *What to say? Something.*

"You're making too much of it," she said. "It's really nothing. I saw Doctor Thorne yesterday and he said I'm severely anemic." He actually had said she was anemic when he reviewed her hospital tests. "It makes me have these kind of weak spells sometimes. He put me on a good iron regimen."

"That's it?" Linda looked at her suspiciously. "You're not keeping anything else from us?"

Mercy Grace forced herself to laugh. "No. I promise, Mother Hen."

Mercy Grace excused herself a few minutes later, saying she had to get back to Eudora's Parlor so the manager, Ruth, could go to a doctor's appointment. Two blocks from the café, she drove into the empty parking lot behind the Elks Club, put her hands over her face, and burst into tears.

Three days later Mercy Grace noticed Harley sitting on a bench in front of the hardware store a few doors down from the post office. He grinned and winked at her. She fought down the bile rising in her throat, looked away and ran right into Johnny Costello.

"Hey, Mercy Grace!" Johnny grabbed her arm. "Didn't mean to knock you over."

"Oh, sorry, Johnny. I wasn't looking where I was going."

"How're you doing?" He gave her a quick hug. "Karen said you haven't been feeling well."

"I'm okay. A little under the weather for a bit." She knew Harley was watching them. "How about you?"

"I'm good," Johnny said. "Terrific New Year's Eve party this year, as usual."

"I'm glad you weren't on duty so you could come."

"Well, it was a fine kick-off to 1962. Looks like we're off to a good start with a couple of new businesses coming to town."

"I heard that. It's good to see some of the Main Street merchants making improvements, too. What do you think of the hardware store's new sign?"

They both turned and looked toward the hardware store where Harley was sitting on the bench. Mercy Grace wanted Harley to think she was pointing him out and talking to the chief of police about him. She knew she had hit the mark when he got up and slouched off down the street.

"I hadn't noticed they put up a new sign. Looks good."

* * * *

"There was a man in here asking about you earlier," said Sandy, the manager of Eudora's Attic, when Mercy Grace stopped in to pick up the week's receipts the following afternoon.

Mercy Grace's heart stumbled a beat or two. "Oh? What was his name?"

"He didn't say. He just nosed around for a while. Asked a few questions. Didn't buy anything."

"What kind of questions?" Mercy Grace made sure her voice was steady.

"Like, how long you've been here. Where you came from. That kind of stuff. Said he thought he knew you from somewhere."

"What did he look like?"

"Not like anybody you'd know. Kind of creepy."

61 – FALLING APART

Mercy Grace snapped the suitcase closed and set it on the floor near the bedroom door, ready to go in the morning. Thank the Lord there was a trade show in San Francisco and she could get out of town for a few days. Maybe get a good night's sleep for a change, away from Gazely Creek, away from Harley. She needed it. She felt as raw as hamburger meat.

Yawning, she kicked off her shoes and turned down the bed covers. Just as she pulled her dress over her head, a strange feeling shivered her from head to toe. She glanced uneasily around the room. The window blinds were still up! *Settle down. No problem.* Second story. Nobody could see in.

Mercy Grace couldn't shake the uneasiness as she put the dress on a hanger in the closet. Keeping her eyes on the open blinds, she quickly crossed the room and flipped a switch, plunging the room into darkness except for the faint glow of a streetlamp on the corner. She felt her way to the window, peeked out, gasped, and flattened herself against the wall, heart pounding.

Harley! He was out there! Leaning slightly, she looked again. It had to be him. He was slouched against the lamppost, cigarette glowing in the dark.

She lowered the blind and rushed for the phone, knocking it off the bedside table in the darkness. The dial tone droned on and on as Mercy Grace clutched the handset to her chest. Who was she going to call? The police? And say what? Harley hadn't actually done anything to her. He had hardly even spoken to her. She put the handset back in the cradle.

Mercy Grace climbed into bed, still in her slip, pantyhose and underwear, and pulled the blankets tightly under her chin. Leaning against the headboard, she sat wide-eyed and shivering, but not from the cold, throughout the night.

* * * *

Mercy Grace was up before daylight. Exhausted, she stumbled through a shower, shampoo, and styling her hair. She took extra care with her makeup in an effort to offset the dark circles under her eyes and the gray gauntness of her face. She was falling apart and she looked it.

She was constantly on edge, not knowing when he was going to pop out of nowhere or what he was going to do or say.

She loaded her suitcase in the trunk of her car and double-checked the house door locks. She drove around to the front of the main house, stopped in the circle drive near the front door, and left the motor running while she dashed inside to the office. All she needed was the company checkbook for the trade show and she could be out of there.

Clutching the checkbook under her arm and in a hurry, she opened the door to step onto the porch and saw him. Harley was leaning against her car, arms and legs crossed, grinning. Her legs went out from under her for a second and she grabbed the door for support. *Steady. Breathe. Don't let him win.*

Slowly and with an exaggerated show of faked calm, she locked the door, walked down the steps and toward Harley. Could he see her heart thumping under her blouse? She forced herself to look directly at him and said, "I don't know who you are, mister, but if you don't get off my property right now, I'm calling the police."

He laughed and she clenched her fists to stop herself from hitting him.

"Looks like you done yourself right proud, Laney." He turned and looked at the old mansion. "Maybe ole Harley hit the jackpot in more ways than one. I took care of you when you needed it. So now you can do the same for me and do it in style, looks like to me."

"I beg your pardon." She reached for the door handle and keeping her voice dead calm, added, "You've mistaken me for someone else."

"Well, you play the hoity-toity all you want, sister, but I know you.

Colored hair, fancy talkin', and fancy clothes don't change nothin'." He gripped her arm.

"I don't know what you're talking about." She pulled her arm but not hard enough to escape his grasp. As scared as she was, she needed to hear him out, know what he had to say, so she would know what to expect.

"Sure you do, Laney. You left me for dead so I couldn't collect what was comin' to me after all them years puttin' up with your sickly mama and bringin' you up from a snotty-nosed young-un'."

He narrowed his eyes and peered closely at her. "But ain't I lucky? I heard they was work to be had out here in this Gazely Creek, so I high-tailed it out and sure enough I got me a job on the graveyard clean-up crew at the strawberry plant down the road. And here you turn up like a bad penny. Yep. It was a good day when I decided to come to this here California." He tightened his grip on her arm. "Now, ole Harley's gonna get what's comin' to him in spades."

"I don't know you. Now, let me go." She jerked her arm free.

"You ain't gettin' away from me again, Laney. You owe me double-down now, for trying to kill me. I'm gonna take what's mine. You know I will."

"I am not who you think I am. Leave me alone." She slid behind the wheel. Harley leaned into the window as she inserted the key in the ignition and turned over the motor.

"I knowed you since you was still peeing your pants, Laney." His lips pulled back, showing brown-stained teeth. "You could paste hen feathers on your head and dye yourself green and I'd still know you."

"You're crazy, mister!" She couldn't stop the trembling of her voice.

"Soon, Laney," he said. "Real soon." He pursed his lips in a kissy motion.

Mercy Grace dropped the car into gear and hit the gas pedal. The car shot forward. Harley threw up both arms and jumped back to keep her from running over his foot.

As soon as Mercy Grace cleared the railroad underpass north of town, she pulled into the empty parking lot of a seedy would-be nightclub and put her head back against the seat. She gave all her attention to just breathing. It was almost an hour before she felt steady enough to drive to San Francisco.

* * * *

Mercy Grace was back in town before noon three days later. She parked in the carport and took her suitcase out of the trunk. Fumbling for her house keys, she walked to the side door into the kitchen. Then froze. The door wasn't standing open but it wasn't fully closed either. The door, frame, and lock were badly damaged. *Harley! He had been in her house…was in her house…waiting. Come to collect his "fun"!*

Mercy Grace dropped the suitcase and ran to the car. She drove directly to the police station.

* * * *

Johnny Costello strode into the office and eased his bulk onto the edge of a desk near where Mercy Grace waited in a chair by deputy Fred Croft's desk.

"I wonder why he only broke into the house and not either of the stores," Johnny said. "That's where the money would be, right?"

Mercy Grace knew why but she said, "Right."

"He could have broken in any time in the last three days, but there's nobody there now. I even looked under the beds." Johnny grinned, leaned over and patted her hand.

"Thanks." Mercy Grace managed to smile back. "I wasn't about to go in there by myself."

"Good girl. We don't get this kind of thing around here very often, so I'm guessing it was a transient."

"I hope so." She *felt* it was Harley who broke into her house but couldn't prove it. Couldn't prove anything and even if she could? Even one word could be the match that lit the fuse to the hidden dynamite that would explode the life she had so carefully built, the life she loved.

"We'll do our best to find whoever it was, but he's probably long gone.

"Probably." *Not a chance. Harley's sending a message. He's going to get me. Soon.*

"I took the liberty of calling a locksmith and a handyman to get your door fixed, so they're probably there by now."

"Thanks, Johnny. I really appreciate it."

"Gotta take care of our girl. I left a deputy out there until you can go through the house. It didn't look like anything was disturbed—which is funny for a break-in—but if you find anything missing, give George a list. We'll add it to the police report."

"Okay. Guess I better get back out there." Mercy Grace stood and hugged Johnny. "Really—thanks, Johnny."

Just as she opened the door to walk out, Fred called after her, "Get a dog, Mercy Grace!"

Mercy Grace sat in the car, drumming her fingers on the steering wheel for a couple of minutes. *Get a dog.*

She drove straight to the pound.

62 – THE END OF THE ROAD

Thunder, a ninety-pound, two-year-old Bull mastiff-golden retriever mix sat in the passenger seat like he was the king of the road, his big pink tongue hanging out. Mercy Grace had been hesitant, even a little fearful, when she first saw him. He looked like he meant business, with the massive head and jaws of the mastiff. Just right to scare the stuffing out of Harley, hopefully, but was he too much dog for her to handle?

The shelter staff assured Mercy Grace that Thunder had the gentle heart of the retriever. His master, a retired bachelor schoolteacher, had been killed in an auto accident less than a month earlier, leaving the orphaned Thunder homeless.

It was obvious he had been well loved and well trained. He flawlessly obeyed a series of commands from the shelter attendant, and, like a gentleman, sat in front of Mercy Grace, extending a paw to shake. Thunder rubbed against her and pushed his head under her hand to be petted. She fell in love. Why hadn't she gotten a dog before?

* * * *

George, the deputy, was leaning against his patrol car watching the handyman put his tools into a red metal box when Mercy Grace parked in the carport. Thunder closed his mouth and stood up, his red-bronze fur touching the headliner of the car. His ears perked up as he ducked his head

302

to look out the window at the two men. He didn't bark.

Mercy Grace held her palm toward him like the shelter lady had shown her and said, "Stay." Thunder sat back down but watched her intently.

"Hey, you got yourself a buddy." George unhooked his thumbs from his gun belt and pushed off the patrol car.

"Yeah. I think he'll be a deterrent to anymore break-ins," Mercy Grace said. "Maybe I'll sleep better anyway."

"Looks like he can do the job," the handyman said. He ripped a sheet off a pad and handed it to Mercy Grace. "You can send me a check. The locksmith said he'll mail you a bill."

"The chief wants me to wait while you have a look around to see if anything's missing," George said.

"Right." Mercy Grace inhaled deeply and entered the house. Just knowing Harley had been there, looking at her things, maybe going through her things, made her want to throw up. There was no sign Harley had touched anything until she got to her bedroom. The panty drawer of the lingerie chest was not quite closed.

Mercy Grace hesitated with her hand on the knob then yanked it open. Her usual neatly folded rows of panties were in a jumble. It was easy to see that the only pair of black panties she owned, a pair with fancy lace she had bought on a whim, was missing.

She said nothing about the missing panties when she reported back to George.

* * * *

Thunder accompanied Mercy Grace everywhere dogs were allowed. He lay on a bed at her feet in the office or stood silently by her side as she waited on customers in the stores. He heeled at her side walking the streets downtown and waited at the door for her to exit stores. At night he slept on the floor by her bed. In just a few days, he became so attached, he dogged her every step, even waiting at the door when she went into the bathroom.

A week passed with no sight of Harley, but Mercy Grace knew she hadn't seen the end of him. One night, as she lay in bed reading, Thunder raised his head. The hair stood on his back and he growled, a deep guttural sound that earned him his name. The blinds were closed but Thunder walked to the window.

Mercy Grace turned off the lights and felt her way to stand by Thunder. "Good boy," she said, patting him on the head with one hand while she pulled the blind away from the window an inch or two with the other.

Harley was there, just like before, leaning against the lamppost, cigarette glowing.

Mercy Grace went back to bed. She did sleep, but fitfully, waking up several times to reach out and pat Thunder on the head, just to be sure he was there.

* * * *

On Saturday night, about ten o'clock, Mercy Grace let Thunder out before going to bed. Usually he was prompt about doing his business, so she stood just inside the kitchen door, holding it not quite closed while she waited for him. There was a sudden spurt of barking, then silence.

Mercy Grace eased the door open a couple of inches to look out and was instantly thrown backward onto the kitchen floor as Harley slammed into the door like a runaway bulldozer. Before she could scramble up, he was on her.

"Thunder!" she screamed.

"Ain't no dog alive don't like a hunk'a meat," Harley said, his mouth against her ear. He pinned her to the floor while he kicked wildly at the door, trying to kick it shut. Mercy Grace tore at his hair and bucked her body under him with all her strength, throwing him off balance. She couldn't let him close that door.

Mercy Grace saw his fist coming at her face and jerked her head aside. She heard the crack when his knuckles smashed the floor.

"Shit! Shit! You bitch!" he yelled and flapped his hand back and forth while trying to hold her down with his other arm. Mercy Grace hit him as hard as she could on the side of his head.

Just then there was a snarl, a blur of bronze fur, and Thunder was on him. Harley rolled off her and put his arms up to protect his head from

Thunder. Mercy Grace scrambled up.

"No! Thunder, down!"

Thunder sank his teeth into Harley's arm and Harley slammed the dog's head with his other fist.

Oh, Lord. Thunder was going to kill Harley right there in her kitchen.

"No! Thunder! No! Down."

The dog hesitated. She grabbed his collar and dragged him off Harley. Harley scrabbled up and grabbed his bleeding arm as he backed toward the door.

"You'll pay for this, Laney." Harley's lip curled in a snarl.

Thunder pulled against Mercy Grace's grip on his collar, his lips pulled back from vicious looking teeth, a low growl rumbling in his throat.

"Next time I'll kill your son-of-a-bitchin' dog," Harley said, then he was out the door and into the darkness.

Fighting to control Thunder, Mercy Grace managed to slam the door shut. She released Thunder's collar, locked the door and then collapsed onto the floor. The dog pushed against her, nuzzling her face. She put her arms around his neck, her face in his fur, and surrendered to the terror. She shook so hard she thought her teeth would rattle but she didn't cry.

Mercy Grace had reached the end of the road and she knew it. She couldn't take this anymore. Tomorrow. Tomorrow she would decide what to do. She would run or she would go to the police. Either way, the life she had so carefully built was over. She should have let Thunder kill Harley. No. That was the one thing she couldn't do. She had already killed the bastard once.

63 – MAMA

The next morning, Thunder's freight-train bark jolted Mercy Grace out of a zombie-like sleep and she was standing on the floor before she even knew she was awake. She looked around her bedroom in confusion. *Ten o'clock!* She had never slept until ten o'clock in her whole life, even if it was Sunday.

Bedlam, with Thunder barking and the doorbell ringing. The doorbell! *Harley.* No, Harley wouldn't ring the doorbell. Would he?

Mercy Grace pulled a robe over her pajamas and raced down the stairs barefoot, with Thunder right behind her. She caught a glimpse of herself in the hall mirror and ran a hand through her hair. If it was Harley, maybe the sight of her would scare him to death.

"Sit, Thunder. Stay." Thunder sat, his eyes on the door. Mercy Grace took a deep breath and opened the door part way.

"I knew you'd be a redhead," the woman said.

What? Mercy Grace gaped at the woman. She was tall, string thin, and a redhead herself. Her purple coat was as shabby as the cheap suitcase sitting at her feet.

"Excuse me?" Mercy Grace's mouth was so dry her words sounded like crumpling paper.

"Mercy Grace French?"

"Yes."

"I'm Ruby Jo Cassity." The woman shifted uneasily from foot to foot in her scuffed shoes. "Your mama."

Mercy Grace went cold to the bone and grabbed the door with both hands. No! She couldn't take anymore, not one more thing. Not now.

Please, don't let this be happening.

"Excuse me?" Mercy Grace said again, her voice trembling in perfect rhythm with her shaking legs. She swallowed, trying to moisten her mouth. "I don't…" She shook her head. She was overwhelmed, plunged into a bottomless pit, the darkness clutching at her, dragging her down, down.

No. Wait. Yes. *Yes! This could change everything.* It wasn't the end of the road. This could fix Harley. Who would know their own child better than a mother? She was Mercy Grace French once and for all. Ruby Jo Cassity was the proof.

Mercy Grace inhaled deeply, steadied herself, and opened the door wide. "Come in," she said.

Ruby Jo smiled nervously, picked up her suitcase and stepped in, then hesitated. *She's scared.* Mercy Grace's heart softened toward the woman.

"I don't know about you," Mercy Grace said, "but I really need a cup of coffee. Just leave your bag here in the hall." Thunder followed them into the kitchen, staying close to Mercy Grace.

How was she going to manage this? Out of nowhere, she suddenly had a mother. How to make sure Harley knew that? How to explain to her friends?

Mercy Grace watched Ruby Jo out of the corner of her eye as she made coffee. Ruby Jo sat, clasping and unclasping her bony hands on the table top. She reminded Mercy Grace of her real mother, Mattie—gaunt, gray, whipped.

Thunder curled up near the door, his eyes following Mercy Grace's every move. She put cups, spoons, cream, and sugar on the table. As soon as the coffee was done, she poured them each a cup and put the pot on the table between them.

Mercy Grace took a couple of sips and said, "How did you find me?"

"I went home, to Freeburg."

"Freeburg?"

"Texas. The old home place. There was hardly anybody I used to know still there, but one old neighbor was positive Mama and Daddy had moved to Gazely Creek, California. It was the only lead I had, so here I am. I asked around. Nobody knew Mama and Daddy, but everybody knows you."

"Why?"

"Why?" Ruby Jo looked startled. "Because you're my child."

"It's been almost thirty years."

Ruby Jo's hand shook, rattling the coffee cup in the saucer. "Mercy Grace…" Tears welled in her eyes and trickled down her face. She wiped them away with her hand. "I was so wrong. Everything I thought, everything I wanted, everything I did, all wrong, and the worst was leaving you. I shouldn't have done it."

Mercy Grace felt a hard-edged urge to strike a blow, to inflict at least some pain on behalf of that little body buried somewhere in the desert. "Why did you?" She pinned Ruby Jo with a cold gaze.

Ruby Jo looked away. "It was the only choice I had." She took a sip of coffee, then studied the cup intently for a minute. Turning her eyes back to Mercy Grace, she shook her head. "No," she said. "I don't want to start this way. That isn't the truth."

The truth. Mercy Grace cringed.

"I promised myself I would be honest with you if I found you." Ruby Jo picked up her cup and put it down again.

Honest. Mercy Grace's empty stomach clenched and churned. If there had been anything in it, she would have thrown up. *Oh, Lord.*

"I'll tell you anything you want to know," Ruby Jo said. "and I won't blame you if you don't want anything to do with me."

"Wait." Mercy Grace pushed her chair back and stood. Thunder raised his head. "I'm not ready for this." She needed to get off by herself for a few minutes and think. "I'll tell you what. I'm a mess. I need to shower and dress."

"Okay."

"Would you like to rest for a few minutes?"

"I really would. I been on a bus for a long time."

"Are you hungry?"

"I could eat."

"Okay, as soon as I shower, I'll fix something."

Thunder padded along behind Mercy Grace as she carried the flimsy suitcase up the stairs. It was so light it couldn't have much in it. Mercy Grace opened the door of the guest room closest to the hall bathroom and set the suitcase inside. She opened the drapes and said, "I won't be long. The bathroom is right next door."

"Thank you."

* * * *

Mercy Grace stood in the shower under water as hot as she could stand it. Would Ruby Jo make things worse or better? And what about Mercy Grace's own web of lies? Now she would have to tell even more. Maybe she should just run —get away from it all.

Or maybe she should tell everything and file a complaint against Harley for stalking her. Her life would be over. She wouldn't be Mercy Grace French anymore. Laney Belle Hawkins didn't have a life. So who would she be? No! She *was* Mercy Grace French.

But Mercy Grace French had a mother. If Ruby Jo spent much time here, would she somehow figure out her daughter was a fraud? What then? Would that be a worse blow up than Mercy Grace just confessing right now? Surely it couldn't be any worse.

If Ruby Jo's presence convinced Harley he was wrong, wouldn't that solve all the problems? That could work as long as Mercy Grace could hide the truth from Ruby Jo.

But then maybe it would only be short-term. Maybe Ruby Jo would visit for a while, then move on. Maybe Harley would give up and move on, too. That would be perfect. Mercy Grace's life would go back to being perfect. But, for now, she had a mother... and Harley.

Mercy Grace left her hair damp and dressed quickly in black Jax pants, a light grey crop top and a pair of black slipper socks. There was no sound except the clicking of Thunder's nails on the hardwood floor as he followed Mercy Grace down the hall to Ruby Jo's room. She put her ear to the door and listened. There was no sound.

Mercy Grace knocked lightly twice, then eased the door open. Ruby Jo was lying on her back, asleep, mouth slightly open.

"Ruby Jo," Mercy Grace said. Then, "Mother...?"

Ruby Jo turned her head on the pillow, blinked a couple of times, and smiled. It was a wobbly smile, kind of like a baby who isn't sure whether it wants to laugh or cry.

64 – TRUE CONFESSIONS

Mercy Grace tucked her legs under her in a big, soft chair by the fire with her umpteenth cup of coffee. Thunder lay on the floor nearby. Ruby Jo sat on the sofa holding her coffee with both hands, her feet planted flat on the floor. It was early afternoon, but the living room blinds were still closed.

Mercy Grace had turned on a couple of lamps and lit a fire, so the room felt cozy and snug like a cocoon. They sat in silence for several minutes, sipping their coffee, each lost in her own thoughts.

Ruby Jo stared at the fire like she was watching a fascinating movie playing out against the flames. Mercy Grace studied Ruby Jo covertly. How old was she?

Mercy Grace did some quick calculations. Ruby Jo was not yet forty-five. Still young, but she looked ten-to-fifteen years older. Hair still red but lank, her skin sallow and thinly stretched over lovely cheekbones. The beauty still lingered, not in vibrant technicolor as Mercy Grace was sure it had once been, but softened and a little fragile, like a flower pressed between the pages of a book.

Ruby Jo finally broke the silence. "Thank you for lunch. And for not kicking me back to the street right off."

"You're welcome."

"Your place is really nice. You've done well for yourself. I'm proud of you."

"I had a lot of help along the way."

They fell into silence again and Mercy Grace waited. She was not about to spill her secrets and, just when she thought her "mother" was of the same mind, Ruby Jo said, "What happened to Mama and Daddy?"

"Grandpa was run over and killed by a car right here in Gazely Creek. Grandma died of cancer a little after that. I put flowers on their graves once in a while."

"Oh." More silence. Then, "When did they die?"

The sudden clang of the alarms going off in Mercy Grace's head were so loud she almost jumped out of her chair. The dates were right on the tombstones, so she swallowed hard and said, "Grandpa died in March 1935, and Grandma died a couple of months later in May." Mercy Grace braced herself; she knew what was coming.

Ruby Jo's head snapped up and she looked at Mercy Grace. "But you weren't even three years old!"

"No."

"But, what…"

This wasn't going to be one of Auntie Fairy's little weenie truths. This one was going to be more like the whole cow.

"I was too young to remember. I just know what I was told." Mercy Grace gripped the arms of her chair. "It was just lucky, I guess, that one of Grandma's neighbors, Elsie Pinter, was from Ardmore.

"About the time Grandma realized she wasn't going to make it, Elsie made a trip to visit her grandchildren."

Mercy Grace knew she was talking too fast so she took a deep breath and made herself slow down.

"Grandma begged Elsie to take me with her to Ardmore, to Uncle Horace, so that's what she did. Aunt Vera was already dead, so Uncle Horace's neighbor, Auntie Fairy, pretty much raised me."

The noose of deceit was tight around Mercy Grace's throat and she felt the creaking of the gallows trapdoor under her feet. She held her breath waiting for Ruby Jo to call her a liar.

"Oh, Lord!" Ruby Jo's voice was ragged. "I'm so sorry, Mercy Grace. I should have been there to take care of you. I'm so sorry."

Mercy Grace let go of the air in her lungs and the tension eased out of her muscles. Okay for now. Hopefully, Ruby Jo would never compare notes with Mercy Grace's friends, who thought she had been raised in Little Rock. Mercy Grace had no idea what to say, so she remained silent.

"No," Ruby Jo said, and in the firelight Mercy Grace could see tears shimmering in her eyes. "Sorry is not what I am. I don't know a word for what I am. Regret isn't a big enough word either, although regret eats on me day and night."

Ruby Jo set her cup on a side table. "I sleep with regret and I wake up with regret. Regret should be my name." She arose and walked to the fireplace, then stood, staring into the flames, her back to Mercy Grace.

"Mama... she was a good woman..." Ruby Jo passed her hand over her eyes. "Just one more day with Mama, just one more day so I could tell her... Oh, God!"

The sob that escaped from Ruby Jo's throat was so raw with pain Mercy Grace felt the iron fingers of anguish clench her own heart.

"I mean, after the boys and all... I broke Mama's heart. Daddy's, too." Ruby Jo glanced over her shoulder at Mercy Grace, seeming unaware of the tears running down her face and dropping little spots on her dress.

Mercy Grace thought about Alma's letters.

"She scares me... I fear for her... Homer and me, we don't need no more heartbreak. I think my baby girl is dead, Horace."

She couldn't stop the tears flooding her own eyes and quickly brushed them away.

"I should've married Berlin Jacobson. Oh, that would've made Mama so happy. But then, I wouldn't have had you." Ruby Jo's attempt at a smile didn't quite work. "Or I should have stayed married to Milo French. Milo was a good man, too. Your daddy."

"Why didn't you?"

"It's kind of hard to explain."

"Try."

Ruby Jo sighed deeply and turned to fully face Mercy Grace.

"Truth," Ruby Jo said, sounding like she was resigned to something unpleasant.

Mercy Grace tensed. Whose truth?

"Truth," Ruby Jo repeated. "I promised myself that if I found you, I'd tell you the truth. It's going to be harder than I thought."

Mercy Grace relaxed. Okay. Ruby Jo's truth.

"For as long as I can remember, the inside of me was filled up with something, like angry hornets, always busy, busy, buzzing and stinging, never giving me a minute's rest." Ruby Jo returned to the couch and sat. "That doesn't make any sense, does it?"

"I think I know what you mean."

"I never had any peace as a child. I always thought I was born to the wrong folks by mistake. I thought they were beneath me."

Ruby Jo's voice broke. She swallowed and continued.

"I thought Berlin and Milo were beneath me. I believed I was destined to be a rich and famous movie star. Everybody told me how beautiful I was. All the other girls were jealous, so I knew if I could get to Hollywood, it would all happen like magic."

"Did it?"

Ruby Jo laughed. It was not a pleasant sound. "No."

"What happened?"

"Oh, I got to Hollywood all right, right after I run off and left you with Mama." Ruby Jo hesitated and then she said, "No question about it, I was beautiful and so were thousands of other young girls just like me, chasing a dream. We were all in a row, like so many dominoes."

"Did you make any movies?"

"As a matter of fact, I did." She laughed that laugh again, so brittle it sounded like it would shatter. "In a little gem called "She," you could see the back of my head in a crowd scene. Then there was the "Gold Diggers of 1935." I was a hotel maid who carried an armful of towels down a hallway.

"In 1936 I was a saloon girl in "San Francisco" and an Indian girl in "The Last of the Mohicans." Then, in 1937, I got a speaking part. I was a woman on the street in "Way Out West." I said 'Look!' but it ended up on the cutting room floor."

Ruby Jo picked up her coffee cup, looked in it, and set it down again.

"Like so many other girls, my greatest performances were not in front of a camera. Oh, I thought I was hugely successful. I got to hang out on movie sets and actually met a lot of the stars of the day.

"I remember when I was an extra in "Angels with Dirty Faces," I think about 1937 or '38. I missed my ride and Humphrey Bogart offered to take me home. We… ummm… he was the nicest man. You know, he once said he made more lousy movies than anybody in Hollywood?"

Ruby Jo laughed and it was so genuine Mercy Grace laughed, too.

"I didn't get a lot of parts in movies, but I was always getting calls to go out with this struggling star, or maybe an older established star who was beginning to fade. I was busy with fancy dinners, fancy cars, fancy hotel rooms. I wore fancy clothes provided by the studio. I went to fabulous parties. Somehow I had enough money to get by with a small weekly retainer from a studio and a little here, a little there."

Mercy Grace listened with her mouth open. She couldn't help it; she was fascinated.

"I felt like a star," Ruby Jo said, "but I was so dazzled by the fake glamour, the handsome men, the wicked parties that I didn't realize I was being passed from man to man like a bottle of moonshine in a dry county."

Ruby Jo studied her hands clenched in her lap. "My life changed so slowly I hardly noticed. As I got older, the studio retainer stopped, the men were less handsome, the parties more and more seedy.

"That's not all of it." Ruby Jo looked like she was trying to make up her mind about something. "But I don't know if you're old enough to hear it."

"I'm twenty-nine."

"That's not the kind of old I mean."

"Oh."

Ruby Jo nodded, like she had decided, and said, "I told it like they—the men—were predators and I was a victim. They were and I was, but that was only one side of it. At the same time, I was a predator, too. A friend of mine once said, 'Ruby Jo, you gobble up men like a hungry bear with a honeycomb.'"

Ruby Jo's face reddened, but she went on. "It was Wick."

"Wick?" Mercy Grace remembered the name from Alma's letters. Wick, the outlaw. Dead outlaw.

"I knew him for less than two days. You're not going to believe this." Ruby Jo chuckled. "Wick made me see dragons. Well, one dragon, but he was a beauty. It was like the dragon had always been inside me, but Wick woke him up and got that old dragon to make fire.

"It burned me white hot without consuming me. I became everything beautiful that ever was and grew bigger and bigger until I was nothing."

Ruby Jo stared off into space and the wonder in her voice made Mercy Grace wish she could get a peek at that dragon. Ruby Jo turned to Mercy Grace. "Are you a virgin?"

Mercy Grace inhaled sharply and her eyes widened. "What's that got to do with anything?"

"I don't think you have any idea what I'm talking about."

Mercy Grace didn't want to admit it, but she said, "No, not really."

"Well, never mind. The point is I was always looking for a man who could get that dragon to make fire like Wick did. All those men but never found one." Ruby Jo shook her head and went silent for a minute or two.

Then Ruby Jo looked directly at Mercy Grace and raised her hand a couple of inches out of her lap as if in supplication. "One morning I woke up and I knew what I was and … Oh, God! I knew what I had given up… and for what… *for nothing?*"

The anguish in Ruby Jo's voice and in her eyes was a brutal razor that sliced Mercy Grace to her core. Mercy Grace put her fingers across her trembling lips and swallowed hard. Ruby Jo leaned forward against her knees and clasped her hands behind her head, sobbing.

Mercy Grace moved to the couch and put her hand on Ruby Jo's back, but she couldn't speak. Ruby Jo sobbed for a few minutes while Mercy Grace patted her.

Ruby Jo sat up and wiped her face with her sleeve. "I couldn't go home. I was so ashamed. Now I know there was nobody there anyway."

"What about Milo?"

"I couldn't go back to him. I don't think he would have wanted me anyway, not after what I had done. I thought Mama was raising you up. I knew you were better off with her. I just didn't know…"

"So, what did you do?"

"I'm a fairly good piano player, and I have a passable voice. I got pretty steady work performing in bars for a little money and tips. When my looks started to go, that dried up, so I got a job as a waitress at a truck stop.

"That's where I met Joe. He was a truck driver. We were together until a couple of years ago. He fell asleep at the wheel on a long haul and drove himself off a mountain."

"I'm so sorry."

"No need. I hardly remember what the man looked like." Ruby Jo blinked and a look, like she had chewed something rotten, flashed in her eyes. She lowered her gaze to her lap. When she spoke, the loathing and disgust were obvious in her voice. "How did I get to be that woman?" Her words were an anguished cry. "Oh. God, Mercy Grace. I don't want to be that woman."

Ruby Jo bowed her head, her shoulders sagged and her hands shook in her lap. Silent sobs rocked her thin body. "I don't want to be that woman," she said again.

With tears in her own eyes, Mercy Grace slid off the sofa and knelt in front of Ruby Jo. Leaning forward, she put her arms around the older woman and held her tight.

This poor woman…she's been through too much. She has paid enough. Mercy Grace was jolted by a powerful feeling, a feeling of… *love* for this stranger who could have been her mother.

She rocked Ruby Jo gently, as she would a baby, and spoke softly in her hair. "It's okay, Ruby Jo… Mother. Everything will be okay."

Finally, Mercy Grace stood and poured a small brandy for both of them. They sipped the liquor in silence. Mercy Grace tried to think of the right thing to say, but before she came up with something, Ruby Jo spoke.

"I thought about telling you how I was passing through and wanted to spend a little time getting to know you, but that's a crock. I'm dead busted, used up and worn out. I don't even have money for a bus ticket out of town and nowhere to go if I did. And that, Mercy Grace, is the truth."

Ruby Jo sat quietly, hands in her lap, looking at Mercy Grace like she was waiting for the executioner's ax to fall.

Mercy Grace hesitated, sighed deeply and said, "We'll see how it works out, Ruby Jo… Mother. We'll give it a try."

There, Mercy Grace. You gave me your name and your life. I'll give this a fair trial. I'll do my best to take care of your mama and see how it works out. So, now, we're even.

65 – DOUBT AND CONFUSION

"I want to earn my keep," Ruby Jo said as she cleared away the dishes from the scrambled eggs and toast she had ready when Mercy Grace came downstairs. "I can clean house and cook a little. Maybe do some yard work. I don't want to be a burden"

"I have a cleaning woman twice a week, a gardener once a week, and one of the high school boys every day to clean up after Thunder." Hearing his name, Thunder raised his head and wagged his tail from his bed near the back door. "But, I'm not much of a cook, so maybe we could share that."

"Deal." Ruby Jo refilled their coffee cups. "I'll try to find something to earn a little money, too. You have any ideas?"

"As a matter of fact, I do. I help Ruth in Eudora's Parlor, but Sandy at the Attic could use some help. I've been thinking about hiring somebody part-time to start, maybe full-time later."

"Do you think I could do it?"

"Of course. You'd catch on in a day or two."

Mercy Grace studied Ruby Jo's shabby dress, rundown shoes, and lank hair. "But first, I think we should take today and have some fun. Let's go shopping in San Jose. Maybe I'll check with a couple of salons and see if we can get your hair done. How's that sound?"

"Oh, Mercy Grace!" Ruby Jo ran her thin hands down the front of her dress. "I don't have money for anything like that."

"I know… Mother. It'll be my treat."

* * * *

Mercy Grace looked carefully around the café as she slid into the booth opposite Linda and Karen. No Harley, thank the Lord.

"What's up?" Linda leaned forward over the table. "You said you have something to tell us."

"Yeah, you sounded so mysterious on the phone," Karen said.

Mercy Grace pulled off her gloves and put them on the seat by her purse. "Let's order, then I'll tell you."

"Oh, come on!" Linda and Karen chimed together but they grabbed their menus.

As soon as Marie, the waitress, walked away with their orders, Mercy Grace said, "You remember I told you my mother had abandoned me when I was a baby and I thought she was dead?"

"Yes."

"Well, she's here."

"*What?*" Karen sloshed coffee out of her cup.

"She showed up at my door Sunday morning."

"Just out of the blue?"

"Yep. I opened the door and there she was."

"What's she like?"

"What's she want?"

"Whoa, one at a time. She's still beautiful in a faded kind of way. Life has pretty much beat her up and she's full of guilt and regret."

"Well, she should be! Running off and leaving a baby." Karen pressed her lips in a hard line.

"What does she want?" Linda asked again.

"A place to rest for a little while," Mercy Grace said. "Maybe a place to stay."

"Are you going to let her?"

Mercy Grace waited for Marie to serve the food and walk away, then said, "Yes. At least for a while.

"Can you forgive her?" Linda paused in slicing her roasted chicken.

"Yes. I think so. I want to. She is my mother."

"I don't know if I could."

"What I really wanted to talk to you both about," Mercy Grace said, "is that you'll be meeting her sooner or later. She's had a really rough time. Please don't ask her any questions or bring up anything about me growing up. It'll just make everything more difficult for everybody."

"We promise," Karen and Linda said together, like a pair of twins. "We won't say a thing."

Later, Mercy Grace spoke to Ruby Jo, "You'll be meeting my friends sooner or later. I've never told them anything about my past, so it would be better if you didn't say anything."

* * * *

Mercy Grace took the week off and, except for the lunch with Linda and Karen, stayed away from town. She didn't see Harley under the streetlamp, but every night at ten o'clock, Mercy Grace asked Ruby Jo to step outside with her while she walked Thunder on a leash within the circle of light from the carport. "It's silly, I know," Mercy Grace confessed, "but I'm kind of scared of the dark." A better explanation than the truth.

* * * *

"Whatever happens, I want you to know, Mercy Grace, how much this week has meant to me," Ruby Jo said over a late breakfast on Sunday morning just one week after her arrival. "I know you've got a lot to hold against me and I appreciate you not throwing it in my face."

"There's no changing the past, Mother. It's over and done with." Mercy Grace studied Ruby Jo over the rim of her coffee cup.

With just one week of rest and good food, a new hairstyle, and some new clothes, Ruby Jo looked like a different woman. The gray was gone from her face and she carried herself taller. She truly was still beautiful. But it wasn't just her looks. She seemed to be finding peace with herself.

"Besides," Mercy Grace added, "I've enjoyed having you here." She realized it was true.

"Well, I can't thank you enough." Ruby Jo slipped Thunder a piece of toast under the table.

"I'll tell you what," Mercy Grace said, "Why don't we go to lunch tomorrow and I'll start showing you the town." *And if we're lucky, we'll run into Harley and I can give him something to think about.*

* * * *

Mercy Grace and Ruby Jo went to town just about every day on one excuse or another—window shopping, manicures, picking up a few groceries—but Mercy Grace didn't see Harley until Thursday. He was sitting on the bench in front of the hardware store across the street as they came out of the bank.

"I need some screws to fix that upstairs towel bar," Mercy Grace said, leading Ruby Jo through the crosswalk and toward the hardware store. Harley watched them through squinted eyes. Just as they were no more than three feet from Harley, Mercy Grace exclaimed in a strong voice, "Oh, you know what I forgot, Mother? Milk!"

From the corner of her eye, Mercy Grace saw Harley's eyes widen, then narrow with suspicion as he watched them enter the store. When they came out a few minutes later, Mercy Grace ran into another stroke of luck as Mrs. Payton was just going in.

"Oh, Mercy Grace! I've been meaning to get back to the Parlor. Do you still have that sweet little needlepoint footstool?"

"I believe we do, Mrs. Payton. Stop by anytime. By the way, I'd like to introduce you to my mother, Ruby Jo. Mother, this is Eleanor Payton."

Mercy Grace couldn't see Harley, but she felt him and knew he was hanging on every word. The two women chatted for a minute and when Mercy Grace and Ruby Jo turned, Harley was gone.

* * * *

Mercy Grace wanted to push her advantage while she had it, so they went to town for something every day for the next three days. Mercy Grace didn't see Harley in the daytime, but she saw him by the lamppost every night. The fourth day, as Mercy Grace and Ruby Jo were walking down the street toward their parked car, Harley stepped out of a doorway directly into their path.

"I don't know who you're trying to pass off as your mama, but I know you, Laney. This shit won't work." His face was contorted with anger. "Two can be more fun than one, but I guarantee I'm gonna do you first, you little twat. And I'm gonna give you some extra for all the trouble you've caused me."

Ruby Jo grabbed Mercy Grace's arm and shrank back, but Mercy Grace stood her ground. "Do I have to get the police to make you leave me alone?"

"Why haven't you got the police already, Laney? Huh? Answer me that."

"I thought you'd realize your mistake and leave me alone. I suggest you do just that or I will go to the police." Mercy Grace took Ruby Jo's arm, stepped around Harley, and led her to the car.

Ruby Jo glanced over her shoulder and said, "Who was that awful man?"

"Just some idiot who has me mixed up with somebody else. Don't worry about it, Mother."

Mercy Grace opened the door, then turned and gazed directly at Harley over the roof of the car. He apparently was not expecting her to look back because there was a look of confusion, even doubt, on his face. The expression was replaced with one of pure hatred when he saw her looking at him. An icy shiver raced down Mercy Grace's spine as she slid behind the wheel and quickly closed the door.

66 – SURPRISE!

Mercy Grace wanted Harley to stew and fret for a while, so she and Ruby Jo stayed busy at the stores and home. Maybe he would conclude he had been mistaken. Not likely, but Mercy Grace was encouraged by the fact she hadn't seen him under the streetlight since the last incident in town.

On Sunday, March 4, Mercy Grace awakened feeling more hopeful than she had in a long time. She decided to celebrate by driving to Monterey and treating Ruby Jo to lunch on the wharf or maybe in Carmel.

It was a little after ten when Ruby Jo called up the stairs, "I'm ready when you are, Mercy Grace."

"Coming." Mercy Grace grabbed her purse and coat and started down the stairs where Ruby Jo was waiting in the hall. Mercy Grace had almost reached the bottom when the doorbell rang. Thunder barked behind the closed kitchen door and Ruby Jo said, "I'll get it."

Ruby Jo opened the door and, over her shoulder, Mercy Grace saw a stranger—a tall, broad-shouldered man wearing a camel-hair topcoat. The man removed his hat and smiled, then his eyes widened and his face froze with shock.

He stared, speechless for a moment, then said, "*Ruby Jo?*"

His deep, smooth voice flowed into the room and curled around Mercy Grace like a hug. He sounded like he could be a radio or television personality and he certainly had the looks for it. A flash of attraction did a little dance low in Mercy Grace's stomach.

When she saw Ruby Jo stiffen and grab the door frame for support, she wondered how this man knew Ruby Jo. Mercy Grace dropped her purse and coat and hurried to the door. She put her hand on Ruby Jo's shoulder and saw that Ruby Jo was as shell-shocked as the stranger.

Before Mercy Grace could speak, Ruby Jo blurted, *"Tully?"*

"What's going on, Mother?"

The stranger swung his dark eyes to her. He swallowed hard, giving his Adam's apple a spasm, and said, "Mercy Grace?"

"What is going on?" A little tremor of uneasiness niggled at her. *"Who are you?"*

The man twirled his hat in his hands. "I'm your brother. Tully French."

The little tremor exploded into a brain whiteout of disbelief and shock as Mercy Grace's legs went out from under her. Her bottom landed on the floor with a plop and she sat open-mouthed, clutching a fistful of Ruby Jo's skirt like a three-year-old, staring up at her worst nightmare.

No! She shook her head. *No. Please. I really can't take any more.*

The man squatted in front of her, put his hand under her chin, and held her face gently. "I'm sorry, Mercy Grace. I really didn't intend to spring it on you like this."

67 – THE BAG MAN

"I don't know about you guys, but I need a little more than coffee," Mercy Grace said, as Ruby Jo brought a tray with a coffee pot, cups, and cream and sugar into the living room.

While Ruby Jo served the coffee, Mercy Grace poured a double shot of brandy into three crystal glasses, handed one to Tully and Ruby Jo, then seated herself in the chair opposite Tully in front of the fireplace.

"I am sorry, Mercy Grace," Tully said. "I planned to ease into this, but I was just so shocked to see Ruby Jo. I don't know why I hadn't thought about her being here. It shouldn't have been a surprise."

"How did you find me?" Before Tully could answer, Mercy Grace added, "Why did you find me?"

"Why?" Tully crossed his long legs and Mercy Grace noticed his expensive Italian leather shoes. "Because I promised my daddy. It was the last thing he asked of me before he died."

He turned and looked hard at Ruby Jo. She said nothing, but her coffee cup rattled in the saucer as she set it on the side table.

"Daddy more than doted on you, Mercy Grace. You brought color, purpose, and joy back into his life. You restored his faith."

Mercy Grace cradled the brandy glass in her hand and watched him as he talked. His face, like his voice, was smooth and strong, broad at the cheekbones and full-lipped, with well-shaped eyebrows and a small cleft just above a square chin. His hands, holding the brandy glass, were slim for a man, the nails neatly manicured.

"Mama and Daddy wanted more babies more than they wanted

anything," Tully continued, "but I was the only one. Then Mama died and I saw Daddy empty out, like a pail of milk spilled on the ground." He passed a hand over his eyes. "I wanted to be enough. Oh, I knew he loved me, he showed me every day, but I wasn't enough to fill the hole Mama's death left in him. But you did, Mercy Grace.

"It was like he was giving Mama a bit of her dream and, by doing that, he had a little of her back. His sun rose and set in you."

He took a sip of brandy and was quiet a minute.

"When we came home late at night that day and found you and Ruby Jo gone, Daddy became a crazy man. Our friend, Jube, drove all night so we could be at your grandparents' house the next morning. They said Ruby Jo hadn't been there. We had to get back home and tend the hogs, but Daddy said to tell Ruby Jo to wait there for him if she showed up. She could go if she wanted to, but he wanted you. He didn't think Ruby Jo did."

Out of Mercy Grace's line of sight, Ruby Jo made a sound that shot a sharp pain through Mercy Grace's heart like a fish hook in the mouth of a trout, but she did not turn and look at Ruby Jo. She kept watching Tully.

"We went back two days later and the place was abandoned. Neighbors said the Cassitys had gone to California." Tully swirled the brandy in the bottom of his glass. "We were pig farmers and in the middle of the Depression. We could hardly feed ourselves, much less the hogs. There was just no way we could look for you in California."

Tully downed the remaining brandy in one swallow and Mercy Grace noticed his hand trembled as he set the glass on a side table. He gripped the arms of the chair.

"That's when Daddy died. His body walked around after that, but there was really nothing left of him. About two years later, I found him in the hog pen one morning. Heart attack, probably."

He turned and looked at Ruby Jo. "You killed him, Ruby Jo," he said, and his voice was so cold Mercy Grace shivered. "You killed him as surely as if you put a bullet in him."

Ruby Jo flew off the couch and knelt by Tully's chair, tears flowing unheeded down her face. She put both hands on his arm and looked at him steadily even though she was visibly shaking.

"There are a lot of things I could say, Tully." Her voice was thick. "I could say I was young and stupid. I could say I was selfish and thoughtless. I could say there was a wildness in me I didn't understand and couldn't control. All of that would be true but none of it means anything.

"There is nothing I can say or do that will change what I did to your daddy and to you and to Mercy Grace... what I did to my mama and daddy... what I did to myself. There is nothing I can say that will take away the regret that eats at me every day. There are no words to say I'm sorry, but I am sorry, more than you can know."

Tears were almost choking Ruby Jo as she continued.

"It's even worse than you think, Tully. After all this time, I've just now, a couple of weeks ago, found Mercy Grace. I can't ask Milo or Mama or Daddy to forgive me, but I've asked Mercy Grace. And I'm asking you. Can you forgive me, Tully?" She squeezed his arm with both hands.

He looked at her. "I don't know."

All the breath left Ruby Jo. She slumped to the floor and curled into herself, her hands over her face. Mercy Grace slid to the floor and wrapped herself close around Ruby Jo, holding her in her arms. The raw agony and distress of Ruby Jo's sobs were so sharp that Thunder began howling in the kitchen.

Tully sat unmoving in the chair, but when Mercy Grace finally glanced at him, tears were rolling unchecked down his face.

* * * *

After Mercy Grace and Ruby Jo regained control and washed their faces, they regrouped in the living room. Tully replenished the brandy glasses and handed one to each of them.

"So, why now, Tully?" Mercy Grace asked. "Why are you just finding me now?"

She was emotionally exhausted and beyond questioning why he had to show up in her life. Her web of lies was squeezing tight around her like a shroud, but there was nothing she could do about it now. In for a dime, in for a dollar. Besides, it could be a good thing. Just one more nail in Harley's theory that she was Laney Belle Hawkins.

"You may remember, Ruby Jo, the big black car that used to drive real slow down the road a couple of times a month?" Tully said and Ruby Jo nodded. "Turns out that was Mama's parents, Grandfather and

Grandmother Oakley. Ever hear of Oakley Bag Company?"

Both women shook their heads and Tully continued.

"My great-great grandfather started making burlap and canvas bags and sacks way back in the eighteen hundreds. The business came down to his son and so on."

"And now it's yours," Mercy Grace said.

"Yeah. I guess you could call me the bag man." He laughed for the first time and it softened the angular planes of his face. "Except now we make all kinds of bags, not just burlap and canvas. You know those fancy department store bags with logos? Specialty holiday bags? We make those. In fact, if it's a sack, we probably make it."

"So how did you get from a pig farmer to a bag man?" Ruby Jo asked and laughed, too.

"Mama was brought up an only child in a wealthy home in Dallas. Grandfather just about had a heart attack when she decided to marry a pig farmer. He absolutely forbade it and, when she rebelled and did it anyway, he disowned her and cut her out of his will.

"When she didn't repent and showed every sign of being happy instead of miserable and crawling back home, Grandfather began to regret what he had done. He and Grandmother did everything they could to make things right, hoping she would forgive them. They tried to see her and sent letters, gifts, and money, but Mama wouldn't accept any of it. She never forgave them."

Tully glanced at Ruby Jo and took a sip of brandy.

"I don't think it was for herself that she wouldn't forgive them. It was because they disrespected Daddy. She loved him so fiercely. Of course, she wouldn't let them see me either, so I didn't know anything about them. I always saw that car go by, and it even stopped once when I was down on the road and the people spoke to me. I imagined all kinds of scenarios, but I never dreamed they were my grandparents.

"A couple of times I heard Daddy tell Mama it was spooky how the Oakleys seemed to know what was going on at the farm almost before it happened, and it was true. Turns out Grandfather had our closest neighbor on the payroll and installed a phone in their house, so whatever the neighbor knew, Grandfather knew it, too."

Tully picked up the brandy decanter and looked at both women. They shook their heads, so he added a splash to his glass.

"I didn't pay much attention when Daddy mentioned strangers named Oakley and I didn't connect them to the big black car that drove by regularly until after Daddy died."

"I saw that car several times myself," Ruby Jo said. "At first I thought it was… somebody else."

"The undertaker had barely taken Daddy away before Grandfather and Grandmother were there. They took me back for the funeral but, other than that, I never went back to Kendalia again. From then on it was a big fancy house, servants, private school, and private tutors. I was numb with shock for quite some time."

Ruby Jo shook her head and said, "Do you ever stop and think how different your life would be if I had stayed with your Daddy?"

"Of course. At first I questioned everything. Why Mama had to go to the cellar that day. Why you had to run off with Mercy Grace." He looked at Ruby Jo as he spoke. "Why Daddy had to die. Why I was left all alone.

"At first I was so angry, I couldn't think straight. I was mad at everybody, Mama, Daddy, you, the Oakleys." Tully uncrossed his legs and planted his feet on the floor. Leaning forward, he continued, "But the Oakleys were patient and kind. They made sure I was busy with new things and new people just about every waking minute.

"In time, I realized I could never go back to the way things had been no matter how mad I was. You want to know the truth?" A small grin played at the corners of his mouth. Mercy Grace and Ruby Jo nodded.

"I became seduced by the Oakley's status and lifestyle. What I really wanted was Mama and Daddy back but with everything the Oakleys offered… but that's a kid for you."

He paused, looking at Mercy Grace. "But why did it take me so long to look for you?" He leaned back and crossed his legs again before answering.

"Well, for a long time it was school, school, school, then college, and in between, Grandfather worked my tail off. Our main office is in Dallas and our actual factory is in Birmingham, Alabama, but we have warehouses in Buffalo, New York, and Oakland, California. I had to learn every phase of the business from the ground up and become familiar with every operation at every location. I even learned to make bags on the production floor.

"Grandmother died not long after I went to live with them, but when

Grandfather died just two years ago, he left everything to me. As much as he had prepared me, it still took some time to hit my stride, but I never forgot my promise to Daddy. So." He threw his arms wide. "Here I am."

"How did you find me?" Mercy Grace asked.

"It wasn't all that difficult. It took a private investigation agency about three days to find a number of Frenches but only one Mercy Grace. And here you are."

"Yes, here I am." The unspoken question in her voice was *what now?*

"First things first," Tully said. "I would like to take you ladies to dinner. Is there a good place nearby?"

"There are several in Gilroy just down the road, or a good place over in Hollister if you like Mexican."

"You choose."

Okay, but Ruby Jo and I need to freshen up a bit."

* * * *

Later, as they were sitting at a candlelit table at Henri's in Gilroy, with the muted sounds of dining and conversation in the background, Tully looked over the top of a very large menu at Ruby Jo. He reached over and touched her hand.

"I'm working on it," he said.

The corners of Ruby Jo's mouth turned up in a small smile and she nodded.

Mercy Grace decided that if she had to have a brother, she was glad it was Tully.

68 – THE TOURISTS

Tully stood at the window in an upstairs guest room and looked at the back of the grand old mansion that was an antique shop and the barn remodeled into a second-hand store off to the right. The early morning sun washed the buildings with a pearly patina and turned dewdrops still blanketing the expansive grounds of the estate into tiny winking crystals. Impressive.

Tully wasn't sure what he had expected, but it wasn't this. He had come prepared to be disappointed. His memories of Ruby Jo hadn't instilled confidence in her parenting skills, so his expectations of his sister ran the gamut from a slattern housewife with a dozen kids and a no-account husband to a brassy waitress, to much worse.

Instead, he found a smart, confident, obviously successful businesswoman who was even more beautiful than her mother but in a less sharp-edged way. He liked her.

So, now what? Tully's plan had been to find Mercy Grace and say hi and bye to fulfill his promise to his father as fast as possible and get out of town. He had allowed ten days for the mission because he didn't know what he would find or how long it would take.

Now, instead of hightailing it back to Dallas, he was thinking he should take those extra days and spend the time getting to know his sister. Yep, good idea. He was due some time off anyway.

He followed the smell of bacon and coffee and found Mercy Grace and Ruby Jo already in the kitchen. A small blue vase with half a dozen daffodils sat in the middle of the table set for three. Ruby Jo was scrambling eggs and Mercy Grace was pouring orange juice. They both looked up.

"Good morning."

"Good morning," Tully said. "It smells awesome in here."

"Have a seat. Hope you're hungry." Mercy Grace filled the coffee cups.

Tully noticed how slim and fine her hands were with neat, short, plainly manicured nails. She was dressed in a soft ivory sweater and charcoal wool pants. Her red hair, a softer, less bronzy color than Ruby Jo's, was held back with a hairband this morning. He wondered where she got her sense of quiet, elegant style. Certainly not from Ruby Jo.

"I'm starving," Tully said and sat in the chair at the end of the table.

When breakfast was finished and they were having their third cup of coffee, Tully said, "You know, I'm in Oakland a couple of times a year, but I've never spent any fun time in San Francisco. I have a few days now, so I'm wondering if we could play tourist and you could show me around... if you have time, that is."

"I wouldn't be much of a guide," Mercy Grace replied. "I'm just in and out of the city for the occasional trade show."

"Well, that's great then. We could learn how to have fun in the city together. Just pack a bag for three or four days and we'll make it a real adventure."

Tully paused, then added, "You too, Ruby Jo," and held his breath. *Say no!* He really wanted to spend the time getting to know Mercy Grace.

"Not me." Ruby Jo stacked the dishes from the table and carried them to the sink. "I promised Sandy I'd relieve her two days at the Attic this week so she can go see her new grandbaby in Hollister. But, you go, Mercy Grace. It would do you good. You never do anything."

Tully let go of his breath and waited for Mercy Grace to answer.

"That actually sounds like fun," Mercy Grace said, "but I won't leave you here alone at night, Mother."

Tully thought that was a little odd and noticed the look of concern on Mercy Grace's face.

"He wouldn't bother me." Ruby Jo turned from the sink and looked at Mercy Grace. "You think?"

"Who?" Tully's muscles tensed.

"Oh, just a case of mistaken identity." Mercy Grace waved her hand in dismissal. "But, he can be a nuisance."

She took a sip of coffee, then put her cup down and stared at it for a couple of minutes, obviously lost in thought. "I'll tell you what. Ruth's son, Bruce, is a big bruiser of a kid. He's a student at San Jose State but he's home every night. I'll bet he could use some extra money. If I can get him to sleep over, I'd love to go!"

"Great!" Tully slapped the table with his palm. Thunder raised his head, looked around, then went back to sleep.

* * * *

They arrived in San Francisco late in the afternoon and checked into adjoining rooms at the Mark Hopkins Hotel on Nob Hill. After their bags had been delivered and the bellboy tipped, Mercy Grace freshened up and changed into a dress for dinner. They found their way to the Top of the Mark and were seated at a window table with the city below sprawling out to the bay.

"What would you like to drink, Mercy Grace?"

"My friend, Linda, got me started on Tom Collins, so that's what I always have."

"Tom Collins it is." Tully gave her order to the waiter and ordered a Rob Roy for himself.

When the drinks were delivered, Tully raised his glass and said, "To family found."

Mercy Grace clicked her glass to his. "To family found," she repeated.

"I have to confess, Mercy Grace, you're not what I was expecting at all with Ruby Jo for a mama, but it seems she's just arrived on the scene, too. So who raised you to be such an outstanding young woman?" Tully noticed her blush and smile.

"Uncle Horace and Auntie Fairy."

"And where was this?"

"Ardmore, Oklahoma." She slowly turned the drink glass with her finger tips and looked out the window.

"What was it like growing up in Ardmore, Oklahoma?"

She shrugged. "Okay, I guess."

Okay. She doesn't want to talk about it. Maybe it wasn't that great, or maybe there was another reason?

Tully ordered another drink and told her more about his childhood, then they moved on to talking about business, his and hers. The golden blaze of the western sky slowly faded to pink, then lavender and finally dark purple beyond the lights of the city. She seemed perfectly willing to talk about her adult life but changed the subject when it came to her childhood. Tully didn't press her.

They had dinner at a little Italian restaurant off Union Square and turned in early. The next day they walked Fisherman's Wharf and ate shrimp out of a paper bag and sidewalk crab cocktails out of paper cups.

After insisting Mercy Grace take a late afternoon nap, Tully took her across the bridge to Trader Vic's for dinner.

"I've been here a couple of times with guys from the warehouse," Tully said. "It's really a fun place."

"This is different," Mercy Grace said, wide-eyed, as Tully guided her across the little wooden bridge and through the flaming tiki torches.

"No Tom Collins for you, my girl." Tully seated himself after holding the chair for Mercy Grace. "You must have one of Vic's famous Mai-Tais."

"Oh, my!" Mercy Grace exclaimed after one long draw of the drink through a straw. "What is this? It's wonderful."

"A lot of rum and a little fruit juice. Be careful. It can knock you on your keister."

The restaurant was busy and they had both finished their drinks before their food arrived.

"Can I have another?" Mercy Grace had her elbow on the table and her chin resting in the palm of her hand. She grinned at him and tucked the paper umbrella from her drink in her hair above her ear.

"I do believe you're tipsy, Mercy Grace."

"I am not. See, I can put my finger on my nose," and she did.

"How about this? Eat your dinner and, when we get back to the hotel, we'll go up to the Top of the Mark and you can have a Brandy Alexander. You'll like it."

Mercy Grace pushed her lower lip out in a pout and then she grinned. A jolt of desire hit Tully right where it counted. *Whoa. Where did that come from?* He forced himself to look at the plate of coconut shrimp the waiter placed before her and said, "Wow. Those look good."

* * * *

The next day Mercy Grace picked up a cherry blossom painted fan in a chintzy souvenir shop in Chinatown and held it up to cover her nose and mouth. She twirled around and spun to a stop in front of him, looking up and batting her eyes over the fan. He was looking down at her and the fleeting look she saw in his eyes was so intense, it took her breath away.

He grinned and said, "Careful there, little one."

They wandered the shops, had tea and dim sum. Mercy Grace bought a Chinese teapot with little cups and a silk, two-piece, multi-colored lounge pajama set for Ruby Jo. Just after dark they found a small "hole in the wall" and ordered Peking duck for dinner. By the end of the day, Mercy Grace had decided that brief look in Tully's eyes had meant nothing. He was her brother, after all.

* * * *

"Today's the tour," Tully said after breakfast on Thursday morning.

"I thought you didn't know anything about San Francisco."

"I said I hadn't been here just for fun, not that I didn't know anything about it. So, lucky you—at least we won't get lost."

They drove out to the beach past Playland, up to Coit Tower, along the Embarcadero, and down Lombard Street on Russian Hill. Mercy Grace held on to the car's chicken strap as Tully negotiated the steep, sharp switchbacks.

"They say this is the crookedest street in the world," Tully said, "but it really isn't. That honor goes to Vermont Street right here in town."

Lunch was at Tommy's Joynt on Van Ness where they consumed thick sandwiches of roast beef on sourdough rolls and ate an entire crock of pickles, all washed down with draft beer.

"No trip to San Francisco is complete without shopping at I. Magnin," Tully said as he helped Mercy Grace out of the car in a parking garage near Union Square.

"Oh, I don't want to shop, but I'd like to just look."

The prices took her breath away. On the second floor, Tully took a soft moss green cashmere robe off the rack and held it up against Mercy Grace. She ran her hands down the fabric.

"It feels like a kitten."

"It's perfect with your red hair."

Mercy Grace checked the price tag and made a face, "Oh, sure."

Tully turned to a nearby clerk and said, "We'll take it."

Mercy Grace grabbed his arm, leaned in close and said, "No, we won't," as the clerk walked away.

"Yes, we will. You're my baby sister. I can give you a gift if I want to."

Over dinner at a small French restaurant on Maiden Lane that evening, Mercy Grace said, "You know, when this is over and we settle up, I'm going to pay for half the trip."

"You will not. It was my idea. When it's your idea, you can pay."

"Deal." Mercy Grace held out her hand. They both laughed and shook on it.

They were the only ones going down in the elevator after their customary Brandy Alexander nightcap at the Top of the Mark that evening, but they were so close their shoulders touched. Tully leaned closer and sniffed.

"Wow. You smell good."

"It's Desert Flower body lotion. I get it at the drugstore in Gazely Creek."

Tully smiled down at her it and tapped her nose with his finger. "Well, it practically makes me drool, so keep wearing whatever it is."

On the last day, they shared a picnic of Italian salami, slabs of Stilton and aged Cheddar cheeses, olives, pickles, sourdough bread, and white wine in Golden Gate Park, then spent the afternoon at the zoo. During dinner that evening, Tully said,

"You're awful quiet tonight."

"I was just thinking. I've had such a good time, I don't want to go home, but I guess nobody could live this way all the time." She twirled the dark red liquid in her wine glass and took a sip.

"Probably not, but we can always do it again sometime."

"I hope so."

* * * *

Tully said goodnight to Mercy Grace at her door. In his own room, he stripped to his boxers, stretched out on the bed, put his hands under this head on the pillow, and absently stared at the ceiling.

What a puzzle his sister was. On the one hand, she was smart and sophisticated, especially when it came to her business, but on the other hand, she was naïve and uninformed. He smiled as he remembered watching her out of the corner of his eye as they checked into the Mark. He could tell she wanted to ogle all the opulence and grandeur, but she did a good job of hiding her awe as she stood waiting for him. She took an almost childish delight in her new discoveries—the view at the Top of the Mark, Mai-Tais at Trader Vic's, Brandy Alexanders, Peking duck, the ride down the crooked road.

He laughed out loud as he envisioned her tucking the paper umbrella in her hair and, just that afternoon, waving and laughing as she rode her white steed round and round on the carousel at the zoo. He could almost bring back her smell—Desert Flower. There wasn't another woman he knew who would have admitted she was wearing an inexpensive drugstore body lotion.

And that woodsy green robe. He would have spent his last dollar to buy it for her. He could just see her in it, soft against her ivory skin, sliding down, baring her shoulders... He sat up and swung his feet to the floor.

What was wrong with him? He had to stop that kind of nonsense. He couldn't remember when he'd had such a good time with anybody, so that's what he needed to think about. Yep. Having a baby sister was just all right.

69 – AWAKENING

"Did you see any sign of that man while I was gone?" Mercy Grace asked Ruby Jo after Tully left on Sunday morning. She'd almost said "Harley." *Be careful.*

"No, but then I didn't have any reason to go into town and, of course, Bruce was here."

"Good. Maybe he's gone." Not a chance. He might have some doubts but he wouldn't give up easily. She knew he figured her debt to him was way too big to walk away.

"So you had a good time?"

"The best. Who would have thought having a brother could be so much fun?"

Tully had promised to visit again. She could hardly wait.

* * * *

For days, Mercy Grace's body was in Gazely Creek but her mind was in San Francisco. She slowly came down to earth and settled back into her routine. Tully called to say he arrived home safely and what a good time he had. After that he seemed to find some reason to call every few days.

She saw Harley under the streetlamp a few times and in town once or twice over the next month. He didn't approach her, but she could feel his hatred as he watched her. Maybe he was more unsure of himself than she thought.

But as long as he was in town he was a risk, so she didn't let her guard down. She was watchful, stayed away from town unless really necessary, double-checked the locks, and didn't walk Thunder at night by herself.

It was not quite five weeks after San Francisco when Tully called to say he had business in Oakland and was hoping he and Mercy Grace could "do something" again.

"Is there anything special you'd like to do?" he asked on the phone. "I only have four days."

"I'll plan something," Mercy Grace replied. "And I'm paying."

"Oh, no you're not."

"Yes, I am. We had a deal."

"If you pay, I'm not going," Tully said.

"Well, if you pay, *I'm* not going," she retorted.

She could hear him sigh on the other end of the phone. "Okay. We'll split it. How's that?"

"Deal."

* * * *

They stayed at a quaint little bed and breakfast in downtown Calistoga. A tour of the wineries around Napa consumed one day. They dined in small, quaint restaurants and cafes. Everything, it seemed, was "quaint." Mud baths and massages on two afternoons left them drained and relaxed, so they had picnic "dinners" and wine delivered. The proprietor allowed them to eat at a small table on the back porch overlooking a tee on a small nine-hole golf course.

"You play golf?" Tully asked, reaching for a piece of cheese.

"Never learned. Never had the opportunity."

"Well, milady, we have to fix that pronto. Tomorrow we'll start with some putting and hit a few balls on the driving range."

* * * *

"You're a natural putter, but your swing leaves something to be desired," Tully said the next day at the driving range, laughing as he watched Mercy Grace swing the club and miss the ball by at least a foot.

He knelt down in front of her. "Your grip is all wrong." He rearranged her hands on the grip and stepped close behind her. "Here. Let me show you." His arms went around her and his hands closed over hers.

Mercy Grace felt him, warm and strong. against her back and had a sudden urge to snuggle into him. *No. Not good.* She felt his body go rigid just as her own muscles tensed.

What was this? Surprised and more than a little confused, Mercy Grace snapped her head around to look at him. Because of his height, he was leaning over her so his face was very close to hers and their eyes met. She stood very still. He blinked, let go of her hands and stepped back.

"I think we better get a pro to give you lessons," he said.

When Tully hugged Mercy Grace goodbye two days later, he made no mention of coming to Gazely Creek again.

* * * *

What was going on? Mercy Grace was distracted and listless. She wasn't sleeping well. Linda had been a little tart with her when she turned down a second lunch invitation. Thunder followed her around all sad-eyed and droopy as if he shared her confusion.

All she could think about was Tully. She remembered practically every minute of their time together, but what occupied her thoughts the most was the golf lesson. She wasn't sure what she had felt, but she experienced it again every time she thought of him holding her.

But what exactly had happened? Was it just her imagination? Whatever it was, it couldn't happen again. But maybe it was just her. He probably didn't notice anything at all. But why wasn't he calling as usual? She put her hand on the phone to call him a number of times, but didn't.

"You seem a million miles away," Ruby Jo said at dinner one evening.

"Am I? Got things on my mind, I guess."

"Be careful, Mercy Grace."

Something in Ruby Jo's voice made Mercy Grace look up from buttering her bread.

"Why? Have you seen that man coming around again?"

"I'm talking about Tully."

"Tully?" Mercy Grace felt a little jolt of uneasiness. "Tully wouldn't hurt me."

"No, but you could really hurt yourself. And him. Just be careful."

70 – PLAYING WITH FIRE

Mercy Grace was preoccupied but she did notice that Harley was appearing more frequently, circling closer and closer now. He was back under the streetlamp most nights and always seemed to be about when she had to go into town. She was constantly on edge, expecting him to approach her or try something. How could she get him to accept she was not Laney, once and for all, and leave her alone? There had to be a way without completely destroying her life.

Then, all thoughts of Harley flew from her mind when, four weeks after Calistoga, Tully called. Mercy Grace held her breath when she heard his voice.

"Hey, I've missed you," he said, sounding perfectly normal and at ease. "I'm in need of a Mercy Grace fix. Can you take a few days off next week?"

So maybe it was just her. She relaxed her grip on the handset. "Sure. What do you have in mind?"

"I don't know. Plan something. Surprise me."

* * * *

Tully acted like nothing had happened, so Mercy Grace decided to put the golf incident out of her mind and act the same. They cut over to Santa Cruz from Gilroy and spent a day walking on the beach and wandering the town. The second day they visited the boardwalk, ate hot dogs and cotton candy, and drank soda pop. Tully won a stuffed monkey from target shooting and she won a goldfish by tossing pennies but couldn't take the fish with her.

Mercy Grace screamed like a crazy woman on the roller coaster. Tully put his arm around her at the peak of the first insane plunge of the cars down the steep tracks and held her tight until the ride ended. When the Ferris wheel stopped for a couple of minutes with their car at the highest point, Tully squeezed her hand until the wheel started moving downward.

Mercy Grace didn't know what to think, but Tully didn't seem to pay any particular attention to the physical contact.

On the third day, they drove down the coast and along the 17-Mile Drive, lunching at Pebble Beach Golf Course. Tully said nothing about a golf lesson. That evening they had dinner on the wharf in Monterey, in a restaurant that barely clung to the shore, with the main dining room suspended on pilings out over the water. They could hear the surf breaking almost under their feet.

They made small talk broken by moments of silence. Several times Mercy Grace glanced up, found Tully looking at her intently, and her heart kicked into high gear.

What was happening? Whatever the quivering of her insides meant, it couldn't be good. But, Lord, she didn't want it to stop. Something in both exciting and terrifying, seemed to be coming alive for the first time. She felt something was being demanded of her but she didn't know what.

The setting sun had left just a bare blush of lavender on the horizon when they left the restaurant and walked along the boardwalk. They stopped and leaned against the railing, watching the surf foam around the rocks below. Mercy Grace didn't know what to say, so she said nothing. After a few moments, Tully spoke.

"Mercy Grace." But her name didn't come out whole. It sounded shattered, like a dish dropped on a stone floor.

She turned to him. He wrapped her in his arms and held her tight against him. She could feel the thud of his heart under her cheek, and she wrapped her arms around him.

"Just think," he whispered into her hair, "a few months ago I didn't know you." Just that. But the tenderness of his voice, the yearning she clearly recognized sent goose bumps racing over her skin and she shivered.

He kissed the top of her head, stepped away and took her hand, leading the way back to the car.

The next day they drove down Highway 1 and toured Hearst Castle at San Simeon. It was a long tour and late when they left the estate.

"You know what?" Mercy Grace said, "It's not too far to the Madonna Inn at San Luis Obispo. I hear it's really exceptional and worth seeing."

"I wonder if we could get in without reservations?"

"I don't know. It's a pretty big hotel"

"Let's give it a shot.

* * * *

"Two rooms for my sister and me," Tully said to the reservations clerk.

"Do you have a reservation, sir?"

"Nope. Spur of the moment."

"Let me see what we have." The clerk turned a couple of pages in a large black book and said, "We only have two rooms available. One is the California Poppy with one King bed and the other is our Pick & Shovel Room."

"Pick & Shovel?"

"It's our Western theme suite, actually three floors. There's a master bedroom and bath on the main floor with a large living area. The second floor bedroom has two double beds and a bath and there are two twin beds in the attic room. That should give you and your sister plenty of room."

Tully looked at Mercy Grace and raised an eyebrow. Alarm bells went off with a clang in her head. *Sharing a room, you're playing with fire. But, oh, I want to be burned. No. You don't. There'll be no turning back. Don't be stupid.* Before she could decide what to answer, Tully said to the clerk, "Sounds great. We'll take it."

It was true. The Madonna Inn had to be one of the most unique hotels in the world. The Pick & Shovel room was definitely Western and rustic with wood ceiling beams, a fireplace, tile floors, a massive red leather couch that could only be custom-made, and a bar with tractor-seat stools in the living area.

As soon as the door closed behind the bellboy, Tully picked up the

343

phone and asked the bar to deliver bottles of liquor and ingredients needed for Rob Roys. "And have an antipasto platter and whatever other appetizers you think we need sent up," he added.

Mercy Grace unpacked her toiletries and lay her nightgown and robe on the bed while waiting for their order to be delivered. She slid onto a stool just as the door closed behind the server and began sampling the appetizers while Tully made drinks. He came around the bar and handed her a drink. Sitting, on the other stool, he clicked his glass to hers and said, "To…" hesitating, then "new adventures."

"To new adventures," she replied.

But their conversation centered on past adventures and most sentences started with, "Do you remember when…?" or "Do you remember that…?" They laughed and teased each other. *Talk about the past good times; just don't talk about now.* Tully made more drinks and most of the appetizers disappeared.

Finally, Tully glanced at his watch. "Good golly! I didn't realize it was so late. We need to get some dinner into you, my girl. We'll order room service."

"I'm not really all that hungry, so make it something light."

"Okay."

"While we're waiting, I need to get out of these travel clothes. I'm feeling a little grungy." She was also feeling a little buzz from the Rob Roys. Not drunk, by any means, but warm and fuzzy.

Mercy Grace took a quick shower, then stood wrapped in a towel debating whether to put on a pair of slacks and a sweater or her nightgown and the soft green cashmere robe. *Put on the pants and sweater. Put on two pairs of pants!* Nonsense. The robe was certainly decent, even appropriate. Nothing suggestive about it. After all, it wasn't a negligee and she wanted to be comfortable.

Besides—she glanced at herself in a mirror—her face was bare of makeup and her hair was still wet. Kind of like a drowned rat. Well, not a rat, but maybe a kitten. A long way from being a *femme fatale!* She laughed at herself and ran a hand through her wet hair.

Tully rose and pulled out a chair for her at the small table brought in by room service.

"It smells heavenly," Mercy Grace said and flicked her napkin open. The linen-covered table held crocks of French onion soup with crusty cheese topping, Caesar salad, sourdough bread and butter. and a bottle of red wine.

"You'll have to come to Dallas sometime," Tully said as he poured the wine.

"I'd like to. What's it like, your place there?"

Tully told her about his house in University Park, the one inherited from his grandparents, and about the Oakley Bag Company headquarters in downtown Dallas. Then they sat on the sofa and watched the latest episode of "Dr. Ben Casey" followed by the late news.

"Sleepy?"

"No," Mercy Grace replied. "Not yet." It wasn't that she wasn't sleepy; she just wanted to be with Tully a little longer.

"Okay. Me neither." He searched for old movies and found "Casablanca" just starting. "How's this? I've seen it a dozen times but I always like it."

"Me, too." She curled her feet under her on the sofa and he sat beside her.

They talked little as the movie played and somewhere along about Sam being asked *"to play it again,"* Mercy Grace put her head back and fell asleep. The next thing she knew, Tully was shaking her shoulder.

"Hey, sleepy head, movie's over."

"Oh, okay." She blinked, yawned and stretched. She took Tully's extended hand and stood but lost her balance for a second. He grabbed her by the shoulders to steady her.

"Whoa! You okay?"

"Yeah, fine," she mumbled, still a little fuzzy with sleep and drinks.

"That's it for you, milady." Tully picked her up in his arms and carried her to the bedroom. At the door he set her on her feet.

"Thanks," Mercy Grace said and tipped her head to smile at him.

"You're welcome," he replied and laid the tip of his finger on her nose. He just stood there, looking at her, his finger on her nose, and she could hear him breathing. Then, slowly, he traced his finger down to her mouth and ran it softly back and forth across her lips. Mercy Grace held her breath. *Oh, no. Yes! No. No.* She didn't move or blink.

Tully groaned and put his palms on each side of her face, then lowered his mouth to hers. The world she knew shattered into a million pinpoints of fierce white light, then slammed back together with a flash of brilliance that took her breath away.

She put her arms around him and held on. He kissed her forehead, her cheeks, her neck, her ears, and her mouth over and over, his hands in her hair, making sounds she had never heard before. She kissed him back, caught in a whirlpool of a new and startling desire that pulled her down, down into the unknown, spinning faster and faster. She was on fire and silently screaming, *oh, Tully, burn with me! Burn with me, baby.*

Holding her tight in his arms, he walked her backward until the back of her legs hit the bed and she fell across it, with him on top of her. With his mouth still working wildly on hers, he raised up, reached between them and pushed her nightgown and robe down. His hand slid down her neck and covered her bare breast and she strained against him.

Suddenly, like he had been jolted with a cattle prod, his body went rigid, then he scrambled off her and off the bed. She raised up on her elbows, her gown and robe down around her waist, and looked at him. He stood with a hand over his eyes, shaking his head. He said something Mercy Grace didn't understand, then he turned without looking at her and stumbled from the room.

Mercy Grace curled up where he had left her on the bed, her arms wrapped around her knees. She shouldn't have let it go so far. No, it was what she wanted. She hadn't realized how she ached for him to touch her, kiss her, until he did. Now, she wanted him to do it again. No. That couldn't ever happen again. *He was her brother. This couldn't be, ever again.*

She would tell him everything. Yes, that's what she would do. No! There was Harley and Ruby Jo and all her friends and her life, everything she had built. Not to mention the legalities, maybe even criminal charges for stealing an identity. No. Telling was the one thing she could not do

It was such a tangle. She finally crawled under the covers to toss and turn all night, her thoughts and emotions writhing and striking at her like a den of sharp-fanged snakes. She awoke exhausted the next morning. Tully came down the stairs dressed and carrying his bag. He didn't look at her.

They hardly spoke during breakfast and on the drive home, only saying what was necessary, neither speaking of what had happened the previous night.

Tully didn't have a rental car. She had picked him up at the San Jose airport and he asked her to drop him there without going back to Gazely Creek.

"Just drop me at the curb," he said. "No need to come in."

So she stopped at the curb near the departure gates, got out and opened the trunk. He pulled out his bag, stood for a minute looking at it, then he raised his head and looked at her. What she saw in his eyes was like a blast of buckshot to her heart, pellets of pity, love, desire, fear, and, yes, anger, shredding her insides and making her stagger. She steadied herself against the open trunk lid.

"Tully…"

Tully cupped her chin in his palm and said, his voice hoarse and ragged, "God help us, Mercy Grace." And then he was gone.

71 – A DARK ALLEY

Mercy Grace told Ruby Jo she was really tired from the trip and stayed home the next day. She lounged around in her pajamas, tried to read or watch TV, but couldn't keep her mind off what had happened with Tully.

What *had* happened, exactly? Nothing she hadn't wanted to happen, hadn't been on edge hoping would happen, if she was truthful, ever since the golf lesson. And, when he finally did take her in his arms and kiss her—boy, did he kiss her—it was beyond anything she had imagined. He ignited something in her so combustible that if someone had struck a match in her vicinity, she would have burst into flames.

She wanted him; no question. When he fled the bedroom at the Madonna Inn, he left her teetering on the edge of a chasm she had never been near before but felt desperate to plunge into, head first. She didn't know what awaited her, but every square inch of her skin, every nerve in her body, every imagination of her mind told her it would be an exquisite burning.

But was that all it was—lust? She relived every minute they had spent together in her mind. Collapsing into a chair by the window, she covered her face with her hands. Did she love him? Yes, she loved him desperately, but she couldn't have him.

He believed he was her brother and she could never tell him otherwise. It would be like setting a bulldozer with a maniac driver loose in her life. So many explanations to so many people, especially Ruby Jo. She thought she had just found her daughter, and now to lose her again. No. They had formed a close bond and Mercy Grace couldn't—wouldn't—do that to Ruby Jo.

She had no doubt if Harley was positive she was Laney, he would act for sure, even recklessly, to make her pay. Then there was the possibility of legal, maybe criminal—even prison—consequences to her for stealing Mercy Grace's identity. No, she would never reveal her secret, not even for Tully. Especially because of Tully. What would he think of her? What would they all think of her?

* * * *

Ruby Jo had already gone to work the following day and Mercy Grace was just walking out the door when the phone rang.

"Mercy Grace?" Tully said before Mercy Grace even said hello. He sounded terrible.

"Yes?"

"A friend of mine has loaned me a cottage in Carmel for a couple of days. Can you meet me there tomorrow?" The words stumbled into each other, like he had to get them out before he changed his mind.

No! Don't do this. I have to. I have to. With only a moment's hesitation, Mercy Grace said, "Yes."

Tully gave her the address and told her where to find the key. "You'll probably be there before me."

"You must have barely gotten off the plane and you're coming back again?" Mercy Grace's voice was low and soft.

"Yes. I'm coming back."

Mercy Grace got through the day but she couldn't have said how because her mind was not on the shop. A dozen times she picked up the phone to tell Tully not to come; she wouldn't be there. It was insanity.

Then she thought about the Madonna Inn, how he had brought her to the brink of something demanding, exciting, even dangerous. Something that might destroy her, but, oh, she wanted it, whatever it was, so every time she dropped the phone like it had bitten her. She would meet him and let the devil take the consequences.

* * * *

Mercy Grace told Ruby Jo she had just learned of a large estate sale in Monterey and needed to check it out the next day. What was one more weenie truth? She arranged for Bruce to stay with Ruby Jo a few nights, then packed her bag for Carmel. She didn't know what she would find at the cottage—no room service, for sure—so just before ten o'clock in the evening she jumped in the car for a quick trip to the liquor store before it closed.

"Cape Fear" with Gregory Peck and Robert Mitchum had just opened that night at the little movie theater, so all the Main Street parking was taken. Mercy Grace swung down the nearest side street and when she saw that was full, too, she said, "Oh, crap."

She sat with the car idling and looked down the alley at a dimly lit off-street parking lot behind the liquor store. Her mind was on tomorrow but, out of habit, she looked all around before she parked and got out of the car. She hurried around to the liquor store and grabbed a few things—ingredients for Rob Roys, a couple of blocks of cheese from the limited selection, and some crackers.

Mercy Grace surveyed the street again as she exited the store. The tavern and the hotel café were still open, but there was no one on the sidewalks. No sign of Harley.

She hurried into the dim alley and juggled the liquor store bags in one arm while she inserted the key in the car door and turned the lock. Suddenly, out of nowhere, her body was slammed against the car, knocking the breath of her and jarring her teeth as her face hit the top of the car. The key, still in the lock, punched into her right side. She dropped the bags.

A hand seized her wrist and twisted her arm behind her back, bringing tears to her eyes. She smelled him. *Harley.*

"I've got news for you, girlie." His mouth was against her ear. "I don't give a shit who you are and I don't give a shit who your pretend mama is. I'm done waitin'. You ain't jerkin' me around no more. You look like Laney, so you can just pay up for Laney. Pretty as you are, you'll do."

"No!" Mercy Grace said out of the corner of her mouth not squashed against the car. The acid of fear seared her insides, seeped through her pores and burned her skin.

"Now, here's what you're gonna do, girlie." He jerked her arm up a little more and sent a jolt of new pain across her back. "Open this door real easy like and slide over into the passenger seat. I'll drive." He laughed and she felt his wet tongue circle her ear. "I know a place that's real quiet. Nobody to bother us. You're gonna have so much fun."

"No!" Mercy Grace tried to kick him in the crotch but her backward kick missed the target. He tightened his hold or her arm and said,

"You little bitch!"

"Hey! You there!" a male voice shouted from just a few feet away, and a couple getting into their car on the street near the end of the alley stopped and looked toward them.

Harley's hold on her loosened a little as he turned toward the sound. Mercy Grace brought the elbow of her free arm up and back as hard as she could and caught Harley under the chin.

"Shit!" Harley said, releasing her and striking a glancing blow on the side of her head with his fist as he turned away and fled. Mercy Grace saw stars for a minute and clung to the car to keep from falling.

"You there! Stop!" the man said, shaking his cane at the disappearing Harley. Mercy Grace recognized Mr. Ambrose on his way to the tavern for his usual nightcap. With his poor eyesight and the darkness, it was unlikely the old man would recognize her unless he was within arm's reach.

She grabbed the sacks from on the ground and threw them into the passenger seat. At least one bottle was broken. She slid into the car, started the motor with shaking hands, and sped out of the alley. As she turned onto the street, she could see Mr. Ambrose in the rearview mirror, still shaking his cane.

Her hands trembled on the steering wheel.

Go to the police now. He's going to kill you like he did your mama.

She slowed down as she approached the street that led to the police station, then sped up and passed the corner. She would go to the police, but not tonight. That would mess everything up and she wouldn't make it to Carmel tomorrow. Nothing must stop her going to Carmel; she had to see Tully.

72 – CARMEL COTTAGE

"You're white as a sheet." Ruby Jo was sitting at the kitchen table with a glass of milk and a plate of cookies when Mercy Grace walked in. "What happened? That man again?"

Mercy Grace nodded. She didn't trust herself to speak just yet. If she did, she'd burst out screaming and never stop.

"Here, sit down." Ruby Jo pulled out a chair for her. "I'll make some coffee. Or would you rather have some brandy?"

Mercy Grace shook her head.

"I don't know what's going on with that man, Mercy Grace, but you have to do something about this. I'm afraid he's going to really hurt you."

"I will, Mother. As soon as I get back from my trip. Right now I just want a shower and the bed."

Mercy Grace threw all the clothes she was wearing into the trash, and then stepped under scalding water in the shower. She scrubbed her ear so hard she thought it would fall off.

There was no way she could sleep. What she really wanted was to get in the car and head for Carmel tonight, but Bruce wasn't coming until tomorrow. Ruby Jo couldn't be left alone.

Mercy Grace put on pajamas and climbed into bed, then patted the covers on the other side of the bed. Thunder cocked his head and looked at her.

"Okay, come on." She patted the bed again and Thunder hopped up and sprawled out, fully taking up his side of the bed. "I'm sure I'm going to regret this, so don't get too comfy." Thunder's eyes were already closed.

Mercy Grace dozed fretfully, resting a hand on Thunder's neck most of the night, and was up and on the road early. She drove by rote, her mind blasting her with thoughts as rapid fire as machine gun bullets.

The raw fear from her encounter with Harley still clung to her like sweat on a hot summer day, but she pushed it to the corners of her mind. She would deal with that when she returned home.

Right now—Tully. What did it mean, Tully coming right back? Was he regretting what happened? If so, why was he coming back? Did he want to move forward with this… what was it? A relationship? How could that be? He thought she was his sister. He wouldn't be wanting to move forward, just the opposite. So why *was* he coming?

Maybe a better question was why she on her way to meet him? The whole thing was impossible. And what did Tully think of her meeting him in the privacy of the cottage, thinking she was his sister?

Harley no longer cared whether she was Laney or Mercy Grace, so hiding the truth provided no protection against him now. But still, even with the change in Harley's motives, she couldn't just blow up her life. She had worked too hard and too long. Whatever the answer, exposure wasn't it.

Mercy Grace arrived at the beach cottage in Carmel in early afternoon. It was gray-shingled, with a steep roof and large French casement windows overlooking mini-dunes of sand, sea grass, and driftwood. Standing on the porch, Mercy Grace could see a small sheltered beach and the ocean beyond.

She chose a lovely bedroom with lots of flowered yellow chintz to deposit her bag. Then she made a pitcher of Rob Roys and spread out the snacks on a big stainless steel island in a kitchen with a Mexican tile floor and lots of white cabinets. Now what? A walk on the beach? No. Tully hadn't said when to expect him and she wanted to be there when he arrived.

Mercy Grace settled onto a chaise near the window and picked up an issue of "Life" magazine with a picture of Bob Hope in an Indian headdress on the cover. She thumbed through a few pages. The sun fell through the window and across the lower part of her body. It was warm and peaceful. She put her head back and fell sound asleep.

She awoke with a start with a crunch of tires on the gravel driveway. Where was she? How long had she slept? *Tully!* She jumped up, ran to the door and opened it just as Tully stepped onto the porch. He had a two-day stubble of beard, looked rumpled and wasn't carrying a suitcase. His face was drawn and there was a look of weariness about his eyes.

Tully stood just outside the door, looking at her for a long moment, and then passed a hand over his eyes. Mercy Grace didn't know what to say or do, so she waited.

"I had to see you again to be sure," Tully said, his voice slow, deliberate.

"Of what?"

"Whether or not I can be around you and be a brother." He put both hands in his pockets and took a step backward. "I told myself I could… that the other night was just temporary insanity, but…oh, God, Mercy Grace!"

The abject sadness on his face brought a flood of tears to Mercy Grace's eyes. He reached out, wiped her tears away with his thumbs and then rested his palms on her cheeks.

"I cannot do it, Mercy Grace. The love I have for you is not brotherly. Sooner or later something awful is going to happen if I'm around you." The words were moist and thick and he swallowed hard. "I can't see you anymore. I'm sorry. Please understand." He turned and was down the steps in one leap.

"Tully… wait! There's something…"

Tully jumped in the rental car, slammed the door and slung gravel every direction as he sped away. Mercy Grace slid down the wall and sat on the floor in the open doorway. What just happened? Never see Tully again? Is that what he said? *He said he loved her.*

She couldn't think straight anymore. Conflicting thoughts banging into each other. Raging emotions hammering her, first one way and then another. And fear, always that layer of fear. All of it writhing like a ball of snakes in a boiling cauldron. How did her life get to be such a mess? Just a few months ago everything had been perfect. When had it fallen apart?

Harley. Ruby Jo. Tully. They had torn up her life. It was their fault. What right did they have to come into *her life*, into *her town* and ruin everything? *How dare they?* A searing anger obliterated every other emotion.

Mercy Grace put her head back on the wall, closed her eyes, clenched her fists, pounded her heels against the floor with a rapid-fire tat-tat-tat, and shrieked at the top of her lungs.

When she was screamed out, she took the pitcher of Rob Roys, a glass, and a platter of cheese and crackers out to the small table and rocking chair on the front porch.

The more Rob Roys she drank, the madder she got. *Who did they think they were?*

She wasn't going to take it anymore. She never asked for a mother or a brother. She had been doing very well, thank you, so they could just go live their lives somewhere else and leave her alone.

And Harley. There had to be a way to get rid of Harley without upsetting her own apple cart. What she really wanted to do was shoot him. Too bad Thunder hadn't killed him that night. Auntie Fairy would figure out what to do in about one second. *I want Auntie Fairy!*

Tears pooled in her eyes and ran down her cheeks. *Help me, Auntie.* She bawled like a newly branded calf until she ran out of Rob Roys, her nose dripped, and she got hiccups.

Mercy Grace sat on the porch until the moon was high in the sky. She tried to focus her blurry vision on the golden path the moon laid down on the ocean and her blurry mind on hearing an answer in the whisper of the waves rolling onto the sand. But the waves were like an old phonograph record stuck in a groove. *This is on you*—wave comes in. *Figure it out*—wave goes out.

Maybe it was right there in front of her. Just walk down to the beach, then across the golden bridge, all the way to that big moon. Disappear again... forever.

73 – THE BLAME GAME

The next morning Mercy Grace made it as far as the San Juan Batista turnoff before she had to get out of the car and walk around a bit. A sharp-edged ache delivered a hammer blow right to the middle of her forehead precisely every five seconds and her stomach was in all-out rebellion. What idiot would drink themselves into this condition? Never again.

Obviously alcohol didn't make one smarter or more clever, for she hadn't solved a thing in her stupor. Her thoughts still twisted and turned in her mind like a jungle of poisonous vines. *Ruby Jo. Tully. Harley.* Around and around.

Ruby Jo. Mercy Grace had begun to not only understand Ruby Jo as she heard more and more of her story, but had come to care about the woman. She enjoyed Ruby Jo's company and the woman was certainly a big help in the Attic. She had taken to the secondhand store like she was born to it.

And, Mercy Grace didn't have a mother in her life… at least not until Ruby Jo came along. Nothing wrong with having a mother. Besides, she owed it to the baby Mercy Grace.

Mercy Grace could work around Ruby Jo and stay safe. It was Harley and Tully who made such a mess of her life. Tully, the forbidden brother. Harley, the coward that preyed on women. That thought startled her. *That's him all right, mean sniveling little coward. Why didn't I see that?*

The July midday sun beat down on her as she leaned against the car. A trickle of perspiration ran from her hairline and down her cheek. Still, she stood unmoving, her attention caught by a hawk riding a current of warm air, circling, circling high above. That was her. Caught in a whirlpool of doubt, indecision, and fear. And, yes, anger. She clenched her teeth and balled her hands into fists. What right did any of them have to come into her life and threaten everything she had become?

Then, the little thought that had been wiggling around in the back of her mind, probing for an opening to make itself known, jumped out and whacked her right between the eyes.

Harley and Tully aren't the problem, Mercy Grace. You're the problem.

I am not.

Yes. You are. You got yourself into this mess.

It's not my fault. I was minding my own business...

How long are you going to wallow in self-pity? Fear? You used to be in charge of your life. Why have you let these people take control?

But, I didn't let them. They just barged in...

Enough. Stop the blame game. You're a bigger coward than Harley.

I am not!

Then tell Tully everything.

I can't.

You love him.

Yes.

Then it's simple. Tell him the truth or never see him again. Choose.

Ah. Back to Linda's simple question. Which choice scared her most? Both terrified her, but the one she could not live with was never seeing Tully again. Okay, I have to tell him.

Good. But first, you have to take care of Harley.

Mercy Grace pushed off the car, inhaled and exhaled deeply and said aloud., 'Okay. Exactly how am I supposed to do that?"

She waited. Her mind didn't answer.

* * * *

The next morning Mercy Grace was sitting on the sofa in the living room, her legs curled under her, drinking her third cup of coffee, and thankful it was Sunday. She needed the quiet time. An elusive idea about how to deal with Harley had been hovering in the shadows of her thoughts and she needed to think it through. The TV was turned on low and a show about canning and preserving vegetables was playing in the background when Ruby Jo popped in the door.

"Hey, Mercy Grace, I want to wear my new dress to work tomorrow but I don't have any red shoes. Can I borrow yours?"

"Sure. They're on the top shelf of my closet."

Ruby Jo clattered up the stairs and Mercy Grace leaned her head back against the sofa pillow and closed her eyes, the drone of the TV becoming white noise in her ears. She dozed until she had a sudden funny feeling that someone was watching her. Her head snapped up and she opened her eyes to see Ruby Jo leaning against the door frame definitely staring at her.

"What?" Mercy Grace sat up and put her feet on the floor. Ruby Jo looked odd, her face drawn and her eyes red-rimmed and puffy, like she had been crying. "What's the matter?" Mercy Grace put her hand on the arm of the sofa to push herself up, then stopped, wariness making her hesitant.

"When are you going to tell him?"

"Who?" Mercy Grace leaned back in the sofa. *Bad feeling. What's she talking about?*

"Tully."

"Tell him what?"

"What he needs to know." Ruby Jo propped a fist on her hip.

"What are you talking about?" Uneasiness crawled on Mercy Grace's skin like a rash needing a scratch.

"You'll figure it out. I wouldn't wait too…" Ruby Jo turned away as the doorbell rang. " "I'll get it."

"What now?" Mercy Grace threw her hands up and flopped back on the sofa as she heard a murmur of women's voices in the hall.

"Okay, we want to know what the hell is going on, Mercy Grace, and don't give us any more crap," Linda said as she and Karen walked into the living room. Ruby Jo gave a fluttery wave as she passed the door and headed upstairs.

Linda and Karen had shown up unannounced, so Mercy Grace was still in her pajamas. Both women seated themselves without being invited.

"You've begged off lunch four times in a row," Linda said. "Have we offended you in some way?"

"Good heavens, no!"

"Then what's the problem?"

Mercy Grace was truly stumped. No lie sprang to her lips, so she sat speechless, staring at her friends.

"Does it have anything to do with that man?"

That brought Mercy Grace's voice back. "What man?"

"Then it wasn't you in the alley behind the liquor store?" Karen said, sounding just like her cop husband.

Mercy Grace's heart gave her a couple of ninja kicks right to the ribs. Had Mr. Ambrose recognized her? "What are you talking about?"

"I ran into Fred in town yesterday and he said old man Ambrose had come into the police station with a story about a woman being assaulted a couple of nights ago. He said it was you at first. Then he said it might've been Gloria Helmsted or maybe Kelsey Clark. By the time he finished the story, he had named half a dozen women."

"Could he identify the man?"

"No. Said he hadn't seen him before, but Fred said as confused as the old man is, it was probably nothing more than a couple of kids making out in the alley."

The hard knot in Mercy Grace's stomach started to soften a little. "What did Johnny think?"

"I don't think he's heard about it. He's been up in Sacramento the last few days on police business."

Mercy Grace's stomach knotted up again. Johnny Costello ran a tight town. He wouldn't laugh off this incident as easily as his deputy, Fred. Johnny would ask questions. Mercy Grace would probably be at the top of his list. The trail could lead to Harley.

Mercy Grace saw her life unraveling before her eyes as surely as if she had thrown a ball of yarn across the floor and watched it spin out of control.

No more wiggle room. Action was being forced on her. But she wasn't ready. There were still so many loose ends in her plan to deal with Harley. It had to be perfect… smooth. So many things could go wrong. Didn't they say a coward cornered was the most dangerous of all threats?

All the nerve endings in Mercy Grace's body jumped like popcorn in a hot skillet.

She couldn't wait any longer. Tomorrow. There was no stopping it now—her life was on a roller coaster plunging straight to hell.

74 – SHOWTIME

Early the next morning, Mercy Grace opened her closet door to take down a battered box from the top shelf. *Now, why is that box on that end of the shelf? I always put it on the right side.* She shrugged. *Oh, well, I don't know what I'm doing half the time anymore. Lucky I don't forget my name.*

Mercy Grace put the box on the bed and removed Mama's old purse. She hugged it to her for a minute, then positioned it carefully in direct sunlight on a table in front of her bedroom window. Shooting from every angle and being careful to get close-ups of the big dark stain still visible on the side of the purse, Mercy Grace exposed an entire roll of film. By nine o'clock she was on her way to San Jose.

Before noon she had an airline ticket to Dallas for the following day in her pocket and was on her way back to a one-hour development shop to pick up the pictures.

Mercy Grace knew the strawberry processing plant parking lot would be a beehive of activity at four o'clock when the day shift ended and the swing shift arrived, so she could observe and check out the lay of the place without calling undue attention to herself. She arrived ten minutes early and parked at the far end of the lot.

Two super-size overhead doors were open, revealing women sorting berries on conveyor belts near the entrance and a forest of machinery in the cavernous space beyond. Her plan depended on those big doors being open when the graveyard clean-up crew arrived, but she had no way of knowing if they would be or if Harley would even show up for work.

She noted a small one-story building at the edge of the parking lot with a sign on the door that read "Office" and "Monday—Friday, 8 a.m.—5 p.m." Reserved parking spaces beside the building would be in darkness at midnight, a perfect spot to watch and wait without being seen. Satisfied she had prepared as much as she could, Mercy Grace drove home.

She was back fifteen minutes before the swing shift ended at eleven-thirty. Wearing black clothing and cap, her hair caught back in a ponytail, she stood in the dark shadow of the office building, watching as the workers ended their shift, climbed in their cars and left.

A half a dozen or so night-shift cleanup crew members arrived and parked in the spaces closest to the overhead doors, which were open and casting large blocks of light far back into the parking lot. Mercy Grace was shaking so hard she had to lean against the building to keep from falling. She put her hand in her pocket to make sure the envelope was there.

At ten minutes to midnight, Harley's beat-up blue pick-up rolled into the parking lot. He parked beside the last car to arrive before him, in the last slot, at the greatest distance from the open doors. She had to time it just right. He had to be close to the big doors, in full light, close enough to be seen but not heard by the men working inside.

Don't think. Just do it. As Harley slouched toward the open doors, she walked fast in her soft-soled shoes to close the distance between them. When he was in the best spot, Mercy Grace inhaled deeply, clenched her fists and called, "Harley!"

He spun around and, even with the light at his back, she could see the shock on his face. He stared at her, slack-jawed, for a minute, then he grinned. "I knowed it! I knowed it was you. You can't fool ole Harley." Then, suspiciously, "What are you doing here?"

Mercy Grace willed her voice to be steady. "You know nothing, Harley." She stepped closer and took the envelope out of her pocket. Holding it out to him, she said, "I brought you something."

While he pulled the pictures out and looked at them, she glanced over his shoulder at the activity inside the doors. The few men she could see were going about their business. One glanced toward her and Harley, then turned away, easily within shouting distance if needed.

"What the hell is this?" Harley sorted through the pictures quickly.

"It's pictures of Mama's purse, Harley. If you look closely in good light, you'll see the dark splotches of Mama's blood. Do you have any idea what all the police can find out from a little dried blood, even years later?"

Thanks to Joe Friday and the "Dragnet" show she used to watch for that idea.

Harley's head snapped up and he threw the pictures on the ground like they were a fistful of hornets. He squinted at her and she could see the wheels turning.

"Don't even think about it, Harley. You'll never get your hands on her purse. That purse and a long letter about everything that happened the night you killed Mama are in a sealed box in my attorney's safe. He'll only open it if something... anything happens to me.

"And, I do mean anything. If I die from a bee sting, if an airplane falls out of the sky on me, if I choke to death on a piece of meat, that box gets opened. Did you know there is no statute of limitations on murder, Harley?"

His lips drew back from his teeth. "You bitch. It was an accident."

"Was it? Good luck with that story. I can testify how you regularly beat Mama nearly to death and it won't be just me. What about the farmer's wife, Mazie? She saw Mama beat black and blue with her eye swollen shut. And what about burning down the tent?"

Harley shifted from foot to foot as he glanced nervously over his shoulder at the open doors.

"And, that's not all. You're a nuisance, Harley, and I'm tired of fooling with you, so here's what's going to happen." Mercy Grace saw the heaving of his chest and the clenching of his fists but she swallowed and continued, commanding her voice to be hard, cold. "You're going to find another town and another job, preferably in another state. Do you understand me?"

"You can't make me leave me."

"Yes, I can. You see, you're right about one thing, Harley. I've done very well for myself and I have more money than I need. I have enough to hire a couple of private investigators to go down to Rockford, Texas, and nose around, ask questions for however long it might take to find out what happened that night. See what they can dig up. People in small towns see things, Harley. Exactly what did you do with Mama's body?"

Harley made a noise deep in his throat and rocked on the balls of his feet.

Mercy Grace forced her voice to be stronger, a little louder. "Do you think somebody might have seen something? Maybe that farmer's wife, Mazie, is still around. She was an awful nosy woman. Mama told her a lot, you know. And, bones, Harley. You know bones last forever? Just one little bone is all the police would need." Mercy Grace had no idea if that was true.

Harley was breathing hard and his eyes were wide with the look of a trapped animal facing a mortal enemy.

"Give it up, Harley. It's over."

As she said the words, she realized it was true. It was over. Her body wanted to go limp with relief, but she held herself stiff and upright. "If I see you in town again, I will make your life a living hell. You'll be looking over your shoulder every minute. Do you understand me?"

Mercy Grace saw the confusion, indecision, and raw rage in the contortion of his face. His body quivered with the power of it. She braced herself for an attack, waiting to see if he would be so reckless.

"Damn you, Laney Belle Hawkins," he snarled. "Damn you to hell."

He stalked to his pick-up, slammed the door, started the motor, gunned it, and careened out of the parking lot. Two men near the door of the plant looked up. One stepped outside, stared at the speeding pickup, then looked at Mercy Grace.

She forced herself to smile and give him a little wave, then walk casually to her car. In the darkness, she supported herself with one hand on the trunk, leaned over and threw up.

75 – A LONG CONVERSATION

Mercy Grace held herself as hard and cold as an ice cube during the confrontation with Harley, but as soon as it was over, she shook so violently she thought she would knock the enamel off her teeth.

Now, there was no way she could sleep, so she sat in a chair, in the dark, in her bedroom through the night. Thunder lay on the floor at her feet or sat by the chair with his head on her lap.

Mercy Grace didn't have breakfast the next morning, but she did go down for a cup of coffee and told Ruby Jo she would be out of town for a couple of days. It took less than an hour to shower, dress, and pack a small bag. The flight to Dallas wasn't until four o'clock that afternoon, so she decided to use the extra hours to catch up on some paperwork.

It was impossible to focus on the columns of figures, so she paced the small space of her home office just off the kitchen. Should she tell Tully she was coming? No. What would she say when she saw him? How would she tell him? She didn't know. Would Harley really leave town? Yes.

Mercy Grace and Thunder jumped at the sudden assault on the silence when, close to noon, the doorbell rang. Not just a ding-dong but over and over like somebody was really leaning on the bell. They raced for the door, Thunder leading and adding to the confusion with his barking. She ordered Thunder to sit and shut up, then jerked the door open, more than a little irritated at the insistent interruption.

Her world went tilt and she emptied out of every sensation except shock. It was the feeling she had when the roller coaster plunged from the highest peak at insane speed and her stomach was left at the top. She grabbed the door frame for support. She wasn't ready. She thought she still had hours to prepare!

"*Tully?*"

He looked worse than he had in Carmel. His beard was scruffier, his cheekbones more pronounced, and his eyes seemed darker. His jacket hung looser on his frame. If a man ever looked like he was fighting demons, it was Tully.

Mercy Grace clung to the door frame but held the other hand out to Tully. He didn't take her hand and instead rocked back on his heels a bit.

"Tully…"

"No, Mercy Grace. I need to have my say before you say anything… please."

Mercy Grace nodded, her heart pounding, and extended her arm as an invitation for him to come in. He stepped into the hall, but left the door open.

Tully shook his head, ran a hand over his face and then looked at her. The pain in his eyes sliced through her. "Oh, God, Mercy Grace! We've unleashed hell and I'm afraid we're going to be consumed."

"Tully…"

He held up his hand, palm toward her. "No. Let me say my piece."

Mercy Grace waited while Tully stood rigid, a slight frown making a little "V" between his eyebrows.

"All I do is think about you, Mercy Grace. I can't sleep; I can't eat. I can't focus on work."

Mercy Grace's heartbeat kicked into high gear. She wanted to throw her arms around him, kiss away the pain she saw on his face. *Whatever price she paid to be loved by this man would be worth it. But would he want her when he learned she was a liar, a fraud, maybe a criminal?*

"I don't know what to do. I can't be with you and I can't be without you." He put his hands in his pockets. "Everything I know, everything I've been taught tells me that loving you is wrong. But it doesn't feel wrong, Mercy Grace. It feels so right and it's driving me crazy." His chin quivered.

She had to stop him; the pain was too much. "Tully…"

"No. No. I have to say it all. If I don't say it now, I don't know if I ever can. I love you and I want to be with you, the devil be damned. I can't believe I'm even thinking what I'm thinking. Oh, God!"

"I'd be asking you to do something so unacceptable, so repulsive, so unspeakable to others, it would plunge you right into hell with me. It would mean a life in the shadows…" His Adam's apple jumped as he swallowed hard.

A shadow life. Exactly what I have been living all these years.

"The secret would destroy us if it became known," he continued. "So, here's the thing… if you feel the same… do you love me?"

She nodded. "I do, but, Tully…"

"Having the same last names isn't necessarily a problem." He talked fast, words spilling out topsy-turvy. "There are a lot of people with the same last names who aren't related. Or we could get married in Mexico. The main thing is children. We could never have children."

Beads of perspiration tricked from his forehead and into the stubble on his face. "So you have to think about whether you can give up children. I saw my doctor … a vasectomy prevents children."

"*Tully.*" Her voice was barely a whisper. "Tully," she said again, louder, to steady herself. "You haven't…"

"No. My doctor wouldn't to it. He says I'm too young and don't have any kids yet. But I could get it done in Mexico."

"*Thank the Lord.*" Mercy Grace grabbed his arm and squeezed.

"I know what I'm asking, Mercy Grace. I have no right… but I have to try… figure out something. It's all I can think of." His shoulders sagged, everything about him sagged, as he stood like he was waiting for his turn with an executioner. "I can't let you go." His voice was almost a whisper. He reached out his hands to her. The plea she saw in his dark eyes was desperate and savage.

"I have something to tell you, Tully." She grasped both his hands and pulled him gently forward. "Please, come and sit in the living room. I'm going to call Ruby Jo to come over from the store. I can only tell this once."

Mercy Grace didn't trust herself to sit with Tully and not blurt out the truth while waiting for Ruby Jo and she did know she could only tell it once. She busied herself making coffee in the kitchen, trying to think what to say. Ruby Jo walked in just as Mercy Grace handed a cup of coffee to Tully.

"What's going on?" Ruby Jo's eyes widened when she saw Tully and her gaze flew to Mercy Grace. "So, you decided to tell him?"

"Yes. And you."

"What?" Tully's head swung back and forth between them.

"Well, before you do, I have something to say."

"Okay." Mercy Grace inhaled sharply. After that weird conversation with Ruby Jo the day before, what now?

"First, I want you to know I'm not saying this because I want a free ride or to feather the nice nest you've given me here." Ruby Jo picked up a cup, filled it with coffee and sat on the couch. "Thanks to you, I'm back on my feet. I know I could go to Gilroy or San Jose, get a job and take care of myself."

"Okay," Mercy Grace repeated.

"You've given me something far more than a place to stay and a job. Whatever happens, I want you to know, you are the daughter I never had. Nothing can change that."

"What's going on?" Tully put his coffee cup on the table and stood.

"How did you know?" Mercy Grace asked.

"The red shoes." Ruby Jo took a sip of coffee. "When I got them out of the closet, I knocked down a box. A Bible, an old purse, and some letters fell out. I knew the Bible was Mama's, so I picked it up. And I read the letters."

"I'm sorry, Ruby Jo."

"If there's blame, Mercy Grace, it's mine." Tears shimmered in Ruby Jo's eyes.

Tully threw his arms in the air. "*WHAT THE HELL IS GOING ON?*"

"Sit down, Tully," Mercy Grace said and, sitting in the chair opposite his, she began. "This is going to be a long conversation."

76 – THE AWFUL TRUTH

Mercy Grace didn't know where to start, so she took a deep breath and started at the beginning. Keeping her eyes on Tully, she said, "My birth name was Laney Belle. I was born to Calvin and Mattie Hawkins on April 2, 1933, at Menard, Texas."

Tully stared at her in disbelief for about one second, then he jumped out of his chair, almost knocking it over. "Wait a minute." He put his hand on the back of his neck like he had a headache, looked down at the floor, then up at her.

"You're not my sister?"

Mercy Grace saw in his eyes the instant when full understanding registered. *"Damn! You're not my sister."*

He pulled her from the chair, and spun her around, laughing. *"You're not my sister."*

"No, I'm not."

"Damm. You're sure I'm not dreaming."

"I'm truly not your sister, Tully."

Tully pulled her to him and kissed her with such abandon and exuberance, Mercy Grace could hardly catch her breath. She couldn't help but laugh as he set her on the floor. "I'm sorry I put you through all this."

"That's not important."

"There's more."

"Nothing else matters as long as you're not my sister."

"I have to tell it all, Tully. Now."

She settled back in her chair. It took a long time. Sometimes she was so overwhelmed with the enormity of it all and her own audacity, she choked up and couldn't speak. Sometimes she tasted the salt of her tears in her mouth as she spoke. Tully paced and often swore and Ruby Jo wept though almost all the telling.

"And, so, I told Harley he had to leave town and never come back." Her last words were strained and weak with exhaustion.

"That bastard," Tully said. "You should have let me get my hands on him."

"No. I had to do it, Tully." Mercy Grace twisted her hands in her lap, one foot nervously tapping the floor. Every word of the telling had chipped away at her shield of safety and now she was shivering, naked and exposed in a jungle of uncertainty.

She turned to Ruby Jo. "I'm sorry I stole your baby's name. I'm sorry I'm not your real daughter."

Now the tears came in a flood and her body shook with sobs. Tully and Ruby Jo both knelt by her chair and wrapped her in their arms. They held her for several minutes until Mercy Grace cried herself out.

"You shouldn't be sorry," Ruby Jo said, brushing a strand of damp hair off Mercy Grace's face. "You didn't kill my baby. If anybody did, it was me. I'm just glad her name helped you. You make a beautiful Mercy Grace and I'm so proud of you."

"Oh, Ruby Jo!" Mercy Grace started wailing again.

Ruby Jo continued to hug and rock her as Tully took a bottle of brandy out of the liquor cabinet and poured three small glasses. "I think we can all use a little of this."

"So, now you know everything. I'm a liar and a cheat and probably a criminal. I'll go to prison." Had there been any tears left in her, Mercy Grace would have burst out crying again. Instead she hiccupped.

"I seriously doubt it," Tully said.

"I think I will." Mercy Grace couldn't let go of the old fear.

"That's just a fear that coward drummed into you when you were little to keep you a prisoner."

"But what if I do have to go to jail?"

"I don't see why any of this has to go beyond the three of us." Tully poured another splash of brandy into his glass. "I'm not an expert in the law, Mercy Grace, but even if all this did get out, I can't see there being any serious consequences. I mean, who have you actually hurt?" He swirled the brandy and took a sip. "First, somebody would have to go to the law and complain..." He turned to Ruby Jo.

"Not me!" Ruby Jo held up her hand, palm out. "Never. Ever. No matter what. I swear. She *is* my daughter."

"Even if I don't go to jail, I can't go back to being Laney Belle. I *am* Mercy Grace French."

Tully tossed back his brandy and set the glass on the side table by Mercy Grace's chair. He knelt in front of her. "Well, if you marry me, no question your name will be French forever, so no problem there."

Mercy Grace's eyes widened and she inhaled sharply. "Do you mean it?"

"I do." Tully took her hands in hers. "Will you?"

"Yes. *Yes!*"

Tully pulled her close and kissed her while Ruby Jo clapped. "You haven't just made me happy, Mercy Grace. I think you saved my life!" Tully laughed and pushed off his knees.

"But what about this mess I'm in?"

"Have you or Ruby Jo told anyone I'm your brother or mentioned you have a brother?" Tully sat in the chair opposite her.

"All my friends think I have no family, except now, Ruby Jo. I haven't told them any different... I guess mainly because I've been so busy and distracted lately I haven't had time to even talk to them."

"I haven't told anybody," Ruby Jo said.

"People who aren't related but have the same last names do marry, so that by itself is not the real problem." Tully crossed his legs and leaned back in the chair. "Do you have a birth certificate for Mercy Grace French?"

"Yes. It's the only one I have. I never had one for Laney."

"Okay. I've never been married before, so I don't know if a birth certificate is required for a license. If so, we could side-step that by getting married in Mexico. We might think about getting married down there even if there isn't a problem. It might be fun."

Tully uncrossed his legs and stood. "But there are all kinds of situations that could require our birth certificates, beginning with having kids and that will show we have the same father."

"But what can we do?"

"I keep a bunch of hard-assed Dallas attorneys on retainer. Phrater, Mensheim, Starr & Johnston, Esquires, can fix just about anything or at least make it better." Tully paced across the room.

"We'll have to talk to them, but I can think of a few possible options. I remember growing up out in the country at Kendalia. Babies were often born at home without a doctor even present. I'm sure there were instances where, for one reason or another, a birth certificate was never recorded. So that's step one. Find out if a birth certificate exists for Laney."

"And if there is one?"

"Let the lawyers handle a legal name change. People, do it all the time. But your first name only. For a very short time, you'd have to be Mercy Grace Hawkins. As soon as we marry, you'd go right back to being Mercy Grace French. There's no reason anyone would know about it except us and the court. It wouldn't mean anything to anybody in Dallas anyway, and nobody in California would know unless we told them." He stopped pacing and sat in the chair near her. "Whatever route we take on this, it'll easier if you're willing to sell out and move to Dallas with me." He leaned forward and rested his elbows on his knees.

"I will ...but Ruby Jo..."

"Don't worry about me," Ruby Jo said. "You have to do what makes you happy."

"Ruby Jo can come with us or stay," Tully replied. "It's up to her."

"I really appreciate it, Tully. I think I'd like that...maybe I could be a better grandma than I was a mama." The corners of her mouth lifted in the hint of a smile."

"Okay, we'll work on that." Tully laughed. "If there is no birth certificate recorded for Laney, the attorneys will know how to handle that. I know there is a way to solve this without a big upheaval. As far as people in Gazely Creek know, you happened to meet someone with the same last name, sold out, married and moved to Texas.""

"But I'll have to tell my friends a little more than that."

"I'm sure we can figure it out."

"Tully, do you really think we can make it work?"

"Honey, as long as you aren't my sister, we can fix anything."

The End

EPILOGUE

As it turned out, there was a birth certificate on record for Laney. However, a name hadn't been chosen or provided by the date of recording, so the document only stated "Baby Hawkins." It was a fairly simple matter for the lawyers to get a certified certificate in the name of Mercy Grace Hawkins.

It was late August when Mercy Grace and Tully flew to Acapulco and were married, barefoot, on the beach by the equivalent of a justice of the peace. After a dinner of lobster and Mai-Tais, they retired to their pale pink hillside villa with a pool and a view of the ocean. It was there that Mercy Grace first made the acquaintance of Ruby Jo's dragon. Well, not Ruby Jo's exact dragon, but a very close cousin.

As for her friends, Mercy Grace and Tully simply told them the truth. Tully had tracked down a woman named French in Gazely Creek and came to town hoping to connect with a long-lost sister. Instead, he found the love of his life.

YAY! THE END

Thank you for reading "A Shadow Life." I hope you enjoyed reading the story of Mattie, Ruby Jo, Laney, and Mercy Grace as much as I enjoyed writing it.

Your thoughts about this book are important. As an independently published author, readers play a significant role in the success of my books. In fact, they can't be success without you. When people like you write a review, it helps not only me, but other readers in a big way. So, please consider posting a review for "A Shadow Life" on Amazon.

You don't have to be a writer or say anything fancy. Other readers just want to know whether you liked a book. A sentence or two will be a great help. You can find "A Shadow Life" on Amazon by title search. Thank you. It means so much to me.

Leta McCurry

FREE!

A Shadow Life: The Lost Chapter

Laura Oakley
When does love cost too much?

(Note: This chapter does not appear in the published version of A Shadow Life)

http://bit.ly/29020DY

ABOUT THE AUTHOR

Tale-spinner. Revealer of secrets. A dog's best friend. Cornbread and fried okra country girl.

Lives in Southern Oregon and enjoys writing, reading, the open road on a motorcycle (trike–as a passenger), good food, travel and a large, fun-loving family. Favorite destination: Ireland. Author of "High Cotton Country" and "A Shadow Life" and presently writing her third novel, "Dancing to the Silence."

LET'S CONNECT

Readers Club - Facebook:
https://www.facebook.com/groups/1085183758260919/

Web site: http://www.letamccurry.com

I appreciate all your input and comments.

Made in the USA
San Bernardino, CA
03 September 2016